THE SERPENT'S SKIN

It's a cold and wintery night in 1968 and ten-year-old JJ's mother isn't home. The cows are milked, the pigs fed, and her dad won't answer any questions. The four children survive as best they can in a cloud of their father's lies and clear misery, dealing with their mother's absence in their own ways. But it's always been JJ's job to cause trouble, and her sleuthing wreaks havoc in their tight-knit community. Fourteen years on, JJ has a new life, a loving partner and a good job, but she finds herself being pulled back into the unsolved mystery of her childhood. While pretending to have made peace with her father's dishonesty, she organises a final farewell for her mother so they can all put the past behind them. Will the tragic truth finally set them all free?

ERINA REDDAN

◆

THE SERPENT'S SKIN

Complete and Unabridged

AURORA
Leicester

First published in 2021 by
Pantera Press Pty Limited

First Aurora Edition
published 2021
by arrangement with
Pantera Press Pty Limited

A catalogue record for this book is available
from the British Library.

ISBN 978–1–78782–465–2

Published by
Ulverscroft Limited
Anstey, Leicestershire

Printed and bound in Great Britain by
TJ Books Ltd., Padstow, Cornwall

This book is printed on acid-free paper

Dear Reader,

The world is a strange, wild and complex place, and 2020 took first prize in all those categories. I'm guessing that if you are holding this book, it's because you know the power of a book to get you through the hard times.

Books take us deep into the richness of life and we need that. Books take us away from what pulls us into the dark and we need that. Books give us hope and we need that. I wrote *The Serpent's Skin* out of just this kind of need.

My life is so rich and full of beauty and fun and adventure and I'm bloody lucky. But lurking below the surface, like a serpent, is the challenge of the dark I grew up in. The darkness of excruciating poverty. Of the fear and the bitterness it engenders. Of the utter loneliness, the deep isolation.

We grew up on a dirt patch of a farm that we kids loved. The house had been built by my grandfather back at the turn of the last century and it was weathered and worn and the wind whistled through the cracks in the boards in winter and the sun burnt through the tin roof in the heat of the summer. In fact, the Victorian health board made the long trek out from the city just to let us know that our house was UNFIT FOR HUMAN HABITATION. But inhabit it we did — all eight of us.

We grew up and grew away and my father sold

that farm, and the house was promptly demolished to make way for a modern, no-cracks one.

None of us blinked. It was what had to happen. But twnty years on, my brother, a livestock auctioneer, noticed that somebody was waiting for him the whole morning. When he finished, the old guy stepped forward. He'd been to our place back in the day, and at the time he'd had a new Brownie box camera. He'd recently discovered a photo of our house, and had tracked Pat down to offer him the single slide in its plastic sleeve. There were no photos of our place, so Pat developed the slide, blew it up, framed it, put it on his wall and invited the rest of us round.

We gathered in great excitement. But the chattering and banter slid into silence. It was my brother who finally said it: 'How could the old man let us live in that?'

That was the moment the serpent stirred.

I needed to write about that world.

The tribal pulling together in the epic struggle to survive; the unquestioned power of men and the church and the destruction they made possible; the sheer joy of the things that shone light, like the mucking around and the kidding, as well as the incredible sisterhood.

A neighbour from across the creek, a woman with two toddlers of her own, took my newborn baby sister for six weeks when my mother nearly died giving birth. Another neighbour, with six kids of her own, took me at eleven months. I didn't get home for six months more.

I wanted to write about this complex world in which these unseen, unsung and profound acts of love and heroism made so much difference. I wanted to write about the everyday accommodations women had to make against the strictures of patriarchy and what it took to bring it down so that my life could be different. Notwithstanding, we all must fight on.

Books saved me. I never dreamed in that dark time that I would be writing them myself one day: stories that get deep into the bones of the reader and give them hope and strength, which is what I hope *The Serpent's Skin* does for you.

I'm so grateful to you for going on this journey with me.

Much love and take care.

Erina Reddan

To my daughters Maya Verena and Alena Bella, for their courage, their fire, their joy.

To all of us who fight with whatever we have to bring down the master's house.

'. . . the master's tools will never dismantle the master's house.'

Audre Lorde

PART I

BURIED
1968

The past is never where you think you left it.

Katherine Anne Porter

THE BEGINNING

Dad said she'd gone.

I didn't reckon. I reckon she'd had enough, all right, but she couldn't be *gone* gone. Mothers didn't take off. Not any of the mothers I knew. And not my mum. She was too set on yanking my hair into twisty plaits, no matter what I might or might not have done to make her go.

Philly said Dad wouldn't lie. 'Dad hates sin more than he hates the devil.'

'Shut your gob and go to sleep.' I jammed my arms behind my head and got my eyes busy counting cobwebs on the ceiling. You couldn't keep ahead of those spiders.

Philly jumped up in her flannel jarmies. Even in the moonlight I could tell Mum'd ironed em. Those jarmies made me bloody mad. I flung back the blankets and bolted to our chest of drawers, the chill of the floorboards nipping at my feet. I ripped open Philly's drawer. She had her clothes in piles like soldiers, all squared up.

'Get your filthy hands off my stuff,' she said.

'Your PJs are dirty. I'm getting you another pair.'

'You're a lying snake in the grass, JJ.' She pushed back the covers and was on all fours.

'It's on ya collar — bleedin great stain.'

She twisted her head, plucking at her jarmies,

like a maggie, over and over at the ground for a worm. She gave up and launched herself at me, roaring. At nine, she was only a year younger, but so little, I caught her scratching hands easy. She pushed her face into mine and hissed like a cat.

We both stopped, listened. Normally, Mum would be belting down the passageway, floor vibrating, yelling at me to stop riling up Philly again. But this time there were just the rats scratching about like nothing had changed on their side of the wall.

★ ★ ★

There was no Mum the next morning, either, rushing into our room with a big wind: 'That Jack Frost — had the bug in im last night. Jump up and see if you can catch him at it!'

I was awake already without Mum, though. I poked my head over the window ledge. Out past the three pine trees in front of our place there was nothing but paddock after paddock, all silver and emptied over with frost. Inside it was all shivery bitey. Philly had a whimper up about how icy itchy her chilblains were. So I picked up the big warm wind Mum would have made and blew it all over her, dashing her and our school uniforms to the fireplace in the lounge. At twelve and thirteen, Tim and Tessa considered themselves too big to complain about a no-changing thing like the weather. I stabbed at the ashes in the grate for a spark of leftover orange hot from last night's fire.

'Bloody damn!' I said.

4

'You'll go to hell.'

'Least it'll be hot.'

Philly clapped her hand to her mouth and made full moons with her eyes. I dropped the poker with a big racket to cover over her shriek, in case Dad thought about thundering in here. The freeze shivered us up as we ripped out of our pyjamas and into our polo tops and tartan skirts. Philly folded her jarmies so the buttons were in a dead straight line down the front. I balled mine up to shove under the pillow.

★ ★ ★

It was all tight around the breakfast table. Tessa had Mum's apron over her school uniform. Mum always said it didn't matter that the big yellow sunflower with all its joy on the front had worn gone — we knew it was there and that's what counted. The apron was too big on Tessa because she was skinnier than most, but she'd wrapped the straps around and around so they were strangling into her like flat snakes across her belly. She'd got our bread turning brown in the toaster, put out Vegemite and poured milk into plastic cups. Mine was purple like irises. Mum said when I was a kid I wouldn't have any other colour, so the others had to stop fighting me for it. I guess that was after she showed me irises in her book and said they were named after the Greek goddess who carried messages across the rainbow between heaven and earth. A bit like me, she said, cause I sometimes knew more than I should, and where I got that knowing she

5

didn't know but it had to be heaven. I'd made little teeth marks on the side of my cup where I gnawed when I wasn't eating my vegies but pretending I was getting ready to. I settled my teeth into those marks now. They were a bit of warmth in the shiver cold.

Tessa seemed taller today. Her hair already ribboned up. Just as shiny careful as when Mum did it. Had that brave girl look on her face. I wanted to smack it right off. Dad patted her hand when she put his toast on his plate.

Wished I'd got Dad's toast for him.

Dad didn't say anything about Mum. Hunched right over, eyes all high beam on his plate. Tim beside him, carbon copy.

'You right to go to school?' Philly asked me, with a chirp like a bird. Her pixie face above her pink cup. No teeth grooves. Tessa looked up sharp from the sink, like she'd forgotten something and it was a stab in the guts to her.

I pointed at my school uniform to show I was going whether I was right or not.

'So all better?' said Tessa, pretending she hadn't missed a beat, smoothing her apron over the front of her just like Mum did.

'Who wouldn't be after spending a day in bed reading?' said Tim, his spiky crew cut slicked over neat with water. He dropped his eyes straight back to his plate, though. He didn't have it in him to go full pelt on me this morning. He had the toast to his mouth but could only get a nibble in. Still, he was getting through it. It was almost like he expected Mum to come racing through the door with the chook eggs in the collecting tin, rousing at him for leaving food on his plate.

'What would you know?' I said. 'Never read a book in your life.'

'You don't either — just baby stories.'

'Do so. Read *Alice in Wonderland* — the whole book yesterday.'

'Not sick at all, then?'

'Was so.' I jumped to my feet, kicked backwards at my chair. It skidded across the floor and smashed into the cupboard. There was a ghost of a grin on Tim's face. Dad slammed his fist against the table. 'Pick that up,' he roared without looking up.

I had my fists tight, tight, and the blood inside me was spurting like hot milk through the pipes in the dairy. But Tim stopped grinning. Looked away out the window, and just like that the red whooshed out — leaving me just as empty as a wrinkled old balloon skin.

★   ★   ★

Tessa kept checking out the window for the bus on the far hill. She smacked Mum's hairbrush against the bench like Mum did. She should just try to use it on me and then she'd see. Philly jumped good and proper, though, every time, like when Mum was at it.

Tessa got Philly out the door and started her off down the track to where the bus stopped for us on the road. I sprinted out after them, but before I got too far I peeled away to the back verandah to check on the joey. Tessa shouted

7

after me but I didn't bother yelling back.

Tim was already there, hunched over the joey, dipping the tip of the rag into an old tin of milk and sooking it at her mouth. But she kept her black button eyes looking straight, like her head was too heavy to move. I bent to cosy the towel around her and push the clock more against her tummy. We were trying to fool her into living by pretending the ticking was her mum's heartbeat.

'You should talk to Dad about where Mum's gone,' Tim said.

'No, you should.'

A crow flapped to rest on the nearest strainer post. Ducked its head to the side and gave the joey a good looking at.

I pushed the cardboard box with the joey in it snug to the wall. Pulled the scratch of the torn towel over it.

'Anyway, won't do no good, he says he doesn't know,' I said.

'She'd never just up and leave. You gotta ask him again; reckon he knows something more than he's saying.'

I thought about telling Tim it was all my fault, but I reckoned she'd call or maybe even come back today so then I wouldn't have to.

'You're older,' I said.

'You're his little shadow.'

'You just want me to be the one who gets the backhander.'

He squatted forwards, pulled back the towel a bit and reached under to tease the milk rag around the joey's mouth again. 'I'm just saying,' he said.

Tessa's voice yelled for us to hurry up or we'd miss the bus. I got to my feet.

Tim stroked the joey's nose with the back of his finger, not going anywhere.

'Bus, Tim,' I said.

Not a muscle.

'If we miss the school bus, you'll get what for from Dad. He won't be driving you all the way to Chilton.'

Still nothing.

I grabbed him by the back of his jumper and hauled. He fell backwards, but jumped up straight away, wiping his eyes with his sleeve. He scooped up his bag and took off, leaving me for dead.

★   ★   ★

Just before lunch, Mother Gabriel's cracked voice came over the loudspeaker calling: 'Tim McBride, to the office.'

I screwed the lid on my ink bottle real quick and opened my desk to shove in my maths book and ruler. I sat there, fists opening and closing, just waiting for that bell. You never heard Tim's name over the loudspeaker. Mick Watson, Shane Smith, the two Farrell brothers, sure. Tim liked setting everyone else up to get boiled hard in hot water but he made sure to keep his own toes dry as dry. So him being called up like this must've had something to do with Mum.

Reckon Philly thought the same cause she was waiting for me as soon as I got out of the classroom door. Clicking her fingers over and

9

over. 'Why'd they call Tim and not Tessa? She's the oldest.'

I grabbed her hand to stop that clicking. 'Cause he's the boy.'

We raced to where only kids in trouble went, pulling up short under the head nun's window, making sure we were plenty out of sight. Philly danced from one foot to the other.

'You'll wet your pants again. You should have gone to the toilet.'

She shook her little squeezed-up monkey face.

'Look. If Mum is really in there, you know I'll make her wait for you while you go,' I said.

Philly put her hands on her hips and bared her teeth at me. I gave up and let her stay. We turned to the office, screwing up our eyes like it would help us see through the wall. I snuck around to the door to look through the keyhole. Philly was just about inside my shoes, she was that close behind.

The door sprung open and we startled back. Mother Gabriel was as wide as the doorway, what with her habit sticking out all stiff, on top of her being fat. Philly's little fingers bit into the back of me and I put my arms by my sides to make myself so big Mother Gabriel couldn't see her.

'You.' Her stubby finger was pointing straight at me. 'Get the Strap.'

I knew where the Strap was.

I took a step back as if to leave, but I was trying to get a look around her into the office to see if maybe there still was a chance Mum was in there.

'You'll have that Strap on the back of your own legs in a minute,' Mother Gabriel warned.

I had to get going then. I motored Philly behind me fast so she couldn't be seen until we got around the corner. When I let her go Philly scuffed my head with the back of her hand. 'Should have asked if Mum was in there.'

I didn't answer, just got hold of her jumper at the elbow and towed her back to my classroom. Philly was too scared to come in cause kids weren't allowed into classrooms at lunchtime. I raced up to the glass cabinet at the front where Sister Peter hung the Strap on a nail where it could keep an eye on us.

Philly gave me a 'what took you so long' look when I got back outside. I thought about taking a detour to the toilet block so she could get it out of her but, one: Mother Gabriel was waiting, and I didn't want to make her any madder; and two: even though I knew what I knew, there was still a chance Mum could be with her.

Mother Gabriel was right where we'd left her on the step outside her office. She took the Strap and tested it against her hand.

'Has Tim McBride arrived yet, Mother?' I asked, brave as brave, thinking it was one of the Farrell brothers about to be on the business end of that Strap and still wondering what she wanted with Tim.

'Elizabeth Jane and Philomena Anne McBride, get back to your own playgrounds or it'll be you two next.' She cracked the Strap against the door of her office. 'And do that ribbon up properly, Elizabeth. You're a disgrace to St Francis Xavier's.'

We stumbled over each other backing away from her and getting around the corner. We leaned against the wall, Philly shaking, me pretending not to.

'She knew my name,' said Philly, all moon eyes again. I didn't answer, and it took Philly a few seconds to catch on that whatever Tim was called for it had nothing to do with Mum.

'Toilet. Now.' I yanked at her jumper and pulled her upright from the wall.

But we heard Mother Gabriel's grunt and the whack of the Strap. In the distraction Philly twisted away. I got back hold of her again.

Then we stopped.

It was Tim.

We knew the sound of him trying not to cry.

I let go of Philly's jumper and charged around to the office door. I jumped that step and raised my fist to bang on that door. Tim must be feeling real bad about Mum leaving if he'd let himself get caught at something.

Philly flew at my back to stop me, her arms swung around my neck, but I shoved her off and sent her spinning into the dirt. I banged that door right open. Mother Gabriel's backside and all the layers of her habit filled the room. She was hunched over, thrashing the Strap onto Tim's bum. She swung her arm back to lay into him again. Bent over a chair, Tim lifted the back of his arm to swipe at his eyes. All the sorry for him balled up in me and I launched myself dead at her. The shock of the extra weight on her arm turned her right around. She shook me off, her face all red and animal.

12

I stumbled back, hit the statue of Mother Mary holding baby Jesus and sent it smashing to the ground, and went down after it. Mother Gabriel stood over me, panting like she'd been out after the cows.

'You,' she had that finger stabbing at me again, 'I'm not surprised at.' She swung her veil back from her shoulders with a great heave, pushed her sleeves further up her arms. 'Tim McBride.' She was speaking to him but her eyes were square on me, not blinking. 'I'm done with you. It's your sister Elizabeth's turn.'

Tim looked from me to Mother Gabriel. I scooted on my bum away from her boot.

But she got to the door before I could get anywhere near it. 'Get up off the floor,' Mother Gabriel said to me. She flung the door wide for Tim. Yanking her head to Philly outside. 'Get your sister to the sick bay,' she told him. 'Change of underwear.'

Tim didn't move an inch. Nothing but his eyes: at me, at Mother Gabriel, at the door.

'The shame this one is to your father.' Mother Gabriel whacked the Strap on the filing cabinet, still panting. 'Elizabeth's got the devil in her. Now go away while I get him out of her.'

Tim threw me a sorry with his eyes before he took off out the door. Mother Gabriel slammed it closed after he'd gone. She scratched her neck, keeping her eyes right on me.

'Clean up the broken mess you've made of our Sacred Mother,' she said to me.

I gathered some of the biggest bits, got to my knees and on to my feet, the back of my neck prickling up under her spidery stare.

Once I clattered the pieces into the bin, Mother Gabriel finally peeled her eyes from me, giving me her back. Then came the sound of the door locking.

THE THING SHE LEFT BEHIND

I was first in the bus line after school when Philly came pounding across the asphalt, making a beeline for me, her face all scrunched up concerned. I shook my head and she stopped, half tripping over with the sudden of it. I turned exactly away to stare at the rocks in the fence. Still she tucked in behind me and the thing was, Mary McCarthy and Joanne Tyler kicked their schoolbags and shuffled back to let her, sending big blazes of sorry my way. I knew Philly would be picking up those blazes and giving a tight half smile back.

Not me. I had my arms folded and my socks pulled right up to my knees. I didn't even look up when I saw Tommy's scuffed shoes hesitating before me. He and I always stood together, but after a few seconds he peeled away down the back of the line.

When we were all loaded up, Mr O'Brien was about to yank the bus door shut, but Tim just made it, pounding up the steps, with only a whisker to spare. In the window I saw him ruffle Philly's hair beside me as he passed us. Saw her reach up. Saw her hand touch his. Their eyes burning into my back. I squeezed mine shut to stop all that seeing. Tim threw his bag on to the rack above the seat behind Philly's and mine and

15

grunted at Marty McMahon to git out. Marty did.

Only Tessa was where she normally was, up the front of the bus. Bet her lips were pursed tight up, though.

★   ★   ★

After our stop, the bus roared away with a gear grind and a spurt of black exhaust cloud and we all tore off up the track to see if Mum had come home yet. Philly got left behind pretty quick and set up a siren wail. Tessa clicked her tongue and fell back to wait for her to catch up. Tim let me take the lead easy, pretending he was slowing down for the others. He didn't like to be the first one knowing a thing if the knowing wasn't going to be much good to him.

'Mum. Mum,' I called as I slammed the door behind me, the whole house shuddering.

No answer. Not that I was expecting one because I already felt the house was full of empty.

I raced into my bedroom, tugging my uniform over my head on the way. I stuck my legs into a pair of trousers and pulled a jumper over my head. My thumb got caught in the hole at the elbow and I yanked it free. I hung up my uniform as if Mum had been there.

I was so quick that when I got back outside, the others still hadn't turned up. I took off down the back to find Dad. Get to him before the others did so I could ask about Mum and answer his standard question about school without them putting in their two cents' worth about me and Mother Gabriel. He wasn't with the pigs, wasn't in the cowshed, but the ute was parked in the drive, so he was here somewhere all right.

And he better tell me if Mum called, too.

The thing was, I was home in bed sick yesterday, so she would have told me where she was going if she was going somewhere. But maybe I was asleep and she didn't want to wake me.

I'm not much of a sleeper, though, not in the day anyway. And she would have left me a note. Unless she was just going down the paddock, or taking Dad his lunch, or wild to the west wind with me.

All I remember is reading and reading about that Alice. But maybe I did fall asleep because I didn't even hear Mum drive off with Mrs Nolan who'd been around helping Mum stake up the tomatoes. And that's what she must have done because how else did Mum get to the station?

I climbed to the top rung of the cowshed fence to get away from all this scratching in my brain. Squinted and stared.

'Dad.'

I put my ear to the wind. Nothing came riding back on it.

'Daaaaaaaaaaaaaddd.'

Just the mourn of the crow. Nothin sadder. Up there in the gum tree beyond the fence, all by itself, black against the grey of the sky.

Where was Dad? Was he gone too now?

A hand in my gut was starting to fist up. I pressed my forearm into it, but it did no good. I ran to the other side of the fence and jumped up there to get a good look in the other direction. Pins and needles started buzzing in my wrists. Soon they were numbing me up, moving like a wall right through me. I stayed there looking and looking.

Then I saw it.

Something dark down by the lip of the dam where it shouldn't have been. I leaned all the way forwards. A gumboot — adult big and flopped over.

The fist turned into a knife and my guts knew it.

What was it doing all on its own?

'Get down from there.' Tessa came into the shed, all changed and ready to set up for the milking later, as if Mum being gone was nothing out of the everyday of things.

My hands gripped the rail and no words got out of me.

'Would have thought you'd be on your best behaviour after today's performance. Get the hay into the bales.'

I turned and stared.

'That look might work on Mum.'

'Dad,' I got out.

'No, I haven't told him about you attacking Mother Gabriel yet. But if you don't get down this minute, I will.'

'Dad's gone too.' My voice ribboned up with cut and blood. 'Drowned in the dam.'

'Don't be stupid. He's in the training yard.'

Breath hiccupped back into me. I jumped down and doubled over with it, clinging hard to the rail as if I couldn't trust my bones to stand me up. Tessa rolled her eyes, hand on jutted out hip, waiting. 'Finished?' she asked.

The crow took off in a great burst of black. It circled once above the pointy white of the gum's twisty finger branches. I wheeled out of the shed, ignoring Tessa's shouts at my back, and ran to the training yard, heart knocking at my insides. I saw the grey brumby through the scrub first. She was straining and kicking, wild to be back where she'd come from. Dad was hanging on to the rope around her neck, weighting her down. He kept up his murmuring, eyes never shifting, steady on the brumby as if it might break the spell if he looked anywhere else.

'Didn't you hear me callin ya, Dad?'

'Pipe down,' he worked into his run of smooth to the Grey.

'Did ya?'

'I heard you bellyaching.'

'Then?'

'I can't be bellyaching back. You can see I'm in the middle here.'

I folded my arms and planted my feet.

He didn't look over. He was right inside himself, like it was all calm and peaceful in there. The Grey bucked high against the sky, cutting the clouds in half. Dad kept his voice soft and low, like a slow-running creek. Moving forwards to let her buck but holding steady so she couldn't get too far. Like dancing. And then the mare started listening with one ear. Like she wanted to get some of that slow and soft in Dad's voice inside her. I'd seen him do the same with Mum once or twice, when Mum had been upset. Dad could tame the wild out of anything. He was a marvel; everybody said it.

The Grey stopped hiking back against the sky. Stood, quiver still. So Dad didn't move either, just kept eye on eye, murmuring how it was *all good. Better to be off out of the wild, be here where it was safe, where she'd be looked after.* The Grey twitched. Flicked her tail. Dad with his lullaby words. The brumby breathing easier. Dad leaning in, unwinding the rope from his wrist and taking it in his palm where she could see it. Her not backing away.

It looked dead easy. But it was the hardest thing, getting inside yourself enough to tame a wild horse. I couldn't do it. I would be all out there, filled up with the brumby, and feeling all its terror and panic, and in the end we'd both want to take off back to the mountains she'd come from.

Dad rubbed the rope against her neck. She strained away, but let him too.

'Good girl, good girl,' he crooned. 'Done for today, girl.' He backed away, taking her with him, one careful step and then another. Anchored her rope to the peg beside the water trough and slipped through the fence. I came around to his side. Stuck my hand through the fence to pat the Grey. She reared back and whinnied.

'Git.' Dad slapped my hand away. 'That horse has had enough, losing everything and coming to a new place and having to learn new things without you rilin her up.' He tipped his hat to shoot me a quick grin. 'She'll need a bit more time to get used to little savages like you.'

I rubbed my hand where he'd got me, grinned back.

He poured oats into the food trough, shaking the bag empty.

'How was school?' he said.

'Good,' I said, just like every day.

He grunted just like every day, back to the business of getting on and turning off the hose to the drinking trough. The Grey thirsted at the water, snuffling it up.

My shoulders lost most of their tense. I jumped them up and down, circled my neck. So now, if those others didn't dob me in about Mother Gabriel, I'd be right.

'Get up to the shed and help your sister set up for the milkin.'

'Mum call?'

He grunted again. This time with an edge, warning me.

'Did she?'

'Get off with ya.'

Which I took for *It's none of your business what your mother did or didn't do.*

'If she called, you should tell me right now.'

'I'll tell you when I'm good and ready.'

I put my hand up to my forehead to shield my eyes from a sun that wasn't there. Squinted him a good look as he wound the rope around his arms in a circle, nice and neat. He sent me back a look that was all flat-out warning now, nothing but edge, but it was too late: I smelt the spit of guilt on him and I had to know if maybe it wasn't my fault Mum took off.

21

'Did you blue with her? That why she left without saying goodbye?' I asked.

He stopped sharp in the winding, stabbed eyes all over me like he knew what I did and that it was all me in Mum's going away so sudden. I went inside myself, tighter and tighter.

He dumped the rope over the tall of a post and slapped at the rail with his thick palm in a rhythm like there was a bit of music playing somewhere. I was stuck between the hoping it wasn't all me and the not wanting him to be so twisted up. He angled slow away. Good as forgot I was there. But he hadn't. His voice came low out of the hunch of him. 'I love your mother. She's my moon and my stars.'

'I know, Dad,' I said, my heart bursting with a sudden sorry, cause I did know.

'I'd do anything to protect her. Anything. Your mother's a saint.'

I took a step and my hand was on his arm, full of question.

He looked up, nodded. 'I'm all right, love.' He sandpapered his whiskers with the crook of his hand. Straightened. 'Listen, love, you have to be the big girl now with your mother gone. I'll tell you all at the one time as much as I know when I come in.' He collected up the oat bag. Gave it a shake. 'Off and get the kettle on. Tell the others I'll be in soon.'

★ ★ ★

Max gave me the stink eye as I passed. We weren't on speaking terms, like there'd been

22

some betrayal and I was in on it. I wasn't letting him get away with that today, though. I stopped, planting my legs wide.

'How's it going, you old bull?'

The weight of his chest pulled him down as if nothing could go right in his world, while the mucus around his nose-ring shone in the afternoon grey. He finally rumbled out air in my direction and I took that for something and moved on. I was almost up to the chook shed when I heard Philly. I went towards the sound of her sniffles. She wasn't in the shed. She was tucked into the bushes behind it.

'What is it, little duck?' I asked.

She had her arms over her head and her head tucked between.

'I'm the one who should be crying.' I tried a laugh. 'Mother Gabriel lit into me, not you.'

She scratched her nose with the back of her wrist. Pushed back further into the bushes.

'Get any further in there and you'll fall down Alice's hole,' which she was reading now.

'It's the joey.' Her voice all small and wrapped up tight.

The air whooshed right out of me and I stood there like I was stoned up. Then I found something to do and I got in there beside her. Sat in the hush with her, saying nothing. My head down between my arms like hers. Feeling everything close in around us.

'Where is she now, then?' I finally got out.

'Tim put her in the ute for Dad to take down the gully'

'Should we do a funeral?'

The top of her head shook from side to side. I didn't much feel like it either. One thing I did know, though. You couldn't fool a joey. It knew when its mother was gone.

★   ★   ★

At afternoon tea the air was that heavy it was keeping our eyes low on the table.

Dad jammed up his slice of white bread, slow and steady, and started. 'Your mother called.'

Our heads jerked up like we were all connected. Philly jumped to a crouch on her seat. 'Mum's coming home!' she yelled, relief big through her.

'Few days yet,' he said, waving her down. He dipped his knife into the cream. He was all about getting the cream evenly to the crust.

Why wasn't he saying? No matter how much sorry I had for him, he shouldn't be making us wait. The red started beating at the inside of me. Getting a hold. And still he said nothing, all business with the jam jar now. Finally I'd had enough. I leaned forwards, smashing a hammer smack hard against his no talking. 'Where is she then?'

He looked up, long and level, holding his rolled-up jam-and-cream bread like a wall between us. 'Aunty Peg's.'

I shot back against the chair like he'd smacked me one, shaking my head. 'But you never let er.'

'She didn't stop to ask.'

'Why didn't she ring to tell us yesterday?' Philly asked in a small voice, hunched over, her

24

knees tucked into her armpits.

'She thought she'd left a note, see.' Dad cleared his throat. 'She was in a hell of a hurry when she left. Peg had a turn, and your mother couldn't be missing the train to Melbourne otherwise it would have been another day before she made it to Peg's place. As soon as your mother found the note in her handbag this morning, after you buggers had gone to school, she rang. Said she was sorry she worried us.'

He looked at me from under his eyebrows, like he was daring me to say something else. But he was right: if Aunty Peg needed Mum, Mum wouldn't stop to ask Dad if she could go. Only that red was still knocking from one side of my gut to the other.

He pushed my plate towards me. 'Eat up.' Gave me a wink. 'All good, then, after all.'

I looked at my bread with one slash of red across the middle. I waded my knife into the jam and got the strawberry all over.

'I was home, but,' I said, all quiet, as I cut my slice into tiny, tiny pieces. 'Why didn't she say goodbye?'

He jerked his eyes in my direction. He'd forgotten, see.

'Maybe she tried.' He shoved down the other half of his roll-up so he couldn't speak for a bit.

'She probably looked in on you,' Tessa jumped in, like she was Mum. 'Saw you were out like a light and didn't want to wake you.' But then she added, back to her normal self: 'Knew you'd go wild if she told you.'

I grunted, saying maybe could be, maybe not.

'Why'd ya tell us yesterday that she'd gone gone, then?' I said, looking straight at Dad.

He scratched his head and dropped his hand on the table like it was a great sack of spuds. I studied the forever lines on his face but they didn't make anything come clear. 'Didn't know any different till she called,' he said. 'No note, see?' He pushed the cream bottle and the jam jar away.

'Why didn't you call the police, then?'

Philly gasped and Tim went into a coughing fit to cover his splutter.

Not a sound from Dad, though. He drummed the table beside his plate with his thick finger. Finally he cleared his throat. 'We did blue the night before. Thought she might have just needed a bit of time.'

'Must have been a real bad one,' I knifed back, quick as lick.

'None of your bloody business.' He was back on his cream and jam. He looked up to see my eyes all narrow on him. 'What?' Like there was an axe in his voice and he was about to swing it.

'Mum blued with you, not us. Why didn't she ring to tell us goodnight?'

Tessa kicked me under the table. Tim grinned right at me but just so Dad couldn't see. He gave his grin a bit of sauce by slicing his finger across his throat.

Dad's stare was on me. I kept mine on my plate. But Dad surprised us by not going off his nut. His voice, when it did make it out, was full of calm. 'That mad old biddy Peg had one of her worst turns yet. Your mum's had her hands full

26

to overflow.' His axe all packed away in the shed. 'So that's why she couldn't ring to say goodnight to you little buggers. She would of if she could of. Yous all know that.' He rolled another slice up. Looked dead on me. 'Your mother and I blue all the time. Nothin out of the ordinary in that. She's got more important things to worry about now.' He loaded his roll-up into his mouth. 'Any of yous seen your mother's address book?'

'It's in the drawer by her bed,' Tessa said.

Dad grunted, chewing hard and stabbing at his plate to pick up a crumb or two.

'So how long do you think it'll be till she can come home, Dad?' Tessa asked.

Dad tapped the table once more, and then twice. The others all took this to mean *not long*.

Not me.

I reckon he didn't know one way or the other. But I didn't say anything. Because then they'd know that maybe it was a bigger thing keeping Mum away than Peg's turn and that I knew more than I was letting on.

I looked down at the little ribbons of blood bread on my plate.

$$\star \quad \star \quad \star$$

After we stacked the dishes, I got out into it just like Mum told me. The first time she done it, she shoved me ahead of her, digging me in between my shoulder blades, out of the kitchen, past the cowshed and into the top paddock, and straight away I saw she was right. All that soft: the pale of the blue in the sky, the brush of the gold in the paddocks and the clear of the air in between, and all of it going on and on until it reached the end of the world. Melted away the red in me like butter.

This time I had to get myself down in among the grass, below the teeth of the wind, smell the cool of the dirt. After a good bit of sucking the sweetness out of a blade or two, I could see that everything Dad said made good sense. It had nothing to do with me. I wasn't glad Aunty Peg had a bad turn but I was glad as that Peg was the reason Mum'd gone. Now maybe nobody had to know what I did.

I spat out the last of the grass. It was just . . . those never-sitting-still eyes of Dad's, sneaking little looks out the window like there was something he wasn't saying. But maybe he was just all rolled up in missing Mum. Tomorrow was Saturday, though, so she'd definitely be calling us then and she could tell us everything herself.

It wasn't the same out here without Mum, but it was something. Winter safe. Snakes all holed up, sleeping out the cold.

Turned out we were just like snakes. Only they got rid of their skin every summer and we did it every seven years. And not just the skin like the book at school said. Every cell and every bit of us. All newed up every seven years. She'd better get back soon, before I changed up every cell and she wouldn't know me.

★ ★ ★

'You'll do as you're told,' Dad said that night as he loaded the shotguns into the back of the ute after tea, along with two packets of cartridges. Philly stood at the end of the path, not coming one jot closer. Tessa chafed Philly's hand between hers, backing Dad up like always. 'Mum'll be back in a day or two,' she leaned over Philly to say. 'Wouldn't be right to cancel when Mr Kennedy and Pete are already here.' She pulled Philly forwards a step.

Pete walked over to ruffle her head, his flannel shirt flapping wide despite the edge of cold in the air. 'You'll be right, little puss. Just a bit of shooting fun. Same as every Friday night.' He looked over at Dad just like always. Pete had lost his dad a good few years back in his last year of school so every weekend he came over to help with a bit of fencing or feeding out the cows, making sure us kids knew what a giant of a man our dad was.

Philly sharp nodded, like she was trying to be as brave as Pete thought she should be.

'I'll sit in the front seat with you,' promised Tessa.

'That's not fair for you,' said Philly. 'It's your turn in the back.'

'It's what Mum would do,' said Tessa, her lips all folded firm, like that was the end of the matter.

I jumped into the tray of the ute quick smart so nobody'd be thinking I should stay with Philly too. I'd only just got old enough to get out of all that sliding and slapping into windows in the cabin as the ute slammed around the paddocks.

As if that was safer.

I got myself nice and tight into the corner under the driver's side and got hold of the rope tied all around the inside of the ute. Tim leaped up beside me, and Dad and Mr Kennedy grunted their way in behind.

Pete was at the wheel, beeping and skylarking. He put it into gear and nudged the ute backwards, then spun it around, taking off in a great spray of gravel. Mr Kennedy dived for the rope before he was turfed out sideways. Dad banged the roof of the ute.

'Give us a chance to pop a tinnie,' he complained, but laughing, like something was loosening in him.

Tim and I laughed too, letting his loose curl around us. When we got to the back gate, Tim jumped down to open and close it without a whine, all run through with the excitement of things.

It was in me, too. There's magic in spotlighting. I liked the way the grown-ups' voices sounded in the dark. I liked the way they worked together, laughing and joking, making something different from what they did in the day.

Pete careered the ute off down the hill, hurtling over rocks.

Dad hit the back window again. 'Kids,' he growled, but eyes dead on his tinnie where the beer was frothing out.

Pete turned the ute on to the flat, skidded right so we were facing Jean's Corner, then gunned the motor before cutting it.

'Bloody idiot,' said Mr Kennedy.

'Gimme a beer, ya bastard,' called Pete. Dad nodded at Tim, who pulled the ring of a can and angled over to pass it through the window to Pete.

The moon wasn't up to much tonight, so I could only just make out the little stone bench under the apple tree in the elbow of the creek. Mum said there used to be a cottage a long time ago. A lady called Jean lived in it after she had a baby without a husband. The baby wasn't right in the head and it didn't live long. But that Jean never went back to her family. I guessed she liked it in her corner because it was pretty with the gums leaning long across the creek and the water rushing by all day long like a friend. Nothing left now except the little stone cross getting all overgrown by long grass. I wished I knew the name of that not-right-in-the-head baby so I could scratch it back into the cross. Mum said naming a thing meant you knew it, and knowing a thing made it easier to get a hold of. I reckoned every baby needed knowing.

I chewed my nail and made myself look into the dark of another direction because Jean's Corner made me think of Mum again. She came down here for a bit of peace and quiet when she was fed up to the back teeth with the lot of us. Sometimes I snuck down after her. Picked all kinds of different wildflowers. Mum and I would sit on the bench and figure out what they were saying when you put them all together. She always carried them home in her apron, put them in a jar, put them on the table for dinner. 'Make it special,' she said. She shushed Philly

31

right up one night when Philly asked what a bunch of dead weeds sitting on the table was for. Wished now I left Mum alone on that bench sometimes. Let her have that bit of peace and quiet. Maybe she wouldn't have gone.

I looked over to Tim but he was doing his best not to look at Jean's Corner, either. It was in the huddle of him.

'You seen it yet?' Mr Kennedy asked Dad in a low voice like there was a chance Tim and I mightn't hear. He hissed the top of his second tinnie open.

'I'll not look at it, even if you hold it under my nose,' Dad said, all decision and purpose, telling Mr Kennedy what was what. 'And nobody else should either. It's a bad business. Brian and Mary can't hold their heads up.' Dad spat out the side of the ute. 'They don't deserve even a bit of this. That girl ought to be horsewhipped for what she's done to her parents.'

Tim raised an eyebrow in my direction, jerked his head towards Mr Kennedy. But if Tim wanted to know he could do his own dirty work this time. I already had it from Mrs Nolan and Mum that somebody had seen a picture that might have been Colleen, who'd left for the city two years ago, in a dirty magazine. In the nuddy. Or maybe mostly nuddy.

'Yep, horsewhipped,' Mr Kennedy echoed. 'Got your head screwed on right there, Jack. Like always.'

I scrunched my face up into the terrible of it, because a girl shouldn't be doing that. But Dad would never horsewhip a horse so why would he want to do that to a girl even if she did do a bad thing to her parents? I hunched tighter. That wind was picking up.

Dad tossed Tim his shotgun easy and Tim loaded it, perking up.

Dad and Mr Kennedy did some weather and crop talk until Pete wanted to know if we'd be getting going anytime before Christmas.

That Pete. He might always be trying to get into Dad's good books, but he was still a character.

Dad looked at me all curled up and tight in the corner. 'You can have a shot this time.'

'Nah, I'll be right.'

Dad clutched his heart, pretended to stagger. I grinned.

'She's just a little girl, after all,' said Tim, grinning too.

'Am not,' I flicked back. But maybe I was because I was always on at Dad to give me a go, but tonight, with the joey dying and Mum being gone — it didn't feel good.

'You leave her alone,' said Dad, scuffing him on the shoulder. 'She's ya sister. Should look after er.'

'Yeah, Tim,' I said, grinning wider.

'When I'm not around, it's up to you to be the man, mate,' Dad said, all serious.

Tim cut me a look, guilty, hunched over his gun, because he let Mother Gabriel light into me instead of him. But I shook my head at him behind Dad's back, letting him know it wasn't like that.

'Let's get on with things,' said Mr Kennedy,

turning on the spotlight. 'Or they'll hear us coming for bloody miles.' He banged on the roof of the cabin, and Pete let out a whoop and took off.

He belted us in a straight line for the creek at the other end of the paddock. I squatted back low, holding real tight.

'What's got into ya?' Dad yelled at me.

'Stayin out of the wind,' I yelled back. It wasn't the wind. But it was something. I was usually jumping up and down with the different of it.

Pete pulled up sharp at the far end of the paddock and wheeled about, heading up towards the bridge.

'There,' Tim and Mr Kennedy yelled, one voice.

Pete skidded to a stop. Mr Kennedy manned the spotlight. I hopped up to see. Mr Kennedy scudded the light about till it found the target. A small grey body scooting this way and that in ever-smaller dodges until it was nailed to a quiver-still stop. Up on its hind legs, two black eyes, shiny with the thing it knew was about to happen.

Then the shot.

The rabbit's body jerked high and somer-saulted backwards.

Shouts of victory.

Tim leaped out. Came back with the prize, and tossed it in the box. Dad rubbed Tim's head. 'First shot too, boyo.'

'Bet you can't do better,' said Tim. Even in the dark I could tell they were both grinning.

Then Mr Kennedy's voice. 'I'll give ya a run for ya money, but.'

There was a quick knocking from inside the cabin. 'Philly's crying,' said Tessa, getting her head out the window.

'Bloody hell,' Dad swore. Then everybody waited for him to say more.

'Phils.' Dad raised his voice so she could hear. 'Never bothered you before.'

'I don't want you to kill,' came Philly's small voice, all soaked up with tears.

'There'll be no dinner tomorra.'

She didn't say anything. I didn't either, kept my head right down, but Philly was nothing but right.

'How about another few goes and then we call it quits?'

More silence.

'She nodded,' called out Tessa finally.

'Righto. Let's get this show on the road.' He banged on the roof and Pete took off again. But slow, like something had come out of the thing.

★ ★ ★

Next morning we were all jangled up listening out for the phone. Philly picked up the receiver a couple of times to make sure it worked. Tim and I fought over the Milo tin and Dad didn't even notice, just kept his eyes long and low out the window. In the end I convinced Philly to take her mind off things by making pot plants out of old fruit tins to surprise Mum when she came home. She agreed if we did it beside the tanks where we could still hear the phone, which was fine by me cause I wasn't planning on going anywhere.

After breakfast, Tessa snatched the tea towel from me and spread it over the dish drainer, all filled up angry. Philly and I took off for the door.

'Where do you think you're going?' Tessa asked.

'Help Dad,' I lied, quick as quick.

'Not before the school shoes.'

Philly looked stricken and changed direction.

'They get a good shine up every bloody Saturday. Reckon they could do with one week off,' I said, still facing the laundry and freedom.

'Don't be so selfish, JJ. Break Mum's heart if she got back and our shoes were in a state.'

I scratched my ear. 'Reckon it would take a bit more than that to break her heart.'

'How would you know?' Tessa smoothed Mum's apron over her stomach. 'Tim,' she yelled. 'Shoes.'

We heard movement from Tim's room coming our way, so if he was doing it there was no getting out of it for me. I went over to the kitchen hearth.

'Shove over,' Tim said when he got there. He pushed me and I fell, getting polish on the lino. I roared and flicked him with my cloth. He caught it with a grin and then held my fighting fists out at arm's length.

'You take up a lot of room for a little girl.'

'You can't talk. You're not even a teenager yet.'

Tim flicked the cloth this time and got me right in the face. I ignored him. I bunched my hand inside my shoe and slammed it down to the hearth. I slapped my cloth at the outside, back and forwards, big and long.

'Settle down,' Tessa said.

36

'I don't reckon she's at Aunty Peg's,' I said.

Philly dropped the polish tin and it skidded across the kitchen, colliding with the stove. We all stopped to watch it circle and circle, then topple.

'If she was there, sure as sure, she'd pick up Aunty Peg's phone and call us,' I said.

'Don't be stupid,' said Tessa.

I gave the shoe a last blast and put it aside. Picked up the other one. Tucked my hand in its hood. 'Dad's a bloody bugger liar.'

'JJ!' Tessa's voice was knife sharp. 'God will strike you down.'

I dropped the cloth and spread my arms like Christ on the cross, as if to say, here I am, strike away.

'So where else is she, then?' Tim asked, all reasonable.

I got the cloth again. 'Dunno.' My voice was no bigger than a pinhead.

'Reckon you should ring Aunty Peg and find out,' he said. I poked my tongue at him.

'She'll do no such thing,' said Tessa. 'Nobody goes near the phone without Dad's say so.' Tessa got Philly to pack away the polishing. She sent Tim out to chop the kindling. She made me clean the polish off the lino.

★ ★ ★

When Dad came in for lunch he nodded at the shoes lined up square like usual. He sat to the table with a grunt, as if he'd been on the tractor day and night for a month. Tessa had sliced up the corned beef Mum'd cooked the morning she left and had it on the table ready with a bit of lettuce and some boiled eggs, so we all sat. Dad forgot Grace so Tessa reminded him. He gave Tim the nod, and Tim gave Grace a good run for its money. Dad didn't stop him racing through it, though.

'Dad,' I started. 'Dad — DAD.' Not a peep back. 'DAD.' My voice went up, an edge in it.

'Yep,' he said, like he'd been paying attention all along.

Tessa kicked me under the table.

I kicked her back. 'When's Mum gunna call again?'

He grunted.

'Dad?'

'What?'

'Mum.'

He brought his great hammer of a fist down on the table. The salt and pepper shakers jumped out of their skins. 'How the hell would I know?' he thundered. 'How am I supposed to get inside the workings of your mother's head? Why does any sane woman up and leave her husband with a litter of kids? It's not right. She's a selfish b — ' He stopped himself just in time.

None of us moved. Dad never said a bad word about Mum. Ever.

'Don't worry, Dad,' Philly finally said. 'Aunty Peg'll be right in a couple of days.'

'She'll call when she can,' he said, all mild again, as if Philly hadn't said a word.

We got back to the business of eating, not daring to look at each other. I waited until he was up to his cuppa for my next go.

'Dad, can we take Mum's things to her?'

'She's got everything she needs,' Dad said, all final and no more to be said on the matter.

I pushed my chair back, tipping it over. The sound of it clattering behind me as I sped into Mum's room, raced back out. 'What about her weddin ring, then?' I asked, holding it up.

'Shit.' He looked at each of us in turn. 'Where'd ya get that?'

'It was on her bedside table.'

He glared, and then it was like his glare came undone and his eyes got lost.

I picked up the chair and sat in it, closing my fingers over Mum's ring.

'Hell of a rush, she said.' Dad's voice was low and gravelly. 'Must have forgotten it behind.' He had his eyes back under control and had them staring out the window.

I left it go for a while, then I began again. 'Dad.'

It was him and the winter grey outside the window all wrapped up together.

'Dad,' I said again.

We held our breath.

'Dad.'

'Clear up, JJ,' said Tessa, standing up to stop me. 'Your turn to wash.'

'DAD,' I yelled. His hand started trembling on the table and I was quick sorry.

'We have to get her ring to her,' I said, tripping over the words cause I had to get them out before I thought better of them. 'You know how she says she's all naked without it.'

'And you know we don't have the petrol.' He

39

said it in this low and dirty voice as if it was all my fault. But even though he was looking right at me, I got the idea that it wasn't me he was talking to.

'We should get the petrol from Mr Kennedy,' I said. 'Cause what if she's not at Aunty Peggy's any more? If she's gone somewhere else? She might need us to find her.'

'Stop talking rot.'

'Can we call her, then?'

'Your mother's a busy woman, JJ. She'll call when she can. That Peg's a mad old coot. Especially when she's high as a kite.'

I swapped a look with Tim. This was a lot of talking for the old man. He was acting all weird again.

'Reckon she'd have time for one phone call,' I said, pushing.

Tessa saw Dad was about to blow so she grabbed me by the shoulder and hiked me off the seat. 'Stop your bloody lawyering on.' She shoved the plates into my hand and pushed me towards the sink.

Dad didn't even say anything about her swearing.

I didn't either. I was too busy screwing my eyes up tight, tight, to keep it all inside. Tessa had said the thing Mum always said to me, but coming out of Tessa's mouth it didn't sound right.

THE STORY JACK TELLS

Early Sunday I was in my school uniform and Philly was in hers, ready for Mass. She didn't like it, but since we didn't have any good clothes, Mum always made us wear our uniforms. Philly sat, hands clasped, arms long across the kitchen table, like she was in school and waiting for the teacher to give her a gold star.

'What's got you all extra prim and proper?' asked Tim as he hurtled out of his room towards the front door, ready. Philly shook her head. Once and then twice, with a wait like a full stop at the end of each one. Tim stopped short and grinned. He crossed his arms and leaned against the cupboard, waiting for the show to begin.

Tessa came in from outside with the egg-collecting tin. 'This is your job, Philly. Just because Mum's away.' She put the tin on the bench and looked at Tim, then tracked back to Philly, suspicious. 'What are you doing?'

'Waiting, like I should be,' Philly said, her chin tilting up just that bit too much.

'Never known you to 'wait'.' Tessa had her fingers all quoted up. 'Give us a look at you.'

Philly shook her head, twisting her legs under her stool, eyes bulging out of sockets with the worry of it.

Dad blasted on the horn outside. Tessa

marched over to Philly and hauled her out of her chair by the back of her school jumper. Tim saw it straight away. I followed his eyes to Philly's feet. It took Tessa a few seconds longer to get there, but when she did she didn't waste a second. 'Get them off,' she barked.

Mum couldn't have done it better.

Philly shook her head. Dad blasted on the horn twice more. Philly started for the door.

'There's no way on God's good earth — ' more Mum words from Tessa's mouth — 'that you are wearing party shoes to Mass.'

'Just this once,' I said.

'You butt out, Miss Troublemaker.'

Philly half ran to reach the door.

Tessa stretched a hand out to yank her back. 'Get her school shoes,' she threw over her shoulder at me.

'Get em yourself.' I pointed to the hearth where Philly's were the only shoes left. She'd pushed them under the newspaper but the toe of one still peeped out.

'You're where she gets this kind of behaviour from,' Tessa said to me as she pulled Philly over to the fireplace to rip her shiny black patent-leather shoes off.

School shoes on, we all got in the car. I patted Philly's hand behind Tessa's back.

At least Tessa didn't have the nerve to get Mum's Mass book and Mass scarf out of the glove box. I would have had something to say about that. Nobody touched Mum's missal. She kept it tied nice and tight in her Mass scarf. She always swiped our hands away when we tried to help her

42

with the knots. 'Nothing wrong with my own fingers thank you very much.'

We were the last car to pull into the church paddock, just like always. Mum would have been putting her scarf around her neck, making the blue blue of the flower sit right at her throat. Mum and I loved hyacinths. 'Things staying the same,' she said. 'Consistency.' I liked all the 'sssssss' sounds in the way she said conssssisstenssssy.

I rubbed my tummy.

'You sick?' asked Philly.

'Nah, just funny.'

'Cause Mum?'

I nodded.

★   ★   ★

The church even smelled different. We were in our usual pew, right up the front, but there was something dark in the air.

I had a good look around. It was the flowers that made the difference. Big, fat night-red roses from Mrs Nolan's garden. There were a lot of them: regret and sorrow. Not the promise of spring lilacs Mum'd been bucketing the bath water on for weeks. Not that Mrs Nolan would have ever read Mum's flower book to know what's what. I saw Tessa's eyes burning into the flowers, too. She'd forgotten it was Mum's turn for the altar, otherwise she would have made sure Mum's lilacs were up there all right. Tessa tore at a fingernail. She'd missed another Mum beat now and I was glad.

All the mothers were face front to the altar but murmuring to their husbands and swapping side looks at one another. Only an emergency would mean Sarah McBride would let Nancy Nolan do her flowers, that's what they were all thinking. The secret language of flowers. Flowers had a language all right: we spoke it loud and clear at Our Lady of the Rosary.

The altar boys shuffled in from the vestry, frilled up in their white dresses, with Father McGinty and his big beer gut bringing up the rear. Mrs Tyler squidged in behind us on her high-heeled toes, late like usual, all the way to the front pew where the rest of her mob were. She snuck in right as Father McGinty finished his bowing to the altar and turned to face us, staring right over our heads so he didn't have to actually look any of us in the eye. Dad always shook his head at Mrs Tyler being late, but Mum hushed him up, saying it was because she had to iron the boys' good shirts, do the girls' hair, get the roast on, pile the wood on the fire and a million other things before she could get herself dressed, like women had to do everywhere. But since they only lived across the road she could send the rest of them on ahead so it was only her who was ever late.

At the end of Mass, the mothers pegged Dad down on the church porch. He could have got past them down the steps easy if he wanted to escape because no woman ever went into the men's circle. But Dad was in no hurry at all. Only too happy to stop and coat all the mothers up in what Mum called his Big Church Man smile, all serious and holier than thou. Mum hated that look. Dad stood there taking all questions, explaining the last-minute emergency. They knew what Peg was like. They all grew up together around Nulla, went to the same school, same dances, same church; all thick as thieves until Dad threw Aunty Peg out of our house just before Philly was born, and she took herself off to the city to live. There were nods and tsks all around. Tessa stood at Dad's elbow, Tim to the other side, and Philly and me behind, scuffing our feet against the wall, but soft so we could still hear what he was saying. Dad said a neighbour had found Aunty Peg raving in the street and had called Mum. Nobody said boo, cause like Mum said, they all treated Dad like he was some kind of god.

Dad served it all up and then got out free into the open air. He punched one hand into the other as if he'd done something hard but done was done. I elbowed Philly to show her, but she'd been looking the other way. Her eyes were all on Mrs Nolan heading in our direction. I backed away fast, sliding along the wall, but didn't get far cause Philly was in the way and then it was too late.

'How are you, pets?' Mrs Nolan asked, head to the side, her mouth like a small pinched button, even though it was all lipsticked up fire-engine red.

I squashed down the quick lick of flame at the cheek of her saying 'pet' after what she said about me to Mum when they were doing the tomatoes the morning Mum took off. But I had

45

to keep shut about it in case she asked any of her nosy questions in front of Philly. Besides, what if Mum told her one or two things after I did what I did?

So I kept my head down, and Philly and I scuffed and grunted like we always did talking to adults. Philly had one sock up and one down. I was torn between wanting to pull one up because I didn't want Mrs Nolan saying anything terrible about Philly being a little savage, and pushing the other down cause then Philly'd have two relaxed socks. Philly had her eyes on the ground, too, so it didn't take long for her to see the state her socks had got into. A gasp popped out of her and she clapped a hand to her mouth. She put her short sock leg up the wall behind her to hide it from Mrs Nolan.

'We'll set up a roster.' Mrs Nolan patted her handbag. 'Poor love.' She nodded at Tessa, who was moving at a grown-up slow pace. 'Been telling me all about it. She's got a lot on her plate.'

'We'll be right, thanks, Mrs Nolan,' I said in a rush. 'It was just lucky Mum did a lot of extra cooking the day before she had to go.'

Mrs Nolan turtled her neck back to give me a stab-sharp look like something wasn't adding up. But she didn't say what, and I wasn't about to ask in case it ended up someplace I didn't like.

'Best be on the safe side, though,' she finally said. More patting against her handbag. Philly had her eyes glued on it despite Mum being who knows where. That bag was as shiny black as the party shoes Philly had tried to wear to Church.

46

'Just luck I opened up early this morning to check everything was shipshape.' Mrs Nolan tsked. 'And very fortunate I did. Imagine my worry when I saw Sarah hadn't done the altar.' She put her hands up like stoplights in front of her. 'I just happened to have the roses in the car. Saved the day. You never know what will come in handy, I say.'

Is that what you say? I said, but all in my head. Then: *Are you and your roses tooling around waiting for somebody to slip up? Like my mum. Happy now?*

'We don't need a roster, thanks Mrs Nolan,' I said, making my voice loud. 'Mum'll be back in a fair shake of a pussy cat's tail.' I hoped hard that using Mum's own kind of words might add a bit of weight.

Mrs Nolan gave me a look like I had dirt on my face. 'There's Kathy. We'll sort it out.' She headed off to catch Mrs Tyler, patting my arm before I could whip it out of the way.

I screwed up my face at Mrs Nolan's wide, wide back.

Philly looked out to where the other kids were haring about like aeroplanes and windmills. She took a step to go and join them, but Tessa's hand snaked out and grabbed her by the elbow. Philly's face jerked up. Tessa shook her head. We both knew what that meant. We had a sick Aunty Peg and a saint of a mother, so we'd better make her proud. I caught Tommy's eye. He had his hand on the edge of the slingshot poking out of his pocket. We'd made it out of the crook of a good old branch last Sunday and we were going to test it out on the bullseye tree today. I lopsided my mouth and shook my head. He jerked his head saying he understood, scuffed his feet in solidarity with me for a few seconds, then sent me an apologetic twist of his mouth which served as a smile and took off. I didn't mind. I would have done the same.

Philly leaned back beside me on the wall again, her mouth bunched up at the unfairness. We stood there, nobody looking but everybody knowing where we were. Tessa was in the women's circle for the first time in her life.

In the empty stretch of boring, I elbowed Philly and showed her a couple of pebbles I'd taken out of my pocket. I nodded towards Tessa. Philly shook her head as if to ask, *What's wrong with you?* So I threw a pebble at Tessa's back all on my own. Tessa didn't look around. So I threw another — with a bit more force. She put her hand behind her and formed her fingers into a gun.

I let a few more minutes of nothing snail by and when Tessa was good and distracted with the sad of it all, I wandered back into the hush of the church where Mrs Tyler was collecting up the vases on the altar. I was sorry Mum wasn't there to do the flowers. All us girls helped her, but Mum looked to me to get them right because I was the best feeler among the lot of us.

After a while I went up the aisle to the altar rail. I pressed my hands to my tummy while I waited, but Mrs Tyler didn't come out of the sacristy where she'd taken the vases. I scratched my face with my bitten-back nails, then bobbed before the altar, hoping God wouldn't strike me down for going where I didn't belong. I went up the stairs and then behind the heavy red velvet curtains.

Mrs Tyler was there fussing about with goblets and vases. When I was with Mum I loved the feel of all the shiny tin and smooth glass, but now I shouldn't be here because women were only allowed if they were cleaning up after the priest. Which Mrs Tyler was. But I wasn't.

'What's up, love?' Mrs Tyler asked as if she didn't think it strange that I was there at all.

I couldn't get the words lined up right.

She put the gold serving plate she was holding down and came over to me. 'You worried about your mum?'

I nodded. I didn't mind Mrs Tyler because Mum liked her best.

She kneaded my shoulder. 'She'll be back.'

'She wants a roster,' I blurted out.

'Who? Nancy?'

I nodded my head as if I could nod it right off.

'You worried it means your mum's not coming back?'

I kept my head at nodding because that was exactly right. Mrs Nolan was the one who drove Mum away and maybe she knew more than anyone.

'Your mum's helping Peg and we're helping your mum. That's the way things are done.' She looked at the open wardrobe where she'd just about finished putting it all away. Shuffled a couple of vases to the side. Picked up the plate again. 'You mustn't worry. It cuts your mum to ribbons.' She

49

smiled over her shoulder at me. 'She'll be back soon. You know wild horses couldn't drag her away from you little rascals, especially you, JJ.' She tucked the plate under a smaller one.

'Has she rung you?' I asked.

Her hands stopped their quick pecking at the dishes in the cupboard, re-positioning them. 'Are you saying she hasn't called home?'

'Once,' I said, my voice squeaky. 'But she only spoke to Dad. We were at school.'

Her forehead creased.

'I'm worried she doesn't have everything she needs, cause maybe she stayed longer that she thought she would,' I said.

'Your Aunty Peg will lend her what she needs. Lord knows she'll have something to spare in that house of hers.' She tried for a cheery tone cause everyone made fun of Aunty Peg and her keeping stuff.

'She forgot her wedding ring,' I said.

Mrs Tyler's smile disappeared. 'She left her ring?'

I didn't tell her that I was scared Mum leaving it behind meant she'd gone forever, but I could see I didn't need to. The creases in her face cut in deeper. She shoved the last things in fast, closed the cupboard with a bang. She hurt my shoulder with her squeeze.

'Reckon we should take it to her?' I didn't say it was because I needed to tell Mum how sorry I was.

'Could very well be right there, love. Let me speak to your dad.'

I was glad, and not glad.

Dad was all buttoned up in the car. We stopped in at the milk bar to get the mail. Philly and I were out the car door before it had practically stopped, but there was nothing from Mum. There were no corners in Philly's face to hide her disappointment.

'Letter?' Dad snorted when we reported back to him. 'She's only away for a few days. She's not likely to waste her money on a stamp. She'd get home before any letter.'

We got our choc wedges and piled back into the car. We licked at them like it was normal because, no matter what, we knew Mum saved up all week so we could buy them and we weren't going to let her down.

When we got to the hill before our place, Dad kept his eyes on the road. Tim and Philly and I looked at each other, worry bouncing between us in the back seat. Normally Dad didn't do what people called 'driving' down this hill. He usually crept along, taking in all the things that had changed since he was last that way, making a new map of everything in his head.

'Do you want me to check the level of the creek, Dad?' Philly piped up finally.

'I'll be on the lucerne,' I said. 'Tell you how much it's grown.'

'She'll be right,' he said, his eyes still glued to the road, taking the curve down to the bridge more than fast.

Tim and Philly and I grabbed the back of the seat in front and handballed some more worry between us. We made it home in one piece, though. Dad turned off the engine and pulled on the handbrake. He put two hands on the steering wheel and leaned back. After a minute of waiting and watching him, Tessa shooed us in to put the beans on and make the gravy for the roast.

★ ★ ★

'Is he still there?' Tessa asked, a while later, when I lifted the lace to look out the window.

'Stuck like mud.'

'Tell him dinner's on the table.'

Philly went out and that did get him moving, but slow. He didn't even wash his hands. He pulled his chair out and angled it towards the window, his legs stretched long and eyes staring out over the paddocks. He leaned his forearm on the table and drummed his fingers against the tablecloth. Tessa put his meal down in front of him. We all waited until he picked up his fork and speared it into the lamb before we got stuck into ours.

After a while, Dad broke the silence. 'Nobody should be bothering people.' He shoved a forkful of squashed peas into his mouth.

The other kids looked up. I didn't.

'What do you mean, Dad?' asked Tim.

'That's all I'm saying. People have their own worries. And your mother's fine.'

From the corner of my eye, I saw Tim shrug and get back to his eating business.

'It puts shame on this family,' Dad went on, a whine getting in to his voice, 'and I can't be explaining to everybody that your mother has got her hands full with an emergency so doesn't have time to ring every five minutes, and what a drama queen certain people are.'

Tessa looked around, stricken. Then she saw me with my head down, keeping a close eye on proceedings on my plate. Relief that she was off the hook was chased away by a grimace that she should have known a thing or two.

'What?' I burst out, accusing her.

'What, what?' she said.

'You always think it's me.'

'Because it always is.' Her face twisted hard and voice loud. 'The rest of us are doing what we should. Tim's out on the horse, I'm cooking — '

'What about Philly?'

'Philly's a baby,' said Tessa. 'But even she did the folding.'

'I'm not a baby!' said Philly.

I stared knives back at Tessa. 'You're not Mum and you never will be.'

She sprang to her feet. 'You — '

Dad's fist thundered on the table. 'We'll have a bit of peace around the dinner table,' he said. 'Your mother would be ashamed of the lot of yous.'

Tessa sat down, pulled her chair back into the table. 'Sorry, Dad.'

He grunted.

I wasn't sorry. I was glad because me talking to Mrs Tyler had been all forgotten. What I wasn't glad about was that it looked like Dad wasn't listening to Mrs Tyler either, and we

weren't getting in the Holden to go and see
Mum anytime soon.

* * *

When Philly and I woke up Monday morning,
there was a little black body tangled up in the
lace of our bedroom curtain. It was all folded
inside its wings. I yanked the blanket back over
my head, leaving a gap so I could keep an eye on
it. The tousle of Philly's head stirred.

'Don't move,' I whispered.

Philly flipped back the blankets, saw the bat,
squealed, flipped the blankets straight back over
her head.

'Shh. You'll wake it up.' I slipped my feet out
of bed first and followed them down between
our two beds, squishing a pillow to my head
while I snaked over to Philly's bed and slipped
up under her blankets. Her eyes were big in the
dark.

'We can't stay here. We'll miss the bus,' she
whispered after a while.

'We'll have to make a run for it.'

But neither of us moved. Our bodies like two
halves of an apricot.

'I need to wee,' said Philly eventually. That got
us going. We spent a lot of time setting up for a
quick getaway. Then we did it, charged out,
pillows plastered like beanies to our heads. Tessa
had to go back in to get our uniforms.

* * *

The next morning when the sun woke us up, the bat was back hanging there. Philly let out a whimper that went on and on like a train. When it hadn't been there when we got home from school last night, she'd been sure that we'd never see that bat again. In the end we called Tim to bring his air gun. He sent us out of the room and when it was done there was a smudge of black on the white pretend-lace curtain where the bat had been. Philly made me climb up on the bed head and jump the curtain rod down. She pushed both the curtains off the rod, rolled them in her arms and took off for the laundry. She got Tessa to help her and before long those curtains were back up on the rod drying. There was still a dead bat shadow, but Philly pinned it in a way that nobody could tell.

I was all dressed for school and admiring her handiwork when I saw Dad out the window under the pine trees.

He couldn't feel me. He wasn't like that.

I thought everybody could feel things, but there was one time I was tucked in between the two house tanks with my book. Mum had called Dad to help her chase the goats out of her vegie patch where they were doing a power of damage. As Dad shoved the last one out it raced under the clothesline and yanked down a shirt of Dad's. Mum started to chase it, but Dad laughed. 'Let it go, Sare,' he said. He grabbed her from behind, wrapping his arms around her. 'Didn't like it, anyway. Horrible itchy.' I was going to pop out and join in the laughing. But Dad was nuzzling and kissing Mum, all close and unbearable. First

55

Mum leaned into him but then pushed back, swiping at him with her apron.

'Not in front of the kids.' She laughed.

'None here,' he said, pulling her back into his arms.

'What's that, then?' asked Mum, swivelling around, pointing dead on me. 'Block of flats?'

'You've got eyes in the back of your head,' he said, all admiration, letting her go with a final slap on her rear.

'Comes in handy with four kids.'

I was a feeler like Mum.

Now Dad was standing under Tessa's tree. Hands on hips. He pushed his hat back on his head. I was about to turn away to get dressed for school, give him a bit of privacy, when he staggered, his hand stretching out for the tree. But he didn't connect. It was like he gave up on the idea of staying upright and collapsed to his knees, toppled forwards so his forehead was to the ground, back heaving. I was stabbed through with the pain in him.

But what was breaking him in bits? Then it hit me. The big of it stopped my breath hard. Mum might or might not be at Aunty Peg's like he'd been saying, but he was as certain as he could be that she was not coming home. Not on her own.

I pushed back off the windowsill and ran to find Tessa.

'Get the Rice Bubbles,' she said, not looking up from the sink.

'Dad — ' I started.

'Just do it, JJ. For once in your life.'

So I did. But not because she told me.

WHAT MRS NOLAN KNOWS

'Get those ricies into ya,' I said to Philly when she came out of the bathroom, cheeks all rubbed up rosy hard like Alice, which she was still reading. She was just a little Alice kid, trying to get on with things in a world that didn't make sense without Mum.

There was Dad in pieces and Philly still baby-bird small. I smashed one fist into one hand cause I knew it was up to me now.

'Made em myself,' I said.

She spun around twice before she sat, sticking her little finger out as she held the spoon. 'Delicious,' she said in her little-girl posh voice. 'So good, you should open another restaurant at the other end of the house.'

'Madam.' I bowed. 'I spat my best spit.'

She pushed the bowl away.

'In my bowl, not yours.'

She pulled the bowl back to her, her eyes all squinty, head shaking like a little monkey.

I thought I was doing a good job distracting her. But the next thing she said slapped that right out of me. 'Mum'll definitely ring today,' she said.

I hoped like hell she would, too. Otherwise how could I tell her I was sorry and I'd never do it again, and she should come home cause we all missed her and Dad was in bits, and I'd iron my school clothes and not whinge about it and I'd wear that stupid school ribbon, and I'd never say a terrible thing to her again.

'Dad can tell us all about what she says, then.' Tessa came into the kitchen, all school uniformed up.

'He'll be down the paddock.' Philly slurped up Rice Bubbles and milk. 'I better stay home from school to answer.'

'Don't be stupid, Philly,' Tessa said. 'I'm just wrapping up a piece of Mum's apple cake for you to take for little play.'

A spurt of fear jerked my head to face Tessa because I knew good and proper there was no apple cake, and she must know it too, so she was setting out a trap for me and finally I'd have to admit to everything. But when I turned to get in first and accuse her, she was bent down to the freezer pulling out a round shape wrapped in foil. Then I knew. Mum must have made more than one cake the morning she left. It took me a while to get my breath nice and steady after I realised I'd dodged the Tessa-finding-out-what-I-did bullet.

I'd smelled that apple cake smell from all the way down the back of the house where I'd been in bed the morning she left. My tummy had gone back to normal. But the rule, see, was if you if took a sickie cause you said you were sick, you had to stay in bed. So I pretended I had to go to the toilet so I could get a taste, just a tiny bit from the underneath so nobody noticed.

But it was even yummier than normal. I knew

I'd gone too far because I was full as a goog, and because the underneath of the cake looked like a moon crater, all pocked and empty.

When I heard Mum's footsteps outside coming up the path back to the house I froze, then shoved the cake back under the tea towel, backed away fast, hands locked tight behind my back. But I knew it had to be written all over my face. Then, at the last minute, Mrs Nolan, who I hadn't realised had come over, called out to Mum, and her footsteps went back the other way.

I couldn't believe my luck. Then I did need to wee. I straightened tall and rubbed some innocence into my face. Mum wasn't just a feeler, she was a real good one; could feel from half a paddock away, so it took a lot to pull one over her. I scooted along to the toilet, which was up past the underground tank. Normally I stopped to open the lid and get my head inside the cool dark of the tank that went all its echoey way to the centre of the earth. But this time I was all business, heading for the outhouse and hoping like hell the pan wasn't full.

The air was sharp cold, so the warm of the outhouse sat nice on my skin. I peeled my jarmie pants down.

'Yep. Stayed home again,' I heard Mum say from the vegie patch.

'She's a handful,' said Mrs Nolan's hard, polished voice.

I stuck out my tongue and waited for Mum to tell Mrs Nolan she was wrong.

'Always got the knife and fork out, carving us

up,' was what Mum said instead.

I gripped the toilet seat, my skin lit up with buzzing.

'She's not a bit like Tessa. That JJ needs a good firm hand to keep her on the straight and narrow,' said Mrs Nolan.

'Needs something.'

I held my tummy. That cake had got nearly all inside me. Mum'd see. She'd know it was me. Something was clouding me up. Twisting red and slamming about at my inside walls. I jumped off the toilet and pulled up my jarmies. I rushed out and banged the door closed. It didn't make a loud enough bang, so I banged it again and stamped around to the vegie patch.

Mum looked up. Hope in her that I hadn't heard, so I wiped that look off her face quick smart.

'I hate you,' I yelled. 'You're a . . . you're a . . . bum.'

I swung around and took off.

'Elizabeth Jane, you get back here right now.'

But I was back in the kitchen and the slamming of the front door behind me cut off the rest. I went straight to that cake and I lifted that tea towel and I used both hands and I tore that thing apart until it was just crumbs. Now she'd never know that I ate it. I stood back. It wasn't enough. I picked up the plate to throw those crumbs all around the kitchen.

But then I saw on the backbench Mum had set a bed tray for me. It had lilac in a vase and everything. Mum always gave me lilac when I was sick, a little bit of hope I would spring back to wellness fast. It was our special thing. I dropped that plate back on the bench like it burned, stepped back. Hands tight together.

Mum was right. I was trouble. I knew it all the way down into the part of me that went on forever. Past all those watching eyes, down, down, to where there was no more me but it still went on.

I was on the ground, all curled up and folded over. Then there was Mum in the kitchen with me and she had me gathered into her arms, pulling me onto her lap, wrapping me around with the soft of her forgiveness. I burrowed into the cake smell of her. She was the only one who could ever change the colours in me, so I went in and in to her. She held me tight and tight, and rocked me, saying 'JJ' over and over.

After a while the air got lighter. She got up and walked me to the bathroom, wet a washer and washed my face, and the cool of it took another layer of the dark away. Then she walked me back to bed and tucked me in and sat beside me, smoothing my hair behind my ear. All fairy gentle.

When I woke up, she was gone.

Then I found out she was gone, gone.

It was all my fault. Dad was all in pieces under the front trees; Tessa trying to fit into Mum's shoes and mad because she knew she couldn't. Tim so out of his skin he was getting himself strapped at school, and Philly, like a baby chick who had nobody to follow any more. It was too big and Mum hadn't forgiven me after all. But she would.

61

I knew what I had to do. I couldn't wait for her to call in case she never did. I had to go and get her myself. Tell her I'd be better. Make her come home.

'You haven't touched your cereal,' Tessa said.

I gave up and pushed the bowl away. 'Got spit in it.' I tried a half grin at Philly. 'Tim can have it.' I rubbed my tummy, trying to settle it.

'You sick again?' asked Philly.

'Just itchy.'

I ran back to our bedroom and stuffed some after-school clothes in my schoolbag and upended my piggy bank into the palm of my hand. There wasn't much so I did the same with Philly's. Reckon she'd think it was in a good cause.

'Timmm!' yelled Tessa. I made it back into the kitchen just as he came out of Mum's sewing room, which joined up to his bedroom. 'You can have JJ's spit,' Tessa said from the sink, hands deep in the suds, 'or you've missed out again. Bus'll be here.'

'JJ's spit,' he said, sitting down. He wolfed down the Rice Bubbles as Philly and I slung our bags over our shoulders, me pretending mine wasn't fuller than usual. We all took off down the track at the same time, but I ran back pretending I'd forgotten something and shoved a few more things from the kitchen cupboard into my school-bag. I dashed out again, stopping to give Dad's good old dog, Doll, an extra scratch between her ears, telling her to look after Dad for me. Doll's eyes were full of serious, like she understood her job now wasn't just herding up the sheep.

At the school gate, I gave Philly a peck beside

the cowlick in her fringe and she shot off. Tim didn't look back. Tessa and I normally walked together because our rooms were side by side, but she had to go to the church first to say some extra prayers. I left her at the door, then slipped behind the church and dodged through the trees to the back fence, skidded over it and headed towards the main road. I got changed in the bushes and shoved my school uniform in my bag.

While I waited for the school bell to ring, I shovelled in a couple of spoonfuls of Milo that I'd put into a jam jar. Then the bell finally boomed. It took two boys swinging on the end of it. I loved how that bell sounded deep in your belly. The nuns didn't let us girls near the bell rope.

I stood up and went to the side of the road. My feet were sticky to the ground and my thumb was like it didn't belong to me, all stuck out on its own. But straight away a car slowed. I thanked the driver and got in the back seat, hugging my schoolbag close on my lap. I told the driver I was on my way to the city.

'That's a fair hike,' he said, pulling back onto the road. 'I can take you nearly to the freeway. How'd that do ya?'

'Good, thanks.' I shifted on the seat, pulled at the bottom of my jumper.

He tapped at the wheel. 'What's in the city?'

'My Aunt Peg's sick. We don't have the money for me to go on the train.'

'Fair enough.'

We drove on, going back up the road the bus had just come.

'Got an address? For your Aunt Peg?'

'Got everything I need, thanks.' I patted my schoolbag, even though he didn't have eyes in the back of his head.

'Taking time off school, then?'

'Mum and Dad say it's for a good cause.'

'Don't you have a brother they could send instead?'

'Nah,' I lied. Funny that people thought just cause you're a boy you could do everything better. Maybe some could.

I tried to come up with something to show I knew what was what even though I was just a girl. 'Been a lot of rain,' I said. This was how you paid for the ride. We were always shuffling our bums over for a hitchhiker. You met some interesting people. Now I was one of them.

He grunted. I'd done my bit so I settled back into the seat.

He slowed the car at the top of Rileys Lane. 'Good luck, then,' he said. 'Hope your Aunt Peg gets better.'

I thanked him and beamed a smile that curled up at the edges and died before it got a real hold. The slam of the door behind me made me jump. It was only twenty minutes of walking and I'd be on that freeway and then I was really on my way. I plucked at the neck of my jumper. I had thought God would stop me. But he must've thought me going to get Mum was a good idea after all.

I swung my bag onto my shoulder and put one foot in front of the other. Quick as lick, I hadn't even got halfway, another car pulled over. It was

Mrs Tyler's sister. She came to our Mass, too. 'Going somewhere?' She leaned over and shoved the door open so I had to get into the front seat beside her.

'The city.' Before she asked, I gave her the story.

'I'm off to Chilton, so that's a start.'

'Thanks, Mrs Roanan.' I steeled myself because this sister was the talkative one. But Mum must have been wrong because Mrs Roanan didn't say much. Then she remembered something. 'Dear me, I left my shopping bag at home. I'm just going to zip back and get it. Won't take a mo.'

She did a slow U-ey and we turned into her drive. She had all kinds of pink and purple dahlias all along the front of her house. Big petals, the kind Mum and I loved best. A few too many red ones, though. Mum would have told her to get rid of those quick smart. You don't want betrayal and dishonesty right on your front doorstep. Mrs Roanan leaned across me to spring the door open. 'Tell you what, while I'm picking my bag up, why don't you come in for a biscuit. Fresh made.'

My tummy rumbled. I liked the idea because I liked biscuits, and I didn't like the idea because I was supposed to have more serious things on my mind.

'You've got a long way to go.' She smiled, even though that smile wasn't sitting properly. Mrs Roanan led me through the front door and into the kitchen. It smelled baking good, so I thought what a good idea it had been to stop in the end. She got out the milk and poured me a glass and set it down before me. She put one, two, three, four and then even one more biscuit on a plate.

'I'll just go track down that bag, be right with you.' She disappeared into a dark corridor.

I took a nibble. Not like Mum's, but pretty good. It was warm and homey in Mrs Roanan's kitchen. The kind of place you could fill your lungs. The tea cosy was knitted and all pink like a princess dress. There was a set of canisters for tea and sugar and flour set out on the sideboard like they were decorations. They did look good because they were made out of china like houses in a fairytale, with chimneys and everything. I bet Mum would have liked that kitchen, where everything was neat as a pin and there were frilly curtains on the window. My feet twitched, but I knew it wasn't good manners to go looking in somebody else's place so I ate another biscuit.

Mrs Roanan ran in from the corridor, all panty. 'The pigs have got out. I'll just round them up and yard them again.'

I jumped up ready to help. She pushed me back into the chair. 'You'll only scare them, dear. They don't know you.'

I bit into another biscuit. Never known pigs to care about one person over any other.

Mrs Roanan got back in after a while. I'd finished all those biscuits and my tummy was pushing against my trousers.

'I'll pack you a few more.'

I took my cup and plate to the sink. I rinsed them off and stood them in her dish tray. I picked up my bag and stood by the table, waiting.

66

She tilted her head like she was listening to the wind. A growl was making its way up her driveway. 'Listen, love,' she said, turning to me. I could see that smile that didn't sit properly again. 'I'm sorry, poppet, but there was just no — '

She broke off at a knock at the door.

THE THING THAT SHOULDN'T
BE THERE

It was Dad at the door. Mrs Roanan let him in, her smile still looking as if it could slip off her face any second. I saw now it was an apology. So I'd learned something. How to read those smiles.

I wanted to throw myself at Dad and hug him up good, but he didn't even look my way. Mrs Roanan handed me the packet of biscuits she'd made and I didn't look her way. She patted my shoulder. 'Your mum'll be home before you know it, poppet.'

'Thank Mrs Roanan and apologise for putting her to trouble,' said Dad.

So I did.

I slid into the front of the ute and hunched over. It was all black around him. I tightened myself up, ready for him to blow. But he didn't say a word. Then I squeezed myself even harder because he hadn't blown and because he was all screwed down. I kicked at the glove box.

'Stop that.'

I kicked again.

'You hear what I say?'

I heard all right.

I plaited my legs so they wouldn't kick any more. I tapped along the dashboard instead. Then I realised Dad wouldn't like that any better, so I tried to wrap my hands around each other and keep them in my lap. But I must have knocked the glove box because it sprung open.

Dad exploded then. 'Leave that bloody thing alone.'

I shoved it shut quick smart. We drove on.

'What's Mum's Mass scarf doing in the glove box?'

'What're ya talkin about?'

'Mum's scarf. In the glove box.'

'Suppose she can keep her scarves where she wants.'

I felt the vein pumping in his forehead from way over where I sat.

'Her Mass scarf is always knotted tight around her Mass book.' I smacked the glove box with the back of my hand. It flipped open again. 'And now it's all on its own, right there.'

He leaned over and shut it with a bang that meant business. 'How would I know why she stuck it in there?'

'Doesn't make sense. If she was planning to be away long enough to go to Mass she would have taken her scarf as well. You ever seen her in church without that scarf?'

'Stop pushing, JJ.' His voice had that grit of teeth.

Everything got real still and silent like the sky before the storm. And I crawled deeper in and in, keeping my lips buttoned, but it was no use: the thunder came anyway.

He thumped the steering wheel so it bounced. 'It's all push and shove with you,' he blasted. 'You never let up. No wonder your mother — '

He made himself stop mid rage.

It's not like he needed to finish that sentence, though. He was nothing but right. The scarf in the glove box didn't change one thing. Mum was gone. Cause of me. And he was trying to keep it from the others.

I stared straight ahead, bit into my thumbnail, ripped the top of it clean away.

He looked over. Whatever he saw in me changed something in him. 'Just give it a bone,' he said like the bottom of a bucket had just broken and the rage all whooshed away.

He pumped the steering wheel again, but this time as if he were reminding himself of something. He rubbed his cheek, all sandpaper loud.

I did want to give it a bone.

I looked at his face, tired over with lines. I remembered him slumped on the ground under Tessa's tree this morning. I wanted to push it all back inside me. Not just from that day but right back to the morning Mum left. Right back to when I could have made things right. Right down to not eating that cake.

'Sorry, Dad.'

And I was. Real sorry.

★   ★   ★

Later, when we were finishing up the milking and the night was starting to dark up the sky, Philly came skidding into the shed. 'Where's Dad?'

Tim turned off the milking machine so we could hear. 'What?' he yelled.

'It's the police.' Philly was shaking her little hands like she was going to take off for the moon.

That stopped us. We swapped our scared between us. We'd never seen real police, just the made-up ones in *Homicide* on the telly.

'Where's Dad?' Philly whispered.

We all turned to look out into the rising night, trying to spot him.

'Dad,' we called.

He came charging in from the paddock through the holding yard as if he'd been waiting. 'What?'

'Police,' we all hollered together like we'd rehearsed it.

His big hand reached out for the fence to steady himself. He dropped his head to watch his boot scuff at the mud, but not before we saw the same scared in him that was in us.

We waited, holding on to posts on our side, watching.

It only took a couple of beats before he straightened and closed the distance through the already milked cows between us. 'Get the cups off Daisy and Tricksy.' He flicked the words at Tim and me as he pushed past, all grown up and business again.

Tim and I looked at each other and took off after Dad and Philly.

Tessa stood by the police car with the two policemen. All three watched us charging towards them, Dad's gumboots slamming against the ground.

'Mr Jack McBride?' asked the tall one as Dad got within distance.

'Who's asking?'

'Constable Michael McGuire,' he said, 'and this is Constable Steve Jones.'

'You've come to the right place, then,' Dad said. 'Get on with it.'

'Is there somewhere we can talk privately?' said Constable McGuire, nodding at us like we shouldn't be there. Dad nodded back as if the constable wasn't half his age.

'Get back up to the shed.' He flung his arms at us. 'Finish up that milking.'

Tessa shooed us away, trying to lead us back in the direction of the cowshed.

I folded my arms.

'Git.' Dad raised his hand as if he were going to belt me.

I planted my feet wide.

Tim grabbed me by the scruff of the neck and toppled me over, dragging me behind him. Tessa herded me from the rear, like I was a breakaway poddy calf. They didn't let up all the way to the shed. I didn't protest, but as soon as they loosened off I darted back down the track to the ute and hid.

Dad had his arms crossed and so did the two policemen, all of them legs apart. I strained to hear, but I was too far. The petrol tank was closer, but Philly had darted from behind me and snuck in there, with Tim fast on her heels.

I dashed over to join them, but there was no room and Tim shoved me away. He nearly gave us away by elbowing into the side of the petrol tank in the scuffle, which would have made a hell of a din with all that empty echo inside. Instead I ran to the side of the shed. I looked back and poked my tongue out. I was in way closer than him.

But it was too late. They were handing Dad a big thick envelope and shuffling their feet. The short one said how sorry he was. The tall one said nothing, all grim faced. Dad put out his hand, but it was only the short Jones one who shook it. The other turned away like Dad's hand was so much dirt.

The police got into the car and drove away, idling down the track, like they were heading for a Sunday picnic.

Tim, Philly and I came out of our hiding places, not even bothering to disguise where we'd been. Dad was still watching the police car disappear down the track, hands at his hips. There was no breath in the air.

'Get Tess,' said Dad's statue.

All three of us backed away. Not a word between us.

We got to the cowshed. Tim jerked his head, telling Tessa over the noise of the milking machine that Dad wanted to talk to us.

Tessa uncupped Daisy's and Tricksy's udders, Philly untied the leg ropes, I opened the bales so they could back out.

Tim opened the gate and we all shooed them into the holding yard to join the rest of the herd.

None of us stopped to let any of them into the paddock.

Tim turned off the machine and Tessa turned off the lights.

Tessa's hand went to Philly's. I took Philly's other one. Tim went ahead.

She died of a burst appendix, Dad said, when we were back in the kitchen. They'd taken her to a hospital quick smart, but it was too late.

'Who's they?' I asked.

Dad looked like I'd punched him and that reminded me of how he'd looked in the ute earlier when I found the scarf. I zipped my mouth up tight.

Tessa did this kind of animal noise. Philly got her thumb stuck in her mouth and crawled into Dad's lap. Tim stabbed at the fire. I was patting Tessa on the back, but not putting any heat into it.

After a while we got to, 'Does Aunty Peg know?', 'Did she cry?' and 'Reckon she'd like roses in the church for her funeral.'

There was too much empty space around us. The Mum space all empty but all filled in with the knowing she'd never be in it again.

Then I got to the knowing that if she hadn't taken off she would have been with us when her appendix burst. And we could have said stuff, told her how big she was for us. Even made her get better. And then I remembered the next thing: if I hadn't eaten that cake, or gone to that toilet, or heard that stuff, or got red mad and called her a bum. If I hadn't tired her clean out every day of my life, she wouldn't have gone at all. I pinched myself until it cut deep but it didn't help.

That night I got Ted out of the box in the corner for the first time since forever. I got him up into my arms and into bed with me without Philly seeing. The soft of his belly against my cheek was something.

★ ★ ★

Once the word got out, a lot of people came over and that made Dad pull something over his singlet to make himself decent. The men milked the cows and the women brought casseroles. I went up my tree, sat on the plough seat Dad had nailed there for us a long time ago and watched.

Tommy came around after school and I went down to the dam with him. He worried a stick into the mud until he saw I didn't want to talk about Mum. We skidded some stones for a bit, then headed down to the creek to catch frogs. On the way back there was something in the distance that didn't sit right. I told Tommy to go on back without me. He took off his glasses and polished them up. He stumbled when I pushed him in the house direction, but I didn't say sorry.

I watched him go until he couldn't look back and see me, then I ran across the paddock over to Jean's Corner. I was right. Mum's Mass scarf wasn't in the ute any more: it was tied around the bottom of the not-right-in-the-head baby's cross. It was twisted and twisted so you wouldn't know there were even hyacinths all over it. If it hadn't been for the wind moving the grass about when I'd been with Tommy I wouldn't have even seen it. How did it end up down here?

I took off my shoes and peeled off my socks and shoved them hard into the toes of the shoes, pushing until they were tiny balls and I couldn't see them any more. I put my feet into the rush of the creek and felt the ice of it right into my brain. I didn't want to think about Mum's scarf. I didn't want to think about how I couldn't say 'Mum says' any more. What she said was in the past because that was where she was. All those things were coming from behind me now. And in all before me there was no Mum.

THE WORLD WITHOUT HER

'This one?' Tessa held up Mum's navy dress.

Philly shook her head.

'She wore it to Mass,' Tessa said, pushing it further towards Philly, as if shoving it in her face would change her mind.

Philly backed away and screwed up her nose, all brussels sprouts.

I swung my legs, kicking them back under the bed. 'It's gotta have flowers.'

'Don't be stupid, she doesn't have one with flowers.' Tessa hung the dress back in the wardrobe and slid to the ground. Philly slumped with her.

'Maybe there's something in the sewing,' I said. 'Mrs Tyler could finish it.'

Philly jumped up, hope running wild across her little face, but when we all got to the sewing room the basket was empty. She puddled to the floor again.

'We'll sort it out with Dad tonight,' I said.

'Who knows what mood Dad'll be in after all that talking to the hospital and Father McGinty and stuff,' said Philly.

'Reckon he might feel a bit better after talking with Father,' I said.

Tessa and Philly nodded like they hoped like hell, too.

The dogs were going mad so I knew Pete must be coming up the track with the petrol for Dad to drive to the city. I had a thing to say to Dad before he took off, so I left Tessa and Philly to it. By the time I got out there, Pete had taken off to the cowshed to see to the poddies and Dad was siphoning the petrol from Pete's car to ours. Dad was all face screwed up sucking at the hose to get at the liquid. I waited until it gurgled up and he got it swirling down the funnel into the Holden.

'Do you reckon you should take Mum's Mass scarf to her?'

He tore his eyes away from the petrol and locked them on me. Then his face went all soft and collapsy and he turned away to get a good look at the horizon. I knew the taste of sorry again, all dried up bitter. Now Mum was gone gone I had to stop and think more, just like she always said. After a bit, his back went up and down and I got real worried about that petrol. I grabbed the hose from him and held it up so Pete would have enough left in the tank to get him home. Doll came sniffing around and rubbed up against Dad's leg. Dad dropped a hand on autopilot to Doll's head. I pulled out the hose and the funnel and tiptoed off, not wanting to get in the way of the thing Doll was giving Dad.

★　★　★

Once Dad was packed off down the track to the city and Pete had gone back to his own farm, Tessa said Mum was sure to be in heaven, but

78

just in case she had to go to purgatory for a little while we should say a rosary. Philly and I got the beads out from under everybody's pillows and we placed the chairs in a circle facing outwards so when we kneeled we couldn't see each other. Not that Tim would be wiggling his eyebrows to set us off today.

I sat on the floor in the middle of the chair circle waiting for the others. Philly came to sit by me, close, tucking in under my wing. She nudged my shoulder like a foal. 'You reckon it'll be Tessa or Tim?'

I pulled the side of my mouth down at this new worry. Tessa's the oldest so she'll want to lead the rosary, but Tim's the boy so he'll reckon he should lead off. Tim came into the laundry and shucked off his boots, just the way Dad did.

At the sound, Tessa flew in from the lounge, kneeled in front of her chair and took up her beads, feeding through them to get to the right starting one. Philly and I got to our knees too and slid across the lino to slump over the seat of our chairs as well, giving our backs to each other.

'The first Sorrowful Mystery, the Agony in the Garden,' said Tessa before Tim could even get his beads into his hands. He kneeled over his chair without putting up a fight.

Twenty minutes later the lino was getting its teeth dug up good into my knees. Truth be told, it had been biting in a while, but I'd been offering up the pain to get Mum out of purgatory. But I was real glad when Tessa swung on to the final Glory Be. When it was all done, Philly collapsed on the floor. I grinned and leaped like a frog and sat on her. She giggled. Tessa frowned, like she didn't know if giggling *after* the rosary was wrong. Then Tim was on top of us, wrestling me off.

We jumped up and shoved the chairs aside. Philly got the towels from the bathroom and twisted them up to mark out the arena on the ground. Tim, now Gorgeous George Junior, got into the ring first. Frank Knucklebender, me, charged in there after him. Baby Face Davo kneeled just outside the ring and leaned in as far as she could, arm stretching, stretching towards Frank.

Gorgeous George swung low from side to side like he was an ape and then he lunged, going in fast. I dodged, but George turned fierce and grabbed me about the waist and brought me down. He had a knee on my chest and it was pressing in hard. 'Little Sheila,' said Gorgeous George with a big grin. But Frank Knuckle-bender sees red, just like me, and the red exploded out of his belly and rolled Gorgeous George off. He yelped with the surprise, but lurched back around to pin me down.

I flung out my hand to tag Baby Face, but George pulled me back so I couldn't reach Philly. Gorgeous George's arms tightened. Tim's eyes were squeezed shut. He took one hand from around my neck and pounded his fist into my arm.

'Tim,' I yelled. 'Tim, it's me. It's me.'

Tessa screamed at him to stop. He pounded on. I pushed up into him and got my arms around him and hugged him hard. Philly was hugging him from the back. Tessa flew over, grabbed his fist, so then her hands and his were both pounding into my arm. Then she got her hands to his cheeks and cradled him up. The surprise of it stopped him. He slumped over, breathing like he'd been galloping a runaway. Philly lay against his back, Tessa kneeled over him and I was in the middle. Holding on.

Mum would know what to do.

Time slithered like a snake, all silent and like it wasn't there. Eventually Philly got the bright idea to get the Milo tin and four spoons. We lay on our tummies just where we were. Licking the last of it from the spoons before dipping them straight back in the tin again. Tessa too. She didn't even say anything when Tim's and Philly's spoons crashed on the way out of the tin and Milo went all over the floor. She just licked her thumb and pressed it over the little brown dots on the lino, then licked them off her finger. Tim, Philly and I looked at each other, a big question between us. Tim shrugged, and then we were all licking our thumbs and pressing them into the floor.

All the rules were broken and bloody now.

When Tim had had enough he downed tools and lay on his back, staring at the ceiling. Philly copied him. Tessa and I looked at each other and did the same. It was like we were still in the middle of everything and none of us wanted to go on to the next thing.

'Mum would be so mad,' said Tim, a smile swimming in his voice.

'She was Sister Mary of the flying tea towel,' I

said, thinking of her charging at one of us.

'Or Mother Superior of the Sore Bum Order,' said Tim.

'Or Mother Whack-a-lot,' said Philly.

'Monkey,' said Tessa, tickling Philly, who squeaked. Tessa lay on her back again, but this time she was right flat beside Philly.

'Do you reckon Aunty Peg was sick at all?' I asked.

Nobody said nothing.

'Or,' I said, tasting the words as they came out loud for the first time, 'maybe Mum just left us, like Dad said in the first place.'

'You have to spoil everything,' said Tessa.

She said it like a fact.

ALMOST PROOF

After lunch, Tessa spread her hands behind her on my bed, pretend-lounging back. I flicked a page in Mum's flower book. Tessa coughed to get my attention. I held the book higher, turning it into a barrier between us.

'What about Mum's lilac for her funeral?' asked Tessa.

I bought the book closer in so I couldn't see any part of her. Mum and I understood flowers, not her, and I wasn't going to let her in close on this.

'She's not in love,' I said.

'She said it also means the promise of spring.'

'Dead's not spring.'

'In heaven it is.'

I turned the page.

'Maybe you would have been nicer if you stuck with Elizabeth,' said Tessa.

I lowered the book. Tessa was the one who called me Jane-Jane after my second name to start with, because she couldn't get her baby tongue around Elizabeth. When I was old enough I got it nice and short and snappy into JJ.

'What do you bloody want?' I spat at Tessa and her big fat opinions. 'Because if you've got nothing nice to say, you can walk right on out.' I said it just the way Mum did.

She let it go, which was nowhere near like her. Instead she said, 'Reckon we should ring Aunty Peg and find out once and for all if she did have a turn.'

My mouth dropped open.

Her eyes darted out the window. 'Just to shut you up.' She flicked lint off the bedspread.

'I'm good,' I said quickly. After the Milo I saw I couldn't be talking out aloud about why Mum left. Cause if she didn't go to help Aunty Peg, sure as dirt they'd find out it was all my fault she'd gone.

'Philly's right, Dad would never lie.' I crossed my fingers behind my back and added in my head, *Unless he had a good reason.* Maybe God might think Dad covering up for me was a good reason.

Tessa squinted at my sudden change of heart, but then got back on her own track. 'Philly says she heard something when they were fighting the night before.'

'What?' My voice came out a bit hoarse. I cleared my throat.

'Mum told Dad she was leaving him.'

The words struck me like a fist in the gut. This was something new. It'd have to be real bad for Mum to say she was leaving Dad. Nobody left their husbands. Not even if they got beat up. They just went to the neighbour's until things settled down again and the drink made its way out of the father's system.

'What did Dad do wrong, then?' I asked.

Tessa shrugged and picked at the lint. 'Philly

didn't hear that bit.' She locked eyes with me. She had this emptiness where an answer should have been. The nothingness went on and on so I stopped looking before we both got drowned deep.

That gumboot by the dam. I caved over, stubbing the edge of the book into my gut hard, panting and desperate for air, just like Dolly after a full-tilt chasing after runaway sheep.

'What?' asked Tessa, on alert.

I shook my head. 'Nothing.' Because it couldn't be anything. Mum's boots were right where they should be, standing tall and neat between Tessa's and Philly's in the middle of the puddle of the rest of ours. I straightened back up. Closed the book.

Dad would never. He loved Mum. More than any of us.

Then the new thought. Mum told Dad she was leaving before I ate the cake and told her she was a bum. She did all that baking in the morning instead of the afternoon like normal, and she'd cooked food and put it in the freezer for us. Enough for a few days at least, Tessa said. What if she left not because of what I did, but something Dad did? For a second that perked me up. But then I remembered she was still dead.

Tessa was back at her plucking at the bedspread, waiting. I gave her a long look weighing things up. Squinshed up my face because this new thing meant we had to call Aunty Peg, even if it also meant Tessa finding out what I did.

'We're not allowed to use the phone,' I said.

'We won't tell Dad.'

'What about when the bill comes?'

She shrugged.

'Got Peg's number, then?' I asked.

'In Mum's address book.'

'We'd better get on with it then, before Dad gets there to make her say what he wants her to.' I was starting to get all itchy inside so I shot off the bed, trying to stay in front of it. Mostly because I remembered something. I'd heard Mum asking Dad the other day if we could bring Aunty Peg back to live with us. Dad had said, 'Over my dead body.'

'I need the help,' Mum had said.

'She's a bad apple.'

'One mistake, Jack. A very long time ago. She's a grown woman now. Where's your Christian charity?'

Then Dad's voice had got all fierce and whispery. 'You know we can't have a filthy woman like her under our roof. What would Father McGinty say to us having her back if he found out?'

'It's none of Father McGinty's business,' she whispered back just as fierce.

'I think you'll find that's exactly whose business it is,' finished Dad.

Mum must have been disappointed because Aunty Peg was her only sister and they were orphan girls. Maybe Mum left us to go live with her. Maybe. Except for, she hadn't bothered leaving before and she did take us down the city to see Aunty Peg behind Dad's back pretty often. We knew enough to not let on to Dad.

But what else was big enough for Mum to

leave Dad? Tessa was right. First off, we had to find out if Peg had a turn or not.

Tessa raised her hand to knock on Mum's bedroom door as if Mum might be home.

I pushed her hand away before she could connect to the door and the silence behind it. I leaned the door open. It was all dark and shroudy because of the curtains. Tessa crossed the room to yank them open. Mum's address book wasn't where she normally kept it in the drawer by her bed. We walked around, too scared to move anything. But I told myself to offer the scare up to purgatory for Mum, so I started moving papers on the big round table and that got Tessa to work. She found Mum's book in Dad's drawer, where it shouldn't be. Tessa frowned, turning it over, before her face cleared. 'He'll have wanted to let her friends know.'

I shrugged 'probably', but thought the bush telegraph was plenty fine because all the people who knew her came from around here. We headed to the lounge where Philly was playing with her doll and a handful of pebbles.

'Get the washing in,' Tessa said.

'Can't reach the line,' said Philly without breaking her stride in moving the pebbles from the imaginary kitchen to the imaginary sewing room.

'What's the drum for, then?' asked Tessa.

Philly sighed and got up. Tessa watched her go until she was well out the front door. We turned the phone around so it was between us.

'What'll we say?' I whispered.

'We'll ask how she is.'

'You do it.'

Tessa shook her head.

'Give me the number.' I picked up the phone from its cradle and put it against my ear. I dialled and then held the phone in a way so Tessa and I could both hear.

'Aunty Peg?'

'Who's there?'

'It's me — JJ — and Tessa.'

'Needs a good haircut that Tessa.'

Tessa flew her hands to her twisty neat plaits,

'How are you?' I asked, to get Tessa's mind back on the job.

'Good as gold.'

'Better, then?' I said. *What now?* I asked Tessa with my eyes.

'Nothing wrong that a stiff tot of Scotch wouldn't fix.'

Tessa grabbed the phone, her hands over mine, so we were both holding on. 'Aunty Peg, when did you last see Mum?'

'Why? What's wrong with her? Finally left His Highness, has she?' She laughed. 'Must be why Your Lordship is gracing me with his presence this afternoon. If she's got any sense in her at all, now she's got away she should stay away.'

See, I'm nodding at Tessa. She doesn't even know Mum's dead. See, Mum wasn't at Aunty Peg's at all. See, Dad's been lying all right.

Tessa's eyes were going wild and her teeth were pulling at her lip, but not because Dad lied to us. But because Dad was on his way over to Aunty Peg's and Aunty Peg would tell him we called and he'd know we'd been using the phone. Then we heard Aunty Peg drop the receiver and walk away. Tessa squeezed my arm so hard I wanted to pinch her, but I just held the phone tighter.

I imagined Aunty Peg moving careful like a cat through the mountains of newspapers stacked all over her house. She reckoned things were always whispering at her and she needed them papers to check the truth. Made sense to me. Things whispered at me all the time.

Aunty Peg came back.

'Sarah hasn't been for sixteen and a half weeks,' she said.

'That's a long time.'

'Sure is,' I said.

Aunty Peg's voice changed so she was speaking in a posh accent. 'It's as if she believes I don't speak the Queen's English or that I'm not good enough.'

'Goodbye, Madam,' I said, in the same posh voice. Tessa gave me a look as if I was as mad as Aunty Peg.

'Who shall I say called?' Aunty Peg said.

'It's the electricity company,' I said. 'I bid you good day.'

I put down the phone.

'Good one, Elizabeth Jane,' Tessa said with a grin.

'I hope she doesn't go through all those newspapers looking for Tessa and JJ from the Electricity Company.'

'Dad won't believe a word she says now, anyway,' said Tessa, clapping her hands. We heard Philly coming into the laundry so we ran the address book back to Mum's room to put it exactly where it'd been.

'What are we going to do?' We sat in the muddle of blankets on the unmade bed. Tessa was scratching her head and looking at the blankets as if she was planning to make the bed right then and there. Mum would never have left it like that. I hooked her back to the big thing before us. She was wringing her hands like there was a sudden frost on. 'I don't know — Dad — he's not like that. He wouldn't tell a lie. He'd rather die.'

'But Aunty Peg said,' I listed them off, 'she hasn't seen Mum, didn't have a turn, didn't know Mum had appendicitis.'

'I know, I know.' She was squeezed up and twisted in. So was I. All these lies soring up Dad's mouth. I was as sure as sure now. Mum wouldn't want me doing all that lying, too. I had to tell Tessa. Now. About maybe it was me who made Mum leave. But the words didn't know how to say themselves, like they didn't have the get up and go to get out my throat. What did come out was this terrible strangled cat noise.

Tessa's face jerked up, alarm switched up high. She gave me a quick thump on the back. I yanked away, heaving hard to get my breath right. I held up a hand to let her know I was fine, which maybe I was and maybe I wasn't. It took me a while to get myself straight. She had her forehead all scrunched, waiting. I shrugged my shoulders up and down a couple of times real fast to loosen the words up. Took a steady breath and started in on everything I'd done.

I got right to the end. Tessa didn't interrupt

once. I sat back, twisting my hands around and around.

Tessa furrowed up her eyebrows again, clicked her tongue. 'Don't be stupid, JJ. You are a pain, but you've been the same pain forever.'

I scratched hard at the palm of my hand and it felt good to get at the itch. What Tessa said made sense and it was like something had been smashed up good. Mum hadn't acted like something was broken between us. She'd rubbed my back and washed my face. I rounded out my eyes and smiled, all hopeful. But Tessa didn't smile back and then I lost mine as well.

'If Dad wasn't covering for me,' I said, 'then he lied for himself. That blue they had. Maybe it was real bad. Maybe Dad's got something real bad to hide.'

'It's probably just a mistake,' she said. 'Let's see what he says first.'

'But Aunty Peg's calendar is never wrong.'

She nodded, all serious, caught between the two true things — Dad would never lie and Aunty Peg's calendar was as reliable as the sun — and now there was one true thing less in the world.

I caught Tessa's hands to stop them flying about and putting little knives into me.

★ ★ ★

Dad was curved over the steering wheel, like he'd been yarding up cattle for a month, one foot in the car and one foot out.

'Don't move the curtain, Monkey,' said Tessa.

Philly rolled her eyes. *I'm not a baby,* she was

saying. I didn't reckon Dad was going to notice a bit of lace fluttering, ten yards away inside the house. He wasn't even paying attention to Doll, who was dancing about the car door and barking her head off.

Dad fell himself out of the car and we didn't need binoculars to read him up. He was as slow as Old Mr McKenzie, who barely got to Mass once a month. He put on some speed for us though as he came through the laundry and threw the mail on the kitchen bench, all pretend energy, hiding all that sad in him. He sent a quick look around the room where Philly was lining up sauce bottles in the cupboard, I had the end of the broom and Tim was brushing down the hearth. Tessa didn't need a cover to be in the kitchen.

'Hi, Dad,' we chorused, as if we'd been rehearsing.

He grunted. Tessa pulled him out a chair, then took his dinner off the stove with a tea towel.

'Dad?' gasped Tessa, letting the plate clatter to the table. There was a red shape like Tasmania beside his left temple that was starting to bruise up. We all swooped in to investigate.

'Just a scratch.' He pushed us away, straightened the plate, picked up his fork, daring us. 'Rosary Tuesd'y night, funeral Thursd'y.'

Tessa ran to the freezer. Philly dropped to the ground and crawled under the table. She squeeshed herself up into Dad's lap as Tessa got back with ice wrapped in the tea towel. He waved it away. 'Knocked my head on the car door. It's nothin.'

Looked something to us.

He made way for Philly. She laid her cheek

against his chest. Despite the extra trouble getting his arms around her, Dad shoved in a mouthful of meat.

'Going to be a shiner,' I said. That damned car door. It was better than somebody socking him one, though. Which was a stupid idea because nobody would have a reason to hit him when he was just visiting hospitals and funeral parlours and stuff.

He grunted, threw in another mouthful.

We watched as he drank his food back like it was a bottle of beer. When he was done, he shoved his plate away and sat back, an arm around Philly. She hadn't moved an inch.

'Did you speak to the hospital, Dad?' asked Tim.

'Yep.' He slid Philly off and went to the fridge, hunching over the opened door, his back to us. He clenched up his fists and pumped them open and shut. Tessa and Tim's eyes widened, but they didn't look at each other. I looked at everyone.

'What about Aunt Peg? How did she take it?' I asked, my breath not coming out.

He reached in for a tinny and came back to the table, pulled the ring right off in one go. 'Dropped around.' He tipped back his head to take a long gulping swallow. It was like the beer was alive in his throat.

'Then?'

'Said she'd known since they were kids that Sarah wasn't going to make old bones.'

I was nearest, so I took Philly's hand.

'She'll be up on the train Sund'y and stay for the funeral.'

'Isn't she supposed to be having an episode?' I asked.

'She's better,' Dad said. 'Been on her feet since yesterday, when your mum — she was out when your mother had the attack. Didn't know anything about it. Thought your mother had come home.'

Tessa refused to catch my eyes.

'Your aunt took it bad. Thinks it was her fault. Like her having a turn made your mother die. Mad talk.' He flicked a crumb from the table. It shot right by my arm, soared into the air and landed on my sock. 'She's got it in her head there was no episode and she never saw ya mother.'

Tessa gave me a triumphant look, which she squashed quick smart before somebody caught her.

'So I don't want none of you buggers buggin her about it.'

A DEFINITE LIE

Dad was in a right stink. Sal had picked that moment to get down to the business of birthing. No manners. I felt the empty Mum-space scrubbing at my insides. Not even the sight of the heavy old sow swinging low and full of piglets from one side of the pen to the other made a difference.

'Git around her on the other side,' Dad said.

I chased the other pigs away and gave Sal a slap towards the birthing pen.

'Watch it,' said Dad as a couple of the others nosed at my bum. 'Come behind, come behind.'

Doll set up a bark from the fence, busting to get in with us and get at the herding.

'Away with ya,' Dad yelled, flicking his hand towards the milk shed. Doll backed off a couple of steps then came back sharp as Sal shoved past me, stumbling me and then pinning me against the wall.

Dad waved his arms, roaring at the top of his lungs, giving Doll, who was barking like mad, a run for her money.

Me pinned and petrified, a bunny in a spotlight. Sal was squashing the breath out of my lungs and didn't even know it. Dad came in fast. He leaped over the other pigs, pulling his belt off as he came. He whacked into Sal, then got his shoulder to the back of her and heaved her off me. She squealed like we'd stuck her with a knife and took off. I ran to the fence and rolled under quick smart.

Dad fell against the wall, catching his breath, then flicked his belt at the nearest pig. He stood up and threaded the belt back through his trousers, tilted his head to me to get back in there. 'Keep ya eyes open this time.'

'You keep your dog away, then.'

'Cut the back chat.' He grinned, reaching out a hand to scruff up my head. Normally I'd lean right into it, and I wanted to because he'd just saved me from Sal, but I didn't know what to do with all those lies between us, so this time I pretended I hadn't seen and ducked away.

We yarded up Sal, and Dad swung the lights up, going into the big shed to switch them on. I got busy settling Sal.

'What are you doing?' he asked, coming back.

'Makin her comfy.' I pushed hay in around Sal as she lay on her side.

He shook his head. 'She's just a pig.'

'It's what Mum always did,' I said. 'Reckon she'd know a bit more about birthing than you.'

'I'll leave ya to it, then,' he said. 'Mrs Tyler'll be here before you know it.'

I sunk down into the hay beside Sal and curled up along her back now that she and all her blubber were resting. I liked her big and slow, and the way her belly went on and on. I jumped away, though, when Mrs Tyler darted into the pigpen in case the newness stirred up Sal. But she didn't even look up. Mrs Tyler settled in the corner on a hay bale, putting her crochet bag beside her. It was for Mrs Tyler's cousin's firstborn; having a baby, she told me, the first of the new generation. She was using real nice wool, all soft and lemony. Reckon that baby would feel real good wrapped all the way up in it.

I got my book, and sat in the corner on the ground, looking up from Heidi and Peter's goats every time Sal grunted. After a while, Mrs Tyler stuffed her wool back in the bag and kneeled beside Sal the way Mum did, pushing at her side and listening, ear to belly.

'She's gone off the boil,' she said, blinking in the gloom. 'I'll just pop down to the house and get a cuppa.' She gave me an encouraging smile. I wondered if she remembered that she'd told me Mum would be home soon. 'Sal will be a while yet. Off you go, too.'

I found Tim and Tessa by the woodpile. Tim was up on blocks with an axe in his hands.

'Go,' yelled Tessa. She clicked the stopwatch.

Tim bought down the axe, hard and clean, slanting in one way and then the other. Three chops each way. I dodged as a chip soared straight for my eye. Tim jumped around on the blocks, fast like the champion woodchoppers did it at the Show and started in on the other side. Chop chop chop. The axe bit deep into the wood. But still the log didn't break in two. He jumped around again and did the same on the other side. Still not getting through. Tim threw the axe to the ground, collapsed, panting on the woodpile.

'Doesn't matter,' said Tessa. 'I messed up the timing anyway.'

He grunted, then noticed me. 'You keep ya mouth shut.'

'About what?' I grinned. 'Bout that log needing a man to get into it?' I muscled up my arms above my shoulders.

Philly raced towards us, panting. 'Dad's saying stuff to Mrs Tyler,' she said as soon as she was within reach.

We took off. Tim left the axe right where it had fallen. Dad would be plenty mad, but I didn't stop to put it away, either. We pelted in under the kitchen window, colliding with the wall and each other like a pack of puppies.

' . . . change her spots, Kathy. And you know what a handful Peg is, and that's when she's not having a stark-raving-mad-as-a-snake attack. Night before she had her attack, Sare told Peg she had a gut ache — that was it.'

Tessa refused to look at me.

Mrs Tyler's voice murmured something.

'Peg's been a blasted nuisance from start to finish,' said Dad.

'Not entirely her fault, Jack.' We heard this time because Mrs Tyler's voice had gone up sharp-like. 'She was never the same after she went to live in that house without Sarah's steadying hand, so far away except for the odd cuppa if any of us happened to be in town needing the hospital.'

'Wasn't my problem. This is a good Catholic household and no place for a woman with loose morals.'

'It's me you're talking to, Jack. Peg had those

same loose morals all along, as we all well knew, and they hadn't bothered you before. It's a wonder Sarah even let you send her away.'

'The kids were growing up. We'd had to put them first,' Dad mumbled. 'Anyway.' He put some grit into his voice. 'Can't afford to have Peg goin off like a two-bob watch right now. She's all agitated and on edge because she's got it into her head it was her fault. Her havin a turn and then Sarah getting appendicitis and Peg having to make the call to the ambulance. I asked the doctor to give her something to calm her down. Doc said best nobody brings up how Sarah died with her so as not to set her off.'

Tessa ignored my pinch at this string of lies, pretending she was hard at listening.

We didn't hear Mrs Tyler's reply again.

'Appreciate that, Kathy. If you would put the word around.'

We listened longer, but it was all pigs and scones and tea and casseroles. Philly started pulling my hair, not in a hurty way, but like she had nothing better to do. I slapped her hand away. Tessa put her finger to her lips. Tim got the next idea, which was to take off for our trees out the front of the house. Getting snug into the umbrella of them was like something warm in the cold. Tessa's was the easiest tree for Philly to climb so we all squashed onto the wooden platform Dad had made for us in that one. Tessa laid out the biscuits she kept there for 'guests'. One butternut snap each.

Philly bit in. Took it out of her mouth and tried to break it in half with her hands. She stood up and smashed the heel of her boot on it. We all looked at the biscuit, still intact.

'Coulda broke a toof,' said Philly.

'Won't break in half,' I said. 'Must be somethin in the air today.'

Tim punched me.

'I'll just suck it,' Philly said.

Which is what we all ended up doing.

Tessa stayed right out of it, having a different conversation with her eyes telling me to keep my mouth shut. Which I did, but only because it was all mud and cloud in my head. Why did he tell us Aunty Peg didn't know about Mum's appendicitis but he told Mrs Tyler it was Aunty Peg who called the ambulance? That red was building right up. A while later, Dad came around the corner of the house. 'JJ, where the bloody hell are you, you little bugger?' We all froze. He stood with his hands on his hips. Face wild. 'I'll skin yer alive when I get my hands on you.'

'What'd ya do this time?' Tim grinned. I ignored him and scrambled off the platform and slithered down the trunk on the far side so Dad couldn't see me. As soon as he disappeared back around the side of the house, I ran up the other. Met him at the kitchen door.

'Want something, Dad?'

'That sow is birthing right this second.'

'But Mrs Tyler — '

'You know better than that. Your mother never abandoned the post. Not once. I thought you were still up there. What gets into you, JJ? Bloody rocks for brains. I swear sometimes there's a bit of Peg in you.'

In an instant the red steamed up from the volcano in my belly. 'Why did ya tell Mrs Tyler that Aunty Peg phoned the ambulance when you told us Aunty Peg didn't even know about Mum's attack?'

'Listening at the door?' He snarled and turned to spit. 'What I tell Mrs Tyler is my business.'

'And what I tell Mrs Tyler is my business.'

He started. I'd done a lot of things before, but I'd never threatened him. He thrust a finger in my face. 'You say nothin.'

I was pumping red and I could feel my eyes all narrow and slitty. I just kept my stare on full beam.

He leaned into me. 'I told that to Kathy so she wouldn't be bothering Peg and givin her more grief and distressing her — Peg's recovering from a turn and twisted up enough already. Satisfied?'

I was big sorry. But my mouth hadn't caught up. 'With all this lying you're doing you're going straight to hell when the devil gets his hands on you.'

I marched off before he could thump me. After a couple of steps, I looked back ready to run in case he was coming after me. But he wasn't. He was all crumpled on the ground. The red whooshed away and I ran back. 'Sorry, Dad. Sorry. I didn't mean it.'

'Get out of here,' he said. 'Git. If we lose any of them piglets it'll be on your head.'

I walked backwards, eyes plastered to his bowed head, just hoping. I got even with the toilet and still there was no sign of soft in him. I turned and raced to the pigsty.

101

Mrs Tyler's crocheting hadn't been touched and she was down on her knees in the straw beside Sal. 'Not long now.' When I didn't say anything, she looked up. She was up on her feet and had me gathered in an instant. She drew me back onto the straw and into her lap. It wasn't like Mum's lap, but it was something. I was filled up and over with no more Mum. It was all around me.

Mrs Tyler clucked her tongue like I was a chicken. She gripped me strong and rubbed my back, hard enough to stop me headbutting into her stomach.

'Look!' she said after a bit, like she was changing the subject.

I wiped my eyes.

'You want to be the first to welcome it into the world?'

I scooted in quick before the next piglet landed. I scooped up the first little scrap, just bigger than my hand. I held it up to my face and stroked its soft pale skin along its side. Brand new and not knowing the world and all that was coming at it. I put it in front of its mother's teats.

The others came fast. Little blind things, feeling their way over each other to the milk. When we had them all, I said, 'No runt.'

'See, love, everything'll be all right.' Mrs Tyler brushed back my hair from my face. 'It'll all be right in the end.'

We only lost one of them twelve piglets. And that wasn't on my watch. Sal squashed it the next night when Steve, one of Mrs Nolan's workers, was there and should have known better. 'Bloody fool,' as Dad said.

Still. Losing just the one was pretty good.

Maybe Mrs Tyler was right, but the end was a long way off to wait for everything to be all right.

WHAT JJ OWES JACK

Philly had a good idea. We were going to pick one thing each to put in the ground with Mum. We had to be ready by the rosary in a couple of days. Philly was putting in a runner she did for Mum last Christmas. It had hollyhocks on it and sat on the table beside Mum's bed under the alarm clock. Philly chose hollyhocks because they were big and white and looked real nice. Reckon Mum never told Philly what hollyhocks were really about, but I read it in Mum's book. Ambition, women's ambition, and you just had to take one look at Philly to know she was full of determination to get things right her way. I didn't like that it was going under the ground and getting buried with Mum, but on the other hand Mum would like a bit of Phillyness in there with her.

Tim hadn't made up his mind, but Tessa was putting in a cushion she and Mum made together. It was black and white for Colling-wood, which was our team. I knew what I was doing, but I wasn't telling anyone in case they tried to stop me. I was putting in Mum's special brooch that she brought out when we needed a bit of magic. I reckoned she needed a bit of that under the ground with her. Only thing was, I didn't know where she kept that brooch.

Dad was out doing the morning milking so I had a bit of clear. Before I could stop myself, I knocked on Mum's bedroom door and thought about how funny it would have been if I heard Mum's voice. Something tingled at my neck. I believed in ghosts, just like Mum. She once told us she saw her mum and dad after their car accident. Great Aunt Dot, who brought her and Aunty Peg up after, didn't believe her because Mum was only nine when they died. Told Mum it was just the shock of losing them like that. Aunty Peg believed her, though. That was the good thing about Aunty Peg. She was a believer.

I didn't know where to start in Mum's room. The drawers were all shut up closed. I poked about in Mum's jewellery box. Nothing. So I fell on my knees and started going through the shoeboxes.

'Dad's going to be sooo mad,' said Philly, walking in a good while later. She dropped the pile of clean clothes on the chest of drawers.

'You get out of here,' I said. 'He asked me to clean up.'

'He didn't ask you to throw everything everywhere.'

I looked around and I saw. It was like all of the guts of the wardrobe had been spewed into the room. I bit down on my lip to stop the panic rising up. 'You're just a baby, what would you know?'

'I'm going to go get him right now.' She swung on her foot.

But I was too fast. I lunged and grabbed her ankle and down she went, fast and loud. She flung her hand and caught the stand-up lamp and down that went with her, smashing to the floor, the glass splintering into a thousand tiny bits as far as the door.

There was blood on her chin and I scuttled over to wipe it with my jumper and to get her to stop yelling. But Tessa was in there, and hard on her heels Mrs Nolan, who looked like she'd never seen the like of it in all her life.

I knew this for sure because that was what she said later when she had Dad buttonholed to the table. 'It looked like a bomb had gone off in there and in the middle of it all sat JJ as if butter wouldn't melt in her mouth.' We heard a teacup being moved across the table. She'd stopped by this morning to drop off a casserole and Steve for his piglet shift. She'd stayed to help all day given the mayhem she'd found. She was still there at dinner and sent us away after so that she and Dad could have a quiet word.

There was no hope of that because she was doing the talking and her voice could carry clear across a paddock. We'd taken off all right, just as she told us to, but doubled back to huddle in a pack out of sight beside the fridge.

'Have you thought about what you're going to do?' Mrs Nolan dropped her loud voice to soft like a cushion as if Dad could lay his head right on it.

But he didn't seem to feel the same because all he did was grunt.

'Now that Sarah's gone,' clarified Mrs Nolan. 'With the kids.'

'They'll be right,' said Dad.

'Kids are a handful,' she pushed on. 'Four of them.' Making it sound like Dad's particular kids were even worse than the normal variety.

Dad took a loud slurp from his teacup the way he did when he was with just us, so we knew he was no longer on his best behaviour.

Mrs Nolan didn't take the warning. 'You have to think what's best for them. Man like you is too busy to be fussing around with kids underfoot.'

'All good, thanks, Nancy.'

'Girls need a mother. Specially your girls, just at that age.'

Dad didn't say anything this time, which Mrs Nolan read in a completely different way from us. We heard her charge on as if the gates had been opened.

'I've spoken to the ladies of the district and Jessie is happy to take Philly, which is very good of her given that Philly is still so young and Jessie has those twins already. I could take Tessa — '

'That won't be necessary, thanks, Nancy,' said Dad as if he meant it this time. As if he'd finally woken up to what Mrs Nolan was saying. 'We won't be splitting the family. That's not what Sarah would have wanted.'

'Sarah wouldn't have wanted you to be left with all of this,' Mrs Nolan said. 'At least think about JJ.' Her voice dropped lower again. 'She's not quite right. I mean what's she doing spending so much time with that Tommy Rielly? She should be helping out in the kitchen. Somebody has to teach her how to be a proper girl now that Sarah's gone.'

'JJ's all right.' There was a stop sign in Dad's voice.

Tessa, Philly and I were biting through each other's palms with our fingernails. Tim was right there with us, but he was less worried because nobody would think of taking a boy from his father.

'You weren't there, Jack. JJ attacked little Philly. There was blood and glass everywhere, not to mention the mess. JJ must have thrown everything helter-skelter. I put it all back in order and now I wish I hadn't so you could have seen. I wasn't going to mention this until after the funeral, but in the light of recent events . . . I don't think you know the magnitude of the danger Philly is — '

'Philly's in no danger,' said Dad, cutting her off, but still mildly. 'JJ's got a temper on her, but she means well.'

Tessa and Philly got tighter hold of me.

'On the day Sarah left, she told me JJ needs — '

'I won't be saying any more on this, Nancy. I can see you and the other women have done some thinking and I appreciate it, but Sarah wouldn't want the kids leaving their home, going to strangers.'

'Strangers? My home, or Jessie's or Mary's, who is more than happy to take on a handful like JJ, near saint, is nothing like a stranger's.'

'My kids would be honoured to be looked after by any of you women,' said Dad with just the right amount of honey, and Tessa and my eyes snagged on each other at this strange tone in him. 'But the thing is, Sarah and me, we love these kids. And Sarah, she wouldn't want me to give them to anybody, no matter how good they were.' Dad's voice cracked and wavered.

We were all fitting ourselves into the shape of the next second. We could hear Mrs Nolan's silence it was so loud. It was like she was as unprepared as we'd been. But she surprised us, too.

'You're right there, Jack,' she said. 'Sarah wouldn't like it.'

I let go of the breath I'd been holding.

'But Sarah's not here any more.'

Panic flew my eyes wide and snagged them on Tessa's.

'You may have to face facts,' Mrs Nolan said. We heard the sound of a chair going back. 'But we'll leave that for after the funeral when you're back to thinking straight.'

'Facts?' he said, his voice on the rise. 'Let's talk facts, then. What did Sare say to you? You drove her to the station the day she left. It could only have been you.'

Mrs Nolan didn't speak for a beat and I wanted to squint around the fridge, just enough to see what her face was saying, but I didn't. None of us did. We heard the chink of china as the cups and saucers were swooped over to the sink.

When her voice came it was full of stiff. 'Indeed. I'll tell you one thing for nothing, Jack: she didn't say one word about Peg having had a turn.'

Tessa gripped me. I gripped her back.

109

'She must have found that out when she arrived at Peg's,' Mrs Nolan went on.

'She told you that's where she was going, then?' Dad asked, a quiet of desperation creeping into his words, as if he knew he were admitting something but he just had to anyway.

'Not in so many words.' Mrs Nolan sounded uncomfortable, like she was squeezing words out though her own tight straw. 'She asked me to take her to the station because you were busy. All she actually said was that she had a spot of shopping to do in town.' Mrs Nolan's voice stayed all clipped and hard edged. 'Told me she'd get the school bus home. I knew she always dropped in on Peg, so I assumed.'

'Is that a fact?'

The tick of the clock was the only loud thing now.

'She have any other friends down that way?' Dad asked, low and dirty.

'Not that I knew,' Mrs Nolan clipped back. 'What exactly are you asking, Jack?'

Dad didn't say anything for a long while.

'Funeral,' he finally said. 'We don't want any of her friends to be missing out. And it seems you women know a deal more about a man's wife than I'd have reckoned on.'

'We'll keep the meals up,' Mrs Nolan said, ignoring his words like everything was bang-on normal. 'We've got the spread covered for the funeral. We've booked the hall if that suits. Expect there'll be quite a few there for Sarah. Such a tremendously good woman.' I caught Tim's look, which was just as full of question as mine about why Mrs Nolan said 'good' as if Dad might ever have thought about arguing the point.

Dad was back to grunting and Mrs Nolan took that as acceptance. After the door closed, we were all ready to skedaddle before Dad spotted us, but he didn't move a muscle. After a long quiet, we pushed back across the lino, slow and silent like mice backing away from a cat. We didn't call out to Dad that night to remind him to do our prayers. We did them for each other.

A CLUE AT LAST

The next day, Dad said we wouldn't be going to Mass. We'd never not been to Mass. We looked at each other like this was maybe even bigger than Mum dying. But I kept my mouth tight shut because after Mrs Nolan trying to take me away and Dad saying 'no' at first but then letting Mrs Nolan say 'maybe after the funeral' I was on my best behaviour. I had to even those scales up, which were pretty heavy on the giving-me-away side after I told Dad the devil was after his soul. He hadn't even looked at me since, although he hadn't parceled me out the door quicks sticks with Mrs Nolan either, so that was a shine of hope.

But my very *best* hope was staying exactly out of his path, out of the way of temptation. So instead of going to Mass I went all the way down to Jean's Corner to sit by the apple tree. There weren't any flowers about so I just had to say it all to Mum without their help. Told her about how I couldn't stop sassing Dad, because as soon as I got one thing straight in my head another thing that didn't fit would go pop and the red flooded in. I promised her I'd be stopping all that, though. One hand on her scarf, the other on my heart.

Even though I was on my best behaviour when

I got back, with the others all helping Dad feed out, I still went looking for Mum's special brooch again. I snuck into her room and went through her ottoman. Dad gave the ottoman to her when they got married. It was pale green with roses and forget-me-nots — love and remembrance. Being lovingly held in someone's thoughts, Mum said. I thought that was giving Dad too much credit.

I got my shoulder under the lid of the ottoman. It weighed a tonne. My heart was loud and boomy in my ears, and I was worried the lid would collapse, catching me like a mouse in a trap, all wriggly and broken. But my panic got the lid heaved up enough so it stood open by itself. The first layer was lemon tissue paper. I flattened my palm to it. It was pale and full of fairyness and I drank it up through my skin. Lying underneath the tissue paper like a secret was a smoky pink dress covered in white snow-drops and done up with black flower buttons like I'd never seen. Around the neck were tiny light-green sprigs dancing in a line. I lifted the dress to my cheek and smoothed it on my skin. But there was a stab of empty cause it didn't smell like Mum.

Then the empty all filled up red because Mum kept this magic to herself. This soft, shiny thing. Snowdrops were for hope and she should have shared them with us. But she kept it from us. Just all for herself — and I didn't like it one bit. I folded my lips together, hard like stones. Big panty breaths, pushing out and in, like Max when he was filled up mean. I dropped the dress on Mum's bed and ran to her drawer for scissors. I yanked it open and shoved things around, flying her lipsticks out of the bowl and into her rollers. Something in the mirror caught my eye. It was a wild thing. I looked up, stared straight into her wild-girl eyes. I jerked away and saw my hands shaking. I put one hand in the other and nursed it like a baby. Felt the gentle of it. I backed to the bed and sat on the edge, one hand still tucked in the other. I lay down across Mum's dress and changed hands so the other one would get the gentle too.

A bit of new came up in me. And it wasn't red. It wasn't any colour. The big of it scared me. Then it came out, a high, long, sad thing, and then a breath and there it was again. I wrapped my arms around myself and rocked. Back and forth until the moan of it ended. After a while I was worried that I'd snotted on Mum's dress. I jerked up. But the wet was on the bed. I sat up and smoothed the dress out, spreading the skirt wide like it was dancing all by itself. I laid myself carefully on top of it, face up, my arms where the sleeves were. Then I was glad the dress existed because now she had something pretty to wear when she went in the dark of the ground.

I was all wrung out, but I got back somehow to the ottoman — I still had a job to do.

I found an apron she'd made when she was a little girl, and a few baby scribbles on butcher's paper.

I was almost to the bottom of the things and I was thinking I might not find her brooch there after all, and where else could it be? But there it was, stuck in the corner. I opened the lid of its little navy box and got to my knees straight to say a big thank you to St Anthony for finding it for me. The lilies around the woman's face on the brooch stood out like wedding-cake icing. Mum said lilies were for beauty. But I didn't know if that meant they made you beautiful or you had to be beautiful to wear them. Mum always looked beautiful when she wore the brooch. She said she was gunna leave it to one of us girls when she was gone. I supposed that was Tessa, but that wasn't going to happen now.

* * *

The whole house shuddered as the front door banged shut. Tessa's voice yelled at us all. 'Father McGinty's car is coming up the track.'

I froze. Cast wildly around Mum's room, but saw that I hadn't upset too much this time. Tessa made Dad's bed every morning now so it was as straight as. She even swept up the rice Dad put under his knees, since he'd taken to saying the rosary, praying for Mum's soul every night. I didn't reckon Mum's soul was that black that she needed all that pain and prayer, but it was like Dad couldn't hear us when we tried to get him to see reason. I bunched up Mum's snowdrop dress and folded it back into the ottoman. Father McGinty never came over.

Philly squealed into the house, Tim on her heels, just as I dashed into the kitchen from the other direction. Tessa barked out orders about kettles and scones and teacups.

'That's girl's stuff,' said Tim.

'I'll call Dad,' I said, running right through the kitchen.

Tim jerked me back by catching at the back of my jumper and ran out in front of me, yelling for Dad at the top of his lungs.

I winged out my arms, proper mad, but Tessa whirled me to face the fridge. 'Jam. Cream. Hurry.'

So I did.

'Do you think Father is coming to tell us off for not being at Mass?' whispered Philly as she set Mum's best tablecloth out.

My eyes went wide for a second, mirroring hers, before I came to my senses. 'Probably just wants to see how Dad is, Dad being the President of The Knights of the Southern Cross and doing the collection and everything.'

All the tight went out of her little body and she had enough left to smile some relief. Dad had been so happy the night he was elected President a few months back. Funny to think that now, how happy he'd been. We'd all been. Came home roaring with the drink in him and waking us all up from our beds and on a school night, Mum squawked. But she was laughing when she did it.

Tessa ran back from the crystal cabinet in the lounge with Mum's crystal cream jug and sugar bowl. Normally we walked slow if we had to carry Mum's wedding things. Not this time. Tessa dumped them on the table, panic-signing at us to fill them. Philly and I went into overdrive. Philly spilled the sugar, but I swept it

116

onto the floor and told her with my eyes not to let out a peep.

'Where's the car now?' asked Tessa, throwing frozen scones on a tray and clattering them into the oven, fidgeting with the dial to make the gas real low.

Philly ran-jumped onto the bench to get a better look down the drive. She squealed, which was all Tessa and I needed to hear.

Tim came running back in, his arms loaded up with wood. He stacked up the fire nice and high.

'Where's Dad?' Tessa asked.

Tim didn't face us. 'He says he'll be in when he can.'

We all stopped short. Dad always, every time, dropped everything for Father McGinty. As Mum said, the Church was first, second and third for Dad. And the priest coming to your house was . . . I couldn't think of a word because it never happened . . . an honour, maybe. And Dad was coming when he could?

Tessa fell on to the nearest chair. 'What are we going to tell Father?' she asked, her face full of big and scared.

None of us had any ideas.

'We could hide,' Philly finally whispered, which I thought was a good idea, but it was too late.

We heard Dolly barking up a storm as Father McGinty pulled on his handbrake to park beside the ute. All us kids glued to the window, one eye watching as he opened the door and heaved his big body out of the car, the other on the cowshed, praying like mad we'd see Dad heading this way.

'What was he doing?' I asked Tim.

'Dunno,' said Tim. 'Nothing special.'

Father McGinty adjusted his long black robe over his belly. A priest didn't belong on a farm. They belonged in their big red brick house beside the church. He looked around at the broken-down dray and the rusting combine. Mum would be having a fit. But his expression didn't change, so that was something. I suppose he thought somebody should have been out there greeting him by now, instead of Doll jumping all over him with a fierce bark on her.

Tessa made her lips into one long line and took off her apron. She turned to me. 'You go the back way to the cowshed and you make Dad come. Right now. You hear?'

I stared back. She just pushed me ahead of her. 'You're the only one who can make him do anything, so get.'

I took off, leaving her to go in the other direction to greet Father. I ran like the wind, filled up with this new thing that she thought Dad might listen to me.

'Dad,' I yelled with all my body before I got there. 'Father McGinty's here.' I stopped short when I tore into the dairy. There he was, all hunched over a milk can, in a ball, like he was hiding, just like we'd wanted to. 'Dad,' I said, making my voice gentle. He looked up, then. Wiped his wet eyes with a brush of his forearm.

'Why you crying?'

'Not bloody crying,' he said. He straightened.

'Nothing to cry about. Your mother's dead, is all, and now we have to bury her.'

'Bet that's why Father's here, Dad.' Trying to get my voice as soft as Dad's talking to a skittish foal. 'Came personally, cause you're so important.'

He bit his lip. 'That, or something else.'

'What else?'

He looked blankly at me a good long while until I was full up on fright. Then he started like he saw me for the first time that day. 'Nothing. Nothing it could be.'

'You gotta get up there, Dad, otherwise he'll think there's something up.'

He grunted. 'Right.' He grunted again. 'Right. You were always the clever one.' But he didn't say it like a compliment.

★　★　★

'I'll have your room, Tessa,' said Aunty Peg when she arrived off the train after Father McGinty had gone, and we'd done the dishes and Tim and Tessa and I had been over everything.

'Dad was out of his mind,' was Tessa's opinion. 'You said he was crying. It was the grief talking.'

'But to avoid the priest,' Tim said. 'That's not natural. That's not Dad.'

'Shut up, Tim. What would you know?' Tessa said. 'You're just a boy.' As if that explained all his shortcomings and should be the end of it.

Tim and I exchanged a look behind Tessa's back because being a boy had nothing to do with anything.

Dad set down Aunty Peg's suitcase in the middle of the kitchen like it was the final step of a very long journey.

'My room is all ready for you, Aunty Peg,' said Tessa. She'd even put wattle and lilac in a vase by the bed.

'Take this case in, then, Tim,' said Aunty Peg. 'I'll get started on the vegies.'

Tessa smoothed Mum's apron over the front of her. 'All done, Aunty Peg. Cup of tea?'

'Rots your gut,' she said without blinking.

Dad rolled his eyes behind her back and passed the suitcase to Tim, who took off with quick feet. I was betting he'd be out the window of Tessa's bedroom just as soon as he'd dropped Aunty Peg's case.

'I've got to set up for the milking.' Dad disappeared out the front door.

Aunty Peg pulled out two chairs. She sat on one and hefted her feet onto the other. 'Drainage,' she said to the air. 'That was the trouble with your mother, no drainage from the brain.'

I stepped back out of Aunty Peg's line of sight and crossed my eyes. Philly giggled.

'Giggling's for babies,' said Aunty Peg.

Philly stepped back beside me to poke her tongue at Aunty Peg's back.

'That's why she married your father.'

Tessa sat opposite Aunty Peg; Philly and I pulled out two other chairs. This was getting interesting.

'Could have had James Ryan, the one with the hardware place in town. Mad for her, he was.' She looked straight at me. 'Get me a glass of water, will you, Philly?'

I nudged Philly.

'She meant you,' said Philly, elbowing me back.

'She said you.'

Tessa sighed and got up from the table.

'Philly a bit lazy?' asked Aunty Peg to Tessa, meaning me. She turned back to me. 'Give us your hand.'

I held one out, but only got it halfway before she tipped forwards and yanked it towards her. She bought it almost to her nose and stared hard into it and ran one cold finger across the middle of my palm, then she nodded like she found what she'd expected and flung back my hand. She started to ferret about in her handbag as if she'd moved on to the next thing.

'What did you see in Philly's hand, Aunty Peg?' asked Philly, grinning.

'Hasn't got enough layers of skin between her and the world. She's all trouble that one.'

'Philly always is,' I chimed in, grinning myself. Philly crossed her arms and shook her face in mine.

'James Ryan?' I prompted Aunty Peg.

'Had prospects. Instead your mother chose love and dirt. Where'd that get her?' Aunty Peg looked from one side of the room to the other. 'Eating dirt for breakfast, lunch and tea.'

Tessa swung around from the sink, a brewing storm. I stepped into the gap. 'But Mr Ryan hasn't got any hair.'

'Bald as an egg then too, but at least she would have known what she was getting into.'

'She didn't get into it, though, did she?' I said. Seeing as I was Philly for the minute I was using up my free ticket.

'So she ended up with you lot. Half killed her, you did. Especially you, Philly. Nearly did for her. Poisoned her from the inside.'

Tessa dumped the glass in front of Aunty Peg on the table and said she had to go check on Dad and those cows.

'Me too,' I said. 'JJ will stay with you, Aunty Peg. She's really sweet.' I skipped away.

Tessa came marching back and yanked Philly from her chair. 'JJ's not sweet at all. I need this one to collect the eggs.' The words could hardly get through her tight-together teeth.

*　*　*

It wasn't until Philly and I got to the chook shed that I saw Philly's hands were shaking. I nudged her. 'I was just kidding back there with Aunty Peg. You're not any kind of trouble.'

She pursed her lips up like they'd been button closed. I nudged her again. 'What's the matter?'

'Nothing.'

I took the collecting tin away from her. 'It's not nothing, little duck.' The chooks clucked around us. 'Missing Mum?'

She nodded. I narrowed my eyes, but she turned her back on me, clucking at the chooks. They followed her to the wheat bucket. Mum said Philly was our queen of the chooks.

'Move over, Baby Beak,' she murmured.

The chook stretched its neck into its breast

122

and let Philly take two eggs from under her. If I was trying to get under that chook, she'd be pecking me with that beak of hers, which was a lot sharper than a baby's. Philly got the wheat out to them, but not in her usual arch of rain. Instead, she puddled it out of her bucket onto the ground.

'Let's go, Philly,' I said. I couldn't breathe through the sad. Was it because this was what Mum and Philly used to have together? Like Mum and I had flowers? Like Tessa and Mum had baking?

★ ★ ★

'Your father told you I'm mad yet?' asked Aunty Peg, biting into the chicken. She was eating both the drumsticks when usually Philly and I got one each. Dad's eyes stayed pointed on his plate, just where they'd been since he sat down.

'Are you?' Philly asked Aunty Peg.

'Eat,' Dad said.

'Been mad with grief since I was five,' said Aunty Peg. 'You never get over a thing like that, your parents dying when you're young.' She looked around the table.

Dad belted the table with his fist. The salt and pepper headed for the ceiling. 'That's enough, Peg.'

She waved her chicken leg. 'Not you lot.' She looked around at all of us. 'You're all too old to be affected. You don't have the gift, anyway. Besides, Sarah wasn't good at painting, was she?'

Dad put his palms in the air. 'Don't ask.' His

voice weary with the weight of it.

But I did. 'What's painting got to do with the price of fish?'

Aunty Peg looked at me. 'Which one are you again?'

I shrugged.

'Sassy, aren't you?' She picked up her knife and fork and headed for the roast potatoes on her plate. 'Sarah was like that.'

I sat up straight.

'Sarah would tell you the blue sky was yellow and you'd believe her.'

I sagged. Nobody ever believed me.

'Why didn't you have kids, Aunty Peg?' I asked.

'Bleed you dry. Look at Sarah. Went into the ring eight times.'

Philly plucked at the neckline of her T-shirt. Tessa and I frowned at each other.

'Less talk, more eat,' said Dad.

'It was so, Jack bloody McBride,' said Aunty Peg. She sniffed. 'Not so handsome any more, are you? Where's all that charm now?'

While everybody else was gasping at a lady swearing, at the kitchen table and in front of children, I asked, 'Where are the rest of us?'

Aunty Peg bent down with a groan to look under the table. 'Not there.' Then she laughed as if she'd told us a great joke. 'Eight pregnancies. Every one made her sick as a dog. But this one,' she gestured with her knife towards Dad, 'wouldn't let her be.'

'Be quiet, woman,' thundered Dad. He leaped to his feet, the chair screeching backwards across the lino. 'Have you got your pills?'

Aunty Peg waved her fork.

'I suggest you take them if you want to stay here even one night. I've about had enough of you.'

Aunty Peg shook her head from side to side, mimicking him.

Dad stalked off, leaving his food uneaten.

'You don't frighten me, Jack McBride. That's what the doctor said, fair and square. She nearly died with the last one, Philly, or JJ, was it?'

'Instead she died of something else,' Dad yelled back.

'True enough.' Aunt Peg turned. 'Dead now, so what does it matter?' She cut into the pumpkin. 'What did she die of again?'

'Burst appendix, Aunty Peg,' said Tessa.

★   ★   ★

Dad came into our room that night for the first time since Mum'd gone.

'Can Aunty Peg stay a few extra days?' I asked, wanting him to feel better after the day he'd had being mad with grief and then mad with Aunty Peg. I squashed down what he'd said in the dairy until it was flat into the mud and I didn't see it any more. Tessa had to be right. Dad had been full of normal when he'd had his cuppa with Father McGinty. Talked about the hymns Mum liked best. Father McGinty had found a better reading than the one they'd picked out together in the presbytery the other day. Dad had sandpapered up his chin, allowing as how that

125

was a good one and just right for Sarah, and thanking Father McGinty for coming all that way to suggest it. He was just like always.

'Cheeky bugger.' He swatted me now as I lay in bed, with a ghost of a grin, but there was no fuel in his tank. 'Been saying ya prayers?'

We nodded. 'We say them to each other,' Philly said.

'Good girls.' He sat on the side of Philly's bed. His eyes travelled the ceiling, corner to corner. 'Your mother would be proud of yous,' he said.

I blinked. Not once but three times. 'Why?'

'Why?' he echoed, searching my face for answers. 'She always was' was the best he could do. For me, it had been a serious question. If I knew, I'd do more of it.

'Is Mum our guardian angel now?' asked Philly.

'Reckon so.'

'So can we pray to her?'

'Reckon she'd like that.' He kneeled down beside Philly, turned our bed light off. We all said our Hail Marys together. Afterwards, he leaned back on his heels. 'Don't listen to Peg, girls.'

'Peg was right, though. I did nearly kill Mum,' said Philly matter-of-factly, her hands tucked under her little monkey face.

I saw it then — that was why Philly had been upset in the chook shed. She must have believed Aunty Peg telling us she'd poisoned Mum from the inside when she was growing in her. I put my hand across the space between our beds, but Philly just looked at it like it came from *The Planet of the Apes*, so finally I snuck it back under my covers.

'Peg's a sick woman,' said Dad.

'Why isn't she up at The Hill, then?' asked Philly.

Dad sighed. 'She should be, by rights. But it's not a nice place. Your mother was nursing up at that loony bin on the night shift for years.'

'If they put Aunty Peg there, she could have ended up like Old Mary,' I told Philly with authority.

'Who's that?'

'Don't go frightening ya little sister,' Dad said. He got to his feet and lifted the blankets to Philly's chin. Smoothed them down.

'Night, little chickens,' he said.

'Night, Dad.'

He closed the door just enough to leave a strip of light across our beds. I wished he'd smoothed my blankets as well. Maybe he thought I was too old now.

We listened to the thud of his footsteps back to the TV.

'Who's Old Mary?' Philly whispered.

'They locked her in a padded cell and had one little slit that they opened to give her food. Mum said she was wild. Said she was the only one who could calm Old Mary. Mum was worried about her when she quit but more worried about me cause my hair had turned to straw and fallen out with her not being around in the nights, so she had to stop work. Mum reckoned they would have put Old Mary in a straitjacket.'

'What's a straight jacket?'

'One of them things you can't move in, it's like torture.' I had only the haziest of ideas. 'It's white all over, white for madness.'

'Do you reckon Aunty Peg is as mad as Old Mary?'

I considered. 'Aunty Peg can still cook and stuff; don't reckon Old Mary could have done that.' Mum said Aunty Peg wasn't mad all through. Said she made a meal of it whenever she got around Dad, just to rile him up good. So maybe she was also as brave as brave.

'I'm glad Aunty Peg isn't up at The Hill,' said Philly. 'But she'd better go home after the funeral.'

THE MORE THAT DOESN'T ADD UP

The next day I was staying out of Aunty Peg's way and her cut-cut eyes. I wandered across a paddock or two and found myself on top of the gully. Before I could give myself a chance to say no, I skidded down the mud into the long, dark crack between the two hills to kick at a few old bones. I squatted to line them up to see if I could tell which bone had been what. But give them enough time, all bones ended up dried out, white and cracked through so you couldn't tell the difference. The skulls were good, though. I did a better job there.

I got hold of a beauty, almost perfect, little lamb's skull, I reckoned. I rubbed the dirt away and stared long and long into the black hollows, trying to put the eyes back and give them a bit of spark. One day Mum's head would be all empty gone like this. I traced the eye sockets of the lamb with the tip of my finger. I wouldn't want Mum's bones to be here, kicked around and left for dead. I was glad she died in a hospital where there was somebody to look after her.

The craw of a crow came long and sharp. I looked up and found her standing bold as bold on the short limb of a stunted tree in a crease in the hill. Not much got a hold on living in this gully, so I reckoned good on the tree for giving it a go. The crow gave another long moan across the valley. Against the greys and pale winter greens there was a slice of orange on the ground under the tree. I stopped breathing. Mum had an apron with oranges on it. I knew it couldn't be; Mum died in a hospital with all the doctors and nurses, not here, all alone and forgotten, but I was up and running over there before my brain could tell me otherwise. The lamb's skull, forgotten, bumped away down the hill. The crow took off in a hell of a panic seeing me rushing hard at it.

I could tell, way before I got there, but I kept going anyway because I couldn't stop, my feet kept running, as if the devil was after me. My chest was burning and heaving, but still I kept going.

At the tree, I collapsed over the torn strip of faded orange ice-cream container and cradled it to my heart as if it really was a piece of Mum. I hiccupped out a strange wailing that sounded like it belonged in this place of old skulls and dry bones, so I let it go and go with nobody to hear but the dead. I wondered if Mum could hear me, and decided she had to because she was an angel now. After a while, the animal in me faded away and I was just crying normal, thinking about Mum and all the good things we did. I was the lucky one who got to sit beside Mum when we shaved the hair off the dead pigs last spring. She gave me one of her aprons, not the oranges one, and I tied it around me good. She had to tie Philly's for her. I got to the stool beside Mum first and Mum cuffed at Philly for whingeing about it.

That day it was a cold coming-out-of-winter day so I had my gumboots close to the flame under the old bathtub. Mrs Tyler told me to worry about my boots melting, so I dragged them back under me. But when she looked away I scooted them to the flame again, keeping my hands close to the water warming in the tub.

Then the 'look outs' and 'mind your noggins' as Dad and Pete came in loud, hefting one pig over our bathtub, and Mr Kennedy and Mr Tyler brought in the second for the other tub. Pete pretended to drop his end on Tessa's head and she screamed. Then the laughing and cuffing and carrying on, and the worrying about being splashed. Mrs Tyler put the radio on to 3XY for music. Tim grinned at me. It was all ABC and *Blue Hills* where Dad was concerned, but he couldn't argue with Mrs Tyler, over to help. Then the razor blading. Philly nicked herself straight away. I shook my head. Mum told Philly to get herself a Band-Aid from the packet on the bench and get back on the job. I hid my smile in a tricky bit on the stomach, getting in right close. Mum patted my hair back behind my ear and told me I was doing a real good job this year, not leaving one hair behind and that would make the butchering and the cooking that much easier. I was all warmed up on that and I folded my boots under my stool. In the nick of time, I'd say, because they did feel kind of melty.

She had a winning way with her, Mum did. That's what Dad called it. She'd always roll her eyes and swat him, tell him he was carrying on. He'd just laugh, dodging her tea towel and get in there past it to tickle her, her pushing him away and laughing back. But Dad was right. Mum was magic. And he'd never have hurt her and left her here to rot because he'd never do anything bad to her. I felt a flush of hot that I'd even for one moment thought it. I scrunched up my face, though, because there must have been something wrong or why'd she tell him she was leaving him?

Suddenly there was an almighty crash just along the way on the far side of the boxthorns. I jumped to my feet, fright spiking through me. Backed away hard into the tree. Then I saw it was only a roo as it gained the ridge and bounded away. But I was all jangled and rawed up, and had had enough of all those dead things, so I took off the other way. I ran and I ran and in the end I saw that I was running to the top paddock where Dad kept the Grey.

Dad said you can't name a brumby until it's broken in. You could only name it when you knew it, through and through. So it had to be special and not any old Tricksy or Daisy. Dad had told me I could name her this time. Only with Mum and everything, he'd probably forgotten. But I'd thought of a name already.

I saw that I was running towards her because it was time she got that name, broken in or not. Ever since the police came, she'd been thundering from one side of the short paddock to the other. Dad saying she'd have to wait with everything he had on his mind. I reckoned it was because there was no pool of peace inside him to get the brumby to and convince it to stay.

No more waiting for the Grey any more,

though, just because Dad wasn't right enough in himself. I got up close, but I couldn't see her. I slid under the fence and charged up to the far end and then slowed right down. There was a shadow on the dirt, up in the corner, butted up against the rail. The brumby was lying still and flat, not a twitch. From where I was I could see flies buzzing around her face. All the gloss had gone from her coat.

I came to a complete stop. Hands taking their time getting up to my waist, head shaking one side to the other. Dad'd be sorry now. When I'd done my fair share of lip biting and head shaking, I slipped back through the rails and got to the chook shed and sure enough Philly was on her haunches there, teaching school, her pupils pecking around her paying her no mind. I sent her to find Dad and get him to come to the top paddock quick smart.

'Why?'

'Just get him, and get those eggs in to Tessa or she'll send Aunty Peggy after you.'

Philly snapped up tall; Aunty Peggy fear flew across her face. She ran off.

I bit my lips some more, put my hand down to touch the warm of one of Philly's girls, but she saw me coming and went for a peck. I snatched my hand back and took off back to the top paddock. I leaned on the rail a moment with my head tucked in and hands dark over my eyes, but then I gave myself a good talking to and made myself get back through the fence.

I squatted down next to the Grey. I put my hand on her long neck. Felt the stiff and cold

133

coming back at me. Squeezed my hand down into it to see if I could make a difference. But it all held and there was no difference that could be made. I snickled in close and laid my cheek against her neck, closed my eyes and went deep into the dark with her.

I heard Dad's boots coming through the boxthorns. I held my breath and when he was close enough to see, his suck of air was a knife in my belly.

'Come away from there, JJ.'

'She's gone, Dad.'

'I've got eyes.'

'She was fine this morning.'

Dad saw I wasn't going anywhere so he swung in under the fence and got over to me. He hunkered down beside the brumby on the other side. Hand on her flank.

'I named her all ready for when she was broken in.'

He nodded.

'Silver.'

He nodded again.

'But she went too soon.'

'Reckon we can make an exception. Be a help to give her a name. To know she's still here, a part of you.'

Dad's hand was moving over Silver's flank, back and forth, as if he was feeling what was under her skin.

'Are you going to drag Silver down to the gully?'

He shook his head. 'Knackers this time.'

One of them crows landed on top of the

closest straining post. Head to the side, one fat gleaming eye all narrow and fixed on Silver. I stood up. Hands on hips, staring down the barrel straight back at it.

'She'd had a gut full,' said Dad. He was looking at Silver and nowhere else. 'She was left too long between the home where she came from and the lucerne paddock here where she was ending up. She got too filled up with sad.'

'And whose fault was that?' I asked, suddenly all dirty and thinking about all those dead bones down in the gully and how Silver and Mum were going to end up just like them.

His head jerked up. I scrubbed at my eyes with my forearm. Sawing like blazers as if I could rub the red right away.

'What are you on about?'

'You didn't look after her like you said you needed to.'

He stared hard right through me.

Out of nowhere I took off towards that crow, arms out, aeroplane ready and screaming. Red swirl rising and me just ahead of it. I swerved around and headed back in his direction. He was on his feet, legs planted wide.

'You killed her,' I screamed.

Dad raised his hand as if to stop my words dead. I pulled up short. The breath in me tearing at my lungs, heaving my chest up and down, real quick.

'There was no killing here.' His voice low, quiet. 'It was her choice. Just her time.'

'You left her in limbo, then, where nobody loved her and nobody could say her name.'

'You're talking rot, girl.' But there was still no heat in him. He stabbed the heel of his boot into the mud, forehead low, keeping a close eye on what he was doing.

I backed away from all the holes in him. But still I couldn't stop myself.

'God sees everything,' I said. I reeled off and under the fence and was away, running fast from all that seeing.

★ ★ ★

Dad was asking for our things so we could put them in with Mum tonight at the rosary. He didn't look at me and I didn't care. I wasn't giving him mine because if he knew it was Mum's brooch he wouldn't let me put it in. Only trouble was they all thought I hadn't got something. So I raced back to my room and shot about trying to think of a good enough idea to keep them off the scent.

I wasn't coming up with anything, and Tessa was yelling to hurry up. I stood at the end of my bed, shaking out my hands and thinking I'd better come up with something quick smart. Then I realised I had to sacrifice Ted. I snatched him off my pillow. It wasn't like I ever played with him any more — well before Mum died, anyway. And I wasn't playing with him now, just holding tight to him when the light went off. And now Ted had to do this thing for me. Had to go into the dark and be with Mum, who made him in the first place.

I raced out of my room. I was happy about

this Ted business because Mum would have something of me after all. I slid through the lounge in my socks and it was only when I was just about into the kitchen that I saw Dad poking at the fireplace. There were a few bits of white paper with gold edges on top of the logs, curling and blackening with the heat. The end of Dad's poker burying a square of black deep in the hot orange. I was in mid slide, so I couldn't stop, even though I put my hand to the wall.

Dad came hurtling into the kitchen after me. 'In the car. You're keeping us all late.'

I thrust Ted at him so he'd see there was a good reason. 'Ted's going in with Mum.'

'Where have your brains got to, JJ?' he said, ignoring Ted. 'Should have sorted that out well before.'

I tucked Ted back under my arm, got into my shoes and followed him out the door. It wasn't so much what he said as the way he said it. I missed his half grins and winks behind Mum's back, but I guess he'd just about had enough of me. I dragged down the side of my mouth. I'd had enough of me. That was for sure. Couldn't keep my mouth shut for quids despite all my hand-on-heart promises to Mum. I held Ted tight to my stomach all the way, even though Tessa offered to put him in the bag with the other things.

'He's right with me till we get there,' I said. She didn't argue. It was Philly who leaned over and said what I saw in Tessa's face. 'Are you sure you want to give Ted to Mum?'

I was sure, but I didn't trust myself to do

anything more than nod and stare out the window.

I couldn't see out the front window because Aunty Peg's big hat in the front seat took up the whole view. She'd taken some of the lilac from the vase Tessa put in her room and tucked it into the headband. Mum said she and Aunty Peg had had lots of fun times, like hiding Great Aunty Dot's teeth from her. Mum and Aunty Peg sounded good and naughty when they were kids. I wondered if I'd grow up good like Mum or mad like Aunty Peg.

★ ★ ★

Father McGinty had never said a word to me, but I could see he had ideas of changing that tonight. Dad and Father McGinty said a few low things together, and then Aunty Peg stepped forwards, sending Philly and me into giggles with her curtsey. Father McGinty nodded as if a curtsey was to be expected, then he turned to Tessa and shook her hand with both of his and then Tim's. It was my turn next, but I kept my hands around Ted. He ended up ruffling my head and just patting Philly on her shoulder. He said things to all of us, but I didn't know what they were.

Aunty Peg greeted Mrs Tyler and Mrs Nolan and the others like friends she saw every day. Mrs Tyler put a hand on her shoulder and leaned in for a quiet word.

Tessa pulled Philly after her, and Tim and I followed up the aisle. We got to go in first and have a private moment with Mum before everyone else. It wasn't really 'with' Mum because the coffin was all shut up tight on account of us kids — Mrs Nolan said it wasn't right for children to see dead people. Dad agreed, said he wanted us to remember Mum how she was, not stone cold in a coffin. Aunty Peg had snorted and asked him what he had to hide. Dad swore.

I swore too because with the coffin all locked up how would I get Mum's brooch in to her? But then I heard Aunty Peg saying they'd have to leave the coffin open at the funeral because there'd be a bigger crowd, so we would just have to put up with seeing our mother stone-cold dead, then. I winced; she'd be in that plain old navy dress Tessa had picked out in the first place. Dad wouldn't hear of Mum wearing the pink snowdrop dress because it wasn't a party she was going to.

★　★　★

Tessa got our things out of the bag and handed them to Tim and Philly. She nodded at us to put them in the basket at the foot of Mum's coffin. Tim went first, looking as if he didn't know what to do. In the end, he placed the Donald Duck comic in the basket with his two hands and did a kind of bow. That seemed good to me so I did the same thing with Ted.

Dad put in an envelope and Aunty Peg swept off a set of bracelets from one arm and then more from the other, and let them drop into the basket with a hell of a racket. I sat in the front pew beside Dad, who was all kneeled over. I wished I'd said goodbye to Ted. Properly. With words, not just all that squeezing. I knew he wasn't real or anything. But he was something.

Then the others came tiptoeing in and we began. Tessa's eyes were crinkled up as she gave the Hail Marys in her loud voice, as if they could bring Mum back. Tim's eyes were closed, too. Philly was mumbling along like it was a song, Dad was running the words over his tongue like water over stones in the creek, and Aunty Peg was mumbling, rocking forwards and backwards.

I couldn't catch on to the rhythm; I was always a beat behind, and out of nowhere I dropped my beads. Tessa glared at me as the clatter of the rosary beads exploded against the floorboards. Dad didn't even open his eyes, but I saw by the big sigh in his next 'Hail Mary, full of grace' that I was a long way from being full of grace myself.

I scooped to pick them up, making another racket, but then I didn't know where we were up to. I looked over at Dad's beads and tried to X-ray through his hand, but he had them beads all bunched up inside his fist.

It was the same story everywhere I looked. I felt a rise of panic like vomit in my tummy. My eyes zoomed back in on Dad's beads beside me. There was a smudge of ash on his left hand. I reached over to rub it away. Then I stopped like I'd been burned.

I squeezed my eyes tight and counted backwards from ten like Mum taught me. I got to zero and started again. Dad had a frown waiting for me when I opened my eyes. So I started into Holy Mary, Mother of God, just saying anything to put him off the scent. He closed his eyes and bowed his head.

I squeezed my knees together, but the storm was building. Mum would want me to stay real still. Real, breathing slow, steady. But those bits of gold-edged paper curling on the top of those logs in the fireplace were big in me. Then too big. I tugged on Dad's sleeve. He opened one eye, but whatever he saw on my face made him close it quick smart. I tugged again. He shook his head to warn me. I put my rosary in my pocket and took Dad's wrist and squeezed. Tessa leaned right over Dad and smacked my hand away. I felt my eyes get smaller, so I tried to open them wide, wide. But it was no use.

'Dad,' I whispered.

He just made his 'Blessed is the fruit of thy womb' louder. That made the red get louder in me. I'd seen those gold edges before, every week, right in God's house. I got off my knees and stood up to whisper in his ear. 'Dad, why were you burning Mum's Mass book in the fireplace?'

His eyes sprung open. He turned his head and stared. I was looking straight into those big staring brown eyes of the bunny caught in the spotlight before we found out Mum was dead. All the red whooshed away in me with a puff. I got back to my knees quick smart and got those beads out and sorted. Eyes closed and like I planned never to open them again. Not if I had to see that look in my dad's eyes.

We got to the end of the rosary and everybody shifted so eventually I had to open them. There was nothing of that left in Dad's eyes, and maybe I'd imagined it.

Dad thanked people for coming and shook their hands. He talked to this one and that one. He didn't talk to me and he didn't look at me.

MRS TYLER'S SUSPICION

Aunty Peg's voice was all through the house singing 'Amazing Grace', only putting 'Sarah' for 'Grace'. She couldn't make it quite fit, but she said that wasn't going to stop her singing it at the funeral.

Dad said, 'Over my dead body,' and Aunty Peg said, 'If needs must.'

Us kids took bets on who would win. Tim and I were going for Aunty Peg. We reckoned mad beat angry every time.

By the afternoon, Tim didn't like the look of one of his ferrets. He yelled for me to come take a look. He was on the ground with his face just about in the cage. Longtail did look a bit yellower than normal. Tim twanged the bars of the cage. The other ferrets all rushed to the other side. Tim pulled his hand away. Longtail stayed right where he was in the corner.

'We'd better change the water, clean out the cage, give im some extra meat. See if he perks up.'

'I'm busy,' I said.

He got to his feet, dusted off his hands. 'It's Mum's funeral tomorrow,' he said, as if that should make me think again. When it didn't, he added, 'And you know she'd want you to help me.' But there was something angled up about him. He got the straw from the hay bale in the corner. He was no way looking at me, but I was looking at him real good.

'Not doing it,' I said.

He ignored me.

'Get Philly to help you.'

'Gut ache.'

I knew what she was really doing. She was writing a poem for Mum's funeral. Said she was going to ask Mrs Tyler to read it.

I folded my arms.

'Mum's watching,' he said. 'Sees everything,'

I looked up to the sky. Screwed my face up as if considering the matter, then dashed to the bench to get the big rubber ferret gloves before him, but he got there first, not fooled for a second. He didn't grin like he normally did when he got the better of me. I folded my arms again. He pointed to the sky.

That wasn't what made up my mind, though. I saw what I'd been looking at in him. He wasn't going to let another thing die. Not the day before we put Mum in the ground. I had one big sigh and I let it out as I picked up the bucket and lid from the bench. 'Give me just one of your gloves, then,' I said.

'I need both in case they get away. Bite your toes off.'

I shoved at him, but squatted down to ready the bucket on the ground. He caught the first ferret in the cage and dropped it into the bucket. I smashed the lid on top fast before it could jump out. Black Claws rammed his head against it. Tim got Sulky ready. We counted: one, two, three. I pulled back the lid and in she went. Once they were all in, he put the ferret brick on top.

Tim looked at the empty cage, his hands at his waist. He was all still. Then he itched the back of his neck. He scratched the side of his face. He got down onto his knees and examined the bottom of the ferret's cage.

'Hurry up.'

'Fleas,' he said.

'They'll run out of air if we don't let them out.'

I hated ferrets and their sharp, sharp teeth, but I didn't want them to suffocate while Tim was looking for imaginary fleas. He didn't seem to care that more things were dying now.

'Why did you ask Dad about Mum's missal?' he asked, eyes still stuck on the bottom of the cage, his back to me.

'Didn't,' I said.

Tim pulled at his collar. 'I heard you, JJ, at the rosary.'

'It was nothing. I got mixed up.'

'Why was the old man so upset if it was nothing?'

'Don't know why it has to be such a big secret,' I blurted out despite my good intentions to keep my mouth shut.

'He burned it, didn't he, JJ? He burned Mum's Mass book?'

I sucked my finger. 'Dad's allowed to burn what he likes.'

'It wasn't the book he was burning, but,' Tim said.

'It was so,' I said, the red starting to get its claws in me again. 'I saw it.'

'It's what was inside the prayer book,' he said.

I frowned, trying to get ahead of him. 'Yeah, like Dad wanted to burn all the prayers,' I said scornfully.

He didn't react, his face all muscle still and serious. 'Remember the police gave the old man an envelope?' I nodded. 'I went in to see him about the tractor pump that night. He wasn't there so I waited. The envelope was on the bed with all the police stuff inside, but her missal was more out than in. She must have taken it with her when she died. She never let us touch it, right? Just between her and God, right?'

I was still too.

'This time I touched it, just to feel something of hers. I found out why she never let us near it, but. She wrote something in it. On the inside cover. I saw it.'

I fell back on my bum with the surprise of Mum dirtying up her Mass book like that. It made not one lick of sense. I kicked out, sending him sprawling for lying to me, then jumped quick to my feet, my fists ready for him, but he just took it, getting himself up as if nothing happened.

'She wrote an address,' he went on, as calm as calm, ignoring me.

I let go of my breath. 'That's why she didn't take her Mass scarf with her.'

'What?'

I told Tim about Dad having her scarf in the ute and how it had ended up down at Jean's

Corner. 'She didn't need her scarf because she wasn't going to Mass. But she did need the book because she wanted that address.'

The ferrets were banging away in the bucket.

'Why didn't you say anything?' I asked.

He shrugged. 'Didn't know it was anything special until he burned it.'

'What are you two buggers up to?'

We jumped. Dad blocked the light through the door.

'Ferrets,' Tim said, quick as a flash. 'Longtail looked a bit crook.'

Dad grunted. He had his back to us, sorting through his tools on the bench. 'Seen the shifter?'

Tim scratched his neck again. I was full sorry for him, with this thing that was too big and him not used to things like that — not like me. But I was beginning to feel itchy, too.

'What was the address in Mum's missal for?' I asked Dad before I could stop myself.

'What're you talking about?' Dad's voice was all dirty.

'You know, her Mass book.'

He threw down the hammer with a great bang. Turned. 'Not again, JJ. You're always making trouble where there's none to begin with. How'd ya know about the address?'

'I shrugged. Just do.'

He gave me a long stare then turned back, throwing tools about, making a hell of a racket, like he was all about the shifter.

'Maybe she was bored, looking after Aunty Peg,' I said, trying to find a way out for him. 'Got doodling.' Even though I knew Mum would

147

never go writing over her Mass book for nothing.

He turned back to us, using the bench to hold him up like he had no stuffing in him. 'Just stop it, or you'll end up like your mother.'

I blinked with the knife of it. I buttoned my lips up good and tight, not letting one more word escape. But out of nowhere, for the first time I ever knew, Tim didn't back off.

'JJ being like Mum wouldn't be so bad seeing as how Mum was so good,' said Tim.

I blinked with the surprise of it.

Dad stared too. 'You're not wrong there, son.' He paused. 'But sometimes she had a mind of her own and it didn't do her any good. She should have been here where she belonged instead of gallivanting about.'

'Or looking after Aunty Peg, like you said she was,' Tim corrected.

Dad blinked twice, redded over. Turned his back like he had business he'd better get back to.

But Tim still hadn't finished. 'Reckon that address must have been important,' he said. 'To write it in her book and never let any of us know about it.'

I wanted to give him one of those kicks Tessa was always giving me.

'Could be, son. We'll never know now I've burned it.'

'Why'd ya do that, Dad?' Tim asked. He was crouching still, like he was all casual, but his neck was ridged up.

Dad scrubbed his face with his knuckles. 'Had to say my goodbye before the rosary, my own way.'

Something started prickling at me on the inside of my skin.

'And you've been ringing around after we've gone to bed, haven't you?' asked Tim. 'All those phone numbers in her address book. She wasn't at Peg's, was she?'

We were on the far side of ordinary now and I was as scared as scared. Dad definitely wouldn't keep me if Tim kept this up.

Dad said nothing.

'Did you go to it?' Tim asked. 'The address in her Mass book?' He was on his feet now, feet planted wide, hands on his hips, staring straight at Dad's back.

I pushed at the bucket. It was lighter than I thought, so over it went. I yelped and raced for the bench, Tim yelped and dived for the bucket. He got to it in time to shove the first ferret out back in and right them all.

Dad didn't move even one muscle. Just watched while Tim and I tipped the ferrets back into their fresh-straw cage, Longtail back to nipping at Bandi like nothing had ever been wrong. But once we locked the cage door tight, Dad was all muscle. He slammed down the mallet he'd been holding. The other tools jolted in the air. 'Expect more from you, boy.' He kicked at the ferret bucket and sent it flying. 'They're your bloody ferrets, so you should be a bloody sight more careful. They're dangerous bastards, especially with your little sister right here. Bloody shit for brains!'

Dad wheeled off out the door, hands full of empty.

Tim stared after him, white-faced with shock. Dad had never spoken to him like that in his life. I kept my head down, torn in a dozen different ways.

★　★　★

Philly had finished the poem. Tessa told her how great it was, but I thought it was dumb — which rhymed with Mum so maybe she should have put that in her stupid poem. It was all 'trees are green, but without Mum they'll just seem mean'. How would that help anything? I was hoping Dad would put a stop to it. I was so mad I left Philly and Tessa to it, and went into the kitchen where Mrs Tyler and Aunty Peg were.

'How are the piglets, JJ?'

'Real good, Mrs Tyler.'

'Got any names?'

'Got them all named up.'

'I hope you've called the one with the funny tail Poppy.'

'Just like you wanted. Poppy's real strong, pushes all the others away for dinner.'

Aunty Peg interrupted. 'So I've packed up two of the blackberry and one of the plum.'

Mrs Tyler nodded. 'We'll miss Sarah's jams.'

'Do you think four dozen scones will do it?'

Mrs Tyler and Aunty Peg went over who was bringing what. Aunty Peg marked it all down on a sheet of paper. She bit at the end of the pen. I slipped under the table when they weren't looking, where I could pull the dark in nice and close around me.

Aunty Peg poured another cuppa for them both. She was all business with Mrs Tyler. So Mum must have been right and Aunty Peg was stacking on her maddy around Dad, but then I remembered the pills. Maybe she was back on them just like Dad told her.

'Sad business, this,' said Mrs Tyler.

Aunty Peg clicked her tongue. 'Couldn't get any sadder if you paid it.' She slurped at her tea. 'But Tessa's very capable,' she said. 'Tim, too. JJ's smart as a whip and that Philly's got all of them wrapped around her little finger. They'll be fine in the end. Just got to get this funeral over with.' She scratched on the paper. 'Think we'll need another urn for the top table.'

'Nothing you could have done about it, Pegs.'

The surprise of it lit up the dark around me under the table. Mrs Tyler had broken her promise to Dad that she wasn't going to say anything about the way Mum died to Aunty Peg.

'The peritonitis would have got her even if she was right here in her own kitchen,' Mrs Tyler went on.

Aunty Peg tsked and tsked, but didn't seem to get any upset the way Dad said she would.

'You know,' said Mrs Tyler, who must have been thinking the same as me, 'you really shouldn't bang it on with Jack. He's convinced you're mostly mad.'

Aunty Peg sighed. 'Just playing to the peanut gallery, Kathy; giving him what he wants.'

'It's a dangerous game, Peg. Jack's a powerful man in the Church. One word from him and he'd have you up The Hill.'

151

Aunty Peg laughed. 'And one word from me would see him burning in hell.'

'Give it a break, Peg. No one in authority will believe a word you say if he's got you up The Hill.'

Aunty Peg's sigh was all surrender. 'True enough. He did enough damage between Sare and me.'

Now it was Mrs Tyler's turn to sigh and it didn't sound a bit like surrender. 'To be fair,' she said, sharp, 'as I've just pointed out, I hardly think he was on his Pat Malone there, Peg. How did you expect to get back in his good books with all your carry-on? You know he's fond of his moral reputation.'

'What I do is my business,' Peg hit back fast.

I wrapped my arms around my legs and pulled my knees tight to my chest, trying to fit all these new things in my brain. Then Mrs Tyler spoke up again with this real even voice like she was deadset on letting bygones be bygones.

'Has your phone been out of order?' she asked.

'No.' But Aunty Peg thought a bit more. 'Although it could have been. I don't use it much.'

'It's just that I would have thought Sarah would have called the kids while she was up the road with you. Lucky it was working when you rang the ambulance.'

Aunty Peg made a noise that if you were Mrs Tyler you might take for agreement.

'Good to see you back on your feet so fast at any rate,' said Mrs Tyler.

'Amazing what something like this can give you strength for.'

152

Now it was Mrs Tyler making a noise that might or might not have been agreement.

I held my hands over my ears to stop it all coming at me: Dad saying Mum had been with Aunty Peg, but Aunty Peg at first saying she wasn't, then changing her mind to agree with Dad; Aunty Peg saying she hadn't had a turn but telling Mrs Tyler now she had. Like different kind of bells ringing all at the same time.

And now this new clanging. The phone was plenty working so if Mum had been there she would have called us.

There was one thing for sure. Aunty Peg and Mrs Tyler weren't quite as matey as they were when they first started counting scones together.

'Sarah's better off out of it, anyway,' said Aunty Peg.

'Don't be ridiculous, Peg. Sarah was fine. Happy.' There was a big full stop in Mrs Tyler words.

'Are you Catholic at all, Kathy? Of course she wasn't happy.' Aunty Peg practically spat the last word. 'I'm the last one to say a word against Jack.'

Which was news to me since that was all she'd done since she got to our place.

'He never left her alone. Always mad for it.'

I heard the clatter of a teacup against the saucer and saw Mrs Tyler rise. I flattened to the wall under the table so she couldn't see me.

'I don't know what gets into you at times, Peg. You have no idea what went on between them. The rhythm method only works if you have plenty of backbone and discipline. Besides I

153

hardly think this is any of our business.'

It was all quick on the packing up and stiff-cardboard goodbyes and the door closing. That shocked me the most because the leaving at our place wasn't at the front door. You walked people out, watched them into the car and waved them down the track. Then they'd gone.

'You can get out from under there, JJ,' said Aunty Peg.

I pressed my back into the wall. Aunty Peg's face looked straight at me as she angled over. 'You've got a black streak in your soul, miss.'

I blinked with big eyes. That made two of us.

IT'S GOT TO END

The next day, without Mum, I did my own pigtails ready for her funeral. I put knots in big white ribbons around each one. They weren't perfect, even I could see that, but they weren't not perfect. I was feeling so good about it that I got Philly sorted out before me in the mirror and started in on her hair. I pulled it all back into a ponytail. She had real smooth hair and one little piece out of place made a bump, so I couldn't get it *right* right. My hands got sore, so I got her to kneel. The best part of the kneeling was that I didn't have to see her little screwed-up face in the mirror at every lump I made.

When I got something close to almost perfect, I let her up. She took one look and pulled it out. Grabbed the brush and ran off. I'd have liked to be like her. All action and no words. It was all burn and scald with me.

After the ferrets and everything, Tim had been quiet last night until Dad asked him whether he thought it'd rain in time for the crops to come up before the summer hot. By the time they'd finished with the ins and outs, Tim was almost back to himself. It was like he'd decided that Dad burning Mum's Mass book didn't mean anything after all. Didn't look at me once, though.

This morning, Tim was Brylcreemed up and ready, although with the crew cut I couldn't see that it made a scrap of difference. Dad gave him a cuff of approval as he dashed into the bathroom with his comb. There was no looking at me from him, either.

None of us needed reminding to be right on time. We were all sitting in the car when Dad charged from the house and leaped in. Tessa sat beside us in the back seat, hands folded over Mum's other handbag.

★　★　★

I ran into the church before anybody else to put Mum's brooch in with her. I stopped short just inside the front door, though. Mum's coffin took up all the air in the church. It was big and shiny, sitting in the aisle at the bottom of the altar. Mum was in that thing. In that long, shiny thing that didn't look a bit like her. It was covered in dark crimson roses. I hadn't wanted the roses too much because they reminded me of the ones Mrs Nolan'd had up on the altar that first Sunday after Mum'd gone. But since the roses were from Mrs Tyler's garden and Mrs Tyler was Mum's friend and that crimson deep was darker than Mrs Nolan's and was right for funerals and all the sad sorry, I kept my mouth shut.

But nothing about Mum's coffin was right.

I bit my lip.

Then I saw it. The something much worse. Mum was still all locked away, the lid closed tight down. My heart took off at a gallop. How was I going to get Mum's brooch in there? My eyes filled up full because I didn't have one idea left. I should have put it inside Ted and then it'd be in there already. I fixed my eyes on Jesus on the cross until I cleared the blur. Tessa came into the church and shoved me forwards. I let the others pass and followed them up the aisle and into our pew.

I closed my face tight tight to work out how to get her cameo in there with her. I just needed to think.

Philly dug into me with her elbow. 'Stop breathing so loud.'

I had to lock my eyes open because that was the only way I could hear my breath. But things were all thick and coming at me. I made myself stare at the roses, hanging on to a bit of their steady.

Father McGinty was saying how dependable Mum was and always there and stuff. Then things whirled and the sitting, standing and kneeling all got caught up together. Mrs Tyler read out Philly's poem and dabbed her handkerchief at her eyes. I kept opening and closing my fists because I'd finally worked out a plan to get Mum's brooch where it had to be, and I was dead scared that somebody would catch me.

At Communion, Dad swung out of the pew, us following, Aunty Peg last. Which suited me because nobody would believe a word she said, even if she did open her big mouth. The McMahons hung back out of respect. So all eyes on us. Dad and the others shuffled at the side of Mum's coffin, heads down, hands glued together. I had a great interest in the wood, trailing my hand along the top. A hundred eyes stabbing into my back.

I only had a second between Tim stepping forwards to get his Communion and my turn, but I shoved the brooch in among the roses. It seemed to go in nice and good. Only a couple of thorns on the way. I didn't dare suck the pin pricks. It didn't feel exactly right because I hadn't got the cameo into the coffin to where Mum was. But I had to find a way to be okay with the not-rightness.

I stepped forwards and opened my mouth for Jesus. When I turned I felt all the stabbing eyes on the front of me this time. I kept my own on the floor like I was praying real hard. And I was. Just not about what people might be thinking.

I followed Dad, Tessa and Tim back into the pew, past Philly's turned knees. She hadn't done her First Holy Communion so she'd had to wait for us all by herself.

I kneeled and gripped my hands together hard, offering up the pain for Mum. After a bit I slid back onto the seat and stared at everybody going past her coffin. Job was done, so things were slowing down to normal, but I had to keep on my toes to see if anybody was suspicious.

I narrowed my eyes on Mrs Nolan as she went past the coffin. She'd be the one to do the looking if anyone would. My eyes were right on her and hers were on the altar, all holy. But that wasn't a good idea because she tripped on the step getting up to Father McGinty. She flung her arm out to save herself and grabbed on to Father

McGinty's lacy dress. He stepped back quick smart before she got a real hold, but that upset the apple cart even more. She crashed to her knees, skirt flying. Mr Nolan turned to right her despite having just had Jesus put in his mouth and being in a Holy State, but she was already back on her feet with the help of Mrs McMahon, who was behind her. Father McGinty stepped forwards to give her the Communion.

I didn't know what was on her face when she headed back to her seat, because Philly, Tim and I had our heads buried deep. We were praying all right — praying that we kept all the laughing pushed down. We'd been in just the right spot to see it all, and see it all we did. She hadn't been wearing the kind of big no-colour underpants Mum did. Mrs Nolan's were big all right, but red and shiny and fierce like a traffic light.

Tessa leaned right across Tim and me and clamped her hand over Philly's mouth. Tessa was so mad she looked set to thump Philly, but she couldn't because we were at Mass. Philly's little eyes, bulging above Tessa's hand, were too much for Tim, and he fell to the kneeler as if he was looking for something. I plastered my praying hands tight against my eyes and filled my chest with big, slow air to stop the giggles getting out.

Tessa dragged Philly over the back of my knees and positioned her handy to her elbow. That was enough to shut Philly up.

But while Tim was looking for that thing he dropped, he dug into my leg and grinned up. I grabbed his finger and squashed it under my knee. I grinned down.

We got all serious, though, when we saw we were on the home stretch of Mum's funeral.

It was like we never saw those red underpants on Mrs Nolan's big bum on the altar.

It was like we'd never forgot for a minute that Mum was dead and we were burying her.

I was looking at Dad because I knew what was next. He pursed his lips and I could see he was gathering things up in himself.

Father McGinty came down the stairs with his incense thing and swung it high over Mum. He nodded and Dad stood. The two Mr McMahons got up, and Pete and Mr Kennedy, as well as young Dave Dillion. Although he sure didn't look young. He did everybody's funeral, though, because he'd fought in the war.

They got around Mum's coffin and the air got heavy. Like they were in a dance, they all swooped at the same second and hoisted Mum into the air and then onto their shoulders. Young Dave stumbled with her weight. Somebody gasped. The men under Mum's coffin got their arms around each other's shoulders and steadied. Seeing those grown men holding on, one to the other — it wasn't something you saw every day.

I squeezed my eyes shut. I tried to stop all that seeing. The priest moved off, starting up the procession.

Tessa marshalled us out into the aisle after the coffin. She took Philly's hand and she took mine. I wanted to pull away because I didn't want Tim to be left with Aunty Peg. But I didn't. All eyes were on us again, full of sorry. Ours were straight ahead, full of stones.

Out into the world we went behind our dead mum, through Dad's Knights of the Southern Cross mates who were lined up on each side like a tunnel, which Dad called a Guard of Honour. They shouldn't be here. Mum didn't like them one bit. She pursed her lips up pin tight once a month when Dad was rushing between bedroom and bathroom, black suited and Brylcreeming his hair shiny.

'Pack of sanctimonious, holier-than-thou men,' I heard her say one time to him.

Dad didn't care. He slapped her on the bum, grinning, because he was excited to be off. 'They're good, God-fearing men, love. Church'd fall down without us pillars.'

She swiped him back. 'It's like a little boy's club for grown men. You're scared of each other's shadows. You'd sacrifice your own mother not to look bad in their eyes.'

Once we were through the Knights, Aunty Peg poked me from behind to keep me going forwards until we were well away so everybody else could file out behind us. Faces all closed up serious. Women and men knotted together giving half nods to each other and scuffing their feet in the dirt: 'Lovely service', 'Didn't Father McGinty speak well', 'The flowers.'

I wanted to stand beside Mrs Nolan to make up for laughing at her. Red undies at a funeral. I could see she was worried everybody was thinking about it because that smile of hers was all stiff and straight. But then I saw something else.

In the long car that they put Mum's coffin in were the roses. And then I knew. Those roses weren't going into the ground with Mum.

I charged over. Banged my knee getting into the back of the car but I didn't reach them. There were hands around my waist dragging me out. I kicked out, but they had me good and proper. They belonged to Mrs Nolan. I couldn't hear what she was yelling for the loud in my ears. But I saw. Everybody was looking, rushing to her side.

I squirmed and kicked out some more. I couldn't get her big filthy red underwear hands off me. And then the noise broke through and there was a scream, sharp and loud, and it was me doing the screaming.

Dad put his big shouty face in mine. He had a good grip on me too, trying to yank me away from Mrs Nolan. I thrashed. Dad ripped me free and clamped me to his side. I saw Tessa's face through the crowd. Her face all squashed and wet.

'It's what I've been saying,' Mrs Nolan shouted, rubbing her elbow. 'You all saw.'

We were in the middle of everybody, and everybody was seeing everything.

'Completely out of control,' she yelled.

'Fat liar,' I said, matching her loudness.

'You can't bring her up, Jack.' Her face wild.

Dad breathing hard. He jerked me closer. 'I'll have you mind your own business.' He was all low and clear.

Then my head clouded up because it wasn't just me any more. There was red underwear and Dad by the fireplace burning Mum's missal, and so much swirl in the air.

But then Mrs Nolan said something and Dad took his arm from my shoulders. He stepped forwards. His hand sliced through the air and he slapped her, hard, right across her mouth. The slap cut through the crowd sharp.

'You shut your mouth about my daughter.'

★ ★ ★

We never went back. Every Sunday Dad found enough petrol for us to go all the way into St Francis Xavier's in Chilton for Mass. Tessa said we didn't go to our Mass any more because they were all busybodies. But not all of them, I didn't reckon. A lot of them had still come to the cemetery to put Mum in the ground. Not Tim, though. He wouldn't get in the car. Tears screwing up his eyes. Everybody stood around watching Tessa try to get him in, waiting for Dad to blow again. In the end, somebody took Tim away to the hall where we were having the spread to wait for us there.

It was true that some people went off with Mrs Nolan, but not as many as you'd think. I think they knew she was trying to put a bigger thing in their minds so they'd stop thinking about her trip-up on the altar.

She went too far.

That's what Dad said.

Dad went too far, too, but I reckoned people thought he was just mad with grief. I heard somebody saying that, anyway. After that, everybody left us alone.

Mrs Nolan was right about one thing, though.

163

I was too much trouble. Dad was real good to stand up for me like he did. I was going to be just like Tessa from now on. No more feeling. Either a thing was a thing or it wasn't. So no more questions about Mum. I wasn't going to give him one reason to send me off to Mrs Kelly, near saint that she may well be. Mrs Nolan could be right about that other thing, too. The thing that made Dad smack her one. Maybe there was the devil in me.

PART 2

UNBURIED
1982

The truth isn't always beauty, but the hunger for it is.

Nadine Gordimer

ANOTHER BEGINNING?

Some days I don't do life. I let it kick on by itself and sometimes those days turn into a week. And knives twist into my mind and grey things up. So on the day of Aunty Peg's funeral it was a matter of forcing myself up and out of bed and forcing myself to go through all the motions to get dressed and ready.

I'd done, it though. And there I was, facing the world outside the gates of St Mary's. And there was the world facing me back, all hooded eyes and watching and hand in hand with silence that licked at all the cracks. The heat was in on it too, eating up the air so there was no breathing, and me in the middle of it, pulling in enough of something to keep me on my feet. For a second I wished I'd said yes to Tye when he'd wanted to come with me. He'd be an extra layer of skin holding me together. I straightened my shoulders. He didn't need to see me taking a trip through the mud of memory lane, especially when I had way too much else I should be telling him. I put my hand to my belly and felt about its flatness experimentally. Hard to believe there was so much going on under the skin. But tests don't lie. I just wasn't sure what I was going to do about this awkward truth.

In my head I'd planned to be the last one

through the church doors, but the tram had charged along and then stopped dead outside St Mary's. So instead I was the first by a long shot. I stood at the entrance to the church grounds filled up with numb until I let myself fall into the wrought-iron gates, headfirst. I found some breath in among things and got my eyes open, weighing possibilities.

I didn't like the immediate ones. The church bluestone shot up into a spire and laid a long shadow back down along the ground. It was dark and solid and sharp edged. My ciggies found their way into the cradle of my palm and then I knew what I could do next. I unpeeled from the gates, went into the churchyard and hid around the corner, because I'm good at hiding. I lit one and chugged on the end, and watched the smoke carve a slow spiral heavenwards. I'd need to make a decision pretty damn soon about whether smoking was going to stay on the agenda or not. But not today.

'You turned up?'

Tessa's voice sliced through the quiet. I recovered enough to wave my hand over myself as if to say it was self-evident. 'Honouring the dead.'

Tessa's eyes swept over my jeans as if I wasn't honouring anything. 'A little more help with the living wouldn't go astray.'

'Wouldn't want to take your spot in heaven.'

'Still a bloody idiot.'

'Dad coming?'

She shook her head. 'Relieved?' she asked, eyes narrowed, thoughts ticking.

I gave the clouds a good going over. There was something, but I wasn't sure it was relief. I flipped open the lid of the cigarette packet and held them out towards her. She looked at the lineup of filters, packed in shoulder to shoulder like soldiers, and for a moment I thought she'd go for one, but the hearse nosed between the gates and she tore off, back straight and equal to any task, just like always.

I dragged at the end of my cigarette for a bit of comfort. Out of nowhere an ache snaked down my arms for Tessa's little boy, Georgie, because it had been a while since I'd seen him. He'd be going on four now. A half laugh coughed into my throat as I thought about the way his eyes gulped in the world, mouth going like a fish. I hadn't even met Tessa's twins who'd already clocked up a few months.

I stubbed the butt of my smoke out under my Docs and rubbed a sheen of sweat from my hands down my jeans. The wooden fence slats separating the church from the high rise listed towards me like they'd had too much to drink. I drifted further away along the side of the church and got myself behind a buttress in the wall where I couldn't be seen at all from the front.

'JJ,' Tessa called. 'We're starting.'

I didn't answer.

'For Godsake, JJ.'

The clouds billowed big like parachutes, full of far-off questions. I shook my head free of them, closed my eyes and counted to ten, going at a good slow jog. Then I pushed off the wall but stayed close enough so I still couldn't be spotted.

At the corner I hovered, scanning ahead to see whether the coast was clear. I raised my wrist. The funeral was just about to start, so I reckoned everybody who was coming must be in there, but I took the stairs two at a time anyway. At the top I congratulated myself that there was still nobody in sight who might have a query or two about what I'd been up to in the last many old years.

It took a few goes to heave the massive wooden door open. Inside, the chill of the marble coated me up close like a shroud. I grabbed a cardi out of my shoulder bag. There was a scatter of people right up the front. I dug a knuckle into my palm as I headed towards them, every step against the tide.

Aunty Peg's coffin was a lighter wood than Mum's had been, but it took up just as much space in the aisle, all final and finished like a full stop. I patted the pocket of my bag where I kept my smokes, then went back to knuckling my palm.

I turned into an empty pew behind the others and kneeled, my elbows on the seat in front of me, head tucked in. It was like slipping into old pyjamas. I studied the women from up home. Funny how none of the men had bothered to turn up to Mad Peg's funeral. But the sisterhood was there. That arrowed a zing of warmth through me. The quiet resistance of women with deep-lined, farm-hard faces gathering to honour one of the tribe, even if Peg was an outsider. Mrs Tyler's face had softened and splayed since I'd seen her last, but still she was trim and bird sharp. I had to look twice at Mrs Nolan. She wasn't just comfortable now, she was more than well cushioned, and her hair greyed over. The years were racing her to death's door. I wanted to reassure myself that she was not just old, but also harmless. I couldn't though, not unless I was going to lie. She'd taken to leaving messages at the boarding house for me since Peg's death a week back. I knew Dad didn't have my number so it had to be either Tessa or Tim who'd given it to her. Whatever she wanted with me, I wanted no part of it. I hadn't seen her since *that day*. One funeral always made you think of another.

I bit my lip to stop it shaking. When she turned her big eyes on me I ducked even further between my arms. She pitched forwards to tug at Tessa's jacket sleeve. She tapped her finger against the page of her open notebook. Tessa bent further in to look, head to the side, then nodded.

The church door banged shut and there was a clack of high heels that echoed in the hollow cavern. We all turned. It was Philly, sailing in like a grand new ship to harbour, making no apology for the racket. She waved and when she reached us she went forwards to peck Tessa, Mrs Tyler, Mrs Nolan and the others, like she was at a gala. She looked the part, too. All black and white, swinging skirt and fitted jacket.

When she was through she came back to sit in my pew. She leaned towards me and rested her head on mine. The soft of it melted into me. I tried out a smile and at first it was like cracking through dried mud. She arched an eyebrow and

I saw that she saw how it was with me. She reached down to the line of her skirt and raised it just enough to show me a flash of frilly fire-engine red. She winked and let her skirt drop. A smile sunshined out of me this time. She has always been able to change the channel in me. It reminded me of Mum, but in a sister way.

The priest hobbled out from the sacristy, old and wobbling like a bowling pin. First Philly and her frilly red knickers, and now him on the verge of toppling over. There was a pop in my head and the air got in and out of me easier. Tessa crossed the aisle to us and slipped in beside Philly, taking the time to ignore me. I was okay with that. Good, actually. Better to worry at the paint of the past on my own without her silent running commentary.

The priest found his mark on the altar and spread his arms over us, making a wide sign of the cross. Despite myself, I felt the blessing. I tightened my fists into shields because I didn't want any blessing from the woman-hating Catholic Church.

'Tim gunna make it?' I whispered to Philly.

'Said he had to finish the drenching for Shelley's dad.'

I guess that was okay; it wasn't like it was Mum's funeral. Philly wagged her finger, reading me like a book. 'First time he's Missing In Action — two-hundred-and-twenty-fifth for you.'

'When you put it like that . . . ' I had to admit.

She nodded, her lips all pursed up saying, 'You know I'm right.' Tessa frowned at us and we both raised our eyes as one and clapped them back on the priest. He gestured to Mrs Nolan and she got to her feet, notebook in hand. She bobbed before the altar and suppressed a groan as she lumbered up the steps. She put her hands on the lectern, cleared her throat and made contact with each of us, making sure we were all across the gravity of the occasion. I kept my eyes well down.

She opened with, 'Peg was a marvellous woman. In the true sense of the word.'

The surprise of 'marvellous' jerked my head upright.

'Peg lost touch with us after she moved to the city: she wanted her life to go a different way,' Mrs Nolan said.

Philly turned to me with a lift of her eyebrow. I knew what she meant. What happened to: *Dad chucked Aunty Peg out. Mum cried. Aunt Peg cried. Mum steadied Aunty Peg's arm as she got into the car. Dad held the door, looking out over the top of the car into the far horizon, face like concrete.* The story Tessa had told us.

Mrs Nolan put her shoulder to the wheel of truth and ground it down into something like normal. In her account of the days of Aunty Peg's life there was quirkiness rather than madness.

Truth was that Peg's madness often came in handy. When I lived at her place, straight out of school, she kept this cloud around my head of what she had said and hadn't, what she'd asked me to do and then hadn't. I couldn't live with the convenience of it for her. That, and all the

173

junk she hoarded and the way it breathed up all the air and leaned in close. In the end I realised that was Peg's way of getting me out the door without hurting my feelings. She hadn't wanted me there any more than Dad had wanted me living there. But in those first few months before I got that dishwashing job, staying with Peg was the only way I could afford going to uni.

At least she had colour, though. Madness had that going for it. She was always crashing through walls other people couldn't see.

Mum was special that way, too. She also saw those walls and decided to ignore the shit out of them. She stood with her back to them, sleeves rolled up, arms plunged elbow deep into the sink, scrubbing hard. Heroic in the epic battle of dirt-poor survival.

I leaned forwards and dropped my head deep into my arms triangled on the back of the pew in front so nobody could see me swipe my eyes across my forearm. My heart cracking and then shattering for my beautiful skin-and-bone mother.

Maybe Mum would have been happier mad. But Peg beat her to it. So she was left with duty. Maybe that's why she left us, looking for that something between the stifling rightness of what everybody expected her to do day after day, and the wild wrongness of mad. The tragedy was, she died in a cold hospital bed before she found it.

For a second there seemed no other option for me than to get to my feet, stumble over the back of Philly's and Tessa's legs and run fast and long, away from all of this. But Philly's hand snaked up between my arms until I caught it between my own. And I held on and on to her until the shuddering passed and something new of my mother came to me.

The clean, sharp poetry of her.

She could stand quiver still in a storm.

One time, in the late afternoon, out of nowhere, the sky darked up and split open, bucketing down curtains of rain after years of hard, drought-baked skies. Us kids got straight out and under it. Dad came racing up from the cowshed and joined in, side-kicking and tossing Philly and me up into it.

Not Mum.

She let her tea towel fall to the ground and just stood there, eyes closed, face turned up to the sky, rain rivering over her.

She was our true north.

In that moment I saw I was looking for my own in-between. That narrow strip between being tied to the oven with short apron strings like Mum and all these other women, and giving into madness like Peg. If I were honest, though, it was always going to be more Peg than Mum for me. But I stayed alert. Never kept so much as an extra plastic bag at my place. Made sure I never did the same thing twice unless I was convinced it was for the convenience of taking the same shortcut, not for the obsessive of it.

Mrs Nolan's voice rose high above my twisted thoughts as she weaved together all those threads of truths and not truths about Peg.

'Picnics by the creek, singalongs around the piano, keeping Great Aunty Dot happy in the corner with a nip of brandy in the teacup.'

The women across the aisle sniggered.

'She wasn't like the rest of us. All that gaiety, smoking when you didn't, terrible flirt, did the things the rest of us couldn't. That's what we loved about her.'

Heads bobbed in agreement.

Mrs Nolan wound up with a hope that Peg was finally at peace and crossed herself. I squeezed Philly's hand and released it.

Before she left the altar, Mrs Nolan spotlighted her eyes on me with furious intent, but I flicked mine away before I got rabbit-stilled.

I lost the next bit of the funeral as my mind focused on the problem at hand, trying to figure out how I was going to keep out of Mrs Nolan's determined-to-speak-to-me way. I wasn't letting her off the hook with something as light as an apology. Not after all these years of silence.

When it came to the end of the mass, I had the advantage because Tessa had us up and out and following this other coffin, as if we were always the ones who had to follow the dead first. It was a slow march down the long pull of the church and out through the doors and under the fresh open sky.

Outside, the sun had its teeth in things. I stopped for a moment, blinking it in, then I touched Philly's hand to let her know I was disappearing around the corner. Once hidden behind my buttress, I pressed back into the church wall. The bluestones had taken on a bit of heat behind my shoulder blades. I fished out my smokes, struck a match, and was taking a deep, filling drag when Mrs Tyler hurtled around the bluestone like a bullet from a gun.

I scrabbled to stub out the cigarette against the stone.

'Don't bother.' She collapsed into the wall beside me and exhaled long and hard. She glanced over.

'Got a spare?' The shock of if pulled an eyebrow up, but I shook one out of the pack for her just the same and she leaned in as I lit it. She took in her first puff in the same drowning way I had. I watched the blue veins ridge across the back of her hand. There was a fragile thing about her up close that I hadn't seen in the church.

'Did she see you coming?' I asked.

She steadied her eyes on me, taking in another long drag. 'Nancy's all right.' She tapped the ash off the end of her smoke and let a sly grin tug at the side of her mouth. 'Busy straightening the priest out.'

I took an equally long drag and slumped back, something in me giving way to this new world order where Mrs Tyler talked to me like I was all grown up. I looked down at myself. I was tall enough for it.

She dragged on her cigarette and turned to examine the now clear blue of the sky. Her hand fluttered, and I thought of a sparrow. When she turned back to me her face was full of the same slow sorry as it had been the day she told me in the sacristy that Mum would be back soon. 'Nancy probably just wants to make sure you made it to adulthood in one piece.' She tapped the sticky ash off. 'How long is it?' she asked, saying the words I didn't want to have out loud and shaped in the world. 'Fourteen years?'

I grunted agreement, although sometimes it felt like fourteen seconds.

It's funny that every cell in your body is replaced every seven years, so after two complete changeovers there's not one cell left of the little ten-year-old me who lost her mother.

Yet, miraculously, the pain lived on in the same old skin, located somewhere beyond blood and bone.

Maybe it suited me; I didn't want to forget Mum. Sometimes I thought I was the only one keeping her alive. Everyone else zipped up tight whenever I tried to bring her up.

Not Mrs Tyler, though, by the look of things. But there was something about the sharpish way she kept looking over her shoulder back to where we could hear the others talking low that made me jumpy. So this time it was me who zipped up. I realised I didn't want to share Mum with anybody after all, not even her best friend. It suited me to have just Mum and me locked tight together in the deep dark below the earth.

I was glad when Mrs Tyler changed the subject.

'Little bird tells me you're up for an award at work?'

'Mm,' I said, wary about where this new subject would take us.

'Smart as a whip, just like your mum said. She would have been over the moon. Nobody else from around home had got close to going to university, let alone the law.'

I noticed my ciggie burning away. It took a

couple of goes to shake ash off the end. She watched me at it.

'We all were,' she said when the job was done.

'Not Dad. Said it was a waste of time. Better off getting a bank job, start paying board. Roared like a bull.'

She laughed and took another puff. 'No wonder you kept at it, then.'

I kicked at the skinny blade of grass that had grown up through the crack in the asphalt.

Mrs Tyler opened her handbag and investigated its innards. She gave me a look and snapped the bag shut, her handkerchief in hand. She dabbed at her forehead.

'Your dad was a bit surprised to hear of the award.'

'How the hell does he know?' I pressed back into the heat of the bluestone. I'd only told Philly and she wouldn't have said a word.

'He said some bloke from your firm rang.'

A cold hand grabbed hold of my throat. I coughed to get it off my windpipe. 'What bloke?' I said when I could.

She shrugged. 'Had a plummy voice, your dad said. Very posh.'

Bloody Maurice. It was my business. I ashed my smoke again. I did owe him. Going above and beyond for me like no other lecturer. He stopped me from leaving uni more than once. Even gave me a place at his firm. But this was crossing a line. He had no right to talk to my father.

I pushed down against the dart of red shooting up from my gut.

Maurice had this idea that I was dragging the past around behind me like an anchor. Shit! What if he pumped Dad for answers? The thought of them talking scraped at my insides. Dad, stitched up with fury that a daughter of his had broken from the tribe to go to university in the first place, and Maurice, who expected me to make partner and broker peace in the Middle East some day.

'What'd they talk about?' I managed to ask, voice steady as if I were asking what the time was.

'Your dad didn't let on.' She grunted. 'Keeps his secrets tight, that one.'

I stared, jolted by this abrupt new turn in the road. 'What do you mean?'

'I think you know what I mean.'

I stoned over.

'You know.' She tapped at the end of her cigarette again, all careful casual. 'With Peg gone . . .'

I scratched my eyelid so I didn't have to look at her.

She was all eyes watching. After time stretched out about as far as it could go, she went on like some kind of relentless machine. 'You're the only one.'

She was right. I was the only, only one. The others had all let Mum and all the mystery go a long time ago.

'Peg ever say anything about it all?' she asked.

'Never to me.'

'You ever see anything while you lived with her?'

'I wasn't there that long.'

'Can't blame you there. But?' she prompted, ignoring my efforts to ignore her.

'Look!' I threw my hands up. 'If the others can forget everything, so can I. Mum's dead! Gone! Buried!'

Mrs Tyler barked out a starved laugh.

'Kathy?' Mrs Nolan's voice sailed through the heat straight at us. 'You seen JJ?'

I flattened against the wall, hiding beside Mrs Tyler and shaking my head frantically. She gave me another measured look. 'JJ runs her own race, Nancy,' she called back at last.

'Dear Lord.' Mrs Nolan's voice continued to sail in from afar. 'I was depending on catching her here.'

I shook my head like it might come off at Mrs Tyler. She grimaced. 'You might have to make it another time, Nancy.'

'It's like trying to pin down the jolly Scarlet Pimpernel.'

Mrs Tyler laughed and waved her cigarette. Mrs Nolan must have headed in another direction because Mrs Tyler turned back my way, fishing with her free hand for something in that handbag again. She kept her fist tight around whatever it was. 'Listen.' She shivered like somebody had walked on her grave. 'I've been holding on to something for you.' She rubbed her chin with her closed fist.

'Come on, then.' I half laughed, thinking it was unlike Mrs Tyler to trowel on the drama. She opened her hand and nestled in the cave of her palm was Mum's cameo brooch.

'Fuck.' My eyes blinked. I didn't move to take it.

'You were so distressed about it not going in with your mum at the time.' Her voice was low and sympathetic. 'I didn't think you could handle knowing it hadn't. So I waited. But it belongs to you girls. It's time you had it back.'

'Yeah, sure,' I said, automatically. She passed it over and I shoved it in the pocket of my jeans without looking at it. A snake's nest of jangle firing up inside me. I stared at the fence like it was my job to keep the boards upright with the force of my focus.

'Peg getting cremated,' she said. 'Suppose that's why Jack's not here. Against his religion?'

'Or . . . ' I grabbed the distraction with two hands, grateful to her. It was a Mum thing to do. That quiet seeing and making something else possible. 'It's because Dad hated Aunty Peg.'

Mrs Tyler's eyebrows shot up, surprised at the corner we'd turned.

'From what Mrs Nolan said in there, though,' I said, 'it sounds like they were all pretty matey before Dad chucked her out.'

This time she got busy looking in another direction. She pointed her cigarette at the listing boards. 'That fence needs bringing down.' She did some more fence inspecting, but I waited. 'They were . . . close when they were younger, going around the dances together,' Mrs Tyler finally said, folding under the pressure. 'You couldn't separate those girls. After their parents died, Sarah would never have survived Great Aunty Dot without Peg's spark. Dot was in her seventies when she got them, and she ran a very tight ship. Didn't believe in kids. Did believe in the Almighty. But Peg could get round her. Naughty as hell. And Sarah was like a mother to Peg. Just about killed her when your dad kicked Peg out. She was never the same.'

'Peg must have had the smarts, though, ending up with her own place.'

'That was Sydney. Never knew his real name. Older fella from Sydney who kicked around with us for a bit. He got lucky one night at poker, won the deed of the Parkton house. Signed it over to Peg as soon as Jack threw her out.'

'Just like that?'

'Well.' She seesawed her hand again. 'He got her pregnant.'

'Peg was pregnant?'

'Happened then. More then than now, tell you the truth, what with the pill.' She examined the remains of her cigarette.

'What happened to the baby?'

I touched my hand to my belly and then realised what I was doing and let it fall before Mrs Tyler put two and two together.

'Miscarriage.' She massacred the cigarette under her heel. 'Filthy things.'

I stabbed at the stones behind me with my Doc. 'Okay,' I said, putting this new thing into what I knew. 'But even though somebody gave her the house, she had to keep paying the bills all these years, somehow.'

'All that hoarding,' Mrs Tyler said. 'Peg went through the mountains of junk she picked up from those garage sales with a fine-tooth comb first, found a lot of things worth a few bob and kept herself afloat.'

'Not only mad, then.'

'She had a solid vein of sanity in there, all right.' She stabbed a finger at me. 'Find it. That'll tell you something about what really happened to your mother. About time we know, don't you think?'

MARKING TIME

'Casual Thursday, hey JJ?' asked Suze as I passed her desk.

'Nope. Casual funeral,' I said, wondering what I'd been thinking turning up to work in jeans. 'Just popped in to double-check everything's set for next week.'

'Hey,' Tye said to me as he dropped a file on Suze's desk, giving her a gratitude smile. Despite everybody knowing about us, he was scrupulous about professional relations at work, but his drawn-together brows were busy asking a lot of questions.

'I skipped out on the spread,' I said, biting my lip. 'With the court date for the Stintini case being moved up ... ' I ran out of steam and investigated the corners of the ceiling.

'That bad,' he said, pulling me down the corridor. He closed the door to the photocopying room behind us. 'You are such a chicken.' He made a few noises he thought a chicken made, although I'd never heard anything like that from any chicken I'd been acquainted with, which I told him.

'Who was there?' he asked, ignoring my careful evidence-based analysis of farmyard culture.

'Not my dad. Not my brother.' He hadn't met

Dad even though we'd been going out a couple of years. I gave him the rundown on who had showed up.

'So you ran away from a few CWA women and their scones.'

'You are such an innocent,' I said, taking a precarious seat on the paper-shredder bin.

He squatted down in front of me getting serious with a few well-honed lawyerly questions that went to the heart of things. He laughed in all the right fire-engine-red-knickers and bowling-skittle-priest places. 'But you're okay?' He ran his golden-brown hand over the sandy pale of my bare arm, his eyes wide and warm. I nodded. It was the truth — if I focused on just what I'd told him. And the thing was, I had no plans to focus anywhere else. Not on Mrs Nolan trying to track me down to apologise. Not on Mum's cameo burning a hole in my pocket. Not on Mrs Tyler trying to rope me back into 'Mum's Mystery'. I'd never not told him stuff before. But since I was busy not telling myself the same things, I didn't consider it deception. It was survival. I was good at survival. Besides, we had bigger things to talk about. I scratched in the hollow above my hip bone.

'Still,' Tye said, leaning in to brush his eyelashes over my cheek, before locking in to me, eye to eye, a breath apart. 'Can't have been easy,' he murmured. 'I don't think you should be at work.'

I shrugged. 'Nobody else's going to sort out the Stintini case.'

He sat back, knowing I was nothing but right.

Everybody had to do pro bono stuff, but I had a habit of taking the no-count ones that nobody else would touch because it would never put them a rung higher on anything.

'Except me.' He smiled.

I grinned back. 'You and all that time you got on your hands.' He was working directly with Maurice on a big case they weren't talking about and his hours had gone from ridiculous to insane.

'I'm free tonight,' he said. 'Fried rice on me.'

It was my favourite. I closed the distance between us to press my lips into the sweet musky smell of his.

★   ★   ★

In the end, what with the jeans and the questions and avoiding Maurice because I needed to take him on about inviting my dad to the ceremony behind my back but wasn't up to it, I gathered a few files and left the office. It was Maurice who put me up for the award in the first place. He'd called me into his expansive, windows-everywhere office at the end of a long day, gestured towards the hard leather armchairs in what he thought of as his informal alcove and told me about the award. I'd argued with him, told him there were plenty of others who deserved it more, had been there longer — Tye, for instance. Maurice raised his right eyebrow in that way that had intimidated many a witness and waited for me to finish. Then he took a long sip of the forty-year-old whisky he was so proud of, swirled the rest of the amber liquid in the glass, the ice clinking into the silence. Finally, his face broke wide in that open-hearted smile few saw. 'You don't get it yet,' he said. 'Good lawyers have good brains, are forensic. They hunt down the facts mercilessly. We have a lot of good lawyers here. Very good lawyers use their gut instinct to make those facts sing; we have a few of those.' He sat forwards. 'But great lawyers have fire.' He pointed his glass at me. 'You've got a lot to learn, JJ, but you could be a great lawyer, and that's why you're Smith and Blake's nomination for this award.'

I shrugged because nobody argued with Maurice unless they really had to and the nomination would come to nothing anyway. Only I'd picked up the gong. The first time Smith and Blake had won the prize in ten years so Maurice was inviting selected clients to a fancy restaurant, turning it into something. I winced. He was stoked. I got it. But still there was a line and ringing my dad without telling me was not just over the line but in another country.

★   ★   ★

Back at the boarding house, I made it past Rat-Tail's room without him coming out to investigate what I was up to and got to Marge's door. I rapped a quick knock and poked my head in, waving a paper bag in the air like a password. She grinned as she lowered the volume on the telly and made an effort to get out of her armchair, but I waved her back and tossed the files on her bed. I flicked the switch of her kettle as she wound up her knitting, skewering it into the bag on the floor by her side. The purple hibiscus on the knitting bag was a lift of colour beside threadbare carpet and rickety pinewood furniture. I wasn't normally a hibiscus fan, it was too postcard and shower cap for me, but in this case it was doing a good job. Besides, a little peace never went astray. I poured her tea into the rosebud cup I'd found in the op shop the week before, liberated the vanilla slice from the bag and put them all on her dinner tray.

'You?' she asked.

'I ate already.' I placed the tray over her lap.

'Not from the look of you.'

'I eat plenty.'

The springs of the bed squeaked as I sat, crossing my legs and leaning forwards to counteract the dip in the mattress.

She clawed at her slice to pull it in half. I knew enough not to try to help her.

'Arthritis bad?'

She shrugged. 'Turn that fan down, will you, love? It'll blow the cake right out of my mouth.'

I squeaked off the bed and notched the fan down and angled it away from her face. Her white hair settled back into its usual helmet as she got down to business. I gave her a turn around Peg's funeral, using a lot more shorthand than I had with Tye because it was a world she understood having been a known offender of the Country Women's Association variety herself back in the day.

'Least you got there,' she concluded.

I got up to switch the kettle back on, smiled. I

had to admit, now that it was over, she'd been right all along. I was glad I'd been there for Peg. For Mum. I patted myself down. I was still in one piece.

'Some things have to be gone through in life, and death is one of them. Can't avoid it. It comes running at you anyway. And if you're not careful it will have a knife in its hands.' She dabbed at a crumb with the pad of her thumb. 'Not that I need to tell you that,' she said, licking her thumb.

I scanned the ceiling, running my eyes over the cracks. I didn't know whether she was thinking about my dead mother or her murdered children.

'Peg would have liked that you made the effort.'

'You didn't even know her.'

'I know her. All us old women know each other. All the lines and wrinkles — they tell the same story. Life has carved itself right into us.'

'Cheery.' I laughed. 'And she was a good sight younger than you.'

'Matter of perspective.' Marge laughed, taking a bite and speaking anyway. 'Suppose someone will have to spend hours convincing you to put in an appearance at my funeral, too.'

'Depends on the quality of the booze at the wake.'

The kettle set up a whistle again. I scooted from the bed before it could get to shrieking.

'What about you?' I asked. 'News?'

Her mouth twisted to the side. 'Any day now.'

I grunted back. We were all skitty with waiting

for the community centre to send her an appointment time to discuss the shit-hole she lived in, we all lived in, only she actually wanted to live here because the alternative was some old folks' home out in Woop Woop. And she definitely did not want to live there.

A door slammed at the other end of the corridor and a few seconds later Rocco's head with his wild mess of curls appeared around Marge's door. 'I'm out for a couple of hours.' His white teeth gleamed. He winked at us. 'Stay away from my Scotch, Marge.'

'Leave your door unlocked at least and give me a fighting chance,' she said. We heard his laugh all the way to the front door. The rest of us couldn't work out why he was even in the boarding house, although he made an effort to fit in by only buying his clothes from Vinnies, but he had too much of the whiff of possibilities about him, all smooth tanned skin and effortless cheer. Even though I had the fancy job, there was never any confusion over me fitting in. I screwed up my face. 'Scotch — is that what he's calling that nasty stuff he makes in his room?'

'All Italians are poets.' She dusted her hands together, the crumbs dropping to her plate. 'Least he's got a bit of sunshine in him.'

'Not this again. I'm happy.'

She pursed her lips. 'Not sure if you have that definition of happy quite pegged.'

I got up to take the tray from her.

'Leave the dishes,' she said. 'Give me something to do.'

I told her I'd see her later, and gathered up my

files and went on down the corridor to my room. I unlocked my door, kicked it closed behind me, threw my bag and files onto the bed, and rolled down after them. Face down, head to the side, muscles melting into the curve of the mattress. Feeling the breath fill me up and abandon me, fill and abandon, fill and abandon. Breathing took a lot of effort when you slowed right down to notice.

PROOF

Two days later, Tessa stood in the middle of Aunty Peg's kitchen with her arms wasp-angled on her waist, just like Mum. 'This changes everything,' she said.

'Which bit of everything?' I asked.

'Obviously we can't just chuck all Peg's junk out now — we have to go through it.' Her head swivelled from one side of the chaos to the other. She stepped around piles of crap and leaned between towers of boxes to snap up the blinds and yawn the windows wide so we could get a better handle on the ghosts of Peg's past. I pushed papers off a chair and perched on it, pulling my knees in tight to my chin, while Philly stood near the front door at the beginning of the path Tessa and I had cleared, like a flighty roo about to spring, her mouth pressed into the smallest line.

'I'm not touching a thing,' she said, her fingers plucking at the seams of her pale-blue skirt.

'Yes, you are! Despite your allergy to the past,' said Tessa. 'We all are.' She turned to me. 'Even you, JJ.'

'Never said a word.'

'You're speaking all the time, just not with your lips.'

I rolled my eyes.

'Like right now you're accusing me of being trivial,' Tessa said, circling her finger in front of my face. 'Because out of everything Mrs Tyler told you, I end up focusing on the practicality of locating the valuables rather than exclaiming upon Aunty Peg's unknown pregnancy.'

She was good.

'Don't be stupid,' I said, bending below the table so she couldn't see how right she'd been. I re-emerged, pulling my shoulder bag to my lap, fishing in its depths for pen and paper. 'But being knocked up out of wedlock. You have to admit — in those days. That's something, surely.'

'It might have been,' said Tessa, 'but luckily fate intervened and there was no baby. Imagine passing her particular genes on.'

I used the back of my forearm to shove things aside to clear enough space on the table so I could begin writing out the list of jobs to be done, just like we used to do every Saturday when we were kids, AM — After Mum.

Philly gingered her way to the table where we were, resting her black leather handbag on top of a pile of newspapers. She snapped her handbag wide, inserted her hand confidently and withdrew a small, clear bag.

'Really, Philly? A sewing kit?' I said.

'Brownie training. Be prepared, JJ. You never do know what will come in handy.' She unzipped the bag with a flourish and handed me a pair of scissors.

'Any other signs of madness?'

'Leave her alone, JJ. It's not as if it isn't well established that if there's a Peg Award to be given out, you'd be first in line.'

I mimicked Tessa, shaking my head from side to side like Aunty Peg used to do at Dad. Philly laughed.

Tessa made a show of deliberately ignoring us and poured herself another full cup from her thermos and slugged it back. 'This is a hell of a job. How am I going to find the time to sort through every bit of all this?'

'I vote we turf it all out as per the initial strategy,' said Philly, half hopeful.

'Now that's short-term thinking, right there,' I said. 'There's gold in them there hills.'

'Laugh all you like, JJ. But it would be just like Aunty Peg to have hidden stocks in the fridge or something.' Tessa swigged directly from the thermos this time. 'How did you live in this, JJ?'

I widened my eyes at Philly, giving her the secret shut-up code. She cocked her head.

'Yeah, how did you, JJ? What was it? Five years, day in day out while you were at uni?'

I gave her a dark look out of Tessa's eyeline. But at least she didn't let on I'd moved out of Peg's and into the boarding house after only a month. I winced on the inside at what a baby I was being, but even now I didn't want to give Dad the satisfaction of knowing that I'd been safely out of the Peg zone all along, just as he'd wanted.

★　★　★

Tessa went to get empty boxes from her car. Philly found a wheelbarrow in the lounge room

195

and wheeled it into the kitchen, tipping it on the side to navigate through the narrow path between the towers of newspapers. Joining me at the table, she picked a pile of things off a chair opposite mine and looked around for a space to lay them. I looked up from writing to dare her. She shrugged, and held her arms high and opened them.

'Stop winding her up,' Tessa hissed at me, coming back through the front door, her arms full.

I laughed, going back to my list.

'Both nightmares! One ignoring the past, the other drowning in it,' Tessa said.

'I am not,' I said back, still like I was about five. Philly didn't bother denying it. She made a meal out of staying contemporary. Besides, she'd worked out who she was years ago and she wore it like skin. She made short work of the rest of the things on the chair and sat, elbows on the table, waiting.

When I finished writing, she cut the jobs into strips while Tessa folded them into a bowl. Maybe I missed this. This together thing. Seeing Philly every few weeks, her 'schedule' permitting, was one thing, but this being more than two, this fitting back into well-worn and oiled grooves was something different, like hands cupped around hot chocolate and staring into flames. For a moment I thought about showing them Mum's cameo, which was with me all the time now, but I let the moment pass because I still hadn't confronted what it meant to me. I didn't yet have the courage to breath air into that dark place.

Philly chose first and pulled out the scrap of paper marked 'fridge', which she immediately tried to barter away, but Tessa and I grinned, arms folded.

'It's only mould,' I said.

She made a face. 'I would have brought jeans if you'd told me.'

'I did tell you,' said Tessa, pulling out a second pair of tracksuit pants and a T-shirt from her bag. 'But I expected no less.' She shoved them towards Philly. 'Nightmare number two.'

'See? You're number one,' Philly said to me.

After we finished the job lotto, I bunched all my tasks up on the table while Philly lined hers up one after the other.

Tessa clucked her tongue at both of us and started on the nearest newspaper tower, checking each one for share certificates or treasure unknown. I rolled my eyes, but got to work on sorting the earrings, bills, tape measures and nails on the kitchen table into piles. We got into the rhythm of things although none of us had thought to bring a tape deck for music.

After we'd been going a while, Philly stripped off Tessa's elbow-length yellow gloves. She sat with a groan at the table, spreading herself long across my now cleared and cleaned table.

'So soon?' Tessa asked, opening the door of the oven and sitting back on her haunches to scowl at the newspapers jammed inside.

'I'm bloody hungry,' said Philly.

'Sandwiches in the bag by the door.'

Philly and I exchanged of-course-there-are stares.

'I've got eyes in the back of my head now that

I'm a mother of three, so you can stop communing behind my back.'

Philly and I poked our tongues at her behind, half expecting her to see that as well.

Philly had the sandwich triangles in designer pleats across a plate pretty quick. Tessa sank into a chair wiping her forehead with the back of her arm.

'Found your diamonds yet?' I asked.

'Shut up. Nobody asked you to come, JJ.' She bent over to pull another thermos out of her bag. 'Mother's helper.' She poured a cup of tea for herself.

Philly slid her plastic cup along the table towards Tessa. Tessa screwed up her face and hesitated, looking between the cup and the thermos as if she wasn't quite sure what to do.

'Hurry up, girlie,' said Philly, in a cockney accent. 'Christmas'll get ere sooner.'

'Is that the perfect-public-relations, run-a-million-dollar-company-one-day girl talking?' I asked.

'You can pluck the girl from the farm,' she said in now plummy, cut-glass tones.

Tessa gave in and filled Philly's cup. Philly took a sip and spat it out. Tessa jumped away from the spray of liquid, as I squalled my chair back and roared at the sacrilege to my pristinely clean table.

'What?' said Tessa and Philly at the same time, one challenging, the other accusing, but it was Philly who took the running.

'Mother's helper? What the fuck, at eleven-thirty in the morning?'

Tessa got up to get a cloth from the sink, so we

couldn't see her expression. 'You've got no idea,' she said, quietly, her back still turned.

'I'm the one with the 'allergy' to the past.' Philly made finger quotes in the air. 'But do you see me — ?' She ran out of words. 'Or even her?' She indicated me. 'And JJ's — you know . . . ' She fished about for a word. 'Delicate.' She paused.

'No offence, JJ.'

'None taken.'

I took the flask and smelled it to get myself caught up on the facts. Just warm sweet tea. I splashed a little into my cup and swigged it down. I worked hard to stop my eyes from watering from the extra alcoholic kick. 'Nice drop,' I got out through my coughing.

'Don't encourage her, JJ,' said Philly. 'She's got babies.'

'It's because I have babies,' said Tessa, coming back to the table and throwing down the rest of the contents in her cup, as if Philly's stare might evaporate it before she could get it into her.

I took the cloth from Tessa's hand and started mopping up Philly's mess.

'Does Geoff know?' demanded Philly.

'Shut up, Philly,' said Tessa. 'There's nothing to know. A little softening early in the day makes the rest of it possible.'

'Do you think Mum felt like that?' I asked, not daring to meet their eyes.

'Was Mum sozzled, you mean?' asked Philly, her voice skidding up again.

'I mean, maybe she wasn't coping,' I said. 'Maybe that's why she left.'

Tessa thrust her head into her folded arms on the table. 'I knew this bloody funeral would unhinge you, JJ.'

* * *

Tessa called from the lounge room. 'Finished?'

'Nearly,' we both chorused. We leaped up from the table where we'd been taking a break and each grabbed a side of a large box full of crap and bustled it out to what you might call a lawn if it had ever met a mower. I blinked in the fresh air and slowed again, getting the ease of it inside me. We tumbled the stuff from the box into the skip. Philly let go of her side, pulling her arms together at the back of her so her yoga-limber shoulder blades just about touched.

'Do you remember what Aunty Peg used to say about madness?' Philly asked.

The clouds skidded across the sky. I shifted my feet to get a better grip on the ground.

'Madness is for the brave,' Philly went on, now hugging herself.

'Well. She was wrong,' I said, dropping the empty box to the ground and leaning against the skip. 'Madness is for the mad, Philly.' I didn't say what Aunty Peg had added to me: 'Madness is for the brave, JJ. Just you remember that when your time comes.'

'Maybe it is brave, though. Not caring what others think. Not matching every colour, shade for shade.'

'You are obsessive, even nuts, Philly, but you're not mad.'

I had to admit everyone was probably right: that if anyone did take after Peg, it was going to be me. Sometimes I could already feel it crawling around under my skin. I mean, there were times I was sure Mum was talking back to me when I spoke to her.

I'd felt it more than usual since Peg had kicked the bucket. Even Tye had noticed it. Straight after Philly told me about Peg's heart attack, tiny jackhammers had started in on my nerves all the way along my arms and down my spine. If I'd known Dad and Tim were going to skip out on her funeral maybe I would have done it too. I winced as Mum gave me a clip around the ear from beyond the grave. But then laughed back. Course I wouldn't have not gone, I told her. There was something gutsy about Peg, I added for myself. Like Marge said. You had to honour the quiet fierce of ordinary lives.

Marge knew a lot about that. She'd never told me. I was one hundred per cent sure I didn't want her to, but Rocco had, the words tight and grim. Marge had got up early to cream the milk in the dairy before the kids were out of bed. Her husband was on the tractor already, so she thought the coast was clear. She'd only just sat down to begin when she heard them: two clean gunshots. One for each kid. Then he turned the gun on himself. I did ask once why she kept going. Because she had to, she said. She lived her life because her kids didn't get a chance to live theirs.

The sad of it could strangle you if you let it.

Compared to that, all the muddy, loose ends

fraying around Mum were nothing. The thing was, I might have made it all up, anyway. Maybe there was no mystery. Mum had just taken off to some boarding house without a phone for a break from us. None of it had been easy. You only had to look at Tessa with her kids to see that. And that was with Geoff being a much better husband than Dad had ever been. Had a steady job at the bank, for starters, so there was enough money to keep the kids in warm clothes.

Mrs Tyler had just got caught up in all my drama. But maybe she was right about one thing. Peg dying was an end of an era. Maybe it was time to let Peg carry all our madness with her to the grave. I could be like Philly. I had my career in the right place. Now was not the time to lose focus. I rubbed my arm, hard and fast. I just had to shut down these jackhammers.

★   ★   ★

A few minutes later, Tessa cried out. Philly and I raced back into the house and into the lounge room. Tessa cradled her index finger as blood spurted out. Philly ran to get her first-aid kit from her handbag. I bundled Tessa to the kitchen sink and got cold water coursing over her hand. We both watched the blood spatter and river down the drain with the water. When Philly got back with bandages and ointment, I leaned against the wall for a while, taking in the way their dark heads arched together.

I wandered back into the lounge to see what had cut Tessa's finger. I kneeled over the pile of things she'd been sorting. The broken glass was hidden beneath a calendar. Aunty Peg and her bloody obsessive calendars. I tipped the broken glass into a sheath of newspaper. There was Philly's name on the calendar. Friday afternoon: four pm. I turned the pages over, her name repeated over and over. I hadn't even known. Philly just quietly turned up week after week to visit Peg. The visits lasted forty-nine minutes, fifty minutes, there was one as long as sixty. I pushed the calendar aside and twisted the sheath closed so none of the glass could get at anyone else, laying it in the wheelbarrow ready for the tip.

Back on my heels, I was dwarfed by the mountains of crap rising up and bearing down on me. I stood to even things up and rocked, toe to heel. Heard the snap of Philly's handbag and her telling Tessa to sit and rest. With Tessa out of the picture, I had a window of possibility to chuck rather than sort, so I dropped back to my knees to go at it hard and make a dent in things. I threw the first pile into the wheelbarrow, then picked up the next pile of stuff to hurl. But the burn of Mum's name on a calendar on the top stopped me: *Sarah*.

I dropped it like a scald.

I scratched at my palm, digging right in. Stubbing your toe was bound to happen when you were on the business end of a shovel digging through the past. I pushed out a bit of a laugh at myself and picked up the calendar to throw it in the wheelbarrow. But the bold of the letters dragged at my eyes, tiding them back. I leaned closer. There was something odd about the date. I calculated. It got colder in that room as the answer became clearer.

It was the day Mum left us.

It was proof.

Mum had been here all along. No mysterious boarding house needed. She just hadn't wanted to talk to us. Least of all me. I would have argued her six ways to Christmas to make her come home. I shook my head. She knew she wouldn't have had a chance.

I slumped back on my heels. Rubbed my finger over Mum's name, over and over, like it could tell me something and I would get it if I stuck at it long enough.

So Peg was the liar after all. She'd lied to Tessa and me when we called that day and she told us she hadn't seen Mum.

And then the other thing it meant.

Dad's been telling the truth. All this time.

I curled forwards, gut punched. I had punished him for nothing. He'd never got over Mum and I'd just made it worse with all my suspicion. Even though I stopped asking questions after the funeral, he'd never been the same. Something back then had broken between us. I clamped my hand to my mouth as if that could stop the sudden urge to vomit. I bent again, the other hand to the newspaper stack to steady me, dry retching contorting through me.

Once it passed, I realised that in among it all something good unfurled. It could even be Mum sending me a message — that I could make things up with Dad. I straightened, a lightness rising up out of the unfurl and working its way across my face.

I looked down to see the proof, after all these years, once more, that Dad hadn't lied.

But I'd missed something on the calendar further down and smaller.

She'd stayed only twenty-five-and-a-half minutes.

JACK SKIDS AWAY

The steam of the evening heat had Tye and me up on the roof of the boarding house, our legs dangling over the edge. We licked our ice creams looking down on the top of the trees in the park opposite and over the roofs to the city in the distance. The air so still you could have sliced strips out of it. I was down to the cone, but Tye had a cautionary licking approach that made his last longer. When I'd crunched the last bit I stretched long and laid my head in Tye's lap. He absent-mindedly combed his fingers through my hair. With the stars shimmering above, it should have felt good. But far from fading away, those jack-hammers were busy buzzing up my whole nervous system.

'So,' Tye said after a long while. 'What's up?'

'Nothing,' I said too quickly. I rubbed one hand over the other trying to soothe the buzz.

He wound his fingers through my hair, gathered a clump and tugged.

'Ow,' I said.

'Tell the truth, JJ.'

My hand reflexed to my stomach. To cover, I jerked upright, edged back from the edge and circled my arms around my knees. I cleared my throat a couple of times, but the words were glass sharp and stuck in my throat. In the end, I told him about the shock of Peg's calendar that afternoon.

'So . . . ?'

'That's the thing,' I said. 'I run into the same dot points you do.' I dug into my palm. 'I mean, it doesn't change anything. I already knew she hadn't stayed for long at Peg's. It's just weird to see it in black and white. You know, proof that Dad lied.'

'Proof that Peg lied too.'

'That she did.' I pulled out my ciggies and let my knees drop open. I generally didn't smoke when I was with Tye. He wasn't a fan. 'I guess that's the sticking point. What was so big that those two, who hated each other, came together for a one-time-only alliance?'

He screwed up his face. His lashes long over his angel eyes. 'Except it's not a shared lie. Peg lied saying she'd hadn't seen your mum when she had. But your dad lied saying your mum was staying at Peg's all along when she wasn't.' He widened his eyes. 'They're kind of like opposite lies.'

I tapped the cigarette on the ground. Put the filter between my lips. Held it away. 'And in the middle of all that, why didn't she stay at Peg's? Why spend money she didn't have to stay somewhere else?'

'Unless she had somewhere else to go.'

Something tugged at a thread in my memory. I narrowed my eyes. Something ferret sized. Then it hit me. 'There was an address. But Dad destroyed it.'

'That's it, then. I think you have to ask your dad.'

'What?' I laughed. 'Because of his excellent track record in telling the truth.'

'You were kids back then.' He shrugged. 'Could be something he can tell you now. Or could be nothing. Your Mrs Tyler might be right, though. Maybe now is the time to figure it all out. This thing has been tugging at you ever since I've known you, and you don't like loose ends.'

I sucked at the end of the cigarette as if I'd already lit up. 'You may have a point, Watson.' I blew pretend smoke into the air and shoved the ciggie back in the box.

* * *

My enthusiasm for Tye's calm, rational approach waned the next day, though, when I was in the gloom of Dad's kitchen. I mean, Tye didn't know this world. He'd been brought up in a house of reason: lawyer father, academic mother, one child, framed Japanese prints on the wall. I eyeballed the rat in the middle of this room, up on its hind legs, the black glisten of its eyes lasering me straight back. I balled up a tea towel and chucked it at the rat, missing but not by much. The rat did drop to all fours and lumber off, but took its time about it, making sure I knew who was really in charge.

Dad's kitchen was almost as bad as Peg's. Only there was something darker here. There was malevolence in the dirty dishes jumbled across the sink. The table was crowded with Vegemite and salt and butter and everything he'd had for breakfast, lunch and dinner in the last few days. I backed away and felt for the door behind me. But then I stopped.

If I was to get Dad to admit anything after all these long, rusty, lying years, I'd have to come at him from an angle, a warm cup of tea in my hand, steady.

I scrubbed at my face stuck between the wild need to leave and the pull of making sense of that clue on Peg's calendar, the one clear thing in all the mist and haze of the past fourteen years.

It had to be a sign from Mum that Mrs Tyler was right and it was time to know the truth. Tye was on point, too. We were all adults now. Whatever Dad thought he needed to hide back then could finally come into the light.

'Shit,' I said out loud, accepting that I would be staying.

I picked up the melty butter and the cream tub with its dried, cracked smears and opened the fridge. I shoved them onto the top shelf beside containers marked with the days of the week in Tessa's writing like tiny islands of order. No wonder Tessa bloody drank, having to wade into cleaning this every week.

A whip-red started licking at me so I closed the fridge and went to the sink instead. I could start on something simpler. I knew about dishes: I'd supported myself through uni by dishwashing. I pulled the containers labelled with the rest of the days of the week from the sink, twisted taps and squeezed detergent. I coated up my nerves by watching the listing hill of bubbles the detergent made.

I must have zoned out because the next thing I knew the water was lapping at the top of the sink. I dived to turn the taps off. This wasn't going to work. I had to pull myself together. I straightened my back, opened a drawer and got a knife into the palm of my hand, and headed outside. It was better. The honey smell of the lilac near the tanks plunged me down the rabbit hole back to that other place when I was a kid. And it was a good place, back to BM — Before Mum. I plucked a few petals and crushed them between my fingers, rubbing the crush under my nose, just like Mum and me used to. I sawed at the smaller branches, letting them fall to the ground, and then gathered them into my arms and carried them back into the gloom. I filled a jar with water, wrestled the woody stems into it and set it beside the sink. I kept my eyes on the lilac until the rhythm of the dishes took over, and I wiped all of that malevolence away.

Once I had everything away and things wiped down, not clean but something, there was more air. The clock said that Dad would be in for afternoon tea, so I lit a match under the kettle and set out two cups, two plates, two knives and felt like Noah saving all that was essential.

Then I sat down to wait. The clock ticked. I bit my lip, then started to dig into my palm. The clock ticked. I dug in deeper. The clock ticked louder. I got to my feet, scooped up a pile of Dad's clothes on the chair and walked past the fridge through the lounge and into his room. I dumped the clothes on top of everything else on the bench and crossed the room to yank open the window and spring up the blind. Dust had greyed over the red of the plush velvet of the curtains, cast-offs from the church vestry. I tried to wave fresh air into the room with my hand. But the day was full of burn and still, so I gave up.

The blankets were flung back as if he'd got up in a hell of a hurry, off to fight a war. The creeping enemy kept at bay by the same small things done in the same small way day after day until they bled into death.

I pulled the bottom sheet sharp and tucked it in, then pulled up the top one and the blankets, and got the pillow back to where it had started out. The effort of it heavied up everything under my skin, so I let myself collapse to sit on the side of the bed. Looked out at the lilac, the tanks, the wilting clothesline and all the parched yellow beyond. I was filling up on the forever of it, which wasn't going to do me any good, so I found a distraction. I opened the bedside table drawer.

Looking straight back out at me was a photo of Mum sitting on the front verandah, legs bare and swinging over the edge. My mother looked dead into the camera, a stubby of beer resting on her knee. Laughing. A girl mother, hair flying. Out of nowhere a rage of red volcanoed up in me. Maybe if we'd had this photo of her to look at as we grew up she'd have more dimension now and be more than a feeling in the dark. I narrowed my eyes and considered the wisdom of getting the hell out of there before I did something I regretted. Instead I counted. At twenty I had the red pulled back in and at thirty had it locked down. I pushed off the bed, closed the drawer, took the photo with me into the kitchen and propped it against the jam jar. Then I sat down to wait.

The clock ticked.

This time I ticked along with it, collecting the moments up and building something with them.

'Gidday, love,' Dad said, as if we'd only seen each other just that morning instead of who knew when? He leaned on the frame of the door and shucked off his boots just the way I remembered, although he had to lean down to pry the second one from his foot, his beer gut hanging over his belt. The rough of his cheek pricked me as we pecked hello.

'Nice surprise,' he said.

'Thought it was time.' I poured the boiling water over his teabag and then over mine, keeping a firm boot on the back of the red, keeping it down.

He dropped papers on the bench I'd just cleared. I buttoned my lips against the violation. He headed for the laundry.

'Working you hard?' he asked.

'Pays the bills.'

'Reckon it might.' He came out of the laundry and threw the towel on the back of the chair beside him as he sat.

'What's this, then?' He jerked his head at the photo.

'Keeping her to yourself,' I said.

'Only found it a while back.'

'Why didn't you show us? You know we don't

have photos of her.'

'JJ.' His voice strained, he dropped his fist helplessly to the table. 'You're never here to show it to.'

'Tessa seen it?'

'Always pushing.'

'Has she?'

'Might have.' He raised his voice.

'If she happened to be cleaning up in that particular drawer, you mean?'

'So now that's wrong, too, is it?' He took a sip of tea. Straightened. 'Your mother's dead. A man needs somebody to tidy up a bit and your sister is kind enough to do it. It's none of your bleedin business.'

'A man?'

'I look up to women.' His voice was weedy with emotion and crescendoing. 'Put them on a pedestal where they belong. That's one thing you bloody feminists make sure you miss.'

I lifted that firm boot and the red was back on its feet in a second. 'Do they skin their knees getting down off that pedestal to clean up after you?'

'Get out of here.' He flung his hand toward the door, but only half-hearted. 'You're no good unless you're making trouble.'

I folded my arms on the table, my eyes daring him.

He sipped at his tea, his eyes out through the window and on all that dry out there.

I sipped from the teacup, reminding myself what I was there to do. I followed the lines deepening into craters in his face. I let the clock

213

do more of its work.

'Peg's funeral was good,' I said. 'People asked after you.'

'Many there?' He uncrossed his legs and crossed them the other way.

'More than I thought there would be.'

'Nosy Nancy?'

'Yep. Mrs Nolan did the eulogy.'

He took another sip. Cleared his throat. Rubbed his face. The sandpaper rough of it competed with the clock.

'That so?' His voice wary.

'Funny how people are at funerals,' I said. 'Everything rosy.'

'What'd she say?'

'Said Peg was a great dancer.'

'So she was.'

'Mrs Nolan said you cut a dash yourself.'

'When I was young,' he said, like it was a peace offering. 'I hear she wants to talk to you. Did she?'

'What does she want?'

'How would I know? I don't give her the time of day.' He pursed his lips. 'So she didn't speak to you, then?'

'Like father like daughter. Doesn't get the time of day from me, either.'

A small, satisfied almost smile flashed up on his face for a microsecond. 'What else was said at the funeral?'

'She said Mum and Aunty Peg called themselves Arthur and Martha they were that close.'

He clammed straight up, realising his mistake

214

in leaving the gate open for me. I jammed up a piece of bread for him and poured cream on top. I pushed it in his direction. He was only pretending to look through that window. I should have remembered the thing he did with silence, building sharp corners in it so there was no seeing around them. I should have been prepared.

He wolfed down the bread just like when we were kids. His thick farmer fingers rough with calluses. There was fresh blood on his knuckle. I frowned.

He followed my look. 'It's nothing.'

'Did Tessa tell you she's decided to go through all the stuff at Aunty Peg's with a fine-tooth comb?'

He sat up, a charge in the air.

'Yep,' I said. 'She changed her mind when Mrs Tyler said Aunty Peg didn't just hoard, she 'collected'.'

'Bloody waste of time.' It blasted out of him and even he seemed surprised by the force. 'Find anything?' he asked in a voice he'd deliberately cranked down a gear.

'Not the treasure Tessa was hoping for yet,' I said, moving slowly into position. I tapped the table. 'Did find a calendar.'

He barked out a laugh. 'Plenty of them over at Mad Peg's.'

'Dated 26 June, 1968.'

A look slid out from the corner of his eyes at me before he could stop it. 'Would have been hard for you,' he said. 'Taking you back.' He scratched at his head and bit off another wolf-chunk of his jammed-up bread.

'Not hard, more . . . '

'Got another cuppa there, love?' He was quick to fill my slight pause.

I poured hot water into his mug.

'Needs to be boiled again first.'

'So they tell me.' I kept pouring.

He grunted, shook his head in disgust and stirred the teabag.

'You told the truth,' I said. 'Mum did go to Peg's that day.'

His look was all out in the open this time. He got himself forwards to the table, pulled another slice of white bead from the plastic and knifed the jam right to the crust. 'How'd you finally work that one out?'

'On the calendar.'

'There you are, then. All these years of bellyaching and you've finally got the proof your old man was on the up and up.'

'I've never said a word since Mum's funeral.' I could hear the whine in my protest.

'You didn't have to.' He gave me the ghost of a smile, one like he used to give me back before Mum died. 'Put it behind us, then? Hey?' He shoved the crust in past his teeth, chewing and nodding. Then he sat back, relax running along his muscles as he hummed a tune I didn't know.

'Funny thing, though.'

He stopped humming.

'You also lied.'

The stillness in him shivered like it was the black of night and there was a spotlight dead on him.

'She went to Peg's all right, but she didn't stay.

216

She was there for exactly twenty-five-and-a-half minutes,' I said. 'Where did she get to after that, Dad?'

'Not this again, JJ.' He ramrodded straight. 'How the hell did you come up with twenty-five minutes?'

I worked hard not to react. 'The calendar.'

'You can't rely on that bloody thing.'

'I'm not relying, that's why I'm here. I'm asking you.'

'Asking what?'

'Why did you tell us she was staying at Peg's?'

'Because it's a cold, hard fact.'

I gathered all my nerves and leaned them forwards. 'The calendar says your so-called fact is a LIE. Mum — was — missing — for — six — days before she died.' Each word was an island in a sea of meaning.

He blinked. 'Peg was off her nut. That was why your mother was there in the first place. She'd had a turn. Peg was probably too far gone to write anything sensible down. Peg told you herself, clear as day, when she came to stay for the funeral.'

I thumped the table with all the force I had. 'You know as well as I do that Peg was lying for you. What did you have on her to make her do that?'

'What's this bullshit?' He blustered and looked around as if somebody might spring to his defence.

I leaned all of me further forwards. 'Tessa and I phoned Peg before you visited her that day. She told us 'clear as day',' I put my head on the side to emphasise his words, 'that she hadn't seen Mum for ages.'

His eyes lit up. 'So she either lied to you on the phone or she lied to you in person later.' He leaned over the table, too, forcing me to retreat. 'You just picked the truth that suits you.'

'I'm sticking to the calendar — not being a relative, it can be trusted.'

'For God's sake, JJ. It's never enough for you, is it?' He stood up and flung his arm towards the door. 'You've got my word and now written proof that your mother was there and still — '

Out of nowhere he dropped his arm, went to the fridge and pulled the ring top back from a can. With the door of the fridge still ajar, he tipped the beer straight down his throat. I wanted a drink myself.

'Dad.' I made my voice go soft. 'I know you didn't kill her so how bad can it be? Where did Mum go after she left Peg's? What about that address in Mum's missal?'

He kicked the fridge shut with his foot. 'Kill her? The bullshit that comes out of your mouth.'

'Where, Dad?'

'Nowhere. She was with Peg. Look,' he said, sitting, 'I loved your mother.' He pointed an accusing finger. 'She was my moon and my stars. I'd have done anything to protect her, anything.' His voice rose to a whine. 'Your mother was a saint.'

'Philly heard Mum threaten she'd leave you the night before.'

'Bullshit. It was a normal blue, Philly was just a baby, what, six or seven? She's not

218

remembering straight.'

'Nine.'

He nodded as if it proved his point. 'They don't understand stuff, twist it around. Baby stuff.'

He held my eye, all battle ready, but then dropped his, pushed back from the table to give his beer gut more room. 'When you get older, you'll understand not everything's black and white.'

I sank my head onto my arms on the table, tired through. A fly landed on a crumb on my plate. It rubbed its hind legs together and turned to face me, rubbing again. Dad waved his hand and it took off.

Maybe I shouldn't have let Mrs Tyler's conspiracy set me off. Maybe I should have gone to the beach with Philly and Ahmed today instead of coming here after all. Maybe those big black words on Peg's calendar were just mad scribble and not a sign from Mum. Or, just maybe, I was getting Peg obsessed. I shivered. Definitely I shouldn't have taken advice from Tye, a guy who'd never seen a rat close-range in his life. I sighed and put my head back. 'I want to know, Dad. That's all. It's just a small thing.'

'She was at Peg's.'

I sighed, giving up. 'Was she happy?'

'Happy? What a question.'

'Did she love you?'

He looked up, surprised. 'Reckon she did. Had all you buggers, didn't we?'

WHAT TESSA KNOWS

It was too hot to sleep that night, so around midnight I wandered up to the roof to see if I could catch a breeze. There was already the orange burn of a cigarette end in the far corner. I headed in that direction. Rocco gave a soft, deep-of-the-night laugh when I collapsed into the sixties retro sun lounger beside him. He reached over to offer me a swig out of his home-labelled bottle.

I screwed up my face. 'Not feeling brave enough right now.'

He laughed out loud this time, sucked on his rollie so the end flared up again in the dark. 'Only the wicked can't sleep, JJ. What've you been up to?'

It was my turn to laugh. 'I'd curl your ears just in the telling, Rocco.'

He gestured with his bare big toe at his tobacco pouch. I leaned over to pick it up. Spent a deal of time getting the roll of it right. He lit it for me. I sucked on the end and took the hit. That tiny, satisfying rush to the brain. I sank back into the plastic weave.

'Marge got her date,' he said.

'Oh shit.' I straightened back up. 'When?'

He gave me the details.

I sunk back. 'That's the wicked thing I've been

up to, then. There's a special place in hell for people who don't watch a friend's back. I should've checked in on Friday night.'

'She's a tough old bird,' he said. 'Been expecting it.'

'It's not her I'm worried about. She can't leave me here with you lot.'

'You could always move out yourself, you know.' He turned to look at me directly. 'A big fancy lawyer doesn't need to live in a dive like this.'

'When I get paid like a big fancy lawyer, I'll keep that in mind.'

We smoked some more, although truth was, I let the air smoke down most of mine.

'There has to be another way for her,' I finally said.

'You'd think.' He stubbed out his cigarette, wrangled the back of his lounger so it flattened out and lay fully down, the plastic under his weight squeaking in protest. I did the same and we lay there dozing on and off till dawn.

★   ★   ★

I hadn't returned any of Tye's phone calls since I'd seen Dad. Rat-Tail, our self-appointed message taker, was pulling at his thin, scraggy Rasta-tail at the stream of unanswered messages. Tye and I were always the first in to the office, so he was waiting in the lobby downstairs already when I made it through the revolving doors the next day.

'So my relationship with Rat-Tail has gone to

a new level,' he opened with.

I put my arms around his neck. Breathed him in. Wondered how long we might have for this ease once I'd told him. I couldn't see it as anything but a one-way ticket down Resentment Road. If I wanted it and he didn't? If he wanted it and I didn't . . . I turned my brain off. I'd been around and around these computations too many times already. I had no idea what he would think. Hell, I had no idea what I thought.

'He says to tell you how he likes how polite you are,' I said.

'And?' He waited.

I leaned away to grin. 'Only he can't understand your accent, but!'

Tye threw his hands in the air.

I laughed.

Tye didn't have an accent, but Rat-Tail heard through his eyes, and the brown skin and brown eyes Tye inherited from his Japanese mother confused him.

I used the distraction to make peace with Tye. I grabbed his hands in mine and told him the nothing I discovered at Dad's.

'Okay.' He nodded in his measured way. 'What next?'

'Next I get real busy on my Stintini case.'

Before he could say much, Maurice was there, sweeping us into the lift in his take-no-prisoners way.

He clipped his way through a number of questions to Tye, who'd spent his Sunday working on their case, before turning to me. 'Got the Stintini brief ready, JJ?' he asked.

222

'Yep, yep,' I said. 'Almost. Just a final polish to go.'

'So barely started, then?' He shook his head, seeing straight through me.

The lift doors opened. 'You know where I am if you need me,' he said before sweeping away again like some minor king leaving his minions.

I'd met Maurice the first day of uni. I was early and sat in the very top seat nearest the door to the lecture theatre. He told me later it was his ritual to arrive early for the first lecture of the academic year. I watched this guy, who was supposed to be a God of Law and was the actual Head of the Law School, place his papers on the lectern and stride up and down the platform. He wouldn't have even known I was there but for the noise my pen made when it dropped to the ground and rolled down the next stair. He shaded his hand against his forehead and found me in the gloom of the back of the theatre. He didn't ask me to go down to him. Instead he took the stairs two at a time to get to me. I had no idea that the flowing black gown was not de rigueur. That was another part of his first-lecture ritual. Full academic gear. 'What school did you go to?' was his first question. Which I didn't appreciate, coming from a down-in-the-mouth, library-what-library, but-boy-can-we-put-on-a-mean-mass kind of school. But instead of disapproving, a smile cracked through the seriousness on his face. 'Good. Good,' he said. 'Too many students are spoonfed into this place from nurseries wallpapered with money and schools dripping with gold.' He had a clipped, decisive way of speaking. It was like he knew who he was. I let go of the breath I'd been holding ever since I passed through the mighty sandstone gates of the university.

Turns out he came from a school just like mine. Not Catholic. But the down-and-out part. So when I nearly gave up a few years later, there was enough between us that he offered me a part-time job at his Chambers. That became Articles when I finished, He was a hand on my shoulder, and that has been a good and bad thing. Right now, bad. I had to confront him about ringing my dad. But . . . opening another front right now? It would have to wait.

I sat down at my desk and pulled the Stintini files out. Flipped open the first manila folder. The words on the page pulsed at me, refusing to stay in their straight rows. Flipped it closed. I pushed back in my chair. Bit my lip, dug into my palms, rubbed at the jackhammers pounding away on my arms. Really useful things. I plucked a pen from the re-purposed jam jar, opened the file again. I could ask Suze to do some of the basic work. I'd never done that. Always did my own work. I put my hand to my belly. Felt the quease of it. I really should have tried to get more sleep. I bundled up my files, scribbled out a note and did my own gratitude smiling as I dropped the lot with Suze. I scribbled out another note and left it for Tye. Took a tram home and got straight into the Austin without going inside to run Rat-Tail's gauntlet. I angled the wide bus steering wheel away from the curb and headed for the freeway.

Tessa pulled into her driveway just after me, so I had a moment to gauge her mood in the sliver of rear-vision mirror. There was nothing there but business as she parked beside the front door. I rubbed my palms together and got out, hands to hips, watching. Georgie rocketed out of the car first.

'Hey batboy,' I said.

He flew into my arms. I squeezed my eyes tight to get more of his little body hug, taking the edge off something a few layers down in me. 'You had twins, you smart little guy. How's that going?'

'They don't do much.' He stood back and put his head on the side like a pigeon, his hands behind his back. He shrugged. 'Mum says they'll get better.'

Tessa kicked the door of the Holden, her arms full with bags of groceries. 'Let them sleep,' she called to Georgie, who'd dragged me over to have a look at the twins. 'Leave the back door open.'

'Your mum's spot on,' I said. 'They're like two curled-up grubs who'll grow into butterflies for you to run around and catch.'

I tickled him, lifting him high and soaring him towards the front door. I dive-bombed him to the ground and he took off inside. I got hold of a bag out of Tessa's hand. How the hell do you do the shopping with newborn twins and a toddler? A spit of respect shot out of the tightness I kept around Tessa. All her capable wasn't just a criticism of me. It had a job to do in the world.

There was the ring of a bell deep in my gut. Truth was, I came to her first because of this capable. If anybody had worked out more than me, it was her. I'd found what looked like proof that things were fucked up in our house, but Dad denied it and it was all brick walls and dead ends, so I needed Tessa on my side. But her face was all closed up with the effort of living, and I wondered if I could get past it, back down to when we were kids on the other end of a phone to Aunty Peg.

I didn't have her kind of capable. Maybe you couldn't have a kid without it. I had to think of what would be best for the kid growing inside me. Pretty sure that wasn't me, and yet what do you do with the sadness of letting it go?

The blue-and-green-flecked carpet down the corridor was something good. Tessa was like Mum in this. She needed the ease that Geoff's bank job gave her. Georgie charged straight into the lounge and punched the telly on, full of karate-chopping energy. He settled himself on a beanbag as Tessa and I went past to the kitchen island, dropping bags on benches. Georgie's little face was soft in the curve of his hand as he watched the screen, unblinking as he took in the deliberate and slow instructions of the *Play School* presenter who was cutting shapes into coloured paper. I caught Tessa watching him too, the same softness in her face. She turned back to the shopping, face shuttered up again, and she opened the pantry door. She refilled the flour and rice canisters.

'Georgie,' she called. 'Where's the cereal tin?'

He came zooming over, arms out to the side like an aeroplane, flattened himself to the ground, put his hand behind the back leg of the table closest to the wall and pulled out the canister.

'Why, Georgie, just why?'

'Didn't want the twins to eat it before me,' he said and zoomed off.

'Cuppa?' I asked, happy to be able to laugh.

Tessa fell into a chair. 'Look, JJ, I'm too tired for whatever this is — can we just skip it?'

I put the kettle on. 'Just came to see the twins.'

'You were round at Dad's yesterday. So alarm bells are ringing,' she said, exasperation tightening her mouth up.

I didn't have time for shame about my visiting-the-twins lie. 'He tell you why I was there?'

She shook her head. 'But the last time I saw you, you were flying out of Aunty Peg's like a cat with a scalded tail, and the next thing you turn up on Dad's doorstep. Putting two and two together ... ' She raised her eyebrows and tapped a finger on the table.

I picked up a pillowcase from the pile of clothes on the table and folded it. She tipped forwards and picked up a tea towel. I put the folded case on the table and started in on a pile of baby things.

'Just fold them,' she said. 'I don't iron any more.'

'That's progress.'

She screwed up the tired in her face at me and I wished I could pluck the barb back out of the air so I wouldn't have caused her that pain. We worked our way through the clothes and I wondered if she still thought getting married at nineteen had been a good idea. At least Geoff was a good guy. 'We're going back over to Peg's tomorrow,' said Tessa. She rubbed her nose with her sleeve. 'Dad and Tim are bringing the truck.'

'When did Dad tell you that?'

'He rang this morning.'

'Weird. First he says he'll have nothing to do with Peg's madhouse, then suddenly, after I told him you were sorting through everything not just chucking it, he's changed his tune?'

'Don't be stupid, JJ. He was just letting off steam when he said he wouldn't be there. He always helps.' She folded a tiny romper. 'Why don't you stay out of his way? You've got work anyway. Those law firms aren't charities. You can help with the clean-up on the weekend.'

I turned my head away to hide the eye roll. I got up from the table and picked up a toy car crashed against the windowsill. I took it over to Georgie and put it with a pile of others he had in a box by the beanbag. He looked up and winked.

'When did you learn to do that?'

He winked again five more times, like it was Morse Code. 'Mum taught me yesterday when the twins were having a drink.'

I laughed and winked back. That gave me enough good vibes to get back to the table. I picked up the last of the towels.

'So have you found anything yet over at Peg's?'

'Bit.' She scratched her hair and her hand dropped with a thud to the table. 'Some pearls, a ring, lots of twenty dollar bills everywhere.'

'How much all together?'

'A couple of grand.'

I whistled. 'That's worth it. Actually I've got a day off tomorrow. I'll definitely be there to give you a hand.'

Tessa heaved off her chair towards the kettle and came back with the tea in mugs. 'Listen.' She put them on the table. 'It's better if you don't.'

I smacked my hands open full of the indignant question.

She sighed. 'It's just not . . . calm when you're around.'

'Calm?' I spat the word as if it were all scratched up.

She put up her palms like stoplights. 'Life's hard enough without the drama.'

'It's not me. Life's muddy.'

'Just let us put it all behind us.'

'That's exactly what Dad wants.'

'We all want it. He deserves a bit of peace. He's never been the same since Mum died.'

'Why are you always on Dad's side? What about Mum?' My hand fell to my trouser pocket for comfort, feeling the shape of Mum's brooch.

'We all lost her — not just you,' Tessa said.

'She wasn't just our mother, she was a woman who lived and breathed, and she deserves to be remembered for who she was and what she strived for.'

'She strived,' Tessa made quotation marks in the air, 'for us. Putting food on the table, loving us, keeping us together. You're the only one who doesn't get it.'

'Me?'

'The rest of us are getting on with our lives. You're sitting around rotting in some boarding house dump that's worse than the hole we all grew up in.'

I felt a wildness rip along my spine, red and licking out. I tried to get hold of my breath, send it back into the ground. 'Dad lied,' I said from between my teeth.

'I can't do this any more.' She threw a tea towel across the room. 'I can't stand in the middle looking after you both because neither you nor Dad ever got over losing Mum. The both of you walking around bleeding, one just like the other and the rest of us in between.'

I shook my head, not seeing through the cloudy air. 'You don't look after me — I'm not even around.'

'Present or not, we all know you barely hold things together at the best of times, and since Peg's funeral it's clear you're unravelling, JJ. What does Tye say?'

'He told me to go see Dad.'

She tsked. 'I thought he had a head on his shoulders.' She crossed the room to snatch up the tea towel from the floor. 'Georgie! Check on the twins,' she called. Georgie aeroplaned out again and buzzed through the door. Tessa sat, reining in her frustration. 'Mum spent most of her time protecting you from the world and from yourself. So we do, too. For her.' Her voice on the verge of breaking.

I stood up. Kneaded my palms. I couldn't work the sounds into words and my mouth made shapes but nothing came out. It never felt like she'd saved me from anything. 'Nobody asked you to.' I finally got out.

Her eyes were two pools of pity. I wanted to stab pencils into them.

'Look,' she said, still choked up on her own compassion. 'It doesn't matter where she was those last six days.'

'So I'm right.' I focused on that fact and not her bloody eyes. 'You don't think she was at Peg's, either.'

'I — am — say — ing,' she articulated every syllable, losing all that niceness, 'the — end — is — the — same. She died!'

'Bullshit! If he did something, or she took off with another bloke, we should know. And then he can stop pulling that poor-widow-single-father act.'

Tessa flew her hands to her head and pulled at her hair, which was loose and wispy around her shoulders instead of being swept up into its usual practical ponytail. 'Of course it wasn't anything like that. She loved him. I'm older. I remember. It was just some tiff. It was nothing.' She dropped her hands and sat, leaned her hands long across the table to me, shaking her head. 'Let it go,' she said in a lullaby voice. This time there was some of Mum in her. The soothe in her voice lulled me back into my chair.

'I found proof,' I said.

She jerked against the back of her chair, all lullaby gone. 'I don't want to know.'

But I told her anyway about Mrs Tyler's suspicions and Peg's calendar.

Tessa laid her head on her folded arms.

'You know what that means?' I pushed.

She banged her head against her arms a couple of times. 'This is what makes me tired, JJ. This — '

'Dad and Peg both lied. You can't ignore it any longer.'

She shook her head, but I didn't let her speak.

'Why don't you want to know the truth?' I asked.

'Truth is, you blamed Dad for Mum's death.' Her voice soared and I was glad. 'And you've been trying to make up some drama to give you a reason for blaming him. But it was just you being a baby. Grow up, JJ. Shit happens. It is what it is. You can't trust whatever Peg wrote. Dad did his best. End of story. If Dad did hide something, he had a reason. People hide stuff from their kids all the time to protect them.'

'We're not kids any more. It's time. You're not the only grown-up now. We all are,' I just about screamed.

'What the F are you on about?' Her voice was up, too, but she had one eye on the front door for Georgie's return.

'From the moment Mum died you've been trying to protect us all by keeping a lid on everything, all the 'unpleasantness'.' I air quoted, but did manage to drop my voice to her level. 'But Mum wasn't like that.'

'I'm not trying to be Mum.'

'Really?' I accused. 'You were only thirteen and you never missed a meal.'

'Mum had left a lot in the freezer. It was nothing.'

She started to say something else, but I got in first. 'So why do you drink?'

She backhanded a pile of clothes and they flew through the air and landed in a tumble on the floor. 'I bloody drink because I'm bloody tired. That's bloody all.'

'You bloody drink because you're all bloody twisted tight, but the roar is in you anyway and you can't keep it under lock and key. You know something's not right, but you think you're betraying Dad and therefore failing Mum if you admit it.'

She shook her hands in the air above her head. Her eyes wild and pulled back and behind them something giving way. 'You've got no idea, Miss All-The-Pain-On-The-Outside, and making the rest of us dance to your tune. That's not courage. What's courage is putting one foot in front of another and holding it all together. What Mum did, day in, day out: food on the table, clothes on backs. If you want to honour Mum then get on with your life. Don't you come into my house telling me I'm missing a card from the deck of emotions. You weren't the only one to lose Mum, you're just the only who needs to keep losing her over and over, every day, punishing everybody.'

I backed away from the punch of her words. My skin was peeled back, raw. My head shaking like it belonged on somebody else's shoulders.

She picked up the clothes and she dumped them back on the table. She pulled out a pair of Dad's overalls and started folding them again, pressing things back together. 'What did Dad have to say about all this when you were over there last night?' she asked.

My head wouldn't stop shaking.

'Just what I thought.' She picked up a pair of shorts. 'Peg wasn't right in the head, can't trust anything she wrote. Dad would know. Dad would tell us.'

'Dad would know, Dad wouldn't tell us, hasn't told us, drowns us like kittens in his lies — '

'For fuck's sake. The drama — ' Tessa got to her feet and opened the fridge. 'You think long and hard,' she said, 'about your next step.' She poured herself a wine and sat before the squared-up pile of clothes. 'Unless you think he's murdered her or something, and you know he didn't, then it's not worth it. Leave it alone. You're already on the edge. You need to get a grip. She wanted you to be happy. So be bloody happy and leave this alone.'

'Muuuum,' Georgie yelled. 'They're awake. I'll get em.'

Tessa jumped to her feet and disappeared out of the door, leaving me by the table.

WHAT'S JACK SCARED OF?

The next day, Tye pulled me into the photo-copying room as soon as I arrived at work, took the two lattes from me and rested them on a bookshelf and hugged me tight. 'What the fuck?' he murmured. 'You can't disappear like that.'

'I know, I know.' I groaned back into the smooth of his sweet-smelling neck. Feeling my insides melt. But something else as well. A creeping guilt. I hadn't told him. He had a right to know. If I decided not to go through with it, would I tell him at all? Jack all over again, I castigated myself. I knew it, but it didn't mean Tye'd get the truth in the end.

'Let's go to Mario's tonight.' I squeezed him. 'Drink some wine, eat some pasta, drink some wine.' I'd keep drinking until I'd made a decision. It was like I wasn't giving myself any truth, either.

He squeezed back. 'But you gotta promise. No more disappearing.'

I nodded.

'Also, Maurice is looking for you.'

'Shit,' I said.

I told Tye about going to Tessa's.

He lowered the latte from his lips. 'You left work when you've got the Stintini case about to go to court to go and see your sister? The one who drives you nuts?'

I quickly charged past the concern on his face. I, too, could sense Peg's breath whisper close. Instead I told him about the meals Mum had made ready as if she'd expected to be away. I didn't tell him about the wedding ring she left behind as if she'd expected to never come back.

'Listen.' He wrapped his arms around me. 'Maybe this isn't good for you after all. Instead of chasing it down, maybe now is the moment you should let it go. You're okay, JJ. You're the most compassionate, smart and, yes, *sane* person I know.'

I closed up tight against his words. He always surprised me about how much he knew and didn't say until a moment like this. How the hell did I make enough good karma to get him? On the other hand, his eyes saw too deep into the raw. I pushed away and covered my face with my hands, like a kid who thinks if they can't see the world the world can't see them.

Instead of pulling my hands away, he manoeuvred behind me and placed his over mine, enfolding me. 'You're not like your Aunt Peg.'

I bit my lips to stop the whimper. 'If I made it all up about Mum, I probably am. That's what Peg did. Said any old crap to match whatever the hell mess was going on inside her. It's better to know now, so I can — ' I broke off. 'Prepare,' I finally finished.

He laughed quietly. 'Now that's insane. How you going to do that? Start stacking newspapers in the shed waiting for the moment you might need a shitload to hoard?'

I let a little half-drowned sound escape that could've been taken for a baby ghost of a laugh.

★ ★ ★

I went the long way to my desk so I could avoid Maurice's office. My in-tray had disappeared under the pile of yesterday's documents. I pulled my chair into my desk, opened the large bottom drawer and tipped my in-tray straight into it. I couldn't think with all that swamp. Didn't know how Peg did it, letting things build up into screaming piles around her. I pulled the Stintini files forwards and went through Suze's work. After an hour, my head was exploding with too much information. I dropped it into my hands. Rubbed my eyes. Maybe I did need that day off I'd told Tessa I had. Made a few more notes on the files for Suze. I went by Tye's desk to ask him to cover me while I went out for a while. Told him I'd got a call from Philly who needed a bit of help. Lied. Told him I'd be back. Lied. He raised an eyebrow, but didn't say anything.

★ ★ ★

Aunty Peg's house was peeled back like a skun rabbit — the doors flung open, windows yanked wide. The violence of it stopped me dead. Aunty Peg had filled every space of her house with things, bringing the walls closer and closer until the house fit around her like a glove. I hoped her spirit had long pissed off so she wasn't around for this violation.

'Get behind it, Tim.' Dad's voice from deep inside the house was low and guttural like he was herding up sheep. We could all speak dog.

I wished for a sec that I hadn't skived off work after all so I'd didn't have to face him again. I wheeled my bike up beside Peg's house and leaned it against the wall beside the apple tree. Dad's back came into view, down the verandah steps followed by a couch, then Tim, who grinned.

'Ah, you grace us.'

'As you didn't at Peg's funeral.'

'Gidday, love,' Dad said with a glance as he backed towards the truck. It was his superpower — ignoring stuff.

I kept my distance. I picked up an apple that had fallen from the tree and rubbed it shiny on my jeans, which I'd changed into. When they'd passed, I went in: all that was left of the lounge room were the stepping stones across the floorboards where sofa legs and sideboards had been. The pale vulnerability of them crawled through me.

'Where are the girls?' I called, trying to shut it out.

'We got an early start, been here since five,' said Tim.

I frowned, thinking of how Tessa would take the news they'd been working for five hours, throwing out things she hadn't sorted. And given the haul she'd already scored, she was on to something. It wasn't like her to be late.

I wandered into Aunty Peg's bedroom. It was empty as well and so was her sewing room. I wondered if they'd come across a sewing machine or anything that might have given the room its name. I bit into the apple and its slight flouriness of over-ripe.

'Tessa's going to be pissed off. She's going through all this stuff,' I called.

'We've all got lives,' Dad called back. 'Got to get on with the job and get back to them.'

I grunted and went down the corridor to the back of the house. The door of the spare room was chocked open with boxes. I nudged them forwards and squeezed in. There'd been a bed once, but it was lost underneath garbage bags and piles of clothes. I took another bite of the apple and chucked the rest through the window. I put my hands on my hips, kicked at the nearest bag. So heavy it didn't budge. I got to my knees and opened it. On the top was a ruler, a fan with a dancing Chinese girl on it and a whole lot of wire coat hangers. A sigh took a long time getting out of me. But still. I'd spent the night chasing sleep from one corner of my room to the other, and stubbing my toe against the same thing — Dad was damned keen to get in here and get rid of everything, so there was something he didn't want found. Of course I knew that whatever it was had probably already been shipped off to the tip, but you never knew, and hearing Dad in the next room got me going.

I pulled gloves out of my back pocket, shoved my fingers into them. I poked about in the bag until I hit a lot of rocks at the bottom, and then went through another one a bit half-heartedly. All that uselessness was greying my insides. As I stood to put the box out onto my sorted pile, I banged my shin against a sharp edge. 'Shit.' I bent to rub like mad at it and saw what had got me. It was a rectangle wooden box — all blonde wood. I shoved the stuff off the top of it. It was an old-fashioned butter box. Mum had one exactly the same. She used to set me up by the fire with it and I worked my way through the buttons and ribbons and odd socks, my feet tucked under me, up and away from the licking moan of the wind through the cracks in the wall.

I couldn't get Peg's box open, but it turned out Peg was right: junk did come in handy. I got hold of a nearby screwdriver and I jimmied the lid up. Inside, dozens of hardback notebooks were sardined in. I wiped my hand on my jeans and opened the first one. The writing was all flamboyant loops and loud capitals like Aunty Peg's.

'JJ?' called Dad.

'Here.' I shoved the diary back in the box and pulled a nearby jacket over it.

'We're in there next.'

'I need to bag up these clothes for Vinnies. You can do the laundry first,' I called back.

'Straight to the tip with this lot.' He pushed into the room. 'Rat infested.'

I was about to argue when we heard Philly's voice at the front door.

'Fuck,' we heard Tim say.

'What's wrong?' Dad called, striding up the now cleared and echoing corridor, me in his wake. Philly was kitted out in a matching tracksuit with a mauve sports band around her head. I would have laughed if it weren't for her look of serious.

'Tessa drove into a ditch.' You didn't need to ask questions with Philly. She went on. 'Just shaken up. Last night, ten past one in the morning. She'd been out putting Sophie to sleep. They're both okay. Just lucky Bill Malcolm was passing — he towed her out.'

'Shit,' said Dad. He rubbed his hands together making something of the information. 'But all good now. Let's get back to it.' He turned to go.

'No, Dad. All bad.' Philly put a hand on his elbow. 'She shouldn't have been driving.'

'Why the hell not?'

'She was drunk — and with Sophie in the car.'

'What's she got to be drinking about?'

I rolled my eyes.

'What?' he challenged. 'Geoff's a good bloke. What's wrong with her?'

I pushed past and went back into the spare room. I sat on the butter box and my face found its way into my hands, cradling the sudden heat of guilt. I knew what she had to be drinking about because I had been the one with the shovel digging it all up. I rubbed my arms, trying to coat them.

'Tessa's got too much on her plate,' said Dad, coming into the room, the others behind him. 'Let's get this sorted so that's one less thing she has to deal with. You girls put some muscle into getting that lot into the truck.' He pointed at the crap under the window. 'Get around behind that dresser, will you, mate?' he said to Tim.

I tried to catch Philly's eye. But she was with

Dad: the sooner this was over, the better, and twenty dollars here and there was not enough to change her mind, It felt like the air had hissed from my tyres, too. I had what I needed, anyway. I took a while piling up my arms and adjusting the load to give Dad and Tim time to manoeuvre the dresser out. I had to keep Dad off the scent that I'd found something. Once I was looking at their backs, I dumped the lot, picked up the butter box and disguised it under the jacket. I scuttled with it out the front door and around the corner to where my bike was. I wasn't sure how I'd carry it home in the basket, but I'd worry about that later.

Tim gave me a grin when I got back inside. 'Good to see you back.' He swatted me. 'Have a nice trip?'

'Everyone needs a smoko.'

He grinned. 'Especially you.'

'Shut up.' I shoved him, but my eyes were all over the room, looking for more butter boxes.

'Less talk, more action,' said Dad.

★　★　★

Dad revved the truck as Tim closed up its tailgate. Tim pecked our cheeks, one after the other.

'Stay out of trouble,' he said to me with a further slap on my back.

I darted forwards and punched him on the arm. 'Don't keep Daddy waiting.'

He twisted out of the way and laughed as he swung up into the cabin, the truck taking off before he'd got the door closed.

Philly threw her keys in the air and snatched them back at the exact right second.

'How did the beach go?' I asked.

Her eyes darted sideways. 'We didn't make it,' she said.

'Philly. Not again.' I grabbed the keys in mid air. 'What did Ahmed say?'

She looked down the street. 'It couldn't be helped. Mrs Manto next door needed her pantry done.'

'Really? Philly! If she needed company, couldn't you have taken her to the beach with you?'

'She's a seventy-five-year-old woman, JJ.'

'And you are a twenty-three year-old girl who needs to have a bit of fun. *With your boyfriend.* You can't always be looking after miscellaneous old women. On top of the hours you work. You're already the account manager of their biggest client. Relax. Live a little.' I pressed the keys into her hand, closed her fist around them. 'We all know Ahmed is a saint, but even he's got a breaking point. He's been saying he never gets to see you for ages. You have to start saying no, Philly. You can't be Miss Perfect for everybody.'

She waved my concerns away.

I backed away, hands waving. 'It's your life.' I went around the side of the house to collect my bike. The jacket was there but no box. I looked around, even looked behind the tree where there was no way it could have been. I couldn't work it out. I raced back out to the front.

'Did you see the box beside my bike?'

243

Philly shook her head.

'I had a box right there.' I pointed back around the corner.

'Dad or Tim probably tossed it in the truck thinking it was Aunty Peg's.'

'That's exactly why I wanted it.'

She got her eyebrows low.

'Peg's dairies,' I said.

She held her palms in the air like a shield. 'No. No. No.'

The fury hurtled out of me so sudden I couldn't have caught it even if I'd had a head start. 'Why is it always 'No' with you on this, and nothing else?'

'Because I've been talking to Tessa. If you want to find out if Mum wasn't where Dad said she was, you're welcome, but leave the rest of us out of it. Dad's right. Tessa can't cope. And neither can he. The past is the past.' Philly was all reason and calm.

'That'd be right.'

A kid walked on our side of the street, licking a lollipop. Walking as if she had all the time in the world, taking an interest in things. But Philly wasn't going to give her any more of a show. Discipline was her middle name, so she waited, holding her car keys steady, giving them a tight jingle every couple of seconds.

'I don't want to say it, JJ — '

'Grow a spine,' I goaded her.

'You're fucked up, JJ,' her voice spitting fire.

I stepped back like I'd been winded. From Tessa, yes. Dad, even Tim. But Philly?

'You're out of control. Tessa's right.'

'The world's messy. You can't orchestrate every little thing. People aren't puppets. You can't make the past disappear.'

'I'm glad Mum was in the city when she had her appendix attack. I don't care why she was there. It means she would have got to the hospital faster. If she could have been saved, she would've been.'

'So why did he steal the diaries?'

Philly took a deep breath, turned away.

'Why're you protecting him?' I asked.

She kept moving, throwing back over her shoulder, 'He's all we've got.'

THAT MISSING THING

Rocco was wearing a retro purple velvet suit and carrying a plastic bag in each hand when I skidded my bike to a stop outside the boarding house. He kicked at my wheel.

'What the hell?'

'Where've you been?' His hair was slick with oil.

'Mind your own business.'

'That bird from the community health centre — '

'Shit.' I locked my bike at the side and ran up the steps with him.

Rat-Tail was in with Marge, over at the bookshelf, with a red feather duster. Marge shrugged when I grimaced my sorry.

'Hey JJ,' Rat-Tail said. 'Got this for Marge.' He swung the feather duster.

'It'll make the difference, Rat-Tail.'

'You've got real nice hair, today.'

'Thanks.'

'Done something to it? Looked all greasy yesterday.'

'Just washed it, Rat-Tail. Works really well.'

'Yeah. I'll give that a go.'

I bent to kiss Marge in her armchair. Nodded. She nodded back. All tight and closed except for her eyes — big and shiny.

Philly's floral pink bedspread, matching pillowcase and throw pillows were doing their job.
Rocco pulled the grapes from the bag, looked
around. 'Shit,' he said. I dashed out the door to
my place. Grabbed one of Mum's platters. Stopped,
looked around the room, ran to the drawer, plucked
out a scarf. Ran back.

Rocco pulled out apricots and plums from
the other plastic bag and grouped them artfully
together on Mum's platter. I laid the scarf over
Marge's lamp. Switched it on.

'Get that blasted thing off,' Marge said.

I swivelled at the sharpness.

'Fire hazard.'

Rocco stepped over to high-five Marge, who
looked perplexed. 'You got this in the bag,
Marge. They're not going to put away a safety
chick like you.'

I balled up the scarf into the pocket of my
shorts. Pulled it out again. Laid it over the bed
head.

'Better?'

'Can live with it,' said Marge.

She checked her watch again.

Rocco jammed the scraggy striped carnations
into a glass vase and filled it at the sink. I
wouldn't have gone for them myself, and not just
because they were ugly, but since I hadn't been
there, had forgotten, I wasn't in any position to
complain. Just hope the community worker
didn't pick up on their vibe of refusal. I pulled
the potty from under the bed so that it could just
be seen. I'd ended up paying more than seventy
bucks for it. Vinnies didn't have any so I'd had to

go to the lower end of the antique world.

I switched on the kettle, which began to whistle right off.

I flicked it off again. Turned to Marge, who nodded. The tea leaves were in the new teapot beside the four cups, four saucers and a banana cake.

Rat-Tail counted the cups, then counted around the room.

'Best there aren't too many of us, Rat-Tail,' said Marge. 'Makes the room seem smaller.'

'I'll wait at the door for her, then.' He took off.

'Is that a good idea?' I asked.

Marge lifted a weary hand and let it drop, saying all it needed to say.

Rocco stuffed the plastic bag and the fallen leaves into the rubbish bin and pushed it under the table. Straightened the toaster, the kettle and the two-ring stove, all polished up and glistening. Rocco moved the chair he'd brought from his room an inch or two towards Marge's and the one I'd donated. I was to be on the bed.

I took Marge's hand. Rocco pulled at the velvet collar of his suit. Sat down and bent to tug at the end of his trouser legs. Being so tall he rarely found anything that fitted him at Vinnies. He gave up, crossed his ankles, and stretched out his hands to his knees, eyes on the floor.

The main door slammed shut and we heard Rat-Tail's voice.

Rocco and I exchanged worried looks.

When they got closer, we notched up the worry in the look between us because then we could hear what was being said.

'They're real nice earrings.'

'Had them a while,' a woman's voice replied.

'Must be heavy, but, cause they're dragging your earlobes real bad, down to your shoulders.'

Rocco and I shook our heads.

Marge stared straight ahead.

Rocco tapped her arm. She turned to him, started, then began the struggle to get out of the armchair. On her feet, she quickened to the door and into the corridor.

Marge showed the woman, with her serviceable bob and her clipboard, the building, the bathrooms, the garden, the everything there was to be seen. The woman came in to Marge's room and introduced herself as Shamira, and we took up our positions. Marge sat forwards to pour the tea Rocco had made and handed it around. She cut the cake and passed that around, too. Shamira laid her clipboard on the bed beside me. I tried to read upside down.

We chatted about the weather, the tennis and then the neighbourhood. No, it wasn't as rough as reputation had it. Shamira turned to stab another cross onto her clipboard. After the tea had been drunk and the cake eaten, Marge asked the question.

Shamira pushed her glasses up her nose before she spoke. 'The bathroom being so far away is not ideal — ' She sent a disparaging glance at the elaborate potty poking out from under the bed.

'Am I late?'

We all looked to the doorway.

I jumped up to hug Philly, relieved that she'd turned up after all when even I'd forgotten. She squeezed me back, both of us putting the flare-up at Peg's place behind us.

'You missed the cake, so depends what you had in mind by late,' I said.

Rocco stood to bow. She was bowable, all dressed in a matching magenta dress and jacket with a double string of pearls, not a hair out of place. I introduced Philly to Shamira, whose face brightened at the sight of her grown-up togetherness. Philly said she came to visit Marge once a week — made sure Rocco had done the shopping, I'd done the washing and Marge had got to all her appointments. As she talked she took four Tupperware containers out of her wicker shopping basket and put two in the bar fridge and two in the freezer.

'My job is to tick it all off,' she finished.

Shamira looked from me to Rocco to Marge. The air in the room had lightened, and Shamira started winding things up. Rocco walked her to her car, a perfect, suited gentleman to the last.

Marge blew out her cheeks and dropped both arms to her lap.

Rocco came back rubbing his hands together, Rat-Tail with him. 'Think we gave a good show,' Rocco said.

'Nice touch — all that Tupperware cooking,' I said.

'She didn't have to know I bought it all,' said Philly.

Rocco took out a bottle of Scotch he'd hidden in the wardrobe and poured it straight into our tea cups. Nobody complained.

ORDER INTO CHAOS

I called work, but didn't even try to give much of a reason for taking yet another day off. Just said I wouldn't be in. Hadn't left a message for Tye this time, either. I winced. I mean, what could I have said? Maybe Tessa was right. I was cracking open. But I had to see her. Had to apologise. I picked up some pasta sauce and chocolates on the way and headed back down the freeway. I hadn't rung her in case she snarled at me to stay away. I wouldn't have blamed her. Geoff's car was still in the drive so Tessa was bad enough for him to take the day off. I winced again. She was always so capable. Just like Mum. You didn't see the breaking point coming. I sat in the car, drumming the steering wheel, stopped up with the guilt of having struck the match that lit this fire.

It was Geoff's face at the front door that got me out of the car. I couldn't read anything in his peck as he bent down to greet me. He put the pasta sauce in the fridge. 'Thanks, JJ, kind of you to come by.'

The twins were sleeping and Georgie was at kindy. I was all good to go in and see her. I wanted to ask him how he was, but he sat back at the table spread over with white pages and manila folders. It wasn't clear if he knew this was my fault.

'JJ' was all Tessa said. She was sitting up in bed with a cuppa, looking out the window.

I crossed quickly to her. 'God, Tessa. I'm so sorry.'

She turned to me. 'It's not always about you, JJ.' She put the teacup back in its saucer. 'I'm just exhausted. Twins,' she said. 'You'll understand one day.' She looked out the window again. 'If you ever have kids, that is.'

'What do you mean?' I asked, stung, a protective hand going to my belly.

'You have to have worked out your own shit enough to put somebody's needs before yours.'

'Just like you have,' I said before I could jam the words back into my mouth.

She gave me a 'really' look.

'Yeah, yeah, yeah. I know. Sorry.' I perched on the side of her bed.

'You just can't help yourself, JJ.'

I put the chocolates on her knees and we sat there in silence for a while, both looking out the window at the ducks on the dam sailing to the island in the middle as if they weren't moving a muscle.

'Listen,' she said. 'You do what you like. You always have. But you gotta promise me to leave Dad out of it. I can't be looking after him as well. He's not as strong as you think.'

I leaned forward and cracked open the box of chocolates. Offered it to Tessa who waved it away. I took two triangle ones and jammed them in my mouth at the same time. I needed something to stop up the biting words that wanted to get out at Tessa. She wasn't fooled, though, and

252

sat waiting for an answer, so in the end, given the delicateness of her pink nighty and her unbrushed hair, I nodded. She raised an eyebrow meaningfully, so I followed it up with an 'okay, I promise'.

★ ★ ★

I sat awkwardly with Geoff for a while before I left. Offered him help with the twins and Georgie. He said his mum was coming for a visit, give Tessa a break, so they'd be right. I nodded. Put my hand impulsively to his forearm on the table. 'She'll be all right,' I said.

'Will she?' He looked up, his eyes raw with questions. 'It's like there's this huge empty hole in the middle of her that I can't fill. Not me, not the kids.'

I saw it. I saw what he meant straight away. I wanted to tell him that she was strong. But what did I know?

★ ★ ★

'Listen,' said Rat-Tail back at the boarding house, following me up the corridor to my room. 'You really gotta call that Tye bloke back. Funny name, but. He's bothering me all the time. Real nice bloke, but.' Rat-Tail held out the mess of messages I'd deliberately ignored beside the telephone. His gap-tooth smile dimmed as I grabbed the pink slips and went to close the door in his face. I relented. 'I will, Rat-Tail. Promise. Do me a favour?' I said. 'I've been too busy to drop in on Marge today — could you?'

253

He grinned again, his short, bony body straightening.

'Give her this.' I shoved a paper bag at him. 'One for you in there too.'

Despite the caramel slices, I was pretty sure Marge wasn't going to be happy with me for inflicting Rat-Tail and his enthusiasms on her.

I collapsed on the bed, hands under my head, staring at the map of cracks above me. I tried closing my eyes but they kept flickering back open. The misery on Geoff's face swam through me, the weight of his helplessness. I didn't know him so well, him being quiet, me not having been around much. But they'd both been kids when they started having kids themselves. I lay there long, counting seconds, then minutes, then hours. Time. One second your arms were plunged into the sink up to your wrists, the next you'd fallen through its layers. There was only one true thing I could do for Tessa, for Geoff. I had to find out where Mum had been and why. I was a lawyer. So I should start acting like one. Do what Maurice was always telling us to do — 'Follow the Facts'.

But Tessa was right about one thing. If I was doing her a favour, I had to keep Dad out of it. He wasn't going to help, anyway. So since private facts were off limits, I'd start with the public ones.

* * *

The next day I didn't even bother to call work. I needed to get to the hospital as soon as it opened

254

for business, but standing in the grey functionality of its corridors almost undid me. I hadn't factored in the tiny yet explosive fact. This was the hospital Mum died in. Still. I made myself take one step after the other until I found the medical records desk.

A tall woman with an afro and a white lab coat took the form with all my ticks and crosses and dropped it into the intray beside her.

'Where shall I wait?' I asked.

She looked at me over the top of her glasses. 'Six weeks,' she said and went back to tapping on her keyboard.

I bit my lip to hold back the immediate retort and took a breath. 'Is there any way we could speed the process up?' I asked in deliberately measured tones.

'No.' She didn't look up this time. Somebody else in a white coat came through the glass doors and said a cheery hello as she passed the reception desk with a pile of manila folders in her arms. The woman before me was just as cheery back.

I tracked the somebody else through two sets of glass doors and then left into another room, where I got a glimpse through the opening door of rows and rows of manila folders in boxes.

'It's for the Managing Partner at Smith and Blake on a case of government importance,' I said to the top of her head.

'Really?' She finished clicking on the keyboard with a flourish. She picked up my document and flicked through.

'Sarah Anne McBride, of national importance?'

I nodded without blinking.

She shook her head, opened a drawer and placed another form on the desk. 'You'll have to fill that one out instead, then.'

I pulled it towards me, reaching into my handbag for my pen again.

'That'll be four weeks,' she said.

'Does Mr Smith really have to call you personally?' I said, returning her frost.

'Wouldn't do him any good.' She didn't crack a smile. 'He could try the premier, though.'

On the way out, I tried to slam the door, but being modern and glass it didn't give much satisfaction. I retraced my steps down the long grey of the corridor and sat on a seat where I could track everybody who went in and went out of the records department in the distance. There wasn't that much traffic. After an hour or so, the records woman came out. I hunched away, suddenly interested in something on the wall. She passed me by without noticing. I didn't lose any time. Flew down the corridor, pushed through those double-glass doors, expecting to have to sweet talk somebody, but the desk was empty. I turned left and headed for the records room. There was probably only a slim chance they kept old records with the newer ones, but still. It was what I had.

I rushed along the rows of boxes trying to do a fast decipher of how the records were set up. I'd just figured out numbers against years when a voice stopped me.

'Can I help you?'

I turned slowly, thinking fast.

'Sure.' I smiled brightly. 'Could you point me to the nineteen sixties?'

The man did not smile back. He went to raise his arm, then paused. 'But how did you get in here?'

I made up some story about being directed in here by somebody to get something for Dr Ryan from Cardio, thinking I needed a few facts to tie this lie to the flag of convincing truth.

I'm not sure how convinced he was, but his hand continued upwards and pointed me to the furthest room, and I turned on my heels, checking my watch as if Dr Ryan might actually be sitting there tapping his toes back in Cardio.

I found 1966 in the back corner of the far room and started to work my way up to 68. The bees on my skin got busier as I got closer. I was a cloud of buzz so I didn't hear the far doors opening, nor the footsteps.

I did hear the almost tentative voice, though. 'Miss.'

I turned with that bright smile plastered on again. But it faded fast at the sight of the security uniform.

'You'll have to come with me,' he said with a polite smile, the stubble on his chin patchy because he wasn't old enough to have grown into a beard.

I tried out my Dr Ryan again, but he was firm. Diffident and uncomfortable, but sure of the ground he was standing on.

'Let me just have a quick look — ' I reached for the box of Ms in 1968. I was sure Mum's file and whatever it had to tell or not tell me was only a few beats away. But I didn't make it because, unexpectedly quick, he grabbed my arm and twisted it up behind my back, slamming me into the bookcase. I yelped. Without thinking, I kicked at his shins. It was his turn to yelp but he didn't let go. Out of the corner of my eye I saw the records woman looking grimly at us from the door.

'The police are on their way,' she said.

★ ★ ★

'Really, JJ?' was the first thing Tye said to me when he picked me up at the police station hours later. 'You think Maurice won't hear about this?'

'He's not going — '

'Stop being an idiot, JJ. You're on skid row with Maurice anyway after what you got Suze to do.'

'How did he find out?' I blanched.

'He's Maurice. He knows everything.'

'You saw where Jenna Stintini and the kids were living. We had to figure out where that scumbag husband of hers put the money.'

'Getting Suze to flirt with him at the bar — '

'He's been hid — '

'JJ!' He bunched his fists in the air and waved them in frustration. 'It's not about what you can get away with — '

'Not even Jenna knew.'

'Whether our client knows or doesn't know how we get information on her ex is irrelevant and you know it. Your charm and brilliance won't keep protecting you if you keep crossing lines.' He waved a hand at the police station we were leaving behind. 'Despite Maurice's undying devotion, there is a part of him that's got to be wondering if you're too much trouble.'

'The cops only gave me a warning so it'll be okay.' But I was deflating now, all the raw and rise subsiding on the tide of this truth.

'You attacked the security guard.'

'Not real — ' I tried to break in to protest.

'If you'd had the actual file in your hands, you'd be up for theft of government property.'

'But it wasn't.' I couldn't match his force, though, because he was correct.

'Wait.' He stopped in the street and spun around to squarely face me. He grabbed my forearms. 'You knew all that.'

I scrunched my face.

'What the fuck, JJ? You were willing to screw up your career.'

'It wasn't exactly a thought-through — '

'Shut up, JJ.' His palms in the air. 'You went to your aunty's funeral last Thursday.' He ticked off one on his fingers. 'You avoid me all weekend.' Two. 'You come in late, leave early, then stop coming to work altogether.' Three. 'I didn't realise this was going to set you off like this.'

'If you don't like the view you don't have to stick around.'

He slapped his thigh. 'Get some perspective.'

'My mother died when I was ten and my dad's been lying about it ever since.'

His face came to millimetres from mine, long eyelashes getting there before him. 'Get — the — fuck — over — it.'

My hand reflexed up to push him away, but he grabbed my forearm. We stared at each other, locked in intensity.

I broke first, twisting my arm out of his grip. 'I thought you were on my side.'

'I am.' He didn't blink.

'This is what being on my side means. I'm going to find out.'

'Then get the fuck smarter about it.'

*   *   *

We picked up fried rice, went to the newsagent for butcher's paper and textas and other getting-smarter stuff, and headed back to mine. The itch in me to start on Tye's plan meant we only spent a few minutes saying hi to Marge on the way through, but Rocco was with her so I didn't feel too bad.

Tye was right. I'd been too messy. I'd only acted on part of Maurice's stare-down-the-facts mantra. I had to get methodical.

Tye and I set about establishing a clear record of everything we did and didn't have. By the end of the night, we had a wall covered in butcher's paper mapping out everything I remembered about Mum's disappearance. I was the queen of categories, so it took a while to come up with an information matrix I was happy with: red for facts, blue for memory, green for opinions, yellow for vague ideas and grey for whatever else. On the other wall, above the side of my bed, we made a timeline of Mum's movements those last days. Fact-red only that side. At just after two in the morning, we took our bleary eyes for a walk around everything we had.

The ocean of empty between Mum leaving Peg's place at three-twenty-five and her time of death in the small hours of the night six days later funnelled its empty into my veins.

But Tye shook me by the shoulders. 'That's the point of this exercise, JJ.' His lovely voice soothing my inflamed insides. 'To fill up all that empty.'

THE MISSING PAGES

Tye hadn't wanted to make my excuses at work on Friday. Was worried about the Stintini case. Was worried that I wasn't. I was. Just not enough any more. He covered for me anyway. Said he'd check in with Suze and see where she was up to. He could see I needed to find something concrete to put on the Map of Mum. Had agreed there might be something in Peg's diaries if Dad had gone to the trouble of stealing them. Had helped me take the Map of Mum off the wall and fold it into my backpack. But on the way to Dad's I got more and more wound up because I was doing the exact opposite of what Tessa wanted. But maybe, as Tye said, even if this wasn't what she wanted, this is what she needed. Pumping the radio up to blasting volume didn't help, so I was glad when I arrived and turned down the track to Dad's. I parked the Austin about halfway up between the trees and in the bushes, hidden nicely from roving eyes.

Now that I was stopped, though, I found I didn't want to get out and face what was waiting. The car was a turtle-shell protection around me and my fingers thrummed against the steering wheel. My mind, skittish as a foal, darting forwards and back. The house in the distance hooded and watchful: blinds drawn against the heat. It probably knew I was the enemy by now or was there still a loyalty to Mum in between its cracks?

A bird flew straight at me, tearing away from the windscreen at the last second. It got so close I saw right into the bead of its black eye. I wound up the window and knuckled into my palm. It was only a few seconds later that the heat tumbled me out of the car.

I kept behind the tree line, out of sight in case Dad wasn't where he should have been, but it wasn't as straightforward as I'd planned. The grass was long and snaky between the trees and the fence, and my feet got caught in it. In the far end of the paddock a cow caught me in its eyeline. I froze, but it was too late. It took a few steps towards me, alerting the others. A roan took the lead and trotted in my direction like X marks the spot, the others falling in behind. Big side to side belly joggling. Nothing wrong with Dad's eyes if he happened to be looking this way from wherever he was.

I threw myself into a low huddle run, fast along the grass line as best I could, until I reached the gate where they wouldn't be able to follow. They petered out to a bewildered stop. I wanted to be sorry for them. Max, in the next paddock, took a few hopeful steps towards the herd. But there was a fence between them and a bullring through his nose tethered to a stake, and he knew all of that.

I made it level with the house and got behind the rusty combine harvester that had been peeling paint from its skin since before I was born. As I'd figured, Dad's ute wasn't in the yard, so that was a good start. I filled my cheeks and blew the air out. The morning sun was just getting going on laying shadows down so Dad still had plenty to do, what with only one set of hands left to do it all, and he was farmer slow.

In the kitchen there was a new jacket over the back of a chair like a bruise. Tessa would have been behind getting it for him, as if it could make up for something. There were the remains of only one meal across the table so I knew that if I opened the fridge there'd be a bit of order in there and a fresh set of plastic containers with the days of the week on them. She must have made a quick recovery; that, or such was her level of devotion to Dad's wellbeing.

I checked the benches for Peg's notebooks. I moved through the house, lifting, replacing, being careful. Deep down, I knew I wouldn't find the diaries. It wasn't that I didn't believe he had them, but it was too much to expect that he'd leave them out for me to pop by and pick up. Although I had held out a small candle for finding them in his wardrobe or under the bed.

I investigated the toolshed for good measure. My watch reckoned it was time to get out before Dad came in for lunch, and I did want to go. On the other hand, I still had nothing. I wiped the residue of grease from the tools down my jeans, the smell pinging me back to a time when Dad was just about God, sorting out an engine with a grease tin and a rubber band. 'Give the motor a kick, JJ.' I'd turn the key and away it'd roar.

'Good job, JJ,' he'd say, as if I'd been the one to turn it over.

For a while when I was a kid I'd got it in my head not to go to the toilet at school. I liked the ovals of the plastic seats, but I didn't want to sit on them. I held on and on all the way home on the bus. 'Not again,' Tessa said when I dashed into the clump of boxthorn bushes at the end of our track. Tim got so mad he'd just march off. After a couple of weeks, Tessa took off, too. Nobody told Mum they were leaving me behind.

Then one day I had a spot that was just right between two bushes in front of the strainer post. I got my knickers off and had them bunched up in my hand. I was squatting and about to go when I felt a charge in the air. I went still. A bird was going on in the gum tree above me. But that wasn't it. I went in deeper. It was behind me. I turned as far as I could without falling. Then it broke over me and I couldn't believe I'd missed it. The hissing was coming from a bloody big brown up on its belly aiming at my bare bum. I shot out of there like a bullet.

'Tim, Tim,' I screamed. Tessa pelted back down the track to me with Tim hard on her heels.

'There's a worm. There's a worm. It's up on its hind legs and hissing.'

Tim tore off up the track towards the house and Tessa grabbed my hand and towed me along behind. When we burst into the house, Dad was already there, his shotgun lying across the kitchen table, Tim handing him bullets. Dad's calm hands loading them up, his steady eyes checking the sight line down the barrel of the gun. He swung it up over his shoulder.

'Stay here.'

He slid one foot and then the other into his boots, lifted his beaten hat off the nail and his footsteps thudded down the path. I raced to my bedroom window, glad Philly was out with Mum. I watched Dad until he was a speck swallowed by the trees. The light glinted from the gum tree leaves. I sat by the window making finger patterns in the dust on the glass — rainbows and high half suns — waiting for Dad.

There was one gunshot and, ten minutes later, a second.

As soon as I saw him, moving like a shadow through the gaps in the bushes, I raced out of the house.

'Did ya get him, Dad? Did ya?'

'Got em both, JJ. Snakes come in pairs.'

'Where'd you put em?'

'Over the fence.' He grabbed me by the back of my T-shirt as I turned to bolt off down the track. 'Time for that tomorrow. You get in the house and help your mother with the tea. She'll be back soon.'

He must have seen something missing on my face because he reached out and mussed the top of my head. 'And don't you be doing that any more. Plenty of good toilets at that school we send you to, or wait till you get home.'

I walked beside him up the track, making a game out of keeping in his shadow.

Standing in his shed now, I rubbed my palms along my jeans again, all softened by the idea of

Dad's hand on my head. In that moment I wanted to believe Dad so badly my hands shook. I wanted to believe Tim had picked up the butter box by mistake.

I heard Blue, one of Dolly's, bark a long way off. It was time to get out of there. I took a quick inventory to see if I'd disturbed anything, and then I realised I was busting to pee. I swayed for a moment undecided: the long trip home holding it in or a quick trip to the outback toilet shed?

I heard the flies before I even opened the door. Big, fat, blowsy ones. I held my breath and dashed in, counting. Now it was just Dad on his own, he didn't have to change the pan that often. I had my jeans undone and peeled down before I'd counted to four. I was not even up to twenty-eight and I was buttoning up again. Under a half a minute. Record. That was when I saw the butter box beside the old copper washing machine that was still there from when the toilet shed used to be a laundry.

Bastard.

My eyes took a moment to adjust to the dark. The pale wood of the butter box announcing itself in the gloom. I lifted the lid, but it was all empty space inside. I sat back on my haunches, relief rolled up in the disappointment, like twisting fingers. This box must have been Mum's. I fitted the lid back on, smoothed my hand over it and turned to go.

But there they were — a stack of black notebooks butted against the tin wall opposite the toilet pan. I kicked a can across the shed. It skidded and crashed. I was in after it and kicked and kicked and then missed and crashed my boot into the wall.

'Fuck! Fuck! Fuck!'

All fucked out, I stood there panting in the quiet, hands up against the wall in among the cobwebs.

I gathered the notebooks into my arms and then carried them down the track, tipped them onto the passenger's seat and climbed in beside them. I didn't start the car because my arms were concrete heavy on my lap and the ignition too far to reach.

The cows had ambled back to the far side of the paddock, but Max stared straight at me.

It was Blue's bark, closer now, which finally got my hands working and the key turned. The car got on the track and followed the potholes and curves to the road. It went past Pete's place, down the hill, but not over the creek. The car came to a halt just beside the ford. A full stop. I took my hands off the wheel and they fell like stones back again into my lap. The heat sweated me up and the blood in my head got itself pulsing, so I had to unwind the window, then chock the door open, but it wasn't enough, so I got myself out and wrapped Peg's diaries in a shirt from the back seat and headed down to the cool of the creek.

The sky was burned free of clouds and dragonflies skimmed over the dank, dark surface of the water. As I got closer, a frog leaped from a fallen tree and into the water, its charcoal body no bigger than my thumb, sinking below without a splash.

My feet got lost in the slow cold of the water, the detritus collecting around my calves, clinging and then sweeping away with the current, on to the next thing in the way. I hunched right over and trailed my hands in the chill. A bird called and nobody answered.

I wiped my hands on my jeans and opened the first diary. There was no date. I flipped through the pages. *The sugar tasted like salt today and I saw a box of good cherries at the shops.* No dates anywhere. Oceans of Peg's kind of ordinary. I kneaded my palm. And settled to proper reading.

It was in the fourth diary that I found something. But not words. There were a whole lot of pages ripped out. I ran my index finger along the jagged edge left behind.

'Fuck.'

He was always one step ahead.

TIM'S LEAD

There was one person in this family who might just be on my side. And right then I needed him. I loaded the diaries back into the car and drove the quiet farm roads to Tim's place. As I pulled on the handbrake in their driveway, Shelley was down the steps of the house to greet me, her wide eyes smiling and her fair ponytail swinging.

'Got the jacket you loaned me,' I said as I opened the door.

'Thought I'd lost it forever.' Shelley grinned her big-as-a-moon smile, walking me through the rose bushes and up on to the verandah. I'd often thought she was so sunny because of the roses and all that love and appreciation. Even her dad was a steady, light kind of bloke.

'What's cooking?' Shelley asked, because she was far too polite to ask why the hell I had turned up on their doorstep for the first time in a year.

I shrugged. 'Around at Dad's. Had to pick up something he took from Peg's.'

'Tim'll be in for a cuppa soon.'

'Your dad?'

'Rounding up cattle in the Dargo.'

'Playing house, then?'

Shelley grinned again. 'Think Tim's coming around. He's worried it's a breach of my dad's trust if he sleeps up here.'

The fly-screen of the front door slapped shut behind us and the cool of the dark in the corridor got its arms about us.

'Funny boy, that brother of mine.'

'He's got morals. Like your dad.'

I sewed my lips up tight so not a sound could get out about how Dad might not measure up to his publicity.

I followed her into the solid weight of the Baxter kitchen. The kind of sturdy money could buy. Big-bellied canisters, floral curtains that hung to the floor, a carved oak table. Things that held time.

'You need fattening up,' Shelley said. She put her arm up to showcase her muscles through her own comfortable layer or two.

'Bring it on.' I pulled the cake tin to me and yanked at the lid.

'Help yourself, then.' She laughed.

'I'm practically family.' I had the moist chocolate cake out and on three plates before she'd got the cups and saucers organised. 'Do we have to wait for Tim?'

'Maybe for the second piece.' She sat down opposite. She twisted her hands together and leaned forwards. 'Now that you're here . . . '

'Mmmm . . . ?' I said with my mouth chock full.

'Could you talk to him?'

'About?'

She shrugged. 'You know . . . '

I put the cake down. I kept my eyes on her, emptying the space between us.

'It's been six years,' she said.

'You're only twenty-three.'

'I want babies.'

It was like a stab in my guts, right next to where my maybe-baby was giving growing a go.

'Why don't you propose to him?' I said, trying for lightly.

'He'd just say no.'

She was right. There was a dark place in Tim, deep down below the waterline. He was smart enough to know there'd been something up between Dad and Mum, but not smart enough to know that whatever it was had nothing to do with him and Shelley. I screwed up my eyes for a second. That needed to go on the Map of Mum under 'weird shit'. Tim couldn't make a decision about Shelley until he'd worked out what was wrong with Dad and whether he'd got the same wrong.

'He doesn't listen to me,' I said.

'I know.' She grinned. 'But it was worth a shot. If even you thought he should settle down.'

I leaned over the table to flick her on her arm.

'Why didn't he go to your Aunt Peg's funeral?' she asked.

'You're asking me?'

'Told me he had to finish drafting the last of the cattle before Dad headed off, but Dad couldn't have cared less.'

I took a bite and closed my eyes to get closer to the mint in the chocolate.

I saw Tim, ramrod stiff, refusing to get in the car to go to the cemetery to bury Mum, his skinny body shaking with the effort of keeping the pain all locked away. My eyes flew open at a sudden brush against my calf. Shelley burst out laughing and the cat hunkered back and launched itself into my lap. I got my hand to my heart and cringed away from its settling bones.

'It's only Clementine,' she said.

'Black freakin demon.'

She rolled her eyes.

'Has Tim had any nightmares recently?' I asked.

Shelley pursed her lips. 'A couple.'

I raised my eyebrows over the top of the cake.

'Ah,' she said, realising.

'Yep,' I said. 'Death dredges up a thing or two from the dark.'

The fly-screen door squeaked open and flapped shut.

'Little sister,' Tim said by way of hello. His long, football-fit limbs strode out of the corridor gloom. I slapped his hand away but too late: he had my cake up and into his mouth. He dropped it back on the plate, half of it wolfed away. 'Now that's how you eat Shelley's cakes, JJ. You've gotta commit.'

He went over to the sink to wash his hands. His moleskins, glove-tight and finished by a carefully chosen leather belt; a big improvement on the bit of twine Dad favoured. Why he thought he was like Dad I had no idea.

'To what do we owe this honour?' His back still turned, scrubbing dirt from his nails.

'Been round at Dad's.'

He turned and made a mock sign of the cross, wiping his hands on the tea towel. 'How was he, then?'

'Out.'

He dried his hands and kissed the back of Shelley's neck. 'That so?' he said, his eyes on me. 'Doing the rounds, then. Seeing Tessa next?'

'Nah, did that a couple of days back.'

A look of 'here we go' raised his eyebrow and settled over his face.

'I didn't do anything,' I said defensively.

'I dropped in a casserole this morning,' Shelley broke in to defuse the tension, 'She seemed good, given everything.'

'At least she's sworn off drinking for a bit.' Tim backed off and laughed. He balled up the tea towel and threw it at me.

I caught it and dropped it on the table.

'Now Tessa's off the turps, just you to sort out,' said Tim.

'Roses look good,' I said, deliberately ignoring him, and looking only at Shelley.

He laughed again, showing us his straight white teeth. With that and his mussed sandy hair, he could have been December for sunbaked and farm fresh in the Young Farmers calendar.

'You and the old man. Peas in a pod,' he said.

I snorted. 'Off your pills, mate?'

'Me no looky, me no see,' he said. 'Now, what you need is a boyfriend. Relax you a bit.'

Shelley hit him. 'Leave her alone.'

'What?' he said, all injured. 'You think so, too.'

She screwed up her face, caught out.

'What happened to that Tye bloke?' asked Tim, still full of grin.

'Still around.' I folded my arms, smug, because for once he was way wide of the mark.

'You'd be left on the bench if the amateur psychologists were picking sides.'

His grin widened even further as he tipped forwards to tap the table. 'Yet here you are, still all messed up, JJ. So what do you need?'

'Me. What about you? You should bloody tal — ' I began, but Shelley flicked the tea towel at Tim.

'Stop winding her up.'

He opened his arms wide. 'It's too easy.' The front of his shirt slid open and a glint of silver shone from around his neck. It took me a second to recognise the cross Mum had given him on his first communion. We'd all got one except Philly who didn't make her communion until the year after Mum died. I didn't know where mine had got to.

'Still wearing that?' I asked.

'What?' His hand closed around the cross. 'This?' He did a 'it's nothing' wave with his hand.

But this was what I'd come for. For this small light in the darked-out room I was stuck in on my own. Mum and Tim had been tied up tight together. He saw her in a way none of the rest of us did.

We all knew the story.

Mum had been wearing a new day dress she'd just finished sewing. Nobody else noticed. But after the milking Tim had burst into the kitchen with his little-boy energy. He flew straight at her. He put his hands up to her waist. 'You look real nice, Mummy.' I wanted that seeing on my side.

'Missed a good funeral,' I said. 'Mrs Nolan

had her talons out, though.'

'I hear you kept out of her way.'

'Did you now?' I bit into the cake. 'She tell you herself?' He shrugged a yes.

'She's certainly doing the rounds, then.'

He picked up the slice of cake Shelley had slid before him and bit off half of it in one go again. 'Nancy's not a bad old stick.'

'She's a bloody nosy cow,' I said, with my mouth equally full of cake. 'And I don't need her apology after all these years.'

'Old man's been weird since Peg kicked the bucket,' he said. 'Thought it best to stay and keep an eye on him.'

'You were with him?'

'Needed a loan of his vice about that time.'

'What kind of weird?'

Tim shrugged. 'Edgy. Bit my head off when I told him he needed to put Max out to pasture.'

Shelley shuddered. 'Hate that bloody bull.'

'Like an old man and his mongrel dog,' said Tim. 'Stuck with each other.'

'Max IS a mongrel,' said Shelley.

'I tell him nearly every time I'm over there, but the other day he flew off the handle.' He nodded at me. 'You've got time on your hands, JJ. You should talk to him. Find out what's got him cranky as a cut snake.'

I laughed.

'I mean it,' he said, suddenly serious.

A dead quiet followed.

'I tried,' I said finally. 'After Peg's funeral. Same old. Hasn't told me one straight thing in more than a decade.'

'You think this has got to do with Mum, then?'

I told him about Mrs Tyler. I told him about the calendar, about Peg's diaries. I pulled my backpack closer and reached in to take out the Map of Mum. He reached for Shelley's hand. He watched me, saying nothing as I unfolded it and smoothed it flat against the table. Both he and Shelley moved in closer, his eyes busy on the forest of colours where only red facts should be.

'Mmm,' he grunted. He turned to scrabble about in a drawer in the sideboard. Found what he was looking for. Held it out to Shelley and me. 'If you're after facts, you'd better see this.'

I took the photocopied page in the clear plastic sleeve from him. 'Where did you get this?'

He waved a dismissive hand. 'Round at Dad's. Just gathering dust there. Thought it needed a bit of looking after.'

I ran my index finger over the facts and figures of Mum's death on the certificate. 'Mmm,' I grunted back. 'Nothing we don't know here.'

He nodded. 'But it's something.' He gestured towards my Map of Mum. 'You can turn at least one of those things red.'

He was right. I'd had a question mark over the exact time. And now we had the doctor's name. Shelley found me a red Texta and I made the new additions.

'Reckon you should talk to Nancy. I reckon she's got more on her mind than an apology.'

'She's just a bloody busybody. Mum didn't even like her.'

'Grow up, JJ. She drove Mum to the station. You say you want facts.'

277

'Why haven't you spoken to her, then?'

'I'm not the one constructing timelines and maps.'

He stared me out.

'I'm not interested in her stupid opinions. I'm after facts.'

'In that case, you should check out that address in Mum's Mass book.'

'I never saw — '

'Ninety-five Righton Street, Richmond,' he broke in.

'You remember it?'

He did a half shrug.

'Why didn't you check it yourself all these years?'

'I'm not like you, all broken and bloody, and holding on to all of this.'

'Me?' I exploded. 'I haven't said boo to any of you for fourteen bloody years.'

'You never had to say anything, JJ. It was always saying it for you.'

The cat yelped as I stood up, flinging it from my lap.

'What about you?'

'I'm getting on with my life.'

'You can't even propose, you gutless wonder.'

He glared at me, and sent an uneasy glance towards Shelley, who was busy looking out the window as if she was wondering when it might next rain. But she did her own glaring at me as soon as the coast was clear.

'Maybe I shouldn't be chasing it down then, either,' I said. I wanted to know how far he'd go. He liked to pretend it wasn't any of his business, but underneath I could see he was all burn to know what happened to Mum, just as long as I'd be camouflage he could hide behind.

'Maybe,' he said, calling my bluff. He took his cup and saucer to the sink, rinsing them under the tap.

I let him crash things about a bit. Then he turned back. 'Ever get there to see her?' he asked, tone all reasonable curiosity now, nodding towards the end of his road where the cemetery was.

'What good would that do me?' I narrowed my eyes, wondering what new bait he was laying out.

He shifted like he couldn't find a comfy spot against the sink. I didn't miss the look he exchanged with Shelley, though. 'Dunno,' he finally said.

'What about you? You ever go?'

'Too busy.' He got his arms crossed up.

I let the silence do some work.

'Maybe. Sometimes,' he said.

'Does she talk to you?'

He shook his head like he had to get rid of a fly. 'She's dead, JJ.'

With my elbows to the table, the hollows of my palms made beds for my eyes. The darkness made more things possible.

I felt the heat of Shelley's hand on my forearm.

'Look,' Tim said without any hint of her compassion. 'If you're even half serious, you'll go to that address. But maybe not knowing suits you a whole lot better so you can keep your tortured-soul act up.' He cracked his neck.

'Dad's a good bloke, JJ. Been through hell.' He bared his teeth. 'So either put up or shut up.'

'You can't have it both ways,' I spat. 'You can't figure out what happened to Mum and protect Dad at the same time.' I smashed one fist into the other. 'Because sure as shit he's hiding something fucked up.'

Tim turned away, two hands gripping the side of the sink, shoulders hunching, making a cave for his chest. I felt the strain of all the knots he was tied up in from where I sat, and the red in me dissolved with a pop. I wanted to get up and put my hand to his back. But we weren't like that. In the stillness of him I saw it was even worse for him — I felt the years of its rust — this tug between the loyalty for the lying living and loyalty for the beloved dead. And he didn't have the red to help him.

'Got to get back on the tractor,' he finally said, voice evened out. 'You should go. See Mum. If you think she's got something to say about all this, it'll be there.' He turned fast and pecked Shelley on the cheek. 'Shelley will sort you some roses.'

After he left, Shelley brought the kettle over to pour boiling water into the teapot. She put the kettle back on the stove and sat at the table again. 'See what I mean about Tim?' she asked.

I nodded, still too churned up to trust my voice.

She didn't say anything else. Instead she turned the teapot three times. I stared at the blue rosebuds across the china long enough to let the silver of their outlines put down some roots into me. Blue roses were always tricky to interpret. They weren't in Mum's book. She said they could mean something as simple as love at first sight or as complicated as reaching for the unattainable. She'd taken my two hands and weighed them in hers, smiled her tired smile deep into me. 'Sometimes you got to feel, here,' she placed the tip of her index finger to my heart, 'for what the flowers are telling you. You're a feeler, JJ. That's a powerful thing.' Then she pointed to my head, nodding like it had the same power. 'With this and this,' pointing back to my heart, 'nobody will be able to put a thing over you, JJ.'

'I haven't seen this tea set before,' I said.

'Mum's. Wedding present. Dad had it put away when she died. I was going through the attic.'

'My mum would have liked them.'

'Dad said my mum did.'

'Was it hard for him to see them out and being used?'

'He said you have to draw a line sometime and go on living.'

'Do you miss her?'

'I miss something, but it's all talcum powder stuff because I never knew her. Better than what you and Tim go through, though.'

'Hard to say — ' I began.

'I don't have nightmares,' she cut in. She drained the last of her teacup to make way for the new. 'Go see your mum. At least you had one you remember.'

WHAT NANCY REALLY KNEW

The spray of Shelley's all kinds of red and pink roses across the seat beside me meant that at Tim's gate I could do nothing but turn right towards the cemetery. I couldn't ignore all that love and appreciation. At the wide iron gates I turned off the rumble of the Austin's engine and wound down the window. I couldn't figure out if the hush of the breeze was telling me to grow a backbone and get out of the car, or drive the hell away fast. I had Mum with me every day so maybe I didn't need this under-the-ground, only dirt thing. The crowing stutter of a kookaburra cut into the hush, but I couldn't track it down when I looked for it in the tall pine trees encircling the dead. I opened the car door.

I used to like the weight of time here, with the weeds pushing up through the baked hard ground and the broken gravestones, but that was before Mum went under it. I got the roses into my arms so I could smell them. The Catholics were right up the back and there were a lot of Protestants to get past first.

I couldn't remember where she was so I wandered up one row and down the next, reading names, dates, all the love contained to the most affordable number of letters. Not Mum's, though, I saw when I found it. Dad had spat chips about the *sister* part, but Aunty Peg was paying so there was nothing to be done. He'd sworn out of his window in the ute, Aunty Peg had smiled out of hers, and I'd sat in between.

I kneeled to Mum's grave and felt to see if she was any closer. I couldn't feel her at all. I thought about dumping the roses and getting away, but I was there and she hated dead flowers, so at least I could give her fresh ones. I flicked away the old stems withered dry in the plastic vase at the end of her gravestone. Tessa must not have been for a while. I opened Shelley's newspaper and laid the new flowers out, reds by reds by pinks, just like Mum and I used to. The blooms like velvet footsteps across the newspaper. I took my time feeling out their fullness, texture, height and rightness as I put them in the vase, as if there'd be dozens of Sunday eyes next morning sizing things up, or swimming in whatever it was I was pulling together. I tried to imagine Mum's hand on my shoulder, reaching over me to straighten one rose, push another a heartbeat away. I reached right into the ground for her, right down, but she still wasn't there. I tried not to let it knife at me, but it got in anyway. I attacked the centre of my palm with my nails, then squeezed my hands into fists and held them at my sides. I was trying to stop all the palm attacks because my skin there was a mess. Before I'd even counted to three I was back ripping into the skin again, full up with self-disgust that I'd even imagined there could have been a sign from Mum about what to do next, all neoned up and flashing, just because it was a cemetery.

I punched the newspaper into a ball and jumped to my feet. But a car was pulling up at the gates and I didn't want to get nose to nose with anybody, so I dropped the newspaper and curled up on a grave further along with a tall enough stone for a bit of cover. Chin to knee to chest, waiting for them to get in and get to whatever far corner they were headed to so I could slip out unremarked. I did have something new to investigate for the Timeline, though: not a sign from Mum, but Tim's address. It was something for my mind to work on while I waited to get away from this place of dirt and stones.

It was taking so long, though. I peeked around the headstone hiding me. Shit. She was headed my way. There was something in the way she leaned into one hip. Then she stopped to fan herself with one hand and I knew what that something was. It was bloody Mrs Nolan. She moved her basket from one arm to the other and kept coming. And that meant it must have been bloody Tim! What was he up to? I bet that bastard rang Nosy Nancy. I got one arm to the other around my knees and squeezed, trying to Alice myself smaller. Mrs Nolan's shoes scrunched against the tiny pebbles, closer and then closer. I shrank, dropped my head between my arms, hissed in air between my teeth and waited. And she did turn into Mum's row. She groaned as she got to her knees beside Mum. I hardly let any air out of me.

'I know you're there, JJ.'

Fuck. One hand flew to my forehead, the other close after. Hidden and exposed at the same time.

'No shame in visiting your mother.'

I glanced around the gravestone to look at her. She kept at what she was doing. Big black-red roses sticking out of her basket. I decided to play it as if I hadn't been hiding. Not that I expected her to buy it.

'Just taking a break, Mrs Nolan. Hard work, arranging flowers.'

'Still got a mouth on you, then.'

'They for Mum?'

'Some for your mum, some for mine,' she said, pointing towards the rows beyond to where her mother's grave must be. 'You did a good job.' She snipped off half of the stem of one of her blooms and then did the same with two more, bringing them into height alignment with Shelley's roses. 'You always had the knack.' She placed the blooms in among Shelley's, sat back, head to the side. The new roses pulled the idea of the whole deeper. It was something, adding in that sorrow. She studded one up and down, shifting them all. Again, it was right. I moved to get closer in to them.

'Your mum had the knack, too,' she said.

'She loved your roses.'

'That's why they're here.' She dusted her hands off. 'Didn't see you after Peg's funeral.'

'Needed a smoke.'

She grunted.

'Funerals are difficult,' I said, my voice

heading higher in defence.

She touched this rose and that. Picked at them like guitar strings.

'After what happened at Mum's funeral,' I said, all heckles raised, and sharp with blame.

'Nothing happened at your mother's.' She flicked the cut-off bits away between the graves.

'You attacked me.'

'I tried to help you. You were hysterical with grief. Your father had no idea.'

'You tried to take me away from my family.'

She buttoned her lips, shook her head, looked out through the sighing of all those pine trees. Looked back at me, measuring something. 'I . . . ' she started, then lost her way. Took a long breath in, gathered her words. Started again. 'I felt that without your mother, you were . . . in some danger. You were . . . sensitive, like Peg had been as a girl. More so, because you didn't have her lightness to go with it. You were a broody, fiery little thing. I felt you needed a firm hand to keep you on the straight and narrow. Jack . . . ' She shook her head. 'I didn't think he was the best thing for you.'

'You said I had the devil in me.'

'Peg's devil. I said you had Peg's devil in you.'

Something popped in me. I dropped into a squat, my head buried in the cave of my arms. From the deep dark this new truth came rushing at me. All these years I'd held to this devil thing. It'd made sense. The way Dad had been after that, as if he blamed me for something. But she hadn't meant it; she'd just been worried about me without Mum.

I felt her hand on my shoulder, gentle. 'But look at you. You proved me wrong.'

I looked up. The sorry in her looking down on me. 'I shouldn't have said it at all. But at the time . . . ' She shook her head, did some more looking through the trees. Scratched under her jawline.

I tried to clear the buzz in my head for this new thing she was trying to say. The build of it in her. I stood up, knowing I needed to be on my feet for whatever was coming next. She hadn't been trying to find me at Peg's funeral to apologise. It was for this. What was coming now.

'I was mad with grief myself,' she said. 'Grief and guilt. And a terrible responsibility. You see, at the time, I thought it was my fault you didn't have a mother.' She rushed on now, the words tripping over each other to be out in the world now that she'd started. 'That morning I drove her to the station, I mentioned something in passing that I thought she already knew. But I was very badly off the mark. She didn't know, and I didn't know she didn't know. I thought . . . And . . . ' She shook her hands in the air. 'And now that you've grown up it's time one of you young people knew.'

A terrible chill snaked along my spine.

Was this it?

I wasn't ready, after all. All the not-ready coughed through me like pollution.

'Did you try to tell Tes — ?' I asked to put off the thing right in front of me.

'There's no saying one word against your father with Tessa. There'd be no point telling

287

Philly and Tim, either.'

'I know.' I shoved my fists under my armpits. 'But I bet it was Tim who rang you as soon as I left his place.'

She nodded. 'Yep.'

I couldn't put the knowing off any more. All the dominos that had been set up over the years were crashing down, one after the other.

Mrs Nolan licked her lips and looked out over the dry yellow paddocks beyond the cemetery. 'It's about why your mother threw Peg out of the house.'

'But Mum didn't. It was Dad.'

'What?' Confusion broke across Mrs Nolan's face.

'Mum wanted Peg to stay. Dad said he threw Peg out because she was a sinner and a bad influence on us kids, which we figured out later must have meant she wasn't a stranger to sex outside wedlock. But Mrs Tyler told me at Peg's funeral it was because she'd actually been pregnant.'

'Peg? Pregnant? Kathy say that?'

'Only for a bit.' I shrugged. 'Mrs Tyler said she miscarried.'

Mrs Nolan shook her head as if she hadn't heard straight. 'Can't be right. Peg would have told me.'

'Mrs Tyler said Mum told her. Said it was a bloke called Sydney.'

'No, no, no.' Mrs Nolan shook her head faster. 'Peg and Sydney never had it away.' She plastered her palm to her forehead. 'Sydney wasn't even sweet on her. He was just a fella, bit older than the rest of us, late twenties, who liked her the way we did. She was full of spark and devilry, crossing lines the rest of us were too scared to even look at.' Mrs Nolan let her palm fall. 'Sydney felt sorry for her, gave her the house *because* she'd been thrown her out on the streets, and he'd won the deed gambling the night before. When he sobered up he went back to ask for it, but she'd sorted all the paperwork so he couldn't get his hands on it. He drifted back north eventually, none of us kept in contact.'

'So why would Peg tell Mum she was pregnant to him, then?'

Mrs Nolan squinted into the sun. 'Oh God.' She stumbled back, reached out for something to stop her fall. 'Because she *was* pregnant, they were so close, she couldn't have hidden that. But not to Sydney.' Mrs Nolan's face collapsed and her hand went to her gaping mouth. 'Peg had to lie about who the real father was.' Her wild eyes locked in on mine, communicating a new urgency. I both wanted her to tell me what it was and wanted to back the hell away from it, fast. A noise like a wounded dog came from her.

'It was me. That morning she left. I was the one who told Sarah the truth.' She whimper moaned and hunched all the slow way to her knees. 'I didn't mean to. I didn't mean to. I didn't know. She'd just come back from settling you back to bed. I was trying to make it up to her for having said that terrible thing that set you off. Saying that she'd done a good job with you, given what she'd found out when you were a bub and how the shock must have bled into you, because of how sensitive you were. I thought I was telling her something she already knew. But, to her, it was so much more.'

'What? What?'

'Jack. It was Jack. Jack was the father of Peg's baby.'

'No.' Just the one, horrified word. Not this. Bile shot up from my stomach. I clamped my mouth shut, gasping in air. Dad and Aunty Peg. 'What are you even talking about?' I bent to shake her arm. 'They hated each other.' Then it hit me. That's why they hated each other. 'How can you be sure?'

'She told me herself. Had to tell someone. It had only been the once. Jack had been broke. He didn't know where he was going to find the money to fix the tractor before the harvest. Sarah in hospital with Philly. Both Peg and Jack mad drunk. I assumed your mother had found out because a few days after she came home from the hospital Peg was told to leave.'

My body gave way too and I crumpled to my knees, facing Mrs Nolan.

'She must have realised a few weeks later she was pregnant to Jack. She could never have told me that. Could never have told anybody. No wonder Peg lost her grip on life after she left us. It wasn't the separation from Sarah and the isolation all the way over there, it was the guilt and the lies. It would have eaten her from the insides.'

Mrs Nolan and I locked in together, eyes burning across the abyss, hands reaching. We held, forearm to forearm, drowning in too much knowing.

'That's why Mum left her wedding ring behind that morning,' I said, my voice cracked open, dry.

'Sarah . . . ' Mrs Nolan broke in over the top of my words, not hearing me. 'Sarah looked at me like she'd never seen me before. Her mouth kind of . . . lost shape. I thought she was having a stroke.' Mrs Nolan's wet face looked into mine, pleading. 'I didn't know. We were finishing up the tomatoes. I thought — ' Mrs Nolan released one forearm to cover her eyes, still gripping me with the other hand, panting air in. I inched closer, not knowing what to do, how to comfort her — me. When she spoke again, I could hardly understand her through her gulping gasps.

'I thought . . . ' Her head rocking from side to side. 'At first I thought her distress was because something so private had got out. That I knew about Jack and Peg.' Mrs Nolan slapped her chest for emphasis. 'But then Sarah just kind of lost her stuffing. So I went down after her, both of us in the mud, and I realised she hadn't known about it. That I'd been the one to tell her. I tried to apologise. Tried to take it back. Explain it away; such a long time ago, just the once, both out of their right minds, crippled with sorry ever since, nobody else but me knew, I'd never told a soul. Hadn't. But none of it landed.'

The sobbing overtook Mrs Nolan. Her body racked with the telling. This terrible truth, all these years. No wonder she'd needed to find me, to excavate all of this from her insides. I saw.

My hands dropped back to my lap, now my eyes over the parch of the paddocks to the far horizon, back down the years to my poor, poor mother in that mud.

Mrs Nolan righted herself enough to go on, drawing me back into the more.

'Sarah didn't say a word about it. Just put her palm up to stop me, shut me down. She took off her apron, like she was shedding skin, let it drop to the dirt. She went straight inside. She took pen and paper out of the drawer and disappeared into the bedroom. When she came back out to the kitchen, she picked up an overnight bag that had been packed and ready behind the door; didn't even stop to wash her hands. Didn't say a word on the way to the train. I was bitten through with misery. But at the station she did this one thing.' Mrs Nolan clasped her hands over the top of mine. All of her burning into me, wanting me to understand, to be there in it with her. 'Sarah put her hands out, just like I'm doing to you now.' She shook mine. 'Then Sarah looked straight at me, as straight as I'm looking at you now. 'It's not your fault, Nancy,' she said. 'It's theirs.' Her eyes as clear as clear, but I could hardly see her back for tears.' Mrs Nolan released a bit. 'And that was the majesty of your mother. I thought I was telling her something. But now I realise. I was telling her so much more. It wasn't just the affair. It was the baby they made together and the lies they told together, drawing them in to a circle and leaving her on the outside. Making a fool out of her. Yet Sarah's last words were all of comfort for me.'

Mrs Nolan's folded her lips as if to put a stop to any more of the pain, but she lost the battle and it surged from her, and she let herself collapse the rest of the way to the ground.

I let her go as a fresh horror found me. It made sense now. Why Mum had only stayed twenty-five-and-a-half minutes at Peg's. Just long enough to have it out with her. The crime Peg's even more than Jack's. After their parents' deaths, it was just the two of them, so close they were almost sewn into the same seam.

What a terrible betrayal — skin flayed to bone.

PHILLY'S PUZZLE PIECE

I was completely done by the time I made it, shattered and bruised, back to the boarding house. This thing, it was just too big. It changed everything. How could Jack have done it? This moral man of God. He destroyed so many lives: Peg's, Mum's, ours. He had so many secrets. I stepped over all Tye's messages pushed under my door. But Rat-Tail must have been hovering because he was there before I could even get the door closed.

'He says you got to ring him.'

I couldn't. 'It's too late. Ring him in the morn — '

'He says no matter what time, but.'

'I'm too tired.'

'He says no matter what you're feeling, but.'

Rat-Tail wasn't going anywhere. I knew exactly what Tye would have said to him. I reluctantly pushed past him. 'Okay. Okay.' But Rat-Tail still wasn't letting go. He shadowed me all the way to the phone and hovered.

'Really?' I asked as he watched me, head bent, eyes intent on my dialling fingers, but I knew there wasn't much use expecting him to be anywhere else until it was mission accomplished.

'Hi,' I said for the benefit of Rat-Tail, giving him a significant fuck-off look. He repaid me with the biggest grin and a flare of grateful shot up in me for his sweetness in the middle of all this.

'Don't bloody 'Hi' me, JJ.'

'It's — '

'I don't want to hear it. Maurice says you better call him tomorrow morning, Saturday or not.'

He hung up.

I looked at the phone as if he might still be in there somewhere. Felt Rat-Tail's small, round eyes on me, so I replaced the phone gently. When I looked up, Rat-Tail had disappeared behind his door but it wasn't closed. 'You all good, JJ?' he asked in a little voice.

'Yep.'

His pointed face showed back around my side of the door, all concern.

'You're a good guy, Rat-Tail.'

His face broke open with another of his sweet grins. I returned as much of it as I could.

I numbed my way back to my room. What now?

The springs of the bed squeaked as I collapsed to sit on to it, folding forwards to grab my ankles, just breathing. The desert on the Timeline of Mum's last days radiated urgency into my back from the wall behind me. Because despite all this revelation, there was still nothing to put into all that empty. Eventually I gathered my limbs for the supreme effort of getting up. I Blu-Tacked my Map of Mum back up along the other wall. I picked up the fact-red texta. Then, in big bold letters, right before the red of Peg's miscarriage and Jack throwing Peg out of the house I wrote: *Jack and Peg once, Jack and Peg baby.* I stood away, heart burning, to take in the bold of it. I stepped back in and added: *!!!!*F*!!!!*

★   ★   ★

The next morning, despite Tye's warning, I still didn't ring Maurice. I stayed in bed. I kept my back to the wall where the Map of Mum and all that terrible red was.

Eventually, when the day had stretched long into the afternoon, I dragged myself to upright.

I picked a black dress off the floor and pulled it over my head. Didn't bother with underwear. I pulled a hat down over my hair and stabbed sunglasses on my face, even though there was nothing but grey out my window. I walked to the red phone box on the next corner where nobody could overhear anything, fed in some coins and rang Maurice.

'JJ,' he said, giving me a lot to work with. I pulled up something out of the earth and stuttered my way through an apology and some of the highlights of the past week, but avoided the things that were unthinkable. He let me get right to the end. Didn't interrupt. Silence was among his superpowers.

I didn't like the continued silence so much once I was finished, though.

Finally, he spoke. 'You have a week to sort yourself out.'

'What if I need more?'

'You ring me like a normal adult and we discuss it.'

Red surged through me. This wasn't normal. I didn't feel like an adult. My pillar-of-the-church father had sex with his wife's sister, got her pregnant, threw her out of the house for being a slut, and lied to his wife about the whole thing. That wasn't fucking normal.

'You had no right to ring my father.'

He didn't skip a beat. 'I'm the host. I issue the invites.'

'Not him. If I don't want my lying mongrel father there, that's my business.'

He was all silence.

I was all runaway red, but I still wasn't ready to throw my unwashed past at him to make him understand. Not until I made sense of it, or didn't; not until I'd fitted it into whatever place it would end up in.

'He doesn't deserve to be there. He threw me out because I went to uni.'

'Go back to the facts,' he interrupted quietly, his voice reaching out to steady me. His bloody 'facts sing' mantra. 'That fire in you, JJ,' he said. 'Don't let it consume the facts.'

I felt a swirl of guilt because I knew I was lying: Dad didn't throw me out, I left.

I was drowning in lies: his, mine.

'Here's a fact for you. You can stick your award. I quit.'

I hung up.

★   ★   ★

297

I left the phone box and took off, running, until my thongs tripped me, so I shucked them off and left them behind. Bare feet on hard ground. Eventually I came to a stop, lurched forwards, panting, holding my knees. When my breath evened out I found a tree and leaned back against the ridge of its bark, eyes closed. Minutes or hours ticked by and things smoothed long again so I had enough to look around to see where I'd ended up.

I was where I needed to be. I'd wanted to spare her all of this. Especially with everything going on with Ahmed. But now I couldn't. That thing that had nagged at me all night. I had to know if Mrs Nolan was right. Had she been the one to tell Mum this terrible truth? Or had Mum worked it out the night before in that argument with Dad, and that's why Philly had overheard her threatening to leave? It would make sense of why Mum'd filled the freezer with food. That overnight bag, already packed behind the door before Mrs Nolan had dropped the bomb. And then one thing more, something I remembered. Mum had come tipping-toeing in that night, after she thought we were asleep, to snuggle our blankets under our chins and kiss the top of our heads. If she took off because of all that betrayal, maybe that was enough to stretch across those six last days of Mum. But the way she'd reacted to Mrs Nolan's telling — as if she was hearing it for the first time — I'd bet Mrs Nolan was correct. Which meant there was something else that Philly might know to fill in all that space on Mum's Timeline.

Philly held the key underneath the layers of her denial.

I checked my watch. It was early for Philly, but she might be home. I realised how much I needed her.

She didn't show any surprise when I knocked. 'Call Tye,' she said as she went to close the door in my face. I stuck my leg forwards to stop her. She sighed. 'He's going nuts, JJ. Call him.'

'I did,' I say shortly. 'Are you okay?'

Smudged mascara. Chipped nails. Facts.

She turned away, leaving the door open, and headed to the fridge.

'Are you?' She turned back to pointedly look at my bare feet. She opened the freezer.

I saw the hole on the table where Ahmed's mosaic glass lamp used to be. That was a fact she couldn't deny just because she needed to. I wasn't sure why she was surprised that Ahmed had moved out because he'd been talking about it for weeks. I went up behind her and hugged her hard. She leaned into me for a moment before reaching to topple the container of ice cream down from the top shelf.

She flicked the freezer closed and crossed to the drawer.

'Haven't seen these cow pyjamas since you were fifteen.' I made an effort to be myself so she wouldn't suspect how much shit was going on beneath my surface. If she didn't already know about Jack and Peg, there was no way she could handle that now and I was worried I wouldn't be able to stop myself if she gave me even the slightest opening.

'Surprised you even kept anything so . . . not silky.'

'Not helping,' she said. She only had one spoon. She shrugged when I drew it to her attention. 'He didn't leave you,' she said.

'He didn't leave you, either.'

Philly turned at the sound of the key in the door. Ahmed stopped short, his satchel over his shoulder. 'I thought you were still at work, Feely. I left my soccer bag behind the laundry door.'

I looked from one to the other and made myself scarce. In the lounge my fingers itched to mess up the line of candles on her neat sidetable runner. It was more than enough that the mauve in the runner was the exact same shade as the circles on the couch cushions.

'I'm home early,' she said to Ahmed, 'because I'm in the middle of an emotional distress.' I heard her pick up her keys from the bowl on the kitchen bench. 'I'll leave you in peace to get the rest of your stuff.'

He followed her through the lounge, where I was, laughing as she opened the front door. 'You're wearing your pyjamas,' he said.

She looked down and covered herself with her arms as if she were naked. He reached for her hand, but she twisted away and ran into the bedroom. He tried the handle. 'Feely, open the door.'

'Go away. Don't muddy the waters now.'

'That's life, Feely. Water is always muddy. You move, you stir up the bottom. Being alive is moving. Open the door.'

'Go away.'

'Your head is so hard, Feely.'

I returned Ahmed's wave on his way to the laundry. The strap of his soccer bag went over his head and shoulder in one graceful move as if it knew its place. His aftershaved sweetness filled the air around him. No wonder Philly went for him. That and the way he built a whole new wardrobe with extra shelves at the passing comment from her that it was getting squishy for her clothes in there. He was the opposite of Dad. As Ahmed headed towards the front door, he twirled his finger around his ear in the way Philly had taught him. I didn't know whether he thought I was mad for hiding behind the rocker, or that Philly was mad for locking herself away.

'See you around, Feely. Soon.'

He opened the front door and closed it, staying on my side of the door, in the lounge.

Philly unlocked her bedroom and headed for the table.

'I knew the ice cream would win,' said Ahmed, opening his arms wide for her. Philly had her fists up and flung herself at him. He grabbed her and held her tight. 'I'm not leaving,' he said. 'Just moving out.'

'It's the same.'

'You really need to get used to muddy water. I'm just moving out so I can see you more.'

'It didn't make sense the first time you said it — and not in the seventeen times since.'

'But by number forty, you'll get it. Your head is so full of old facts, it's hard for any new ones to get in.'

'Because this is not a fact. It's . . . ' She threw her arms up and twisted away from him.

'Something different.'

'I'm not your mother. I'm not your father. I am not abandoning you.'

She stopped still. I crawled into the kitchen and hunched against the fridge hoping I could disappear.

'JJ,' she called.

I didn't say a word.

I heard her smack Ahmed. 'JJ told you, didn't she?'

'She gave me a hand to move a few of my things last week.'

'Bitch!'

'Actually, I find JJ very helpful girl.'

I screwed up my face and when I opened my eyes there she was, two inches away. 'What the hell did you think you were doing?' she asked.

'He didn't have a car.'

'You gave him the Cook's tour of your version of our past.'

'Nobody else in this family listens to me.'

'I don't want to be that girl. That sad little girl who lost her mother and . . . you know . . . the rest.' She mocked strangled me in the air. 'It's my life. I get to tell it my way.'

I locked away all the new things I could say about that life and bit my lip to make sure I didn't give in to the temptation. 'You share a bed with him every night. You'd think you could share some head space, too.'

'That's the point,' she said. 'It's not in my head. It's all in yours.'

I bit harder. Held my breath. Reminded myself over and over like a mantra: *Keep your mouth shut, don't break her.*

Ahmed appeared around the door. 'I gotta go. I don't want to be late for practice,' he said, pulling out something from his satchel. 'I've bought you a present.' It was a dreamcatcher as big as the kitchen clock and shot through with reds and pinks and golds. 'Now that I'm not here all the time — it will keep your nights safe.'

'It doesn't match the colour sch — ' she began.

He tapped his foot, his head to the side.

'Ah, that's the point,' she said.

'See, your brain does take on new facts when you give it a chance. A little bit of chaos is good for the soul.' He dropped his satchel by the door. 'I'll be back to pick this up after soccer, so put a nice coat over those nice pyjamas and we'll get some pizza. You can come if you're still here, JJ.'

'Thanks for deserting me.' I forced myself to laugh, which came out more like a hiccup, but I had to try to pull the normal back into me so I wouldn't lose it with Philly.

The door closed on his laugh, which had the lightness of a real one. I slipped away from Philly, grabbed a spoon from the drawer and dashed back to the armchair in the lounge.

She followed me, flopping on to the couch and snatched up the tub before I got to it. She ate alone for a few moments, then extended the tub to me. I dug my spoon in and slipped the cold into my mouth. I was glad to be there with her, just this simple of how-we-are together.

'What?' asked Philly.

She knew me so well. I stared at her, long and hard, trying to work out how I could ask her without telling her anything.

'No. No. I know that look. No.' She dropped the spoon and plastered her hands to her ears. 'La la la.'

'Okay.' I nodded. 'I'll do you a deal — I won't tell you anything, but you have to answer one question.'

'Nothing. I know nothing.'

She picked up the spoon that had fallen on the floor. It was a measure of her distress that she didn't immediately head to the kitchen for a paper towel and a new spoon. She hunched back in among her cows, getting her legs up close to her chest.

'You heard Mum tell Dad she was leaving.' I said it as gently as possible.

Her eyes darted left then right. 'I never told you that. I never told anybody.'

I let her think about that a moment.

'Oh,' she said.

'Yeah, you did. You told Tessa, back then.'

She blanched. 'I was just a kid. Probably didn't hear right.' I saw a flash of the grown-up woman, all bluff and smoke. I bet that worked with people who didn't know her. That's the thing. You might get away with living without a past, but your past can't live without you.

I won the stare-off and she bent to wipe the table with her sleeve. Underneath the glass were three magazines fanned out and a copy of *Alice in Wonderland*.

'That's where my book got to,' I said.

She followed my eyes. 'It's my book.'

'Mine.'

304

She snatched it up and hugged it to her.

'It's got my name on it,' I said. She opened the fragile hardcover of the book and turned over the sticky-taped first page. I pointed. 'See.'

'Just because you wrote your name on it.'

I threw up my hands. 'Okay, so it probably doesn't belong-belong to either — '

'It's mine now.' She put it behind her back.

I brought my eyebrows together. 'Are you reading it at the moment?'

The weight of things in her stopped up her words. Then she made the decision to lie and shook her head.

'So that's why it's sitting out here all on its own, away from its friends, all alphabetically ordered in your bookshelf,' I said, jumping from my armchair on to the couch beside her. 'And that's why it has a nice bookmark with a lovely pompom thing in the middle of it.'

The annoyed dark on her face ripped the years away and she was our little Philly monkey again, as if the past had stretched out its fist and punched me right in the face.

'You started reading after I finished it, the day Mum disappeared,' I said, my voice full of quiet. Alarm lit her up and got her off the couch. She took the book into the bedroom. I watched her and I let her go. For a moment I wanted to ask her to bring out Mum's special pink snowdrop dress so we could both sit under it as we used to when we were kids and missing her. But as much as I longed to feel this thing of Mum's, I knew it would be too much. It would undo me. It was better hanging quietly in Philly's closet rather than dancing with ghosts out here.

When she came back I was pretending to be busy with the ice cream again.

She plumped down on the couch and crossed her legs. 'I'll tell you what I remember, which is almost nothing, but you've got to promise you won't speak to me about it again.'

I nodded, fingers crossed behind my back, though, because she would have to hear it some other time. She had a right to know. When she could bear it. And maybe that knowing could shift something in her. Make her and Ahmed more possible.

'They were out by the tractor the night before she left,' Philly examined her nails and worked her cuticles, 'not realising I was in the long grass behind when they got stuck into it. Dad told her he was the head of the family, he made decisions. Mum flew at him.' Philly was speaking like she'd learned this by rote. I wondered how many times she might have said this in her head. 'She said he was more worried about what the bloody priest and his Southern Cross cronies thought than what was best for his own wife and kids. Told him all this stuff he'd done wrong. How he made Mrs Salvatino pay for their wheat after her husband died, even though the bill had already been paid, blah blah blah, and how she lay in bed beside him at night and she saw as much as God.'

Philly stopped. I knew there was more. I kept my mouth shut.

'So yeah, she said she was leaving,' Philly said eventually.

'She'd known that about him for a long time. Why leave then?'

Philly jerked straight. 'Look,' she said. 'She'd just had it. It happens to all of us. And, she did say — ' She stopped short. Looked at me apologetically.

'Say it.'

'No, nothing.'

'You were going to say — '

'We were so poor and — '

'And she said on top of that there was me.' I jumped in.

'No. No.'

I gave her a look.

'Okay, yes. Yes. But we were all hard. Four of us to feed and clothe. It wasn't just you.' She laid a hand on my knee.

I pulled away. I'd bloody known it all along, but still to hear it from her.

'Look. She said something else.'

I didn't look. Kept staring at that mauve runner.

'It didn't mean anything, but she said she was going to die.'

'What?' I swivelled back, on full wide-eyed stare. 'She was dying?'

Philly's head went into automatic shake. 'No. No. See, this is why I didn't tell you before. It's just a figure of speech. It's simple. They fought, Mum got mad. She took off, stayed with Peg, who made a mistake on the calendar, then Mum collapsed. Et cetera. Coincidence. That's it. You've got way too much time on your hands. Go back to work.' She stood up and paced the room.

Bloody Tye. The thought flashed between all

the other lightning strikes. Keeping Philly up to date with my business. He must have Philly's number memorised.

But I'd got what I came for. This was something else. Mrs Nolan had been right. Mum had a reason to go before she knew about Jack and Peg.

'So what was killing her?'

'Nothing. Nothing. Nothing.' Philly shook out her hands as she walked. 'She said she'd die if she stayed. If things stayed the way they were.'

'Instead she left and she still died.' But I could see it had taken everything Philly had to finally let that 'die' word into the world. With that and Ahmed moving out, I didn't want to push her over the edge. The way I'd pushed Tessa.

'You've got to drop this, JJ. There's no point to any of it. You're going nuts.'

Stung, the red sparked up. 'It's not nuts to consider the crooked road.'

'It's nuts to keep dashing down rabbit holes.'

'It doesn't add up, Philly. Something happened to Mum. You can't run away from it just because it's not black and white.'

'It's not like he did anything terrible. You can't keep making up a mystery because you want colour.'

I slammed down hard on that red but it octopused into too many tentacles. 'She wasn't at Aunty Peg's. It's like Mum waded out into the grey mist and disappeared. Then she turned up dead. If we could just make sense of those last few days it might feel more . . . ' I searched for the word ' . . . more survivable. I just want the truth.'

'The fucking drama.' Philly hit one hand into another. 'Knowing where she was doesn't change the ending. Mum's dead. You're not. That's the truth. Let her go.'

'You don't.'

'Do so. I've got a job. I'm pushing ahead.'

'You're spinning your wheels so fast you've got no time to feel. Why do you think Ahmed had to get out of here? Couldn't live with your speed, filling up all the corners of your life with activity, running from one thing to another.'

She came to a complete stop. Put her hands by her side. She did that thing she was so good at: drawing in everything so it was right where she needed it, close and tight and controllable. 'It's Aunty Peg all over again,' she said. 'All this . . . ' she opened her arms up ' . . . stuff you go on with.'

I put my hands in front of my face and crossed them like I was scrubbing something away, fighting against her tide. 'There's no stuff.'

'There's stuff, all right,' she said. 'Calendars and diaries, and driving Tessa to drink.'

I jumped to my feet, facing off. 'Who told you that?'

She took a step towards me and opened her mouth to say more.

'Shut up. Shut up. Shut up.' I grabbed my bag on the way out and I slammed the door behind me.

WHAT JACK ADMITS

Back at my place I took the red texta in hand. I hesitated. What exactly was the fact I thought Philly had given me? It was so tempting to write that Mum knew she was going to die as a stone-cold fact. Instead I swapped the red out for memory-blue.

I collapsed back to the bed and my eyes went over and over all the things on my wall and across my floor. Waves of hopelessness washed through me. Even with all this revelation there was still not one single fact that accounted for why Mum had left and where she'd been.

My eyes kept snagging on that address Tim had given me. It was in grey for miscellaneous since it might not have had anything to do with anything, but it was all I had. I turned off the light, wriggled out of the dress and burrowed under the doona. I was too done to even do my teeth.

*   *   *

In the morning, though, it didn't feel like I was any less tired. And there was something more, a kind of queasiness like I'd eaten something bad. I lay breathing in the dark under the covers, but eventually I needed to pee. I took my toothbrush and gave my teeth a thorough going-over in the bathroom. Then I spewed in the toilet bowl and had to clean them again. I sank back against the wall. Days were passing. I really needed to talk to Tye. If he'd talk to me. 'He has to,' I said aloud to the air, my hand on my belly.

Back in my room, I took the Map of Mum down, folded it again and shoved it into my backpack, along with an apple and a bottle of water. I considered going back to bed, but instead tugged the bedding up so there was no more temptation. That doona cover was a bloody ugly thing. Only old men didn't mind puke brown. Even Rocco had stuffed his under the bed. Although *Star Wars* wasn't much of an improvement.

Outside, the Austin was waiting for me in the street and I got in and pulled the Melways onto my lap. I figured out the idea of where to go and headed in that direction, pulling over a few more times to figure out lefts and rights because with all the other jangle in my head I could only hold a few streets in my mind at a time.

Hope and dread all twisting together in me. This address might be nothing. Could be something. Maybe I was about to find out where my mum had been. Why she'd really left. Maybe she had a bloke. Could I really handle that? After Jack and Peg?

It could flick Mum's light off in me. And I'd be alone and she'd be alone and that would be the end of it.

Who was I without the bloody great mystery clanging in the heart of me?

Then I knew it. As sudden as shit. That was fucked-up thinking and my life was all angled out because of it.

A couple more corners brought me into Righton Street. The normal of it was an affront to the adrenaline my heart was pumping. I cruised to the far end and stopped at the milk bar. I bought two Mars Bars and stuffed one straight down and put the other in the glove box for later. I got the car back down the right end, parked a few houses away from Number 95 and turned off the engine. The houses were jaw by jaw with short strips of green behind picket fences. Number 95 was not much different from any of the others, although there was a bush of camellias and a spray of impatiens, and the grass was manicured back to a crew cut.

I was glad it was me and not Tim, after all. This kind of thing hollowed you right out. I tried not to let the camellias and their missing-somebody-so-badly get inside me. Instead I tried to fill up with Mum, the feel of her, but there was too much swirl going on. Not being able to get at her dialled the panic up. I put my head down and tried to get more air in and out of me, nice and slow. Even then, my breathing sounded as if I'd galloped the last paddock home.

A bird called and I looked up with the surprise of it. I couldn't see the bird, but the impatiens in the garden of number 95 caught me. Their purple and pinks were so sure of themselves. Mum always stopped at their page in the flower book. Motherly Love, she said. Maybe Mum was in me after all trying to connect in the only way she could through this swirl. I opened the car door.

The front gate creaked as I clicked it open and left it wide after me. I went up the steps and on to the verandah, hearing the hollow of my footsteps against the wooden slats. The doorbell was tarnished from use. I pushed on it. The dring of it loud in the silence of the street. I took a step back and the adrenaline got to roaring in my ears. A kid about twelve opened the door.

'Is your mum or dad home?'

The kid shook her head. And a girl a few years younger than me came up behind her and put a hand on the kid's shoulder. 'What do you want?'

I looked at the sky through the branches of the tree next door. Too blue. And then I realised I hadn't said anything and I hadn't said it for too long.

'How long have you lived here?'

'None of your business,' said the older one.

'Sorry,' I said, shaking myself back into my body and telling myself to be less strange. 'My mum died a while back and she had this address, and I just thought your mum or somebody here might have known her. My mother's name was Sarah McBride.'

The little one shrugged a shoulder, while the older one was all concrete wall, giving nothing.

I cast around for something less confronting and aimed it at the kid who was the friendlier one. 'What's your name?'

'Louise Bridgton,' she answered before the older one could shush her.

'When's your mum back?'

313

'Tomorrow,' the kid got in again.

'That's enough.' The older girl skitted the little one behind her. 'You'd better go.'

I turned. Then I remembered. I took a strip of paper out of my jeans pocket. 'Can you ask her to call me? Just in case she can tell me anything about the people you bought the house off?'

'Sorry about your mum,' said the little one.

The older girl took the paper but scrunched it up as she closed her hand. That single thing, on top of everything else, was so pointy. She started to shut the door with me still standing there. The pointy thing began to spin and it exploded up and out of me. I stuck my Doc in the door.

The girl pushed the door against my foot.

'Get away,' said the kid, her voice all high and quick.

I came to my senses and pushed the door forwards enough to get my foot out. It slammed shut.

'Who was that?' asked a woman's voice from far inside.

'One of Dad's country cousins.'

So there was a woman-slash-mother in there, after all. Which was more than weird. Why did they lie to me? And then to her. I never said I was from the country. The world was bent out of shape. I was so over all this bloody lying. I tried the handle, but the door was locked. I knew it was no use, but the red was out and whipping about, so I screwed it all up for one great kick at the door.

★ ★ ★

314

The smell of bush-hard things was up under my nails as I slammed the car door behind me, my eyes on Dad as he yanked at a prickly pear.

'Saw your car on the road,' he said.

'Saw the ute down here from the bridge.'

'Give me a hand with this bastard, will you? Extra pair of gloves in the back.'

I bent down to pat Blue. She'd got old while I was looking away. She nuzzled her nose into me and I was grateful she hadn't forgotten me. I'd been planning to attack Dad straight away. Had been doing it all the way from Righton Street. I realised that deep down I had thought that address would tell me something. And the crazy-bad disappointment that it hadn't ate me through. There was something at that place that didn't quite add up, but I couldn't work out what, so I put my agitation down to the weirdness of the older one's hostility — that and crashing into another dead end.

So there was just this left. Full-on frontal attack on the open plains. I had to make Dad admit about him and Peg. And see if the shock of me knowing took us to some other place, back to why he and mum argued the night before. I shut the thought of Tessa and my promise to her out of my mind.

But suddenly, with him right there, the puff had gone. I watched him some more as I put on the long, stiff gloves that went over my elbows. It was like I'd been watching the same thing all my life. Dad in an epic war against one thing or another. Getting his whole body twisted, shoulder to the wheel and pushing like he wouldn't take no for an answer. We were in the bottom

315

paddock with the wild apple tree nestled into the elbow of Jean's Corner. No sign of Mum's scarf from around the baby cross left. I looked away from all that gone. Looked to where the sky was a clear blue and the creek was shined up with sun. 'Never known you to attack the prickly pear before.'

Dad grunted with the effort of digging out a large root. 'Things can get away from you.'

The sun went behind a cloud. 'Feeling guilty about something?'

He looked up quick, full of snake. 'What?'

I gave him a long look and left it at that. Dad's mission in life was to leave things alone long enough so they worked themselves out. I remembered back to another day when the sun was also hard and mean eyed. One of the workers had been in the kitchen filling up on lemon cordial before getting back out under the scorch. The kitchen was dark like a cave because of the winter-thick blankets Mum had got up and over the curtain rods to keep the burn of the sun out. Philly, Tessa and I were on the lino. Mum had wet washers for our foreheads and put a bowl of fridge water between us so we could dunk our washers in when they'd warmed up. Tim was on his bed with his own bowl of water and washer, and a Donald Duck comic. The worker had just got his licence, and he had his dad's ute for the week, so he was all fired up and needling every-body. Dad started slapping at his thigh like he did when he was getting fed up.

Tessa told me to stop moaning and get back to my book. I kicked her to shut her up, but I went back to reading anyway. Out of nowhere the worker pretended to trip over me.

'Hey,' I yelled, sitting up, fists ready.

'What?' he said, all innocent, but the grin on him was like he'd won a prize.

'You did it on purpose.'

He did this boxing thing, dancing about, punching the air. 'If you keep those eyes in a book, life's going to come at you with a few unpleasant surprises.'

The roar started in my tummy. When it exploded out, I saw Mum throw her tea towel into the sink like she was about to explode, too.

'Be blowed,' said Dad, getting up from his chair, his legs apart like an old bull. He gave Mum a wink, then swung around to the worker. 'First one to the gate.' He bolted out of the house with the worker on his tail. Tessa, Philly and I jumped up with the excitement. We charged outside, passing Mum, who'd picked up the tea towel and was shaking her head. Dad skidded into the ute and had it kicking over before the car door was closed behind him. He whammed the stick into gear. The worker had made up time and he was in his dad's ute, slamming into his gears. Dad's ute shot off down the track towards the gate. The young bloke shot off at the same time. Only he didn't get far. He'd rammed his gearstick into reverse and taken off in a mighty blast backwards — right through the wall of Tim's bedroom. I could still see the shock on Tim's face above his Donald Duck comic as the tail-lights came to a stop inches away from the end of his bed.

The worker's eyes were just as shocked above the steering wheel. Mum came flying out of the kitchen. The worker ground his gears again and took off. He got to that gate and that was the last we saw of him.

Dad spent a lot of time in front of the hole in the wall, tsking and shaking his head, muttering and measuring, getting his hands to his hips. I was right by his side as I always was in those days, squinting at the hole and holding the other side of the tape measure. After a couple of days, he got Tim to give him a hand to move the wardrobe in front of the hole. 'A bit of air-conditioning, mate, while we source the boards.'

Mum shook her head again.

For days after, Philly and I just had to look at each other to burst out laughing. 'What are yous two always giggling about?' Dad asked over the tea table.

'Nothing.'

Then he dropped his eyes back to his plate, and Philly would smash one fist into her palm and I would do wide, shocked, goggle eyes and we were off again. Even Mum smiled.

She was right, though: Dad never got around to fixing that hole. At uni, I didn't mind the all-nighters because I had left it to the last minute; I minded that it meant I was like him.

'Get in there behind, will you, love?' said Dad, pointing to the prickly pear bush he was working at. I got in there and pulled out branches for him to buzz-saw. We went at a good clip, getting into the rhythm of it. We had a good patch done when he put the saw down.

'DDT in the back, love. Grab it for us.'

He had two DDT packs in the back.

'Expecting me?'

'Just big hopes. Reckoned I'd get through one can pretty fast.'

'Reckon you were right,' I said, taking in the great swathe of prickly pear he'd chopped into.

'What are you going to do once it's all cleared?' I strapped the can onto my back and hauled Dad's over to him.

'Keep it like that.'

'What did you do with Jack?'

He did laugh that time. 'Your mother was always on at me to get this done. She'll be happy looking down now. She didn't want Jean's Corner grown over.'

'Her corner, too.'

'Taught me to swim, she did.' He adjusted the straps and pointed at the place he wanted me to start. 'I wouldn't go near the water before that.'

'Because Great Aunty Patty drowned in the creek when she was just fourteen, and your mother had you all scared of the boogey man in the water.'

'Righto, righto. You've heard the story before.'

I grinned. I was silent a while as I remembered how much pressure I needed to get the spray of poison just right and landing where it should. Dad had us all jet-packed up as kids, and we'd walk the paddock spraying artichokes. The family that poisoned the earth together stayed together. I got back into the swing of things pretty quick and we each took an end and worked inwards.

'It's coming on dark,' said Dad, after a while.

'Best pack up. Suppose you'll want to get off home?'

'I could stay for dinner.'

A trapped look slid behind his eyes. I unstrapped the drum on my back, unsheathed my arms from the gloves. The breeze of the early evening cooled against the sweat on my skin. I stretched my arms in front of me. All the sweetness of being tired in your pores, but not weary with the bone-grinding weight of it.

'Storm coming,' Dad said.

I looked up and the sky looked back, a steady, stormy blue on the edge of night. 'We'll make it a quick bite, then.'

We both got into our cars and ambled across the flat. My brain had flattened out so I wasn't thinking at all. That kind of a sky had that effect; it thickened the air so that thoughts seemed like little things. The ute ahead of me growled with the effort of getting up the hill, and then jarred and jumped over the potholes across the home paddock.

We washed up in the laundry before Dad went to get his slippers. I took out Monday's and Tuesday's dinners and put them in the oven. Now that the moment had come I wanted to push its raft back out into the creek. The physical work had rocked Dad and me into a whisper of tired softness, and that was worth something.

Still, I stiffened my resolve: Jack had a lot of admitting to do, and I'd been down too many dead-end streets.

Dad and I sat over the just-hot-enough food. The cheese of the lasagna spreading and flattening on the plate.

'Where are the pages you took from the diaries, Dad?'

'Used them for dunny paper,' he said without a blink. 'Thought it was funny.'

'Did you read them first?'

'Too dark in there. Would have been a load of rubbish.'

Dad was getting closer and closer to his food, shortening the time between plate and mouth.

'Why'd ya take the diaries?'

'Thought there might be something bad in there.'

I wasn't used to the truth from him. It took the words out of me for a moment. 'Like what?'

'If I've been hiding anything, it was for your own good.'

'So you admit it finally. You are hiding something.'

'I'm not admitting anything. I'm just saying that sometimes a father has to do things his kids don't understand. Can we just drop it?'

'Drop what?'

'Nothing.'

'What?'

Dad shovelled food in like there was no tomorrow. The stones of the wall were mortared back into place. All that whispered softness had disappeared in me and we were back to opposite shores.

'Why did you say Mum had left us that first day?'

'She shouldn't have gone off like that. A woman doesn't leave her family. Wanted to turn you lot against her when she finally got home to punish her for taking off. I was sure she was coming home.'

'So why did you change your mind the next day and tell us she was at Aunty Peg's all along?'

His eyes darted around the room, looking for a hole to crawl into. His eyes ended up on that photo of Mum, which was still propped against the wall on the bench.

'I calmed down,' he said, his mouth full. 'It wasn't right. I shouldn't have been turning you buggers against your mother.'

'Is that so?' I said, and I couldn't keep the scepticism out.

'What else could it be?' He hunkered down into his plate. His eyes slipping sideways to Mum's photo again.

'You know Philly and Ahmed are sleeping together.'

'Stop stirring.' He shovelled in the fork again. He was almost down to the plate-scraping stage. I noticed he was taking less in at each mouthful to make the whole thing last longer.

'Tessa's been drinking for months.'

'What the hell is wrong with you?'

'Me?' I couldn't hear what was going on in my own head any more because cymbals were making such a racket. I scrabbled about in there, but I couldn't get still enough to locate my well-made plan. 'What happened to you when Mum died?' I said, voice pumped up with accusation. 'It was like you'd died, too.'

'Don't talk rubbish.'

'Dad, it was like we were invisible.'

322

Jack tapped the table faster and faster. 'You were never satisfied after your mother died. You carved me up with a knife and a fork, then left me out to rot.'

'You were the parent, Dad. I was ten years old. You left me to rot.'

'Ten years going on one hundred. You were a bloody handful. Still are. Causing trouble from one end of the ship to the other. If Tessa's drinking — if Philly's living in sin — it's your fault. You've never let any of us settle. It's all raw and bleeding and picking at scabs for you.'

The screech of the chair as I pushed it back ripped through the house. 'I haven't said a word to you about Mum's disappearance for fourteen years.'

'The bullshit. You never had to *say* anything, JJ. Your snarky face was always saying it for you.'

I picked up the plate and threw it across the room, smashing it against the fireplace, showering the kitchen with bits of cheap china. The shock of it rushed me out of the house. It was Blue who found her way into my arms, brushing up against the thing that needed to be brushed up against. I pushed my face into the long, tough hair on her neck. Counted down from ten, over and over, and Blue stood there counting with me.

The dark had taken over the sky, layering it now in a thick threat. A flash of lightning split it in two. I went back inside and ignored Dad, who hadn't moved an inch. I went to the fridge and pulled out three sausages. I took them out to Blue and patted her as she wolfed them down. Went back inside.

'Hey, they're for my lunch tomorra.'

'Not any more.'

'What the hell?'

'Blue was hungry.'

'She's a working dog.'

'Everyone needs love, Dad.'

I sat down opposite him again. 'You got Aunty Peg pregnant.'

'The bullshit out of your mouth.'

'Mum's watching everything you do. Same with God. You're down here burning through your heaven points right under their eyes, right now.'

'I'm dead weary, JJ. Just give it a bone.'

'You were tired out years ago from all your lies. Admit it. You and Aunty Peggy. Under Mum's nose.'

'Leave it alone.'

'Where did Mum get to after she'd had it out with Aunty Peg? You know as well as I do that she didn't stay there.'

'You worry a snake's nest long enough, one of them bastards is going to rise up and bite you.'

'That's the plan.'

'I don't know. All right.' His fist slammed into the table. 'I don't know where your mother went.'

'You do because she rang you.'

'I made all that up. Why do you think she never spoke to you buggers? Because she didn't ring. I made it up. That's the lie. And I can't be sorry about it. I didn't want you blokes hurting.'

For a moment I believed him and the anti-climax of it was all cold water. But then I saw a shift in his eyes as they paused on Mum's photo again and then headed back out the window and over the paddock he couldn't see in the night.

'Did she have a friend in Richmond?'

His hand stopped tapping.

'How would she know anybody in Richmond?'

'The address in her prayer book.'

He stood up abruptly. 'You go there?'

I nodded.

He spread his legs, hands to waist. 'And?'

I couldn't work an 'and' off my tongue.

He leaned over to steady himself on the back of the chair.

'I been there, too. The day after the police came, told us your mother was gone. I went to that address. Said they never heard of her.'

'Who did? Who lived there back then?'

'Some doctor bloke.' He rubbed his hand against his thigh. 'I believed im. That doctor, he looked steady.'

'There were two girls there this morning. Slammed the door in my face, actually.' I said. I didn't add any of their other weirdness.

He wiped the back of his hand across his mouth. 'Righto, then,' he said softly. 'End of the line.'

'It can't be.' I balled my fist. 'There has to be something else, Dad.'

'Who says so?' He stared at me. 'Just because a thing is hard to live with doesn't turn it into a crime.'

'What did you fight about the night she left?'

'How can I bloody remember?'

'Really?'

A snakey look passed over his face. 'Peg, then. I probably told her about Peg.'

'So you're admitting it. You had sex with Peg.'

He looked cornered.

I didn't breathe.

'Okay. Okay. The answer is yes.' He held his hands up in surrender. 'It was just the once. Years before. When your mother was pregnant with Philly. Sarah was tired and sick and scared and miserable with being pregnant again. And it was all my fault she was. I was the man. And I just . . . ' He shook his hands in agitation. 'Just. Just couldn't take it any more. And Peg . . . ' He petered out.

'And the pregnancy?'

'I don't know nothin about any pregnancy.' He flicked it away. His eyes flashing between me and the past. 'I felt that bad about it. All those years. I had to finally tell Sarah. So I did that night.'

'Stop lying,' I yelled. 'It was Mrs Nolan who told her about you and Peg. By mistake, the next morning.'

Defeat greyed across his face.

I let him sit with it for a while. But then I didn't. 'But Mum was already leaving you, anyway. Why?'

He held every muscle tight, like an animal in a spotlight.

'Forgot to feed Max,' he got out at last.

'Don't be stupid. It's pitch black, and it's starting to pelt down. Leave him to the morning.'

He stopped still on his way to the door. Turned to point a stubby finger at me. 'When I get back, you be gone.'

'It's going to come out, Dad. It will.'

The first thunderclap came loud and I jumped. Lightning cracked across the sky outside the window.

He got to the door and leaned on it, saying nothing. The air between us thickened until I could bear the tension no longer. But I did.

'You're right,' he burst out. 'Okay! I'm a hypocrite and a liar and all the things you've ever thought I was. She knew it. She knew it, too. That's what we fought about that night. She told me she was leaving because she'd had enough of me.'

I stared at him. This was the tawdry nothing it had come down to. All the puff went out of me.

'I didn't believe her. It wasn't the first time we'd blued,' he said. 'I could have worked on her the next morning. Settled her down. Just like always. But then bloody Nosy Nancy told her about Peg, and she left before I could explain.' His voice went up like he was the victim. 'Tell her how sorry I was. Tell her she was more to me than the air I breathed.'

He held my gaze with indignation for a few beats and then his face collapsed. Shame and sorrow oozing from his eyes like rivers of pain. 'Truth is, I'm down on my knees every day of my life asking for forgiveness. But it'll never come. I'm a sinner.'

Tears blurred my eyes, too. All that rice digging into his knees as he knelt beside his bed every night. It had started back then.

'Your mother was a saint.' His voice broke. 'I was the husband. My job was to protect her.

327

Instead I cast her into hell. I as good as killed her.'

I was full of not knowing what to say. This new father of mine. Raw and broken.

'It wasn't your fault,' I finally got to. 'She died of natural causes. It was just her time. Remember Silver, the brumby? It was just her time. That was all. And the only bad thing was we weren't there to be with Mum. But none of us could have saved her. Not one of us.'

And the truth of it was like water surging through me, gushing and raging, carrying everything before it.

'You made one mistake,' I continued. 'You're right. She would have cooled off, eventually. She just needed some time. She wouldn't have left us.'

His eyes veiled with confusion — lost between the yes and the no of it. His hand dropped from the door handle, he stumbled away, out into the storm. I got the dustpan and broom and swept up all the broken bits of china.

THE SIZE OF TRUTH

I pulled my hair away from my skull as I lay on my bed. I didn't even know how I had got home from Dad's last night. There was pelting rain and hectic, whining windscreen wipers. There was the vomiting pity of all those years wasted, chasing ghosts and shadows. What do you do when you come to the end of a thing? A full dead stop. A thing you thought would end up somewhere. And that somewhere would have made sense of the whole way leading up to it. But instead you were left with palms open, full of empty.

I traced the web of cracks crawling across my ceiling until I came to the end of the line. What did I do now? My hand went to my stomach. Then I let it drop. One thing I wouldn't be doing was having a baby just to fill up the wasteland I'd created.

I remembered that science book I'd had before Mum died. Every cell in our body is supposed to be renewed every seven years. Maybe we were supposed to do that with our stories, too. I'd ossified mine shell hard around me. But this was the fourteenth year. Could I let it shed its skin this time round?

I filled up with the possibility of it, groaning to a sitting position, back against the wall.

I saw Dad hunched over between the trees

that morning before we found out Mum died, I saw him standing in the kitchen in his trousers pulled up by twine, I saw the stubble across his chin, I heard him telling Mrs Nolan that he wouldn't be letting Sarah down again, he'd be keeping the kids, every single one of them.

Mum's Timeline on the wall pulsed at me. I'd been such an idiot. I got out of the bed, took it down and lay it along the ground, like I had that first night with Tye.

How had I stuffed up with Tye so badly? All I had to do was pick up the phone. Even to let him know I couldn't talk about it, but I was alive. Would it have been so hard?

I unfolded the Map of Mum from my backpack and put it beside the Timeline.

And Maurice? Quitting. Did I really do that? I winced. I sat back and scratched my head like I was a mad thing, wondering when was the last time I'd even washed my hair.

I picked up the red texta and weighed it in the palm of my hand. Bloody facts. I finally had them. I knew what had to be known. I uncapped the texta and bent over the Timeline. I added the details of the fight the night before Mum left. Then I leaned further over to add to the Map. I hesitated over using opinion-blue or fact-red. Since it was the end, it had to be red.

I'd found out everything. It had been a run-of-the-mill argument the night before. Maybe worse. Enough for her to need a few days away. But then she found out about Peg and Jack. I could see why he hadn't told her. Mistake? Yes. Gutless? Of course. Flawed? Definitely. But not a

330

monster. He hadn't admitted to knowing about the pregnancy and maybe he didn't know since Peg lost the baby, anyway.

It all added up. Why he hated Peg. Why he chucked her out of the house even though he was as 'loose' as she'd been. Mrs Nolan's revelation accounted for Mum being furious with Peg and only staying twenty-five-and-a-half minutes. She probably slept in some cheap room somewhere. We'd never find out where she'd been those last three days. And Philly was right. We didn't have to.

The futility of it ripped through me. I slashed red across the Map, and slashed it back the other way. I zigzagged that texta back and back and back, again and again, until I couldn't see through the blear in my eyes; until the paper tore and I was running red across the floor.

Suddenly Tye was there, his arms around me.

'What? What?' he asked over and over, gentling me as I sobbed out words that meant nothing. He held me, rocked me, murmured to me. Then I was back in our kitchen the day Mum left. Her rocking me in her muscle-hard arms. Me smelling the dirt of the tomatoes on her apron.

Eventually the grief evened out through me enough for us to lie on the floor, arms around each other, and I was full of the kindness of him coming to check on me in his lunch break even after everything and the not-deserving of me.

'Don't you see?' he said. 'This is what you wanted. Now you can get on with your life.'

'But it's such a tiny truth. How can such a tiny thing set me free?'

He laughed. 'It doesn't matter the size of the truth, it just matters that you finally have the answer: the facts all add up.'

I gave him a lopsided smile at Maurice's words from his mouth. He full-smiled back. Maybe he was right. It just didn't feel like it. Surely, after all this dark time, the truth should come with a marching band and streamers.

'I didn't think you'd come back,' I said. 'After that last phone call.'

'Me neither,' he said, his fingers playing across my belly. 'But Philly rang me about your fight. She wanted me to come check up on you.'

I captured his hand under mine. 'Thanks.'

He smiled back. I took a big breath. If this was the beginning of the rest of my life, I'd better make a start.

'I'm pregnant,' I said, as raw a fact as you can get.

He drew back to look at me, really look at me. He placed his palms on my cheeks and cradled my face, staring deep and deep into me. 'Is that a good thing, or a maybe thing, or a definite not good thing?'

I smiled at his 'JJ-ism' as he called them and shifted so I could cradle his face, too.

'It's an I've-got-no-idea thing.' I paused to search for the first time since I knew there was a baby growing for what the parameters of this might be. 'It feels important that it happened while I was looking for Mum, really looking for her, not just expecting to see her around every corner.'

He nodded seriously.

'So maybe that's enough to bring it the rest of the way into the world.' I paused again, looking for more of it. 'And maybe it's not. It's too early for us. You're even younger than me.' I screwed up my face. 'What about you? What might this be in your world?'

He shifted to lie on his back. He put his hands behind his head and studied those same cracks I'd been considering. 'I don't know yet. It's new for me. What I can say is that I don't hate the idea.'

I surprised myself by laughing at his cautious, careful phrasing.

'How long have we got?' he asked.

'Maybe a few days more. It's just gone six weeks. If we're not going to do it, I think it's only fair to send it off before it's too much, so it can find the right place for it somewhere else and settle in there.'

He laughed gently, turning back over so we could hold each other again. 'Bed?' he asked.

★ ★ ★

When Tye had gone, I did feel more resolved, clearer. So it was a small thing I'd found out. Maybe that's how life was. It had to be enough. But, still, things kept turning me around and sitting me up and turning me around again.

I cast about my room for something to make my mind stop jerking from this to that. I wished I'd bought a telly after all. I turned the radio on. The verdict was in. They were going to try Lindy Chamberlain for murdering her nine-week-old daughter, Azaria, in the shadow of Uluru.

I turned the radio off again.

Aunty Peg's diaries were on the bedside table. I pulled one on to my lap, opened the first page and smoothed it down. *The oranges were lovely today*, I read. The ordinary in it soothed me. I got worried when her writing got loopy and charged across the page. And there were some wild things like: *the rainbow over the house pressed me into the carpet this evening*. But my eyes swept past those bits. For a while I avoided the section around the torn pages. But then I made myself be braver because that's what the truth had to mean.

There was some interesting stuff about money further along from the torn section, which Peg had to have written around the time of Mum's death, although the dates were all mussed up. How she wanted to give Mum the money she'd needed but how Mum wouldn't take it over her dead body. *Now she's the dead one*. Direct quote. That was Peg. Blunt to the point of pain.

A terrible wave of sadness washed through me. It probably meant Mum had to stay in some dive those last days rather than the half-decent place she'd planned on to take some time away from us, further than Jean's Corner where I always tracked her down, further than Peg's where she'd be more worried about Peg, right off into the world where nobody could bother her. Then I shivered and pulled myself together. Knowing what I knew had to mean that I couldn't get pulled back into the deep like this. I had to stay above the waterline. I pulled out Mum's cameo from under my pillow. The truth had to also mean I could finally do this. My fingertip traced the raised contours of the delicate cream curls of the woman's head and shoulders just like I had done as a kid. The clean lines of her elegant beauty and all it had made possible for us in that bare world, with the cold wind always moaning through the cracks and the colour leached from the threadbare carpet. I smiled, pulled back into its magic. Yet I also saw the spot of discolouration which I'd thought back then was part of the design.

Still, this thing passed down from Mum's great-grandmother was full with so much beauty that it was time to share it with Philly and Tessa.

I got out of bed to lay Mum's cameo out in the open on the desk. I considered it for a few moments, then realised I was busting, so pulled a pair of jeans up under my nighty and dragged a cardigan over the top. I checked the corridor and dashed to the bathroom, where I scrubbed my face and cleaned my teeth for good measure because there was no way I was planning on making the trip again any time soon.

Back in my bedroom, I closed the door and fell against it for a moment. The phone dringed at the other end of the corridor. I slid to the floor. I'd been hoping to hear from Philly. I'd never walked out on her before. And now I had something good to tell her that might make it right again, but I couldn't say it right now. There was nothing in the tank.

The footsteps coming down the hall were all in my direction.

'Phone, JJ.' Rat-Tail knocked on my door.

I dropped my head into my hands.

'I know you're in there, JJ. Been watchin. Your brother says it's real important.'

Tim had never called. So I pulled myself upright and followed Rat-Tail back down to the phone. I pointed my finger at him until he'd closed his door and then I said, 'Hello?'

'Old man went and got himself gored,' Tim said.

'Oh fuck.' Guilt lasered through me.

'He'll live. Stupid bugger. Was out in the storm last night feeding that mongrel, Max. He's pretty banged up. He's in the Royal.'

I put the phone down so gently I could hardly hear that final click, as if I didn't want to cause one more terrible thing to happen.

THE MOP UP

It took a while for me to find a park at the hospital. The last time I'd come from work on the tram, direct to the records department. Shame heated through me at the memory. How the hell did I get so off track as to end up with the police? What was I even thinking?

I kneaded my palm all the way to the entrance. Digging in as if I could get right to the bone.

Philly saw me before I saw her.

'Why didn't you phone?' she called out. 'We could have come together.'

'Last time I saw you it was all doors slamming.'

She winced. Folded her arms and looked down to watch her high heel shift on the concrete. I touched her arm. 'It was me. Sorry.'

'You were a bitch, but . . . '

' . . . it's in the past,' I said, finishing her sentence.

She called up a ghost of a smile. 'Something like that. See, it's in your favour this time. Tim says Dad's lost a lot of blood.'

What I had to tell her about Dad, about Peg, that could wait. In the meantime, I slipped Mum's cameo into her hand. 'Mrs Tyler kept it for us.' I folded her fingers closed around it and squeezed. 'Though you might like it for a while.'

The sweet Alice smile she bathed me in was worth the parting with Mum's cameo for now.

We turned at Tim's voice. He was running across the car park. He pecked Philly and then me and folded his arms, legs apart — all serious-man stance.

'Stupid bastard,' he said. 'Don't know what got into him. Should have sent that bastard bull to the knackers years ago.'

'He loved Max,' said Philly.

'Loved that he was as cunning as a shithouse rat,' said Tim. 'Same as him.'

'Hard to send yourself to the knackers, I suppose,' said Philly. 'Wonder what made Max go off like that?'

I groaned. Screwed up my face.

'Fuck me, JJ,' said Tim. 'Out with it.'

I dug into my palm, feeling for the next step. Tim and Philly were all eyes on me.

'Dad and I had a fight last night.'

'You rang him?' Tim's voice was all lit up.

'I was out there.'

'Again? Jesus, Mary and Joseph, JJ. I thought you told Tessa you were going to leave Dad out of it.'

Philly stepped between us. 'Are you saying you left him to bleed to de . . . '

I stepped back like I'd been punched, put my hand up to ward something off. 'Course not.' I winced. 'I left before. Actually, he told me everything. It was . . . good.'

Philly shook her hands in front of my face. 'Don't tell me. I don't want to know.'

'I bloody do,' said Tim. 'What did the old man

say? And what did you say back that sent him out to Max in the middle of a bloody great storm?'

I folded my arms, just like Tim. 'We both said plenty.' I wondered if my voice gave away my guilt. I should have gone out to tell him that I understood everything. Made sure he knew that. Even that I was sorry. Big bloody sorry. Sure, he did the wrong thing, past a month of Sundays, but it wasn't worse than what most of us did in a lifetime. Mum was right. It was just that he wanted to look good in front of the priest, his friends, us. Was that such a bad thing? Especially when the alternative was admitting you had sex with your wife's sister.

'You said plenty about what?' insisted Tim.

'If you think you can blame me for bloody Max — '

Philly stepped in again. 'No one's blaming you for Dad's pigheadedness, JJ.' She herded us forwards. 'Let's just bloody get in there.'

Tim dropped his arms. Shook his head and clipped me around the head, before turning away to walk in with Philly. There was no bloody way I was telling him about everything until I was good and ready.

'Tessa up to coming in?' he asked.

'Probably already up there,' Philly said.

'Where's Shelley?' I asked, bringing up the rear.

'Told her not to come.'

Philly shook her head.

'What are you shaking your head for?' Tim asked.

'She's part of the family,' Philly said. 'You know she loves Dad.'

'Where's Ahmed, then?'

'Shut up, Tim. It's completely different.'

'Cause he's a wog?'

She punched Tim on the arm. He staggered back and crashed into the wall, gripping his arm and wincing as if he'd never play another match.

'And the Oscar goes to . . . ' she said.

Tim straightened up. 'Careful, Philly. That kind of childish behaviour undermines your I'm-the-adult-in-charge image.'

'Shut up, Tim. Dad's lying up there seriously wounded,' she slapped back.

'What's with all white, anyway?' He swept his arm over her white pants suit. 'Somebody will be taking you for a nurse.'

'Doctor,' she set him right.

★ ★ ★

Last time we were sitting around like this was after Mum died. Now, it felt — not good — but something, that all that was behind me. A flash of the Timeline and Map of Mum all squashed up and sticking out of the top of the rubbish bin in my room came to me. I shuddered about how close I'd been to the edge.

Dad's right arm was bandaged up along with the top part of his chest. The grey of the floor matched the grey of the walls, the grey blinds, the steel beds and the metal machinery. Only Shelley's roses made a difference up there on the shelf above the bed where Dad could see them if he could get his eyes open. Yellow for peace. I didn't know about peace. But surrender I could come at.

'If the horn had gone in a couple more inches to the left . . . ' said Tessa.

'Lucky bastard,' said Tim.

'We're coming apart,' said Tessa, eyes darting from one to the other of us.

'How'd ya reckon?' said Tim.

'Aunty Peg dies, Ahmed leaves Philly, Max attacks Dad,' she said.

'You get off your tits and drive into a ditch in the middle of the night,' he said.

She screwed up her face. 'Not to forget, thanks Tim.'

They all looked at me.

'Me?' I said. 'In the pink.'

Tessa rolled her eyes. 'That'd be right. You just got the ball rolling.'

I lifted my eyebrows, but left it at that. I was glad I'd met Tim and Philly first, glad I'd admitted being with Dad when she wasn't there.

'Bloody drama queen,' said Tim. 'You're fine. Dad'll be fine. Ahmed hasn't actually left, and by JJ's own account she's in the pink.' He winked at me. 'I'll grant you Aunty Peg, though. She's still dead.'

'Dad's not fine,' said Tessa. 'Look at him.' He was drugged up and out of it, his face grey and mouth open. 'What the hell was he doing out there at that time of night? He's not a bloody idiot.'

Nobody said a word. I kept my eyes on my shoes. Counting. One, two —

Philly reached for Dad's right hand. I stopped counting. I caught Tim's eye. He gave one short shake of his head, just out of Tessa's range. I agreed entirely. I would not say one word about anything. Tessa's head swivelled to me, anyway.

'It's all your fault,' she said.

Tim jumped in. 'Steady on, Tess.'

'The only thing saving you, JJ, is no smoking gun,' said Tessa.

⋆　⋆　⋆

I volunteered to stay longer so it was me there when Jack opened an eye.

'Hello, love,' he said, his voice all croaked up.

'Feeling better?' I put the straw to his mouth. He sipped and wiped his mouth with the back of his good hand.

'Fair to middling.'

I helped him up on his pillows. He closed his eyes and rested his head with the effort for a moment.

'Brought you some chocolates for when you're up to it.'

He nodded; a pale wisp of a smile was all he could manage.

'Dad.' I covered his gnarled hand with mine. 'I should have stopped you. It was dark, raining, we'd just had that fight. I should have told you I understood.'

He waved my words away. 'I was the bloody idiot.' He sipped from the straw for a while, then looked up. 'Told the others?'

I stared at him a moment, trying to figure out

what he was asking.

'About me and Peg.'

'Hasn't been time.'

'You keep your mouth shut.'

Words stuttered on my tongue, but none of them made it into the world.

'My business.'

'So that's why you didn't mention me being there to Tim,' I said.

He stared out the window just like at home. But red roofs patched across to the horizon here, not burned yellow paddocks.

'They need to know as much as me, Dad.'

'You can tell them when I'm dead.'

'That could be years.'

'Not a chance with you around.'

I winced. He was nothing but right.

★ ★ ★

Tim rang to say he was on his way up again, so I pulled the blankets up to Dad's chin and said goodbye. I was pretty sure there was relief in his eyes. Didn't blame him.

At the lift doors, Tim came out with a cup of coffee.

'JJ.'

'Tim.' I mimicked his business-associate tone. 'Back so soon.'

'Had a few things to pick up in the city before I headed home. I won't get back for a day or two, so thought it was worth dropping in again.'

'I went to that address,' I said.

He stilled. Waiting.

I shook my head. 'Knew nothing. Just another dead end.'

'Shit.'

I was sorry for him.

'And Nancy?'

I punched him. 'You sicced her on me.'

'It's just ... ' He screwed up his face in between apology and acknowledgement. 'You're better at that shit than me.'

I rolled my eyes. 'You're just daddy's little boy and no rockee the boat for you.'

He saluted me with his coffee cup. 'So?' he asked, taking a sip. 'What next?'

'Ummm.'

'What?' he barked.

I blew air out between my lips. I didn't know what was the right thing any more. I was between the principle of telling the truth and the effect that truth would have — on Dad from me telling, and on Tim from him knowing. For all Tim had been pushing for me to follow the clues, he was hoping like hell the trail wouldn't lead to anything bad about Dad.

'She said.' I went slowly, almost as if I wasn't sure what would come out of my own mouth. 'That Dad and Peg.' I screwed up my face. 'You know. Had relations,' I ended limply.

He reared back. 'Why would she say a thing like that?'

'Dad admitted it. Just now.' I pointed up. 'Up there.'

'That bastard.' He punched the elevator button to go up.

I pulled at his sleeve.

He looked down at my hand. 'What?'

'Just . . . don't.' I looked away searching for the thing to say.

'You've changed your tune,' he spat at me.

'He asked me not to tell you. Any of you. He thinks you won't forgive him. And . . . ' I paused again. 'He's suffered so much already.'

'Daddy's little girl is finally putting down the knife?'

I shrugged.

'So what? That's it?' he said.

I shrugged again.

'You gone all chickenshit?'

'What the hell, Tim? You all let him lie to you over and over, right to your face. I was the only one.'

'So why you giving up now?'

'Because that's the big secret he's been covering up. It was one time before Philly. And he's paid for the crime a million times over.'

'That was it, then.' His voice broke. 'Mum found out and she left?'

I fell against the wall. I told Tim what I knew about how it all happened.

'It just doesn't feel enough. Not after all this time,' he said when I finished.

I knew exactly what he meant.

AN UNEXPECTED CLUE

I jumped at the sudden knocking on the other side of my door.

'Come on. You don't stay in bed all day unless you've got someone hot in it with you,' yelled Rocco. He banged on the door again.

'How do you know I don't?' I pulled the doona over my head. 'Go away.'

The thing was, nothing but staying in bed made any sense. Hard to believe you could be skun by a tiny, banal truth. But maybe this paralysis was more because of the massive ocean of guilt that I nearly fatally wounded my father over a concocted mystery I'd blown too much oxygen into.

'We're taking you out,' Roco called.

I burrowed deeper into my bed. 'No thanks.'

'If I can gird my loins . . . ' came Marge's voice.

I swore.

Rocco smashed the door open.

'For fuck's sake, Rocco,' I said, poking my face out.

'Have some pride, woman.' He picked up a dress from the back of a chair and threw it at me. 'Get dressed.'

'Tye's coming over,' I said.

'So he said on the phone just now,' said Rocco.

'He's meeting us at the pub.'

'Then that's what I'll do, too. I'll meet you there.'

'Good idea,' said Marge. 'Make sure you take the time to run a comb through that nest.'

'Nah.' Rocco crossed his arms. 'We'll wait right here for you.'

★   ★   ★

Rocco bumped a schooner of beer down in front of Marge. Rat-Tail leaned forwards to wipe the foam that spilled over the edge.

'Get your own,' said Marge, getting the glass into her hands fast.

'Yours is still at the bar, mate.' Rocco put another before me and took his own chair.

'Yeah. Cheers,' said Rat-Tail. He sat there staring at me.

'If you want that beer, Rat-Tail,' I said.

'Yeah.' He stood up. 'Your eyes are a real nice blue.'

'Thanks,' I said, feeling a microscopic point of colour in all the blah.

'Be better when you get rid of those bags underneath, but,' he said and took off.

'Cheers,' said Rocco, laughing. 'Told him to be nice to you.'

'Good job,' I said.

'Have you heard from the council?' I asked Marge, making an effort.

'They ruled against me,' she said. 'Said the boarding house isn't fit for a person with specific needs like me. I told them it wasn't fit for any of you lot either, then, seeing as you're all a bit special too.'

'Ha ha,' said Rocco.

'They're just waiting for a place in a lovely, boring nursing home to come up before they move me out.'

'How long will it take, do you think?' I asked.

She shrugged. 'The longer, the better.'

'It's not a prison,' I said.

'Good as: they lock the doors to keep the loony ones in.'

I grimaced and took a sip off the head of my beer.

'But we're here about you, not me. I'm a lost cause, being old and all, but you've got your whole life before you. What's got into you?'

'What do you mean?' I asked, although I didn't even have the energy for putting on much faux innocence.

She pursed her lips and gave me a long, disapproving look.

'What do you want from me?' I dropped my head, like it weighed a tonne, onto my knuckles, elbows on the table.

She rolled her eyes. 'We've convened the Inquisition, now you just answer the questions.'

I shrugged.

'How's your father?' she asked.

'Still alive, no thanks to me.'

'Hey.' Tye appeared, smiling his dancing smile and leaning over to kiss Marge, high-five Rocco and pull me into him. 'Has it started, then?'

'So you're in on this, too?' I asked, pushing away.

'Course.' He laughed, pulling me back. 'You need a bit of sense talked into you. All this detective business,' he tapped my head, 'disturbs your brain.'

'You and your father on speaking terms again?' asked Marge.

I shrugged. Told them there wasn't much to tell after all these dark years.

'So he's a saint now?' asked Marge.

I put my head on the side and gave her a questioning look about how hard she was going.

'We're cutting you off,' Rocco said, sliding Marge's beer away from her into the middle of the table.

Marge wiped the table with her hanky. 'It's just that I know your father — '

'No, you don't.'

'What I'm saying, if you let me finish . . . ' She folded her handkerchief to trap the wet inside. She snapped her bag open and placed it in the inside pocket. All precise.

'No need to build suspense,' I said.

'I know your father because all men are the same.'

'Steady on,' said Rocco.

I squeezed Tye's hand.

'Back in my day,' she went on, tipping her head to acknowledge Rocco and Tye, 'they thought they were living gods.' She clicked her tongue.

'Hardly — ' I began.

Rocco put up his hand to stop me interrupting.

'It was all behind closed doors. Good

pillar-of-the-church men in public, but.' She pulled her glass towards her and looked at me over the rim. 'The Catholics were the worst of the lot. Men were the head of the household and nobody said a word. Nobody asked questions. You can't give somebody power without making them accountable. Bad things happen in dark places.'

I blinked. I'd lived a few doors down from Marge for five years now and I'd never heard her talk like this — and didn't want to hear it now, either. 'It's true, he's no saint,' I conceded. I told them what I knew. 'It's just that I gave him such a hard time imagining worse.'

'That's exactly how secrets work,' Marge said. 'They dry your innards.'

She was bang on. 'Nah. That's on me,' I said. 'I should have had more faith.'

Rat-Tail came over. 'Sweet-talked that nice chick over there into another round,' he said. 'Bad teeth, but.'

'Just wanted to get rid of you, mate,' said Rocco.

Rat-Tail grinned. 'Nah. Got a date after her work.'

Tye, Rocco and I exchanged looks. She'd be leaving earlier than usual that night, we reckoned silently across the table. Rat-Tail set the tray down and we all took another beer, with Rocco passing Marge's to her.

'So what yous all talking about, then?' asked Rat-Tail.

'Marge was just giving JJ the benefit of her pessimism.'

350

'Yeah,' said Rat-Tail. 'You don't want to be like that. Life's real good.' He grinned over his glass with froth on his top lip. 'This beer. Real cold, it is, and it gurgles real nice in the back of your throat. And these peanuts.' He reached for the bowl in the middle of the table.

Tye laughed. 'Spot on, mate.'

'What about that address your brother gave you?' asked Rocco.

'Just one more of those dead ends.' I shrugged. 'They were all dead ends because in the end there was nothing much to discover.'

'You're being too hard on yourself, JJ,' Tye said. 'You found out why your mother left without saying goodbye, why she didn't stay at Peg's. That's huge.'

'An extra-marital affair with your wife's sister is nothing to be sniffed at,' added Marge.

'One-night stand,' I corrected automatically. 'Or five-minute stand. And that's scandal, not crime.'

'The real crime,' said Tye, 'was all the lying.'

'Seems to be an epidemic,' I said. 'Even those kids the other day at Mum's Richmond address. Lied. Straight to my face.' I told them the story of how their mother had been there all along in the back of the house, and when I'd gone they'd lied to her about who I'd been. 'Called me a country cousin.'

'Country cousin,' said Marge, placing her glass on the table.

I nodded.

'You sure?'

I shrugged.

She sat back. Opened her handbag. Looked inside. Didn't find what she was looking for. Closed it again. 'I think your mother was pregnant.'

'She'd had a hyster — ' I started.

'You sure about that?' she cut me off. 'Country cousin is what we called a woman up from the country needing an abortion. Stays a day or two to recover and gets on home with no one any the wiser.'

SETTING THE TRAP

I'd drunk enough to put me out last night, but despite that I'd got no sleep. It kept dancing away, soaking up into all those cracks on the ceiling. The thing was, my mother couldn't have been pregnant. She'd had a hysterectomy after Philly. The Catholics' approach to contraception.

Still, there was some dark thing buzzing inside it all.

Truth had to feel better than this. So maybe I hadn't scraped all of it off the sides of this Mum thing yet.

Tye had stayed over and pressed close into my back as ballast against the whirl. In the morning, sitting in my bed, my arms locked around my knees, I watched him leave early to go home and change into a fresh suit. When he'd gone I got out of bed, too. Dressed, got my bike, headed to the hospital.

Dad already had the telly on.

'You're early, love,' he said.

'Was Mum pregnant when she died?'

He immediately clammed up tight. 'What rot're you talking now? They took her baby works out after having Philly nearly killed her.'

'Number 95 Righton Street did abortions.'

'What?'

'Don't play innocent with me. That's why you

came home that day with a black eye. You had a fight with somebody there.'

'What fight?' But he was only half-hearted and then he caved in completely. 'Come on, love.' He scratched his head. 'It was against my religion. He was a baby killer.'

'So you knew it was an abortion clinic all along.'

'If I'd told you that, with an imagination like yours, you would have gone off down a thousand different rabbit holes looking for trouble where it wasn't.'

That right there.

In the past, I would have believed him. I was dead sick of all his bullshit.

'Fuck this.'

'Get your foul mouth out of here.'

'What about your foul opinions?'

'You keep the dirty out of your speech or get out,' he said. His fingers got themselves tapping against the steel of his bed rail.

I got in closer, ready to go on, but a nurse swept in. All small and white and filling up the room. Dad pulled up a smile and plastered it on. I stepped back.

'This another of your daughters,' asked the nurse in an Irish accent, flowing cheer, her face spotted over with freckles.

He widened his smile. 'Second youngest,' he said. 'JJ, this is Maureen.'

'All these girls, you're a lucky man.' She waved at me, while she set Dad up for a blood pressure test.

'Could say that,' he said, his eyes not meeting mine.

She pumped up the bag around his arm, letting it down slowly and monitoring the screen. She sucked in air, shaking her head. 'Blood's up, Mr McBride.' She tapped her head. 'Settle down or you won't be getting out of here anytime soon.' She shot him a wink as she left the room.

He cleared his throat and looked me dead in the eye. 'Reckon it was Peg,' he said.

'Peg what?'

'Reckon that butcher bloke, the abortionist — Sarah might have taken Peg for one. That's why your mother had the details in her missal.'

'Peg was pregnant when Mum died?'

'Nah. Would have been years before. Peg was always putting it around. Your mum had been holding tight to that prayer book for a long time. Remember? Wouldn't let any of us so much as look at it. Reckon Peg was the one who had the butcher's job done. Reckon that's what's behind that address.'

I hated to admit it. He could be right.

But it didn't feel right. I was done relying on just the facts. I had a gut and I was going to use it.

'Bloody Peg,' he said. 'She was — she wasn't a holy woman. That's why I had to get rid of her, out of the house, out of the way of all you buggers.'

'You mean because she was just like you — had sex out of wedlock with you.'

He winced. 'Because she had sex — with anybody. And if she had that abortion, she'll be in hell right now where she belongs.'

Hell wasn't a metaphorical concept to Dad.

His hell was a blood-and-bone affair.

'Jesus Christ, Dad.'

'Don't take the Lord's name in vain,' he said, on autopilot.

'But it's okay to be pretty happy about somebody ending up in the eternal burning flames of hell in perpetual agony.'

'No one forced her to murder her own baby.'

'What about the father? Is he in hell, too?'

He scrubbed one side of his face again. Up and down. I started to think Maureen would be flying in. 'Nothing to do with him,' Dad said. The machine beside him beeped and he just about jumped out of his skin at the sudden loud of it. 'Unless he asked for the thing. But the mother could go away, start a new life, pretend her husband died. There's even adoption.'

'Really thought it through there.'

'It's the Christian thing.'

'Good to see you Catholics see the odd opportunity for charity. I suppose letting her have her kid where she knows people and them supporting her was a charity bridge too far.'

'You're a Catholic, too.'

'Not any more.'

'Your mother and I baptised you — we took you to church every Sunday — even when the creek was up over the bridge in the big flood.' He made a signal like that was all good parenting required.

The machine beside him beeped into life again, sending out rapid fire. Maureen hurtled into the room, with two others hard on her heels. I backed away, making space. Backed right out of the room.

'Marge.' I knocked on her door. There was no answer, so I went on to my room. I'd brought a caramel slice. With all this artery clogging I was facilitating, she wouldn't need to worry about lasting long enough to make it to the oldies' home. I put the slice in the bar fridge in my room.

I looked at my unmade bed. That bloody ugly vomit brown. Even Rat-Tail had a happier one. I straightened the bed so there'd be no getting back into it for me today. My mind buzzing. I pulled out the Map of Mum and the Timeline from the bin. Laid them along the floor. I squatted in front. My eyes darted over them, back and forth. I needed to see connections.

Nothing.

I leaned back against the bed. That's when I saw it.

Hell. I'd written that word in miscellaneous grey and circled it from our conversation the night Max gored Dad. My eyes narrowed. He'd said it was his fault Mum was in hell. That word on the Map of Mum sat right beside the phrase: *Mother was a saint.*

'Saints don't go to hell, Dad,' I said out aloud.

I stood up, trampling the Map and Timeline underfoot.

It was about time.

I needed to shed my skin.

Become somebody new.

Get a whole lot smarter.

I shook the doona out of its cover, balled up

all the ugliness and shoved it into the rubbish bin. I looked at it a moment, sitting there, overflowing and still in my room. I stooped and picked it out of the bin, snatched up my wallet and marched straight out to the garbage bins at the back of the boarding house.

On the way back I stopped by the telephone to ring Tye. 'I'm going shopping,' I said before he even said hello. 'Meet me at lunchtime?'

He let out a whoop. 'Room stuff?'

'Yep. Doona cover, rug, television. It could get wild.'

'Who are you and what have you done with my girlfriend?'

★　★　★

Tessa was already at the hospital when I got there two days later, plans worked over and thought through, buoyed by the whole lot of new spring-green and sun-yellow stuff in my room that Tye and I had gone mad buying, including armfuls of sunshine gerberas. All of that hopeful joy working its way into me.

Tessa was opening and closing the drawers, packing up Dad's things into a suitcase, ready to take him home.

'You'll need that suitcase yourself,' Dad said, his voice high pitched and shocked.

'I'm not going anywhere, Dad.' She was at the bottom drawer, pulling out greying singlets and baggy white underwear. 'And you are.'

'I'm only getting home. Don't need that fancy thing.'

'I've got a garbage bag in my backpack if you prefer, Dad,' I said.

He shook his head, blasting annoyance about him. Tim turned into the room.

'Didn't you get the message?' Tessa said, looking up.

'What?'

'Bringing Dad home today. Told you to visit him there.'

'Well, I'm here now,' he said. 'Back on your feet?' he said to Dad.

'So they tell me.'

Tim looked up as Philly came into the room with an Esky. 'What's this? Bush week?'

'Meals,' she said. 'Save Tessa.'

'Dad won't like your fancy stir-fries full of half-cooked vegetables,' Tim said.

Philly raised an eyebrow. 'It's a sausage casserole, et cetera.'

We all swivelled to Philly. 'You cooked sausages?' Tim laughed.

'I have friends with skills in the ancient art of cooking.'

'Another one for around your little finger, then?' asked Tim.

'It's a talent,' she said.

I rubbed my palm, watching. Tim noticed me. He tipped his head. 'And that's how it's done.'

'What?'

'As if you don't know,' he said. He leaned from the bed over to cuff me. I jerked out of range. 'Phils is a champion at not letting herself be wound up.' He brought his other hand up and managed to cuff me anyway.

'Grow up,' I said.

'Took the words right out of my mouth,' he said back.

'Bit of respect in a hospital,' growled Dad, tapping the arm of his chair.

'Just like the old days,' said Philly.

'What's your excuse, then, JJ?' asked Tim.

'What?'

'Tessa's taking Dad home, Philly's brought food, it's my visiting day. What brings you to the paddock?'

Dad sat up, all ears.

'Mum's birthday's coming up.'

'What're you drivin at?' he snarled.

'It's been fourteen years,' I said.

Everybody stopped, Tessa looking at me like I was some daft cow.

'Remember the good stuff. I mean ... ' I shrugged carefully, nonchalantly. 'We were lucky to have her with us as long as we did. Could have been worse. She nearly died after Philly ... ' I let it trail away.

Dad nodded, but sat up straighter, trying to get in close on what I was up to.

'That hysterectomy saved her.'

'What bloody hysterectomy?' said Tessa.

Bingo.

I watched Dad out of the corner of my eye, watching me.

'You wouldn't know,' I said. 'You were what, five?'

She shrugged. Turned to Dad. 'She didn't have a hysterectomy, did she, Dad?'

'That's right,' he said. Looking everywhere but

me. 'Came whisker close, though, she was that crook.' As though the whisker made up for his earlier lie.

'So let's celebrate Mum,' I finished brightly, now looking around at everybody.

'No need,' said Dad, tapping away. 'I'll pay for a Mass on her anniversary, just like I do every year. You should all come to that, though. Do you buggers good.'

Tim clipped me again, as if to say, *Thanks very much.*

'We'll go as a family. Like the old days.' Dad got himself straighter again.

Tessa zipped up the suitcase. 'Good idea, Dad.'

'I was thinking something sooner than her anniversary,' I said.

'What's your hurry?' asked Tim.

I scratched my palm. 'With Aunty Peg gone, it's the end of an era. We've packed up her place. It's on the market. It feels like something's finished. Us kids will all get a share of the results of Peg's sound financial management, which will open the possibility of something new for all of us. It's time. We should finally put everything behind us.'

Tim folded his arms and sat back. Philly went out the door to tip the water out of the vases. Dad eyed me, searching for something. 'Could be right,' he said, slowly.

'What would we do?' asked Tessa.

'Get the priest in for a blessing,' said Dad.

'If we're going to do this, then we need to do it right,' said Tim, getting to his feet. 'Mum loved Jean's Corner. That's where we'll do it.'

'I'm not getting a priest in to bless a bloody corner,' said Dad. He banged the arm of his chair.

I shrugged. 'Lunch. Dad's place. Sunday week.'

Dad grimaced and looked out the window, trying to figure out if I was up to anything. Tessa screwed up her face at Tim and passed Dad a glass of water, getting in close and hovering beside him.

'Father McGinty's busy, probably couldn't come to just a — ' started Tessa.

'Leave that to me,' said Tim. 'Father McGinty and I are like that.' He crossed his fingers in the air.

'Ever since you painted his arse blue through the hole in the back of the dunny?' I asked.

'He's an old bloke.' Tim grinned. 'Brain soft. What he'll remember is me getting that bloody ten-foot flagpole up on the school grounds a couple of months back.'

Dad shook his head and mumbled.

'Mum gave me a hiding and a half over that blue arse,' said Tim.

'Don't forget to mention that,' I said. 'In your speech.'

'Mother Whack-A-Lot,' said Tim, still grinning. 'She was a bloody firecracker, wasn't she?'

'Bit of respect for your mother,' said Dad, shaking his head. 'Talking ill of the dead.'

'God going to strike him down, hey?' I asked Dad.

'Strike the bloody lot of you, the way you're going.'

'Maybe it's not appropriate to have Father

McGinty around all of this.' Tessa circled her finger around all of us.

'No. He should be there,' I said, so quickly Dad cast another suspicious glance my way.

Philly came back and Tim asked her how she was fixed for two Sundays away.

'I would have thought I could depend on you to put a stop to this,' she said to Tessa.

Tessa shrugged. 'Could finally shut JJ up.'

'There is that,' said Philly.

'Just one rule,' I said.

Everybody looked at me, all still and waiting for something bad.

'No bloody poems, Philly.'

'Mrs Tyler loved that poem,' she said.

'We should invite her,' said Tessa. She looked around at us. 'If we're doing it properly.'

'And Mrs Nolan,' I said.

'No bloody way,' said Dad. 'Leave it just to us.'

'We'll need photos,' I said. 'The one you've got, Dad, and any others we have. I'll come around to dig out her rosary beads.'

Dad struggled out of the chair. Tessa swooped in under his arm. 'Be glad to see the back of this joint,' he said. 'Even with Maureen.' Tim picked up the suitcase, Philly was on the Esky and I came behind with a couple of plastic bags of old roses from Shelley's garden, my arms full of all kinds of love: red for romantic, yellow for peace, white for forgiveness.

Dad said his thanks to the nurses at the desk. We processed down the hall, all as slow as Dad's shuffle. Tessa had been all for getting him a wheelchair, but he wouldn't have it. She'd argued for a walking stick, then, but he'd told her that if he was well enough to leave the hospital, he was well enough to walk out on his own two feet. Tessa had given up, but he was leaning all he was on to her and she was struggling under it.

Philly fell back so that it was just her and me. 'What are you up to?' she asked.

I shook my head, all *I don't know what you are talking about*.

'Listen, if you're serious about finally abandoning your crime theory, you need to be serious about the next thing. You have to contact Maurice and see if he'll let you go back to work.'

I winked at her. 'Mission accomplished.'

'God,' she said. 'What did he say?'

I seesawed my head. 'It took a bit. Not for him to give me the job back. Said he hadn't taken my 'temper spike',' I quoted up my fingers best I could given the roses, 'seriously. But there was a lot of talking to be done about my head, my future. It was either that or the fine Scotch I took him.'

'He's such a softy when it comes to you.'

'I learned from the best of us.' I winked, nudging her.

She grinned.

'How's Ahmed?'

'Fine.' She said too quickly, before grinning again. 'Okay, you were right. And he was right. We do see more of each other.' She screwed up her face into mine.

'So make sure you bring him to Mum's birthday.'

'What about Tye?'

'Course.'

'I just don't want to bring Ahmed if there's going to be any shit.'

'There's always shit, Philly. What family did you grow up in?'

★ ★ ★

Outside the hospital, Tessa opened the car door for Dad and went around to supervise Tim and Philly putting his things in the boot. I put the roses on the back seat.

'Need my wallet, love,' said Dad to me. I separated the plastic bag full of Dad's wallet, cheque book and glasses, and put it on his lap. 'I'll be finding her rosary beads,' he said, his voice low and with an edge. 'No need for you to come.'

I kept mine all cheery. 'I don't mind, have a dig around.'

'You don't come anywhere near my place.' He stabbed the air. 'You hear?'

'Yeah, sorry about the last time,' I said, still all sunny.

He balled his fist and tapped his knee. 'I'm serious, I don't want you there before that Sund'y with the others. And after your mother's birthday dinner, not one word more! Only doing this bullshit so you'll keep your trap shut. Forever! You hear me?'

Tessa opened the driver's door. 'All set?'

I slammed Dad's door and stood with Tim and Philly to wave them off.

CAUGHT

It was on.

At Dad's, I turned the key off in the Austin and the engine cut. Tye and I looked at each other, and for a moment I didn't want to get out of the car. He reached across the red of the leather seats to squash my hand. But it was too hot for long sitting so we got out and unpacked the food. I'd figured out where Philly had got her 'sausage casserole, et cetera' from when I'd asked Marge for some help with cooking a meal for Mum's birthday. No worries, she'd said. Just cooked up a whole lot for Philly the other day. That was Philly's other superpower: she might be all OCD straight lines, but she got stuff done by thinking in crooked ones. That originality is what would take her straight to the CEO's office one day in the not-too-distant future.

Tye went ahead up the path. I leaned against the car, squinting at the old place for what might be the last time. The sun sharpened its edges against the angles of the house; its rusting roof, its listing walls.

I grew up in this shithole. Now I was living in another. In that second I got it. It had been penance. The next second I got something new. I was going to move out.

Tye stopped to see where I was.

'Marge and me are moving out together.'

'I never thought I'd see the day,' he said, dramatically raising the back of his hand to his brow.

I laughed. 'It'll be okay if she's doing the cooking.'

'You'd better factor in a fold-out couch for Rat-Tail and Rocco sleepovers.'

I screwed up my face, but actually even the idea of having Rat-Tail over felt good.

I picked up the basket, peeled off from the Austin and went up the path to join Tye. We went through the laundry and into the kitchen. Into the low hum of ordinary . . . Okay maybe not everyday ordinary: it had that Christmas, dressed-up feel. The table had been brought out into the middle of the room to fit us all and a small table added at the end. Philly had brought her white dinnerware, which put the seriousness into things.

I navigated through the pointy branches of greetings and cheek pecking and held tight to the dive of Georgie into my arms. Wondered briefly what it would be like to have my own little Georgie equivalent.

I caught the look Tim and Shelley swapped between them as I was holding Georgie, but I couldn't read it.

Tim gave Tye a hearty handshake like he was trying to cram a lot more meaning into it than the average. Tye gave back in kind, matching Tim's serious. I loved that about Tye.

'Nice curtains,' I said, surprised that I could do ordinary, too, and my voice got stronger. 'Very lemony.'

'The old man'll have em down quick smart after this,' said Tim. Tessa swatted him with a tea towel. 'You know he likes a clear line of sight to the road,' Tim reminded us. We all knew. Liked to see what was coming at him.

The curtain lifted with a small breeze fanning out over the matching new laminex on the bench. I felt a spit of annoyance with Tessa for even trying to give the old place a facelift, as if that could make a difference to everything. But I realised I was doing the same thing. Bringing in the new, just in a different way. She was wearing Mum's cameo on her blouse and I winked my approval at Philly, jerking my head towards it. She winked back. It would be Tim's turn next.

Somebody had put candles in front of the framed photos of Mum on the bench. Even the one Dad had kept hidden from us all those years was there.

I got my head down and worked with Georgie and Ahmed to thread serviettes through the white chrysanthemum rings I'd made, while Tye joined Philly and Tessa at the kitchen bench. Philly passed him a knife and chopping board, and dumped a pile of piled carrots on top.

Ahmed helped Georgie rainbow more chrysanthemums on each plate while I filled teacups and tiny glasses with water. Georgie got bored, though, and wandered off, so Shelley helped us shape the chrysanthemums into the makeshift vases and arrange them on top of the long white mirror I'd got from the op shop and laid down the middle of the table. We stood back and even Tim broke off his price-of-wool talk with Geoff to twist his mouth in approval at the forest of white, actual and reflected. I was swimming the place in truth. Philly spoke a bit of flower, but if she knew the symbolic meaning of white chrysanthemums she didn't let on.

'Let's get this show on the road, then,' Dad said, rushing out from his bedroom like he had somewhere to go, the smell of Brylcreem strong about the wave of his receding grey hair. He sniffed the roast and rubbed his hands.

'Like the old days.' He looked at my jeans. 'See you've made an effort, JJ.'

'In my own way,' I said.

He tsked, but I shrugged it off. There were bigger things to snag on when you were digging up your mother after fourteen years. 'You're looking back to yourself.'

'Yep, yep. All good.' He shrugged it off as if being gored by your beloved bull was an everyday thing. Despite everything, Dad hadn't been able to bring himself to part with Max, who was still happily plotting conspiracy beside his trough and eyeing off the cows in the adjoining paddock.

He turned to Tye, and I made the introduction.

'Good meeting you, Mr McBride.'

'Beer, mate?' Dad asked him over a shake of his hand. 'Best thing in this heat.'

Tye agreed that it was perfect given the weather.

'What time is Father McGinty getting here?' asked Philly.

'Not coming,' said Tim.

'Did you even ask?' I said.

Tim shrugged. 'The old man told me not to. Said he'd do it.'

Dad had outsmarted me again. I slapped away a barb of disappointment. Wasn't going to let it infect the rest of the day though. Dad beamed his back to me as he got busy with the fridge door and the bottle opener.

I asked Philly to keep an eye on Tye while I went to do something. She frowned into a question, but I just winked, and Tye walked me to the Austin. 'I won't be long,' I said. He put his forehead against mine like a blessing.

★   ★   ★

I bumped down the hill over the flat and pulled on the handbrake at Jean's Corner. I took out the box of garden things and considered my options. I tested the hardness of the ground around the short stone bench, the baby's cross, closer in under the apple tree, then by the creek. In the end I dug close to the reach of the water. I hadn't been able to choose between Purple Loosestrife and its *all that's gone between us* and the wattle, which had so much to say, but in among it was love and protection and the solving of mystery, and I thought there was all of that in the thickness binding Mum and Aunty Peg together. Then the rose bushes: one from Mrs Tyler's garden, the dark red Munstead Wood Rose, one of Mum's favourites because they're survivors and yet so lush. The Bleu Magenta Rose was Mrs Nolan's — because its deep rose purple was as unexpected as Peg, she said. Tye and I had dropped around on our way, told them what needed to be told. They'd held hands across the kitchen table with the pity of it. I dug the holes, poured in water and fertiliser, gentled the plants from their pots, placed them in the ground and covered their roots with soil. I thought of the millions of women who've ever held helpless hands in the face of implacable facts. Watered the plants in. Giving Mum a garden. I stripped off my gloves and reached into the box for the plaque Tye and I had worked on:

Sarah Anne Millet 1931–1968
Margaret Mary Millet 1933–1982

I stabbed it deep into the loosened earth and used the back of the shovel to bang in the rest enough so it would hold.

I sat back on my haunches. It was done. Over. This terrible trail of lies to which they both lost so much. I don't know if this is what they would want. To be together again. But I do know they didn't get a chance to find out. That had to end here.

★　★　★

When I got back to the house, Tessa was yelling for Georgie to come back out the back door. 'Where'd you get to?' she asked me.

'Just doing a bit of re acquainting.' I smiled, shading my eyes with my hand.

'Mmm.' She gave me a sceptical look. 'Dinner's ready.'

'Twins?'

'Down. Your old room.'

'Hope there's nothing catching in there.'

'Better not be.' She laughed.

Inside, Dad scraped his chair to the table and leaned back to get more of a swig of his beer. Tessa went to pick up his plate. He patted her forearm and she smiled.

I took Tye's hand. His other hand came around mine. 'All good?' he leaned in to say.

'Yep.' I bit my lip. 'Done. Now this.' I blew air out and went to pull my hand away to dig into my palm.

He pulled it back and kissed the place I would have attacked with my nails. 'You got this,' he said.

Tessa spooned minted peas and roasted spuds on to Dad's plate. She layered lamb slices beside parsnip and carrots, and put it all before him. Geoff got his own and Tessa moved on to Georgie's plate. Dad sat at the head of the table alone as everybody filled their plates at the bench. He hunched forwards and drowned everything in gravy. He got his knife and fork busy and down went the first mouthful, wolfed in.

Tessa untied Mum's apron and hung it on the hook beside the fireplace, just like Mum used to do. I was still only up to the greens dish when everybody else was settled, the steam of lamb and other things rising. I got my shoulders to my ears and dropped them, and then filled my plate and took my seat beside Tye.

There was that look between Tim and Shelley again.

I bit my lip. Suddenly, I couldn't remember how I was going to start this thing despite all the rehearsal I'd done with Tye. He squeezed my hand under the table. The breath was having trouble getting out of my throat.

'How about you say grace, mate?' said Dad, laying down his knife. Georgie straightened up and big-eyed his face, nodding like a toy dog with a spring-head. Tessa gave him a wink and he stilled to send an elaborate one back.

'Bless us, oh Lord, and these, thy gifts which we are about to receive.'

'Amen,' we answered, although I couldn't be sure there'd been an actual voice out of me.

'Good man,' said Dad, including Tessa and Geoff in his approving look. 'Special occasion today,' he said, and clasped his hands together and bowed his head again. We followed suit. 'Fourteen years since the Lord took your mother to His breast. We don't question His ways, but pray that He takes her from the fires of damnation into the bliss of paradise.' He paused and we waited. 'Amen,' he said. 'Amen,' we echoed.

'Think we can do a bit better,' said Tim, getting to his feet. He looked at Shelley and she beamed encouragement back. 'To Sarah.' He swooped his stubby high. 'To Mum. For the sweet milky tea in the mornings, for the pancakes on Sunday afternoons, and for — ' His eyes skitted along the ceiling.

'For the Hail Marys at night,' said Philly.

'For the good tucker,' said Dad.

'For sewing our dresses,' said Tessa.

'For the paper giraffes,' said Georgie. Tessa's

'shh' was lost in the swivel of eyes towards him. He grew big with the importance of all those eyes on him. 'Grandma made paper giraffes with Mum and Mum makes them with me. She says I can do them with my kids.'

Tessa flushed.

'Now I feel cheated,' said Tim, his beer bottle still charged. 'Where's my paper giraffe?' Philly jumped on board with her own whine about how she'd missed out, too.

'It was just — ' Tessa started.

Tim laughed. 'That was just how Mum was, Tessa. She had something good with all of us. Flowers with JJ, baking and giraffes with you.'

'Settle down.' Dad's voice rose above the wave. 'To your mother. May she rest in peace.'

'To Mum,' we all said.

Tim stayed on his feet. 'We got a bit of news.'

Shelley jumped up and grabbed him around the neck. 'He proposed.'

Georgie bounced to his feet on his seat and jumped up and down, joining in all the clapping.

Ahmed stood up, glass charged. 'To Sheeellleey and Teeem, may the moon hold your love in its arms at night and the sun shine on your lives by day.'

Philly did a proud he's-with-me gesture. The rest of us looked at each other, eyebrows raised, impressed, but not sure how to do the echoing thing with this. Georgie got it, though. 'To the moon and the sun,' he shouted, shoving his empty plastic cup towards the ceiling. That's what we echoed, laughing all around. Shelley grinned at me.

'So, date?' I asked.

'March,' she said happily. 'Wedding at Our Lady of the Rosary.'

'Party back at ours,' finished Tim.

'Dad's moving out to the cottage and Tim's moving in with me,' Shelley said.

'In the big house, Tim,' I chided. 'You'll have to wear your big boy pants.'

He reached across the table to swat me. He took the opportunity to say urgently underneath it all so nobody else could hear. 'You, too. Now's your moment.'

So those shared looks between Shelley and him had been about more than wedding bliss.

And just like that I was back to the numb, shrouding me up. All the adrenaline and purpose of the last two weeks evaporated. I clawed at my palm. Then I stopped myself, fisted my hands and got them down deep between my legs, hard against the wood of the chair.

'Mum would have been fifty-three today,' I said, using the words like a knife through the layers. Tim sat down, nodding like he could see where I was headed. 'Mum would have loved to be here for this. She would have loved you, Shelley.'

Shelley nodded seriously. She knew I was starting whatever it was she and Tim had hoped I'd be doing. 'Mum also loved the truth,' I said. Smiles faded. I kept my eyes on my plate. 'Laid into us if she ever caught any of us with a lie between our teeth.'

'JJ,' growled Tessa.

'Let her be,' said Tim.

'I won't let her turn this into a circus.' Tessa's

voice scratched along the surface. 'Just — '

But I'd lost the rest, anyway. I held still, closed my eyes.

'JJ?' Tim asked. He had those urgent eyes on me again.

'Reckon it's time, is all,' I said, forcing my eyes to look straight at Dad.

'I warned you,' he said, low and snarly. 'I don't know what you got in mind, but scrub it out right now. This is a special occasion and I won't have your mother's memory spat on.'

My eyes narrowed. It was just what I needed. Red reared up in me, snapping through the ropes I'd had it tied down with. 'Because that would be your department,' I said.

'For god's sake,' hissed Tessa, jerking her head towards Georgie.

Philly pushed back her chair to leave.

'You stay right there,' I said.

'I don't — '

'Sit down.' I used all my big sister on her and she stayed put.

'You've got nothin.' Dad's finger stabbed holes in the air. 'You listen to me, JJ. You were a little shit as a kid and you're a little shit now.' His voice slithered out of him low and hissy.

'Don't even try,' I said, the words snarling over each other to get out. 'All those lies tying us in knots so we thought we were going mad ends now. It's truth time.'

He set down his knife and fork, careful on his plate. He pointed his stubby finger. 'Your mother couldn't stomach you another second. She wouldn't have cared about me and Peg. One time a million years before. But she'd had enough all right. You were the thing we fought about the night before. You were why she had that suitcase ready behind the door.'

I gasped, gut punched. A single swing of a machete and the red was felled. Just me left, body panting, eyes wide, rabbit in the headlights trapped.

Dad's face twisted, hate uglying it up. 'Your mother had had a bellyful of your — ' He clawed for the word with his curled fingers.

I felt something against the back of my wrist on the table. I jerked away from the burn. Too late I saw it had been Georgie's hand over mine. He went moon eyed. I reached out to him in sorry, but he ricocheted away, all distrust and fear.

'Get that kid out of here.' Dad flung his arm to the door.

'Dad,' snapped Tessa as Geoff stood and threw down his serviette.

'Come on, mate.' He held out his hand to Georgie, who couldn't get his round eyes off his grandfather, or me. 'See if the poddies need feeding'

'Feed in the dairy,' said Dad in a normal voice, looking at Georgie as if he'd never snarled. Tye, Shelley and Ahmed stayed just were they were.

'Now that's down to you, Tessa,' Dad said, fork stabbing at her. 'You shouldn't be letting a little bloke hear any of this.'

Tessa's mouth fell open, but Dad turned back, all prongs shooting at me now. 'Your fault. Your mother was right! All trouble, You should get out of here right now and leave the rest of us to it.'

Air panted in and out and still I couldn't get any of it into me. Tye's eyes were wild. He was caught between doing and not doing. I doubled over, my fists pressing into my solar plexus, red and black and everything else pulsing hard. In the end, Tye got me a glass of water, a protective hand on my back, rubbing circles.

'Stop it, Dad,' said Tessa.

The sound of Tim's chair screeching lifted my face. He stood, all six feet of tall and hands on hips, staring at Dad. A quiet mantling over him, Some of it even reached out to me. 'What are you saying?' he said to Dad, every word measured.

'Sit down.' Dad hunched over his plate again, shovelling peas into his mouth. 'Said my piece.'

'I won't be sitting,' said Tim.

'Making a fool of yourself, boy.'

'That so?' He was trigger still.

Tessa's eyes darted one to the other and snagged on nothing in between. Philly sat soldier straight, eyes dead ahead, taking in the world beyond the window, as if while her body must be here the rest of her had got away. Ahmed's calm hand on her knee.

'Our mother,' Tim said, face rock hard. 'Your. Wife. Loved JJ.' His voice caught. 'Took the time to see behind all that red shit to where JJ really was.' He leaned across the table towards Dad, loading menace up into his voice. 'And in that place there's nothing but courage. She's been the brave one. The only one of us willing to push hard at the truth for Mum. And all the while you fed her bullshit, fed all of us bullshit, telling us black is white and white is a brown cow. JJ took

378

all your shit because she loved you, Dad. Believed in you. Just like we all did. You threw it all back in our faces. But now the hour is here. So you tell us, Jack. What really happened?'

'Calling me a liar, boy?'

'Am I?'

'A boy who didn't even have the guts to see his own mother buried,' said Dad.

Shelley hissed. Tessa crashed her chair back. 'Have you mixed your meds?' she yelled at Dad.

'What did our mother die of?' said Tim, low and dangerous, not a muscle moved.

Dad pushed back from the table, stood too, legs apart. 'I think you know the answer to that.'

'Perito-bloody-nitus,' said Tim. 'Why would we believe the word of a man who slept with his wife's sister?'

Tessa's gasp was loud as she knocked her empty glass over. For the first time, Philly moved. She rotated her head so her stare moved from beyond the window to Tim. As if this thing could not quite make sense to her. Then, all at once, her head shook from side to side as it hit her. Her palm to her chest, she turned to me, mouthing 'sorry' while her eyes swam. I reached my hand across the table, shaking my head back, saying there was nothing for her to be sorry about.

Dad got his hands on the back of the chair and sent me an accusing look from underneath it all.

'What kind of upstanding, Church-going, God-fearing man does that?' said Tim.

'I'll grant you that,' Dad said, his voice hushed. 'And I'll carry the stain to my dying day. I'm — '

'Park that sanctimonious bullshit,' Tim spat.

'Your mother is in every breath I take, day and night.' Dad's voice was high and windy. 'So don't you — '

Tessa was at his side, a hand on his back. 'Breathe,' she said.

He shoved her off.

'Perito-*fucking*-nitus.' Tim pointed an accusing finger. 'Why don't you tell us, Jack? Why don't you tell us all about what a stand-tall kind of bloke you been?'

Dad straightened, pulled his chair back and lowered in it. 'I'm your father. Leave it at that. Let's put this behind us and get back to Tessa's delicious meal she spent hours about.'

'What killed her?' Tim asked, legs still apart.

'Read the bloody death certificate.' Dad stared up at Tim. 'I know you stole it. So you know as much as I do.'

Tim shook his head, one eyebrow raised, challenging Dad, waiting. We all waited. And the quiet settled in around the waiting. So quiet I could hear inside me again. I closed my eyes and reached in for Mum. The ground cracked open and her absence pussed out, scalding along my skin. I shook my head and widened my eyes as if I were coming up from the dark. I brought my hand up to scratch my palm, but the shake in my hand stopped me. I had to do this thing. Couldn't let it keep blistering up the skin of our lives.

I pressed both palms to the table and stood. 'Why did Mum keep the address of an abortionist in her missal, locked up tight and secret?'

'Abortion?' Tessa spat out the word. Philly

shook her hands in front of her like a shield.

Dad angled his chair to get a good look out the window at what was coming. Steel hardened up his face as if he'd just seen the lemony curtains for the first time. 'You and I talked about this.'

'Yep, you told me she'd taken Peg for an abortion, years before.'

'That's right,' he said, relief in the wash of the words.

'What you forgot to tell me was that it was your baby Peg aborted,' I said. 'Mum didn't just find out about you and Peg that day. She found out a whole lot more. That was the day she figured out you were the father of Peg's baby.' I put up my hand to stop his spluttering from interrupting me. 'That's what Mum figured out when Mrs Nolan told her about you and Peg. That's what drove her away without saying good-bye to me and leaving her wedding ring behind.'

'Bullshit,' he roared. 'Get her out of here.' This time looking directly at Tessa. 'Make sure she never comes near me again.'

Tessa jerked her head in a no. 'Not this time, Dad.'

'You can all bloody get out, then.'

'You didn't chuck Peg out for being a bad influence,' I galloped on. 'You chucked Peg out because she was pregnant with *your* kid and you didn't trust her to keep her mouth shut if she stayed living with us. That's why you banned Mum from seeing her.'

Dad pounded the table with his fist, bouncing the cutlery. 'Happy now?' He glared at me. 'You've

381

got this table spilling over with blood and guts.'

I narrowed my eyes and stared him down. He looked away and got his knife and fork working again.

I couldn't be stopped. 'And what Mum was wild about was that despite all your great Catholicness, you wanted Peg to have that abortion. Wanted it so much you even paid for it.' I slammed my fist into my hand. 'Because where else could they have got the money from? But you wouldn't let Mum have an abortion. That's what you fought about that night. That's what Philly heard.'

His mouth dropped open. Then he closed it and shoved a forkful in. There was something niggling at the back of me that was full of sorry for this hollow man. But I wasn't finished yet.

'Man up, Jack.' Tim said. 'Is JJ right?'

There was just the sound of Dad chewing.

'Oh my God.' Philly bolted up, swiping at her eyes. 'She is. Mum *was* pregnant when she left.' She spun to Dad. 'She said she wanted the money to have what Peg had. You told her you were the man and you wouldn't let her do it. She'd end up in hell and you didn't need that on your conscience.'

We all looked at Philly, then back at Dad.

He laid his knife and fork on the table. He pushed at them to get them positioned just right as we watched. He cleared his throat. He went to say something but coughed. All our eyes on him as he swallowed back beer.

'Not the kind of thing you tell the world,' Dad said into the echo of the empty. 'They wouldn't have let her be buried in sacred ground if they knew she murdered the baby. And that would have killed her. Not being with her people.'

'Would have killed you, you mean,' said Tim. 'It's you who couldn't have lived with a stain like that on your lily-white Catholic reputation.'

'Your mother — '

'The thing I don't get is the death certificate,' said Tim. 'You got some fancy doctor to protect you? How did that happen, do you reckon? Cause it's right here, see.' Shelley passed it from her handbag. Tim flashed it at all of us. 'Says just here.'

I started to speak, but Tessa came over the top of me.

'There were no presents that year.' The handle of the bread knife in her fist stabbing into the table cloth. 'Under the Christmas tree. I thought it was because you'd forgotten, with Mum and everything. But there was no money — you'd used it to buy all them mongrels off.'

'How dare you?' he said, whipping around to Tessa.

But she didn't flinch.

None of us did.

'You've got your truth, then,' he said, defeated. 'Now all of yous get out.'

'You good as held the knife to her belly yourself,' I said.

'Don't talk rot. It was me who tried to stop her.'

'Tried to stop her by not giving her the money.'

He nodded, wary in his eyes.

'And she couldn't have taken Peg's money, not

after finding out about you and her.' I drummed the table with my fingers.

'What?' said Tim, in his seat again.

'She didn't have enough money for a *half-decent* abortion, did she, Dad?'

His hand shook as it reached out for his glass. He saw it too and grabbed it with his other hand to steady it. He felt me looking at him, but there was no meeting of eyes. He went under the currents to duck around the corner before I could catch him, same as he'd done all his life. But everyone else was looking at me, quivering with wait.

'You saying she didn't get that abortion after all?' said Tim.

I kept my eyes, glue tight on Dad. 'It was that address. In her Mass Book.'

'Dead end, you said.' Tim's voice strained at the seam.

'Thought that for a bit. But something kept at me. Couldn't figure it out.' I nodded at Dad. 'You clicked it into place.'

'I told you nothing,' he said.

I coughed out a dry laugh. 'You gave that a run for its money all right. But instead you told me you'd talked to a doctor there the day after we found out Mum had died.' I picked up the death certificate from the table. Pointed to the squiggle signature of the doctor. 'Too bad for you that Dr Steven Bridgton still lives there, Dad. I found his number in the Yellow Pages, easy. I rang when I thought his wife might be home alone. Only took me a few goes and she picked up. She didn't seem to understand me at first, but the facts of how it worked came out of her in the end. She told me women cancelled appointments all the time, some changed their mind, others 'didn't have the money'.'

The tick of the clock was the only thing that breathed in the room. I felt Tye beside me, thigh long against thigh.

'She said backyard abortionists hung around outside the clinic and they'd take whatever money a woman did have and get the thing done.'

Tim collapsed into his chair.

'Is that how it happened, Dad?' I pushed on into whatever was coming at us. 'She ended up in some grubby room with a coat hanger?'

Dad hung his head like some mongrel dog.

'And that's the real reason you came home that day with the black eye,' put in Tessa. 'You got into it with him.'

'He as good as killed your — ' Dad tried to say.

But Tessa wasn't having any more of it. 'That didn't stop you giving him our Christmas money to change the cause of death on the certificate, did it?'

He deflated again.

'Did she even die in the care of a hospital or did she bleed out in some dark alleyway?' Fury strained Tessa's voice. 'Because how come an abortionist was the one to sign her certificate?'

'Hospital,' Dad jumped in. 'He worked at the hospital, too. When the backyarder rang him to say Sarah was in a bad way, he took her in himself. He already had the police in his pocket, but I threatened him with going to the newspaper.

Gave him enough to pay a couple of nurses to keep their mouths shut.'

I let some time snake by, then said quietly, 'But that coat hanger didn't kill just her, Dad, it killed us all.'

'Rot as usual,' he said, trying a last rally. 'You're all fine. Tessa's got her family, Tim's running the most successful farm in the district and Philly's got a good paying job.' He pointed his thick, callused finger at me again. 'You!' His flicked his wrist towards me. 'You're the only write-off.'

'Dad!' said Tessa.

'She is!' He glared at me. 'See, I know a thing or two about you, too.'

I backed away, the air whooshed out of my tyres.

'That poncy bloke, *Maurice*.' He mimicked a drag queen's voice full of venom. 'See, he called again. Said I should talk to you. So you and I both got secrets.'

I shook my head like I didn't know how to stop it going, and pressed back and back through the air until my shoulders hit the back of the chair. How much did Maurice tell him?

'You've skinned me raw here today. You're no daughter of mine.' He stood up, getting power back in him. 'Your mother would be ashamed of you.'

I licked my lips, tasting something new on them.

My father stabbed his finger at me. 'You and me. We're not so different.'

Philly leaped from her chair. 'Stop being a bastard, Dad.'

'No, he's right, Philly,' I said, all slow, still, behind the veil of this something new. 'I tried to steal Mum's records from the hospital and I ended up with the police.'

'Don't be stupid,' said Tye, breaking in. 'You weren't charged. You're nothing like your father.'

I turned slowly to him, half drowning. 'I'm not?'

He shook his head hard.

'You're not,' Philly said, her voice heated in my defence.

'You're right there,' said Dad. 'She's more like Peg. Maurice told me you weren't even living with her when you said you were. Sleeping on a park bench until he sorted you a job and you got into that boarding dump you're in now. Lying to us, all those years.'

'Shut up, Dad,' said Philly. 'Hardly your league. Nobody could live in Peg's nightmare house except Peg.' She looked at me. 'Do you get up every morning? Clean your room? Granted, it's a shithole. Talk to those crazies you live with, look after Marge? Get to work mostly? Win cases?'

I nodded.

'You're not fucking Peg-mad, then.'

'But you are nuts,' said Tessa. She looked around the table. 'Everyone in this family is, in one way or another.' With her eyes dead on me, she said, 'JJ's right, Dad. Mum was the thing holding us together.'

A twisted, tight spring in me released.

Tessa wasn't Mum, but she was doing the thing Mum used to do for me. I gathered all the

387

loose up before it could pour out. We weren't at the end yet.

Dad angled towards the window again. 'At least your mother's not here to see this.'

'There wouldn't have been a *this*,' said Tim. 'It was you, Jack. You and your lies made all this.'

I plucked at the petals in the white chrysanthemum napkin ring. Pulled at each one and crushed them under my nails, making them bleed white on to my skin.

Dad's body jerked up, his face ravaged deep. 'How could I have told you any of that?'

'Dunno, Dad,' I said.

'You think I don't know what I done? You think I don't already feel the heat from the blazing fires of hell on my skin? It was my job to keep her safe. I will not take absolution, I will not clear myself of this sin, because I will not leave your mother in that place for all eternity on her own.'

His face twisted up ugly again. 'You sit there, all powered up on things being as clear as black and white.' He gripped the table edge. 'None of yous know what it's been like for me to keep all of this locked tight, keeping it from yous and the world, keeping your mother's reputation pure and white.'

'None of that shit mattered to Mum,' said Tim.

'Your mother,' said Dad, his voice rising thin, 'was a good, upstanding Catholic woman.'

'Who kept the address of an abortion clinic in her Mass book just in case she'd be wanting it one day,' I said.

'But she was pretty Catholic,' said Philly. 'Why did she even want an abortion?'

That stopped us in our tracks. Dad, too. He licked his lips. Looked shifty again. He searched the bare paddocks beyond the window. He bit his lips and looked at us each in turn again. He slowly rose, a sudden old man, and shuffled to the bench. He brought back the photo he'd kept hidden from us all those years, fumbled at the back of the frame.

We leaned forwards.

Philly saw it first. She recoiled, then stood up, eyes on the door, then half sat again. She stopped in mid air, stuck between whatever she already knew and what she didn't want to know. She looked over to Ahmed, reached across to grip his hand, found enough to sit all the way down. Back still straight.

We all looked back at Dad, who'd worried a corner of white paper out from the back of the photo.

The rest of us got it at the same time.

Finally, after all these years.

Mum's voice.

I wanted to run, too.

Dad had a large enough section of the note freed for him to slide-pull the rest of it out. His callused, farmer-thick hands trembled as they unfolded it four times and smoothed it flat on the table, creases worn thin from many unfoldings.

He stared down, expressionless, knowing the words without reading them.

If there was anyone breathing in the room, I

couldn't hear them.

This was the moment.

If I'd been religious I would've said what I heard was the slow, rhythmic beat of angels' wings, like we were in the presence of something momentous.

He pushed it towards Tessa.

'Just one more lie, then, Dad,' she said. 'You told us there was no note.'

He grimaced. 'Didn't lie. Not the first day, anyway. Found it under the bed the second day. That's why I said first up she'd left us. Didn't know any better.'

He shrugged. 'Couldn't read it to you, though.' He stopped until he found words again. 'It was just . . . not . . . well, you'll see.'

Tessa stared at Dad as she pulled Mum's words to her.

She pressed the back of her wrist into each eye. She dropped her hand to her chest and pressed her palm flat against her heart.

All of us let her take her time.

All of us, suspended between the knowing and the not knowing.

All of us.

When her words came out, they were toneless.

You played me for a fool, Jack McBride. With my own sister. And then that snake pit of lies you had me live in all these years. You are nothing more than a small man, playing at God, rotted through with hypocrisy.

How dare you accuse me of being a sinner for helping Peg get rid of that baby. Your baby. The one you paid to have murdered, making such a show of how it was against your holy principles, and only out of Christian charity and knowing you'd be spending longer in purgatory because of it. Weren't you the saviour? And me forever grateful to you afterwards. I only let her go because of what you'd done for her. The debt I owed you. And didn't that suit your purposes.

Yet you couldn't bring yourself to do the same when it came to me. You'd rather see me dead than risk the world finding out that your wife had had an abortion, in defiance of the Holy Roman Catholic Church. The shame of ex-communication in front of Father McGinty, and the grown men at your club playing at Knights.

You have broken my heart, crushed my soul, destroyed my faith.

But I will do what needs to be done to stay alive. For our living children.

Tell the kids I've gone to Peg's for a few days because she's had a turn and I'll be too busy to call. Tell Tessa I've left a week's worth of meals in the freezer. Do not call me. I don't know if I'll ever be able to look you in your lying, hypocritical face again.

Nobody filled the silence Tessa left. All of us seared in the scorch of Mum's words from the grave. Dad hunkered down in the cave of his arms.

It was both too much and not enough.

'Why was having an abortion the thing that needed to be done to stay alive?' asked Philly, the first to rally. 'When it was so risky back then?'

His disembodied voice, when it came, was muffled. 'The doctor said she'd likely die if she had another one of yous.' He dropped his arms away, straightened against the back of his chair like he was a mighty weight. 'That's what she was talking about that night. But I couldn't give her the money, see?' He appealed to us one by one, passing over Ahmed, Tye and Shelley, as if it were just us again, back in the capsule of the gone-ness of our mother. 'We'd been so careful with the rhythm method for years. Not one slip-up. Except that one night. The night they made me President of the Knights. It was God's will that she got pregnant again. She was in a blessed state. I told her she had to put herself in God's hands. That, if she had an abortion, she'd end up in hell, but if she died in childbirth it was all part of God's plan and at least she'd get to heaven. Told her that her everlasting soul was more important than her earthly body.'

'Shit,' I said, putting all the sorrow of the room into it.

Tessa pressed her lips together to stop something getting out. Tim reached for Shelley. Philly curled into Ahmed, her legs into her armpits just like she used to do as a kid.

I went the other way. I got out of the chair, picked up my plate, and dropped it in the sink. I held out my hand to Tye. He gripped it and together we went through the laundry, down the path, past the hole in the wall, got into the Austin.

Maybe this finally was a big enough truth to make a difference.

Your father forced your mother into a cheap backyard abortion and she bled out in some dark laneway, alone. But not unloved. Facts were funny things.

I looked at Tye and he looked back, bathing me in kindness. He turned his body so he could put his palm on my still-flat belly, a question mark in the press of it. I knew what he was asking. After all this, what life would I choose? Because we both knew I had that choice now. Mum died because she couldn't get a decent abortion. I turned to face him too, trying to read what was in his heart. But in the end it didn't matter. We both knew it wasn't his decision to make. I shook my head. The smallest of movements. I had clear air now for the first time After Mum. I needed to do some breathing for me before I could do it for somebody else. He nodded. The smallest of acknowledgements. I dropped my hand over his, entwining my fingers. He squeezed back, eyes still deep in mine. We held together in that long moment, letting it stretch across time, then I reached for the gear stick.

'Let's get out of here.'

Appreciation

The Serpent's Skin is a love song to the many unseen people who are layered into it. The incredible women and men of the world I grew up in, who struggled every day to make life possible. The women in particular, who are the focus of The Serpent's Skin, who lived with such heart and courage, arms around each other. To my sisters and brother, Therese, Geraldine, Gillian, Patrick and Kate, who lived this world with me, weaving a dirt-raw kind of magic in it all through stories, the Saturday night play and the funny trash talk. To our true-grit parents, Kathleen and Garry, who waged an epic daily battle to keep us out of the wheat field, creek, underground tank, away from snakes, put food on the table and make our clothes.

I am so grateful to the people who laid out a path for me to arrive at this moment, either by backing my work, inspiring me, or suggesting a much better way of writing that sentence. Generous, smart and creative people like Toni Jordan, Alison Arnold, Antoni Jach, my agent, Fiona Inglis, and her Curtis Brown team, and my own fabulous team at Pantera Press, who are creatively inspired and passionate storytellers. Lex Hirst has the wizardry of getting directly to the gleaming gold motherlode in a story and the ability to help you widen it into all that it can be. Lucy Bell has the alchemy of a deep and intense focus that brings it all together. Special mentions, also, to the incredible word wranglers Kate O'Donnell and Rebecca Starford, and Alissa Dinallo, who designed such a gorgeous, sensual cover.

Big thanks to my beautiful, sharp-minded friends and colleagues in the writing world: The Secret Scribblers: Dee White, Karen Mcrea, Sue Yardley, Trudy Campbell, Christine Caley, Lou Mentor, Ian Robertson, Fiona White, Jodie Passmore, Kevin Childs and Trish Staig; The Writerlies: Ann Bolch, Rebecca Colless, Mary Delahunty, Ilka Tampke, Vivian Ulman; The Dodd St group: Caroline Petit, Lyndal Caffrey, Nick Gadd, Lisa Bigelow, Sarah Schmidt, Evelyn Tsitas, Stephen Mitchell; and my Masterclass mates: Anne Buist, Emily Collyer, Anna Dusk, Tasha Haines, Lisa Jacobs, Josh Lefers, Rocco Russo Clive Wansbrough, as well as Jenny Ackland, Serje Jones, Christina Stripp, Donna Ward, Geraldine Coren and Kimberly Duncan and many others who I've worked with through the magnificence of Writers Victoria. We create in unseen places moments of great depth and together we strive to make them more.

I'm blown away by the profound generosity of Graeme Simsion, Christos Tsiolkas, Toni Jordan, Sarah Macdonald, Sarah Schmidt and Elise McCredie, who took the considerable time and focus away from their own work to read The Serpent's Skin and back it. The support of incredible writers, thinkers and storytellers like you all is one of the key reasons why Australian storytelling is still so vibrant, even given all the challenges.

In the power of your work, in your contribution to the cultural conversation and in this kind of support you are a gift to us all.

I'm also grateful to my inspiring and deep-souled friends: Amanda Collinge, Susie Daniel, Clare Kermond and Cathy MacMahon, who went the extra mile to support me, as always, and bring The Serpent's Skin into the world. Thanks also to the generous people who helped me with research on all kinds of random things like legal practice, funeral processes, canon law matters, and how to make friends with the social media beast.

Thanks to the people who keep my heart and soul nourished, laugh at me, and sometimes with me: the man of joy and wild ideas, my rock and home, Victor Del Rio; the deep thinking and sun-hearted Maya Del Rio Reddan; the whip-smart and sassy Alena Del Rio Reddan; the wise, hilarious and original, Andrea Rieniets; my avatar companion through life, Yolanda Romeo AKA Shiel; the clever and creative, Cathy Appleton; my 'oldest friends' Karen Quinlan and Fran Barresi; my nieces, nephews, heart-adopted daughters and the wider Reddan tribe; las mujeres poderosas del Sindicato; and the rest of my Australian-Latino family; the joy-filled and loving tribu Del Rio; my gorgeous Sydney gang; the film crew; the Gaia Girls; the power coaches; the BBS; and my Macedon Ranges friends. For all that we are to each other both on the page and beyond, a big heart-expanding thank you.

We do hope that you have enjoyed reading this large print book.

Did you know that all of our titles are available for purchase?

We publish a wide range of high quality large print books including:
**Romances, Mysteries, Classics
General Fiction
Non Fiction and Westerns**

Special interest titles available in large print are:
**The Little Oxford Dictionary
Music Book
Song Book
Hymn Book
Service Book**

Also available from us courtesy of Oxford University Press:
**Young Readers' Dictionary
(large print edition)
Young Readers' Thesaurus
(large print edition)**

For further information or a free brochure, please contact us at:
**Ulverscroft Large Print Books Ltd.,
The Green, Bradgate Road, Anstey,
Leicester, LE7 7FU, England.
Tel: (00 44) 0116 236 4325
Fax: (00 44) 0116 234 0205**

A SUNSET IN SYDNEY

Sandy Barker

Sarah Parsons has a choice ahead of her. After the trip of a lifetime she's somehow returned home with not one, but *two* handsome men wanting to whisk her away into the sunset. Gorgeous American Josh wants to meet Sarah in Hawaii for a holiday to remember. Meanwhile, silver fox James plans to wine and dine her in London. It's a lot to handle for an Aussie girl who had totally sworn off men! And being pulled in two directions across the globe is making life very tricky indeed . . .

BOUND

Vanda Symon

A brutal home invasion shocks the nation. A man is murdered, his wife bound, gagged and left to watch. But when Detective Sam Shephard scratches the surface, the victim, a successful businessman, is not all he seems to be. And when the evidence points to two of Dunedin's most hated criminals, the case seems cut and dried . . . until the body count starts to rise.

THE GREAT DIVIDE

L. J. M. Owen

In the rural Tasmanian town of Dunton, the body of a former headmistress of a children's home is discovered, revealing a tortured life and death. Detective Jake Hunter, newly arrived, searches for her killer among past residents of the home. He unearths pain, secrets and broken adults. Pushing aside memories of his own treacherous past, Jake focuses all his energy on the investigation. Why are some of the children untraceable? What caused such damage among the survivors? The identity of her murderer seems hidden from Jake by Dunton's fog of prejudice and lies, until he is forced to confront not only the town's history but his own nature . . .